A NOVEL

by Camilla Carr

A Birch Lane Press Book
Published by Carol Publishing Group

A Birch Lane Press Book
Published by Carol Publishing Group

Editorial Offices
600 Madison Avenue
New York, NY 10022

Sales & Distribution Offices
120 Enterprise Avenue
Secaucus, NJ 07094

In Canada: Musson Book Company
A division of General Publishing Co. Limited
Don Mills, Ontario

Manufactured in the United States of America

The author is grateful to the following:
To Edward Swift and Harper & Row for permission to use a few names from *Principia Martindale* published by Harper & Row.
To Bantam Doubleday Dell for their kind permission to use quotations from *The Velveteen Rabbit* by Marjorie Williams, published by Doubleday, A Division of Bantam, Doubleday Dell Publishing Group, Inc.
To Polygram International Publishing Company for their kind permission to reprint lyrics from "Honky Tonk Man" written by Johnny Horton, Tillman Franks and Howard Hausey.

Library of Congress Cataloging-in-Publication Data

Carr, Camilla.
Topsy Dingo Wild Dog : a novel / by Camilla Carr.
p. cm.
"A Birch Lane Press Book."
ISBN 1-55972-013-1 : $16.95
I. Title.
PS3553.A76278T6 1989
813'.54--dc20 89-17375
CIP

To
Edward Anhalt
&
James Stein

Melba Carr
&
Caley O'Dwyer

Colleen Casey
&
Ronnie Claire Edwards

AND SPIRITS OF VIA DE LA PAZ

AUTHOR'S NOTE

Most of the names and locations of the West Texas towns mentioned in this novel, such as Wink, Notrees, Pyote, Wickett, Kermit, Monahans, Andrews, Pecos, Odessa and Midland, are real. However, Highway 158 stops at Notrees, there is nothing between Kermit, Texas, and Jal, New Mexico, on Highway 18, and the real Uncertain, Texas, is actually located on the Texas-Louisiana border. This East Texas town and its inhabitants should not be confused with the fictional West Texas town and characters in this novel.

"O the moon shone bright on Mrs. Porter
And on her daughter
They wash their feet in soda water"

THE WASTE LAND
III. The Fire Sermon
T.S. Eliot

PRO-
LOGUE

UNCERTAIN

ANYONE DRIVING EAST OR WEST through Uncertain, Texas, on Highway 158 wouldn't have seen Baby Flowers out walking until at least a quarter to noon. Baby always woke up at eight A.M., but she never stirred until one of her sisters thought to come in and nod. That meant it was morning and time to get on up. Then one of them would dress her in whatever they weren't wearing that day, feed her whatever Crackerjacks they hadn't eaten, and make their way back into the yard toward whatever rocker wasn't rocking.

When Baby was a baby, the other Flowers would rock her in a tire that hung from the eaves of the porch, but long before Baby grew out of the tire, the porch caved in and nobody thought to build Baby another swing. It had taken every grain of sense from each of the other seven Flowers put together just to come up with the idea of moving their rocking chairs from under the debris caused by the collapse of the porch and out into the front yard where they could all sit back down, rock, eat Crackerjacks and stop thinking so hard.

When Baby saw all seven rockers rocking each morning, she knew she didn't have any place to sit, so off she'd go down the road, hoping to find a good rocking chair.

"Bye, bye, Baby," Petunia Flowers, the oldest at fifty-seven, would call out after her nineteen-year-old baby sister, from her rocker. And six echoes of "Bye, bye, Baby," would follow from Iris, fifty-five, Rose, fifty-four, Daisy, fifty-three, Daffodil, fifty-two, Poppy, fifty-one, and Mum, fifty, from their rockers.

Total retards all, some said their parents had been brother and sister, but nobody could prove it. Some said Baby was the child of Mum, the lone male, and one of the "girls," but nobody could prove that either.

Baby didn't look a thing like any of the other Flowers, for Baby was a beauty. "Looks for all the world like Miss Ava Gardner did back in '44 when Howard Hughes found her," Lottie Shady, of the Uncertain Chapel of Memories Funeral Parlor loved to say to her sister-in-law and business partner, Irene Shady. Baby Flowers was Lottie's favorite topic. She needed a favorite topic all her own, otherwise Irene would go on about *her* own daughter, Mary Jane Shady, the "star," twenty-four hours a day. "Baby's Ava's twin if she ever had one. Looks to me like somebody had her and gave her away, 'cause she sure don't fit with the looks of those other seven Flowers," Lottie would say. "She may be dim in the head, but she's a pure-dee beauty to look at."

"I thank my lucky stars for Mary Jane Shady's looks and brains, even if I sometimes wonder what she's doin' with them," Irene frequently confessed to Lottie. "At least Baby is half-way lucky. She could have got her looks from Mum like Why-vonne did."

"Mum may not be Baby's daddy, Irene," Lottie cautioned.

"Well, he's Why-vonne's daddy, and anybody can tell it from a glance."

It was a well-known fact. Yvonne had grown up in the shack and was raised by the Flowers family seventeen years before Baby, but for years, and especially these days, people went deliberately out of their way to never ask Yvonne Dee Flowers Henderson about her daddy or any of her relatives. Yvonne flatly refused to admit she was related. One night, she told her husband, Bobby Henderson, that her mother had awakened in a strange shack during childbirth, and finding herself surrounded by seven idiots, had died of fright on the spot. She denied knowing who her father was. Another night, she said she and her mother had lived in the house next to the Flowers. Their house burned down and her mother had died in the fire and the Flowers family took her and raised her, but she wasn't related to them. Not any of them.

It didn't matter: one look at Yvonne's crooked teeth, close beady eyes and brown stringy hair with that bald spot in the middle, a dead give-away of Flowers blood, was enough to confirm it.

Baby didn't have a bald spot or beady eyes or crooked teeth. She had long, black, wavy hair that fell to her thighs. It had never been cut in her life. Her eyes were green and clear and bright. Her skin was pale and flawless. And smile! Baby just smiled all the time. Her sisters and her brother grinned. Her half-sister-cousin, Yvonne, grinned. But Baby smiled.

Baby and the other seven Flowers never thought about what their faces did. Yvonne thought about it all the time: she had just enough sense to know the difference between a grin and a smile. She prayed that one day she'd stop grinning and start smiling.

Yvonne, seventeen years older than nineteen-year-old Baby, dearly wished she had been born with any one of Baby's features. She was eternally grateful that Baby did not look like her idol, Kim Novak. "If Baby had have looked like Kim Novak, I'd have had her killed," Yvonne said to her husband, Bobby Henderson, one day.

"I thought you told me you weren't kin to those Flowers idiots," Bobby had replied.

"Well, I'm not!" Yvonne had screamed. "And don't tell me I've got a part-time mind again either!"

"I guess it's just a horrible coincidence that *she* got the looks and *you* got the brains," Bobby had laughed.

"You take that back, Bobby!"

He didn't, but later he wished he had.

Yvonne Henderson spent her life trying to get over her background and trying to avoid the Flowers.

The whole bunch was harmless. The sisters mostly liked to stare happily at the way the sunlight hit their tin can collection. Every now and then Mum would move the cans around with a fishing pole Bobby Henderson had thrown out of his pick-up and into the yard one afternoon after he'd been cleaning out his garage. It took almost all of Mum's concentration to move the pole through all the weeds and stickers toward the can, so he didn't do this too often.

What Mum enjoyed most was peeing on the cans. He liked the tinkling sound it made bouncing off the tins. It reminded him of rain hitting the roof, back when they used to have a roof. But every time he did this, one sister or another would swat at him. This made him stop and think about how it felt to have something hitting at him. But stopping to think made him drop his "thing," since he couldn't think and hold on to himself at the same time. Left unattended, Mum's "thing" would go off like a loose hose all over him. This made his sisters laugh and was the most fun Mum had, so he did this just about three times a day.

The other thing Mum liked to do was wave. All the Flowers liked to wave. Waving was the sisters' favorite pastime, especially since they could keep right on rocking and wave all at the same time. They always waved at the cars and trucks passing by out on the highway, and every morning at 11:40 they got to wave bye-bye to Baby.

"Bye, bye, Baby," Petunia, Iris, Rose, Daisy, Daffodil, Poppy and Mum would call out to Baby's disappearing back. Seven hands fluttered in the air until she was out of sight.

By the time Baby had left the yard, crossed the dirt road and walked a quarter of a mile south, she'd forgotten what she was looking for. The first thing she'd do was stare into the sun as long as she could without blinking. When everything got bright and hot inside her eyes, she'd squeeze them as tight as she could and turn in circles for as long as she could until the light left her head. Then she'd open her eyes and walk in whatever direction she was facing. Every morning, it was always the same direction: west. After two P.M., Baby headed north. By five, Baby was going south. At nine P.M., Baby turned and went back east no matter what.

Each morning by the time Baby Flowers had walked a quarter of a mile from her shack, looked at the sun, spun around a few times and stopped, she was always at the same place: heading west on Highway 158 toward the Uncertain Chapel of Memories, a funeral parlor over on the south side of town. Located on the northwest corner of Highway 158 where it crossed Farm to Market Road 18, it was the biggest intersection in town and the only red light between Midland and El Paso.

The Uncertain Chapel of Memories was exactly one mile from Baby's shack. When it was originally built fifty-six years before Baby was even born, there hadn't been a thing there but two roads (now highways) crossing. Today, the Hoop and Holler Motel for a Dollar sat across the road, Beulah Belle's Chug-a-Lug Liquor Store was on the southwest corner. A man with Shetland ponies you could ride for a quarter, and a tent which housed a Mexican fortune teller took up the space directly across from Beulah's on the southeast side. The fortune teller charged fifty cents and would read cards, a glass ball, follow the lines in your hand or just lean back and think and use her own intuition.

About ten years back, something had told the fortune lady to tell the pony man to sell all but the space they each occupied to the Widders family, who needed some land close to town for their trailer. Kay Widders had two small twin girls to deal with who were continually getting into scrapes over at the Uncertain Trailer Court, and when Sammy Widders offered the pony man one hundred dollars for the half-acre behind him, the fortune lady told him to take it, so he did, even though he had to get rid of six ponies. With so little space left, he only kept three ponies and they had to travel in a circle.

The fortune lady used the fifteen dollars Sammy Widders had paid her to use her influence on the pony man to drive to Lubbock and take a Dale Carnegie course. She told Sammy and Kay's twins, Verona and Morona, that she hadn't gotten much out of it and was glad she could depend on a good pack of cards and her glass ball to get through life.

Kay Widders had placed her trailer right in the middle of the land they had bought, planted poplar trees around the boundary and added a circular driveway all the way around the trees. She was determined to give her children a decent home outside a trailer camp, even if they did have to live in a trailer. Soon she had it planked over and painted, and from the outside, it looked just like a house. It was only when a person went through the low-framed front door with the metal handle that they first noticed they might not be entering a real house, but a trailer house made to look like a real house.

Baby Flowers came upon the Widders' trailer-made-house every morning at 11:45, and by 11:50 she had circled the driveway ten times clockwise. If it was a Saturday, the twins would come out and plait her hair. If it was a Sunday, no one would be home, and Baby would take turns sitting out in each of the aluminum rockers until the Widders returned from the Uncertain Church of Christ. On weekdays, Baby usually just made her rounds on the driveway, unless cars were parked there. On those days Baby would cut her rounds short, so she'd have time to look in the windows and see who was visiting before she went on to the Uncertain Chapel of Memories. Baby never sat out on the aluminum chairs on weekdays. She saved sitting on weekdays for the funeral parlor at the intersection. Right inside the Uncertain Chapel of Memories was a whole set of matching furniture with cushions and covers and springs you couldn't see or feel. For fifteen minutes every Monday through Friday, from twelve o'clock sharp until a quarter past noon, while Irene Shady went to the bank, her sister-in-law and business partner, Lottie Shady, who was minding the store and didn't mind, let Baby come in and rock and sit wherever she wanted to.

Baby forgot all about the furniture in the Uncertain Chapel of Memories as she came upon the Widders' driveway. Something even made her forget to make her circles. Two cars were parked there that she'd never seen parked there at the same time before.

The extra-long purple car with dark windows you couldn't see through and an animal skull on top of the hood belonged to someone whose secrets she knew. She could make out the silhouette of a man sitting silently behind the wheel, waiting, but she knew he didn't own the car; he just drove the owner around and did what the owner told him to do.

Parked nose to nose with the purple car was Baby's most favorite car in the world. Its top was folded back. She circled the car slowly, wondering if its color was darker than the night and who the gleaming lady was standing up ready to fly off the end of the hood and where she thought she was going.

Baby's eyes drifted away from the hood lady over to the trailer-made-house. Whoever was in there was who that hood lady was always trying to escape from.

She didn't hesitate a moment, but walked right past the line of poplar trees into the front yard and up to the first open aluminum window she saw.

Two women were standing up and one was sitting down in a brown leatherette sofa. The walls were covered in brown prefabricated paneling. The floor was covered in brown shag carpet. Hanging on the wall in a brown plastic frame behind the sofa was a depiction of a life-sized turkey made of dried corn, peas, beans and sunflower seeds. This picture always made Baby frown.

She looked at the three women.

The big, fat, flush-faced woman taking up most of the couch and causing it to sink in the middle was the owner of the aluminum chairs and the trailer and the mother of the twins, Kay Widders. She was nibbling on a piece of pink cake.

The one talking was wearing a blond wig. Baby knew it was a wig because it was her half-sister-cousin Yvonne and she wore a wig everywhere she went. Yvonne had painted her face in the same big bold strokes Kay Widders had used to paint her numbered pictures that were hanging on either side of the vegetable-turkey rendering. Baby's eyes went back and forth from Yvonne's bright yellow hair to the yellow dried corn kernels in the vegetable-turkey picture to a numbered painting of a jack-o'-lantern sitting in front of a haystack. She looked back and forth three times before she could make herself look away.

Baby saved the third lady for last because she always needed to look at Catsy Ivanhoe the longest. She needed time to gaze over her long long arms and legs, the slender fingers with shiny green, red and white stones that made little flashes of light without any help from the sunshine. She wanted to stare at all that long black hair, braided and twisted into knots and coils, intertwined with real flowers that looked like they were growing bells. She wanted to make sure the lady was dressed to match the color of her car. She wanted to try to name the different animals it had taken to make the lady's shoes and purse and billfold and belt, which oddly, to Baby, matched Yvonne's car seats. And she wanted to have enough time to stare into the woman's gray eyes speckled with green and try to figure out what she was doing to make the hood lady on her car want to take off.

Shrill, high-pitched sounds sliced through the air. That big smile covered Baby's face. Baby forgot to think when voices started talking. She loved to hear voices talk and so she balanced herself firmly and stared through the window.

Catsy Ivanhoe was propping one of her new alligator custom-made Maud Frizon boots on top of an orange hassock shaped like a telephone. In the midst of what she considered to be an appalling collection of "common" taste, she found the hassock particularly revolting. She caressed the suede of her black Donna Karan dress as she spoke. "Listen, Kay, I appreciate you askin' me to serve on the Twenty Year Reunion Committee of the Uncertain High School Class of 1965, but I didn't graduate with that class."

"I didn't graduate and I'm on the committee," Yvonne Henderson beamed, patting her blond wig. "I'm a volunteer."

Catsy looked at Yvonne standing next to her dressed from the waist up in a purple and orange Yves St. Laurent blouse under a lime green Oscar de la Renta beaded satin jacket, and from the waist down in a tight-fitting, hot pink skirt—the bottom of an Ungaro ensemble. On her feet, Yvonne wore four-inch purple lizard pumps with pink and orange bells on the toes. Catsy Ivanhoe couldn't look away fast enough.

Kay Widders' unplucked eyebrows tried to hug each other. "Why didn't you tell me that, Catsy?" she asked through a mouthful of pink cake.

"I thought you knew, Kay," Catsy snapped impatiently. Kay Widders was so large it was impossible not to look at her, and there she sat, as covered up as possible, underneath a homemade polyester mu-mu imprinted with watermelons, bananas, grapes, grapefruits and cherries. *If she stuck to the fruit on that sack she's wearin', maybe she'd lose some of that blubber!* thought Catsy. "Everybody in Uncertain, Texas, knows I graduated from Wink High School seventeen miles away." Catsy raised a fistful of blood red nails in the air, jabbing south over her shoulder with her thumb and highlighting the prominence of the huge David Webb diamond, cradled in rubies and emeralds, which she wore on her forefinger. "I was the Wink Homecoming Queen my senior year."

"You went to school in Uncertain, Texas, ever minute of your life until your senior year when you didn't get to be the Drum Major,"

Yvonne reminded Catsy. She placed both of her hands on both of her hips so all of *her* rings would show.

"I don't think my reasons for transferring from Uncertain High School to Wink High School are why we're here,Why-vonne," Catsy stated grimly. She swung her foot to the floor and glanced at her gold Rolex watch. She just hated how Yvonne Henderson wore rings on every single finger.

From the moment Catsy's mother sent her to Wink High School over twenty years ago, where Catsy had gone on to become Wink Drum Major, Wink Senior Class Favorite, and Wink Homecoming Queen, Catsy had developed an attitude that she was just too good for Uncertain, Texas. She still loved to distinguish her superiority in every way she could, but in order to appear superior, she needed to be around a few low-life types. Just a few minutes with almost anyone in Uncertain would do. When Kay Widders invited her to stop by, Catsy didn't hesitate. It took a mere thirty seconds for Catsy to compare her own fabulous ranch that sprawled the entire distance between Uncertain and Notrees, Texas, to this pitiful little dark hole of a trailer Kay was trying to pass off as a house. When Catsy envisioned Kay's twin daughters, she spent sixty seconds thanking the stars above for the fact that she was nobody's mother. Even as she wracked her brain, she could think of *no one* to compare those girls to.

Comparisons were how Catsy Ivanhoe came up with how she felt about things. For this reason, she tried to always avoid comparing her husband, Bo Ivanhoe, to Kay Widders' husband, Sammy Widders. Bo Ivanhoe was the wealthiest man in West Texas and that was what counted to Catsy. Catsy told herself it was far more fair-minded to compare Bo to Yvonne's husband, Bobby Henderson. No matter what else he had done, Bobby Henderson had at least approached wealth. Catsy Ivanhoe adored telling Bo Ivanhoe the latest foolish thing Yvonne Henderson had done with Bobby Henderson's new money. She could hardly wait to get back to the ranch and tell Bo that Yvonne Henderson had actually volunteered to be on the Twentieth Year Reunion Committee of a class from which she had never even graduated! No one made Catsy feel more self-satisfied than Yvonne Henderson.

"You only need to have gone to Uncertain High School for two weeks in your whole life to serve on the Reunion Committee," Kay Widders stated, licking her fingers. "Don't ya'll want some of this cake?"

"That doesn't sound right to me, Kay," Catsy Ivanhoe frowned.

"Right or wrong, that's the way it is," Kay said flatly. She spent most of her time dealing with her sixteen-year-old daughters and Catsy thought Kay's attitude showed it.

Seeing no way out, but to give in and get out, Catsy sighed, "All right then, what do you want us to do?" She sat down on the hassock, since she couldn't bear to look at it.

Kay carefully wiped her hands on a paper napkin, thoughtfully placed the napkin on top of her paper plate, looked solemnly at Catsy and Yvonne, and tried to reposition some of her enormous weight by shifting around on the sofa. Two hundred and fifty pounds sunk deeper into a cushion, and a set of springs sang out in misery. Kay settled both her arms in a fold on top of her imposing stomach. "When I accepted the responsibility of heading the Uncertain Class of 1965 Reunion Committee, it never occurred to me that one of my daughters would be runnin' for Homecoming Queen right at the very same time," Kay Widders explained carefully. "Now the Reunion we had back ten years ago wasn't a problem, since the girls were little then, and I would even consider participating in our Thirty Year Reunion ten years away, if I'm still alive. If those twins get married and have children anything like *them*, I may end up in a institution."

"They tried to put me in a institution," Yvonne Henderson grinned, filling the end of a potato chip full of cheese dip. "I never had to count to ten so many different ways in my life."

Catsy Ivanhoe bit her tongue trying not to respond that in her opinion Yvonne should be locked up permanently, and it took the most restraint she could muster to keep from advising Kay not to get her hopes up too high about those twins getting married to somebody. Just as her mind started to wander off and wonder exactly what sort of a person might be attracted to them, Kay's voice cut in.

"We're in a bind here," Kay confessed, sinking deeper into the sofa. "That new rule they passed over at the State Capitol in Austin has forbidden our school children to participate in any extra-curricular activities unless they get their grades up to a passin' seventy average—"

"Does that mean Morona won't get to run for Homecoming Queen?" Yvonne wanted to know.

"No, she's the one with good grades. Verona's the sorry student," Kay replied.

"How could they come up with such different grades?" Yvonne asked in a puzzled voice. "I mean they're—"

"Identical!" Catsy Ivanhoe hissed, her backbone arching.

"They have never done a thing alike except be born together," Kay sighed.

"Well, I hope Morona wins," Yvonne offered.

"That sort of brings me to my point," Kay stated.

"Whoever wins is not going to have a float to ride on, since they aren't allowing the kids to make flowers—"

"They cain't make Kleenex flowers?" Yvonne cried. "What are they doin' in school? It cain't be any fun!"

"It's not," Kay agreed. "I don't know why they even have school anymore. It's just going to be a horrible Homecoming with no floats."

"They've got to have somethin' to ride on!" Yvonne exclaimed.

"That's what I thought," Kay nodded. "So I want to know if they can borrow ya'll's cars?"

"Wait a minute!" Catsy Ivanhoe protested, tossing her long plaited ponytail over one shoulder. "Why are you in charge of what they're going to ride on? That should be the responsibility of the *current* graduating class. It's *their* Homecoming Queen! I thought you were in charge of the Reunion of the Class of 1965— or should I say *your* class, since if you remember, I moved to Wink my senior year and graduated there—"

"Where you were Drum Major, Class Favorite, and Homecoming Queen," Yvonne Henderson smiled sweetly. "Yes, we remember that." Catsy Ivanhoe was about to make her sick. Turning to Kay, Yvonne said, "I will be glad to donate *my* car, Kay, for any reason whatsoever."

"Well, so will I!" Catsy Ivanhoe cried before she could stop herself.

"Floats or no floats, this is going to be a memorable Homecoming if it kills me," Kay Widders beamed. "It's not everyday that the Queen and her Court get to ride around in a big black Rolls Royce and a long purple stretch-out car—"

"I put that car together myself," Yvonne told them.

"We know," Catsy Ivanhoe sighed.

"I didn't do the work, I just picked out how it was supposed to look," Yvonne explained. "It come to me in a dream—"

"We'll hear about that dream later on maybe, Why-vonne," Kay interrupted. "I do have a personal interest at stake concerning what these girls ride in on, since Morona is running for the Queen. When the Homecoming Queen and her attendants ride onto the football field after the parade following the Pep Rally, every eye in Uncertain, Texas will be on those cars!"

Catsy Ivanhoe began to perk up. "I think it will work out best if I drive my own car," she said.

Yvonne thought Catsy had a gift for making herself the center of just any situation. She stared at Catsy, dismayed. *She could stab you to death with those cheekbones!* Yvonne thought to herself.

"Oh, you can drive your car, too, Why-vonne!" Kay suggested.

"No!" Catsy cried. "She'll let her driver drive, won't you, Why-vonne? Think how exciting it will be for the girls to have their own chauffeur!"

"Yes, think," Yvonne muttered in disgust. Catsy Ivanhoe was trying to oust her out of riding in the festivities. The last time Catsy had pulled a fast one on her, Yvonne had retaliated by calling Catsy names. Then Catsy had told her that name-calling was exactly what she expected out of someone like Yvonne. Yvonne had promised herself to never let Catsy Ivanhoe get the best of her again.

"The Homecoming *Queen* can ride with me," Catsy continued, smoothing her black suede dress. "And the runner-ups can ride in Why-vonne's car. I'm sure they won't feel like such losers if they have a real chauffeur."

Yvonne sucked in her painted cheeks, took a deep breath, and told herself to hang onto her wig. She was determined to shake Catsy Ivanhoe right down to the toes of her brand new alligator boots.

"Nobody in my car will feel like a loser!" Yvonne cried. "Not when they'll be ridin' with me, a chauffeurin' driver and Miss Mary Jane Shady!"

The green specks in Catsy Ivanhoe's eyes grew, spreading over the gray, and for a moment she was actually speechless.

"Yes, that's right!" Yvonne Henderson babbled on like she knew what she was saying. "Miss Mary Jane Shady, the only Uncertain star to graduate from the Class of '65, has consented to return from Hollywood, California, and New York City where she has made the biggest name for herself any of us could imagine as a real live big-time celebrity!"

"She's not a celebrity!" Catsy Ivanhoe sputtered. "All she does is those Peanut Butter commercials!"

"Well, she's comin' anyway!" Yvonne cried. "And she's ridin' in *my* car and bein' driven by *my* driver, and me and all the other losers are ridin' with her!"

"This is just too good to be true, Why-vonne!" Kay Widders hollered, rolling all two hundred and fifty pounds of her flesh to a standing position. As soon as she was up and balanced, Kay turned to Catsy. "You are flat-out wrong about Mary Jane's celebrity status, Catsy. Just two nights ago Verona and Morona were watching her on the late-late show in a movie with Fabian!"

"If that's not stardom, I don't know what is!" Yvonne grinned.

"Why on earth would Mary Jane Shady come all the way back to Uncertain, Texas?" Catsy wanted to know. "She hasn't been back here in twenty years. She hasn't returned for one single solitary visit that I know of . . ."

"You can see her on the TV three times a day somedays," Kay Widders went on, to no one in particular. "Not in a nighttime series, and not in a daytime series, but squeezed in between. The twins see her all the time, all dressed up in checks and bows. They've grown up watchin' her sell that Peanut Butter for the past five years."

"Mary Jane Shady's at the top in Peanut Butter," Yvonne stated solemnly.

"You sound just like her mother," Catsy replied.

"I'm glad she's coming. She can crown the Queen," Kay Widders told both of them.

"I'm sorry," said Catsy Ivanhoe. "But I'm afraid I don't believe a word of this. Mary Jane Shady has never come back to Uncertain, Texas and I don't think she's going to return by Friday. I think you are making the whole thing up, Why-vonne, and honestly, I don't know why you don't take the time you devote to these schemes of yours and do something useful, like donate yourself to a charity."

"I did!" Yvonne said. "I donated myself to bein' on this Reunion Committee, and I devoted myself to gettin' Mary Jane Shady to come back and make this the best Homecomin' Uncertain, Texas has ever seen! I cain't help it if you wisht you'd have thought up the idea yourself!"

"Why-vonne, I am not impressed with self-made people," Catsy Ivanhoe said. "Mary Jane Shady is as self-made as you are. When a person has worked that hard at getting to be who they are, it has to have done something to them. I mean, it has to have taken some kind of a toll, you can bet your life on it."

"I'd ask Mary Jane Shady just what kind of a toll stardom has played on her life first thing when she gets here if I was you," Yvonne suggested sweetly. "That's exactly the first thing I would talk to her about, if you get to talk to her at all. You know how it will be with ever-body in town crowdin' around and followin' her ever-where she goes. *I* will put in a good word for you, though, and tell her how much it would mean to you if she will spare some time for the subject of toll-taking in stardom, okay?"

"But ask her first if she will crown the Homecomin' Queen, Why-vonne," Kay Widders said. "Don't get sidelined into a conversation that doesn't have anything to do with the Reunion or the Homecomin' right when she first arrives, hear!"

"We should maybe reserve a question and answer period for one hour at some point," Yvonne mused, sweeping grandly toward the door. "She told me herself she can hardly wait to participate in each and ever event!"

With great flourish, she threw open the metal door, hitting Baby Flowers and pinning her in next to the trailer.

Baby peered through the little screened triangle of the metal door, looking directly into the eyes of her half-sister-cousin.

Yvonne's eyes connected with Baby's eyes. Baby stared and Yvonne blinked. Baby's smile filled Baby's face.

Yvonne felt a cold rush run through her. D"Git!" she hissed under her breath to Baby. Quickly she swung around and waved buoyantly to Catsy and Kay. "Bye, bye, ya'll! I'm off to finalize the arrangements for the arrival of Miss Mary Jane Shady!"

Trying not to run, Yvonne made herself slow down enough to give José, her driver, a chance to get out and open the car door for her.

It was during this moment that Catsy Ivanhoe spied Baby Flowers standing mutely behind the trailer door.

"Oh, Why-vonne!" Catsy cried, thrilled to have the last word. "You forgot your relatives!"

Yvonne pretended not to hear a word as she climbed inside her car. She pretended not to see Baby, and she tried to pretend she wasn't kin to her. Oh, how she hated it when this dimwit relative showed up behind closed doors, in low lit rooms or just walking along on the road in plain sight to embarrass her. How could she ever be who she was trying to be with this halfwit inbred dragging her tacky bloodline through the middle of Uncertain and all over the city limits day and night.

Finally inside her limousine, Yvonne Dee Flowers Henderson collapsed with a moan.

"Now how in spit-fire and damnation am I ever goin' to get Mary Jane Shady to come back to Uncertain, Texas by day after tomorrow is what I want to know!" she screamed.

Seeing that her car was still sitting still, Yvonne gave the window a thump. "Casa! Goddamnit!" she hollered though the glass.

The car screeched out of the driveway, enveloping Baby Flowers in a cloud of white desert dust. As Yvonne watched Baby standing alone, waving, she thought Baby looked just like a little angel about to float up to heaven.

"Oh, God, how I wish she would!" Yvonne said out loud to herself.

Catsy Ivanhoe just stood there and laughed as Yvonne's limousine pulled away. "Poor ole Why-vonne is such a liar," she told Kay. "Both of her legs put together hold up nothin' but pure white trash."

"Do you think she's lyin' about Mary Jane Shady comin'?" Kay asked anxiously.

Catsy looked at Kay incredulously. "Kay, honey, where is your good sense? You're talkin' like you have as many brains as that little imbecile standing in your yard." She gave her hands a small shake in Baby Flowers' direction. "Shoo! Shoo-o-o!" she said to Baby, waving her out towards the poplar trees. "Go on, scat!"

Baby closed one eye, squinted hard at Catsy and smiled.

Catsy felt her hands turn ice cold. "That one gives me the creeps," she told Kay, as if Baby Flowers were a mannequin.

Baby turned and wandered off, heading west on Highway 158.

"She's harmless," Kay Widders replied, going inside her house.

Just as she said it, Baby turned around and started walking backwards, facing Catsy Ivanhoe, but still traveling west and still smiling.

First she unbuttoned her old flannel shirt. Catsy Ivanhoe's eyes grew wide as she saw the first round, hard, perfect nipple exposed, then the other. She could have sworn she never saw Baby actually take off that shirt; it seemed to have slipped away by itself. While she was watching a breeze carry the shirt across the highway where it attached itself to a tumbleweed, she almost missed seeing Baby step right out of her skirt, turn around and keep on walking.

"Kay!" Catsy called. "Baby Flowers is walkin' buck naked down the highway!"

"Again?" Kay asked, sticking her head out the door. "Now why didn't Why-vonne get over herself for a minute and take Baby on home?"

"She doesn't even have on a stitch of underwear!" Catsy declared. "Look at her! There she goes down the road again without wearin' a thing!"

Catsy Ivanhoe felt herself tingling with superiority.

"Maybe you better go get her and take her on home," Kay suggested.

"Me?" Catsy cried, her face flushed from feeling so good about herself. "I don't have time to be takin' care of *morons*! I have a dress fitting with that ex-Hopi Indian over in Notrees in fifteen minutes. He's hand-paintin' me a deerskin dress with rare extinct turkey-feather trim. You take her home, Kay."

"I don't have time either," Kay said, gazing west at Baby's bare back. "The next thing on my list is 'corsages.' Anyway, somebody will pick her up and take her on home."

"It looks like she's headin' for the Uncertain Chapel of Memories," Catsy said, heading for her Rolls Royce. "Let the Shady sisters take her home. I got to go to Notrees."

"If Mary Jane Shady don't show up, do you think Why-vonne will still let me borrow her car?" Kay asked.

"I doubt it," Catsy assured her. "But don't worry, Kay. We'll pile everybody, Queen and all, into Silver Cloud here. We won't even need Why-vonne and her limousine driver."

"That's just if Why-vonne renigs and if Mary Jane Shady don't show," Kay nodded.

"She won't!" Catsy Ivanhoe promised as she started her car and stepped on the gas.

But as she drove away, she didn't believe herself, and by the time she had gone a couple of miles down the road, nothing, not Kay Widders' twins and trailer-made-house, Baby Flowers' bad brains and striptease walks, or Yvonne Henderson's white trash background made her feel a bit better about Mary Jane Shady returning to Uncertain, Texas.

As Baby Flowers came to the intersection of Highway 158 and FM 18, she passed a big sign that Irene Shady had recently placed on all four corners of the highways' crossing. It read:

BAD INTERSECTION COMING UP *RIGHT NOW*.
IF YOU MISS IT AND LAND ON THIS PROPERTY
(an arrow pointed toward the funeral home)
PLEASE KILL YOURSELF.
WE DON'T WANT YOUR COMPANY BUT
WE SURE CAN USE YOUR BUSINESS DOWN AT
THE UNCERTAIN CHAPEL OF MEMORIES.
VENUS 7-0317, AREA 915.

For some reason, people traveling through this part of West Texas were always in a hurry, and more than once horrible accidents had occurred right there at the front door of the Uncertain Chapel of Memories. Lottie Shady looked upon this intersection as an asset. She and Irene brought the maimed in and cared for them until the ambulance arrived. If they died, the appreciative families turned their loved ones over to Irene and Lottie. Lottie prided herself on the location she had been smart enough to purchase years before Miss Deal Grimes, her competitor, had ever come on the scene. Deal's One Call Does All Permanent Rest Center was located downtown which was more prestigious, but not located on a major hazardous highway intersection.

Forty years after settling in Uncertain, Lottie had completely forgotten that she had chosen this location because it was cheap, across the street from the Hoop and Holler Motel for a Dollar, and because nobody else would have it. Today, she just thought how smart she was to have bought here. The property was valuable and fatal accidents happened right and left, so business was good.

As Baby Flowers crossed the big intersection, three cars nearly collided with each other. The green light turned red and two cars went right through it. One car filled with teenagers playing hookey slowed down, rolled down their windows and called out, "Hi, Baby! Where you goin', Baby!", waving and giggling as they sped off.

Baby didn't look left and she didn't look right. She just looked straight ahead at the pale pink two-story adobe stucco building on the northwest corner. A blinking bright blue, yellow, pink, red and green neon sign on top of the roof proclaimed "Uncertain Chapel of Memories." Baby loved to stand and blink along with the sign, following the letters which crawled in a semi-arch above the quasi Spanish motif. The "t" in Uncertain was her favorite letter. It was in the shape of a cactus, which Lottie Shady had chosen as the logo forty years ago.

Lottie had followed her brother Robert and his wife Irene out to West Texas in 1945. Having previously devoted herself to her brother her entire life, she had nothing else to do. She never married and had never been courted and said it never bothered her one bit. She had used the money she received for a dowry to go into partnership with her brother in the funeral business. The Shadys' parents had both been undertakers and Lottie and Robert had lived in the back of one funeral home or another all their lives. Lottie Shady said she never wanted to live any place else.

She had urged her brother to buy the deserted old building out on the highway the minute they saw it. Originally a small hotel built back in 1910, it had been abandoned shortly after the Hoop and Holler Motel for a Dollar went up across the road in 1935. It suited Lottie and Robert's purposes splendidly.

It did not suit Irene Shady. She had wanted to move from East Texas in the first place just to get away from Lottie Shady. And Irene just knew she could have talked Robert into buying a house and maybe going into a different business altogether if Lottie had only stayed in East Texas.

But Lottie Shady had spent every moment since Pearl Harbor waiting for the war to be over and her brother to come home so they could move to West Texas. She had never let anyone forget her predictions about West Texas. In the mid-twenties, she had urged her parents to sell everything and move to Wink just as the great oil boom broke.

"Listen to this!" Lottie had cried, waving a circular she had ordered in the mail. " 'Wink has electric lights, telephones, natural gas, an abundance of soft water, piped in the streets! Wink has schools, churches, lumber yards, picture shows, hotels, laundries, dry goods stores, hardware stores, drug stores, boot and shoe shops, restaurants, meat markets, bakeries, hospitals, confectionery stores, barber shops, filling stations, storage garages, furniture stores, lunch rooms and the city is growing so rapidly that there is room for and need for a great many more stores!' " She clutched the brochure in frustration. No one was listening. Lottie tried again. " 'Oil made Tulsa, Breckenridge, Burkburnett, Shreveport, Ranger, Borger and many other cities—' " she read, *" 'and oil will make Wink!' "* Only her younger brother Robert paid any attention. "They're goin' to need us!" she had warned. "People are goin' to die left and right and *somebody else is goin' to get to bury 'em!"*

Sure enough, a couple of years later, Lottie came through the door waving a copy of *The Ft. Worth Star Telegram.* "I told 'em, and I told 'em!" Lottie told her younger brother. "But did they listen! Did *anybody* listen? Well, listen to this!" She unfolded the paper. " 'Among the Permian Basin oil towns, Wink held the record homicide rate in 1929, about 85 per 100,000 inhabitants, when the national rate was 8.6!' " Nineteen-year-old Lottie Shady threw the paper down and cried. "All that crime! All that violence! All them dead bodies!" she wailed. "And we're missin' it! *We're missin' the BOOM*!"

It had taken her sixteen years and a World War to get to West Texas. Both of her parents were dead and Robert's new wife, Irene, was the only one who opposed. But when they reached West Texas, they confronted something Lottie had not counted on. Wink, Texas already had an undertaker. So did Monahans, Kermit, Andrews and Pecos.

"Now why didn't that occur to somebody?" Irene Shady had frowned impatiently.

Lottie Shady had smiled patiently back. "I don't know," she had said. "It just didn't."

After looking around the Permian Basin area for one week, Lottie determined that Uncertain, Texas was the only place to settle.

With a population of 2,153, it sat almost on the border of New Mexico and served as a community center for ranchers and oil field workers who lived nearby but didn't want to drive into the larger towns for their business. Uncertain had six churches—The Uncertain First Baptist Church, The Uncertain First Methodist Church, The Uncertain Church of the Nazarene, The Uncertain Seventh Day Adventist Church, The Uncertain Church of Christ, and The Uncertain Assembly of God. It had a hospital, a high school, junior high and primary school, a grocery store, a hardware store, a dry cleaners and laundry, two filling stations, a poolhall and domino parlor, a trailer court, a bank, a gift and flower shop, a drug store, a city hall and library, a community center, a swimming pool, two cafes, a motel, a liquor store, a picture show, a pony man with ponies, and a fortune teller. But it didn't have an undertaker.

When the three of them first arrived in Uncertain, they stayed for a while at the Hoop and Holler Motel for a Dollar until they could repair the old hotel. Irene desperately hoped Lottie would fall in love with the Hoop and Holler and stay on and live there. "It's got room service, maid service, hot coffee twenty-four hours a day, is a convenient walk to work and has all kinds of interestin' and eligible bachelors comin' in and out," she repeated over and over to her sister-in-law.

"We sure are lucky it's here close by," Lottie had replied, oblivious to the hints. "It is one of the main appeals of the location. Out-of-towners comin' in to bury people will just love the Hoop and Holler."

With four rooms and two honeymoon suites upstairs, it never occurred to Lottie to live any place but the Uncertain Chapel of Memories. Robert and Irene took a honeymoon suite. Lottie took a honeymoon suite. That left four rooms empty, which Lottie suggested they rent to the immediate families of out-of-town grievers.

"I thought that's why we bought across from the Hoop and Holler!" Irene protested. "No! No! No! I don't want out-of-town grievers upstairs twenty-four hours a day! Anyway, those four rooms are where I'm puttin' my babies!" And she set out to have one immediately, but she didn't get pregnant until 1949.

When she finally did have Mary Jane Shady, she never considered having another. It was the worst birth experience imaginable.

Two miles away, down at the Flowers' shack, a beautiful but homeless young woman had drifted onto the Flowers' place some months back. On the morning of November 9, 1949, she gave birth to a baby that was the spitting image of Mum Flowers. She tied a rope to a tree and hanged herself in the Flowers' yard. It was the first suicide Lottie and Robert had encountered in their four years at the Uncertain Chapel of Memories. They left without finishing their breakfast to go get the body. A few minutes later, Irene's own labor pains started.

When Lottie and Robert returned, Irene Shady was lying, exhausted, in a cherrywood coffin trimmed in pink satin and covered in blood. Mary Jane Shady was screaming between her legs.

Lottie took one look, got the scissors and cut the umbilical cord.

"Well, she ruined that coffin," said Lottie Shady to Robert Shady, who was holding the suicide victim in his arms.

Irene passed out. Robert took Irene out of the coffin and put the young dead woman in. He donated the spoiled coffin to the Flowers family, who couldn't afford a coffin or anything else.

"I named that little Flowers baby Why-vonne Dee Flowers after Why-vonne De Carlo," Lottie told Irene when she woke up. "But you can bet she's not goin' to have any movie star life."

"This one is," Irene Shady told her sister-in-law. She thought her baby's chestnut curly hair and soft blue eyes and china white skin were a good start for something like that.

"What did you name her?" Lottie wanted to know.

"Mary Jane Shady," Irene said.

"That don't sound much like a movie star name, Irene," Lottie Shady replied. "But I bet future readers of *Star World* will get a kick out of knowing that she was born in a casket on the day of a fatal suicide."

Irene Shady fainted for the second time that day. Thirty-six years later, she had never yet gotten used to her sister-in-law or living in a funeral parlor.

Noontime. Still out of habit, Irene expected to hear the train, but the train didn't pass through town in the day anymore and hadn't for years. Sometimes she could hear it at night, but it wasn't like the old days when it came through, stopping, letting passengers on and off. Now it just passed right on through Uncertain. It didn't carry people anymore anyway. It was all freight.

Just the thought of it all made Irene Shady irritable. She had certainly had no intentions of giving a thought to *what* train passed through Uncertain, Texas, in 1985 or 1955 or 1995. When twenty-year-old Irene Shady came to West Texas in 1945, after Robert Shady got home from the war, four years before Mary Jane was born, Irene had never once entertained the thought of ever living in Uncertain, Texas, permanently. But then Robert died and she had Mary Jane to support, and now here she was, forty years later, sixty years old, still running a funeral parlor with Robert Shady's sister.

Irene pushed a strand of graying auburn hair away from her finely lined face. *Why couldn't Lottie have had the bad heart and Robert the good one?* she asked herself.

Lottie's voice broke into her thoughts. "What a shame your very best friend sent her family business over to Deal Grimes at the One Call Does All Permanent Rest Center," Lottie remarked for the dozenth time that morning. "I wonder what kind of friend that is who wouldn't let you embalm her sister?"

Death has a way of mixin' up its victims, Irene thought to herself with a sigh. *I'm givin' myself about sixty seconds to feel REAL sorry for myself and then I'm goin' to the bank.* Out loud, she told Lottie, "I refuse to make Gladys Turner's excuses for her. If she wants to send her sister to Deal, it's her business."

"It sure isn't our business, 'cause we didn't get any business!" Lottie grumbled. She was combing out Wendell Butler's hair, a stroke victim form Georgia, who had died at the service station the evening before. It would be several days before his family could arrive. Irene hoped Lottie would just keep him on the gurney back in the pantry and not move him up front and into the slumber room where they'd have to look at him until his family could cross Alabama, Mississippi, Louisiana and most of Texas to pick him up.

Formerly the hotel's sitting room, the slumber room, off the parlor, was now used to lay out the deceased. Lottie always kept her two most expensive coffins in this room, in full view for potential buyers. The two currently displayed were navy and baby blue and yellow and cream. The other coffin choices were kept in the storeroom and in one of the four unoccupied rooms upstairs. When there was a service, Lottie usually ended up selling whatever was on display in the slumber room.

A red velvet curtain with gold braid could be pulled to close off this room, but it was only done at the family's request. Usually the curtain was left standing open.

The slumber room opened into the parlor, which was filled with two matching gold cut-velvet sofas and four gold cut-velvet easy chairs. During a service, folding chairs were added from the storeroom next to the kitchen and set up in the saloon behind the parlor to accommodate overflow. If the guest list was too big, Lottie and Irene advised the family to take the whole thing into a church. Most families did this anyway.

The saloon and dining room of the old Uncertain Hotel still contained its original eight mahogany stools and fine mahogany bar with a huge mirror cracked in several places from several gun shot blasts. Irene kept a coffee pot perking and fresh donuts on the counter day and night. She set a round oak table with four-high back chairs smack in the middle of the room. That's where she and Lottie took their meals.

Behind the saloon was the kitchen. The storeroom was on the north side of the kitchen and what used to be the pantry was on the south side. The cabinets had been left in the pantry, but today, and for forty years, it had been used for embalming.

Stepping past Lottie and out of the swinging door to the pantry, Irene moved thorough the saloon, crossed the parlor, passed the slumber room and walked up toward the office. The original counter, switchboard and desk were set back from the entry and off to one side.

Irene rummaged around in the desk for a Rolaid. The office bills were in one drawer, the layaway plans in another and the rest was a mess of pencils, erasers, paper, rubber bands, rubber cement glue, paper clips and whatever else Lottie never threw out. The big operation was the death files. Those were stuck in an old safe that sat behind the desk. Lottie had brought this safe all the way to West Texas on the train. It had been in her family for years. As long as she could remember it had held death certificates and the ones in there now went all the way back to July of 1945. It was never locked. No one knew the combination.

On the wall behind the desk was a map of the City of Uncertain, population 1,213. When the oil business was good, the population tripled, even quadrupled over night, but this year it was 1,213.

Lottie didn't have much of an eye for decorating, so Irene voluntarily fixed things to suit herself. Irene had covered the entire space of the parlor wall with Mary Jane's "career" photographs. The effect was very impressive to everyone who came in, and sure made Irene Shady feel a lot better to look up and see Mary Jane all over the wall in various stages of glamour and glory.

Mary Jane as Lady Macbeth in college looking seriously disturbed, holding her hands up to the heavens. Mary Jane with Martha Raye on tour in *Everybody Loves Opal*. Mary Jane on tour with Ted Shackelford in *Play It Again, Sam* before Ted got famous as "Gary" on *Knots Landing*. Mary Jane with Fabian on the set of *A Bullet for Pretty Boy*. Mary Jane on the set of *Slave of the Scorpions* along with Earlene Huddleston, who was one of the extras. Earlene later became Dove Lightlady and Irene was very proud that it had been Mary Jane who had made that name up for her friend, although she didn't think Mary Jane had ever gotten enough credit for it. Whenever Dove Lightlady went on the Johnny Carson Show or Merv Griffin, she always told how she had chosen her first name from her favorite song, "On the Wings of a Dove." What she *didn't* say was that she had been really reluctant to use the name at the time because she had named her little canary "Dove," and her mother, Hazel, thought it might look funny if a potential star had the same name as her bird. Mary Jane Shady had been the one to assure Hazel Huddleston that the little bird would probably die soon, since it was so old anyway, and then no one would know the difference.

Why Dove Lightlady failed to tell the press how all of this came about remained a source of infinite irritation to Irene Shady, but she hung the girl's picture up anyway. Dove Lightlady was a big TV star now, and Irene was certain that Mary Jane had been hugely responsible and wished her daughter had put the same amount of effort into herself.

Even though all of Mary Jane's movie parts had been minor, and the movies forgettable, Irene hung the stills and posters up and down the staircase.

But Irene's favorite picture was one of Mary Jane at a Christmas party with Charlton Heston's head way in the background.

"Look," Irene would point out to whoever would look. "There's Mary Jane with Charlton Heston in Hollywood."

"Did he recognize her?" Lottie had joked.

That made Irene mad. "They're standing together, aren't they, Lottie?" Irene retorted. "Everybody sees Mary Jane on TV now."

"Those are commercials," Lottie replied.

"It's still a role. A running role. Miss Creamy Crunchy Peanut Butter Nutty or Smooth is a role same as Jane Withers as Josephine the Plumber or Madge or Mrs. Folger..."

"What's Mrs. Folger's first name?" Lottie asked.

"She don't have a first name."

"I mean her *real* first name?"

"I don't know."

"See what I'm sayin'?" Lottie asked. "When you're recognized for important acting, people say 'oh, look, there's Charlton Heston.' Not 'oh, look, there's the Ten Commandments Man.' "

Irene put an entire series of Mary Jane as the Peanut Butter Girl in the vestibule of the entry. She had them blown up to life-size. Mrs. Kleebecker's son had gotten this done in Dallas where he was an interior decorator and knew where to get things like that done. When a person walked into the Uncertain Chapel of Memories, the first thing they saw was the vestibule where five life-sized, full-color Mary Jane Shadys stood in the sweetest gingham dresses, hair ribbons, smiling the loveliest smiles and holding up Creamy Crunchy Peanut Butter, Nutty or Smooth, five different jars of them, all alike, for anyone with a death problem, embalming decision or potential casket layaway plan to gaze upon and be uplifted and *impressed*.

The girl in the blow-ups could have been any age between eighteen and twenty-five. She was wearing a simple pale blue shirt-waisted dress with a full white apron trimmed in eyelet. Her thick chestnut-colored hair was pulled away from her face by small blue ribbons. Her complexion was flawlessly healthy, her cheeks flushed in happy anticipation. Her lips, slightly parted, turned up into a winningly satisfied smile.

Then back in the saloon, all over the bar and across from it, were the more serious "career" photos. The tours, and Charlton Heston, and Mary Jane as Elvira in *Blithe Spirit* the winter she was in upstate New York, in Cohoes, near Albany, the winter of '75 when all those people froze. There were several *Blithe Spirit* photos—Irene loved the costumes. They reminded her of the '40s. She had *loved* the '40s, had been a very snappy dresser herself. Irene always referred to this play as "the New York production." Just "New York" sounded better. Sounded like Broadway. Irene knew that. Let 'em think Mary Jane was on Broadway. She should be. She *would* be.

But recently, Mary Jane had sent her mother pictures of some fancy benefit she had attended put on by something call the "UJA." A few of the men in the photos had beards, but *all* of them were wearing strange little black hats which appeared to be far too small for the their heads, in Irene's opinion.

Mary Jane's date was a clean-shaven man named Herman Top, but he was also wearing one of those little black hats.

Irene had headed straight for her beauty operator, Annie Lovejoy with the photos.

"What do you make of this?" Irene asked Annie, showing her the prints.

"Why, that's Herman Top! He's a big star! I've seen him on Johnny Carson!" Annie Lovejoy exclaimed. "I thought he was I-talian, but I guess he must be a Jew because I think they wear those funny little hats."

"Oh," was all Irene managed to say. She wondered why, if Herman Top was such a big star, she had never seen him on Johnny Carson.

"Now, don't worry, Irene," Annie offered. "They're supposed to be real rich."

"Then why don't they buy some hats that fit?" Irene wanted to know. She'd only known one Jewish man in her entire life that she could recall—Avrum Baum, the husband of Daisy Baum, Mary Jane's old piano teacher. Avrum hadn't been rich and the marriage had not been a happy one. Irene remembered that Avrum had been no taller than a gatepost and had a reputation for being stingy. She remembered Daisy Baum telling her that "short and cheap" were "Jewish hereditary traits."

Irene went home, stuck the pictures down in the bottom of a desk drawer and ate three Rolaids.

Mary Jane had talked over the phone about Herman Top like he was some kind of a god, but to Irene's mind he looked just ordinary. Dark hair (what there was of it), a big nose, a mustache, a set of brown eyes, and that was about it. She also thought he looked too old for Mary Jane. She wondered how tall he was. She wondered what the hell her daughter saw in him. She was sure she didn't want to know.

Irene took the photos out of the drawer and threw them as far in the back of the old safe with the death certificates as she could. She wished she knew the combination of the lock. She ate another Rolaid.

"Sometimes I think Mary Jane would have been better off to have just stayed home and married Bobby Henderson," Irene called to Lottie, back in the pantry, as she went upstairs to get her purse. It was time for her to go to the bank.

"*He* would have been better off," Lottie hollered back. She was busy putting rouge on Wendell Butler's cheeks.

Neither of them saw Baby Flowers climb the seven steps that led to the multi-arched portico running along the north side of the building.

Baby opened the front door of the Uncertain Chapel of Memories, jingling the little bells attached to it and wandered past the five life-sized cut-out figures in the entryway. Five wholesome-looking young cardboard figures held five jars of peanut butter toward her.

Baby smiled back at all five cut-outs, waving happily as she passed each one.

"Is that you, Baby?" Lottie Shady called out, hearing the bell. She expected Baby about this time each weekday. "Come on back."

Baby wandered past the parlor and into the saloon, peering through the open pantry door at Lottie's back.

"Well, you got here just in time to help me pick the colors for Mr. Wendell Butler's lips," said Lottie without looking up, as she rummaged through a selection of lipsticks she kept in an old Melba cigar box. "Since neither one of us knew him—he's from Georgia, and I don't know anybody from Georgia, do you? . . ." Lottie discarded an orange-toned Avon for a scarlet red Mary Kay lipstick. "Didn't think so . . . so we can just pick whatever color for his lips that suits us."

She turned to hold out the scarlet red for Baby's approval, and there Baby stood, right by the pantry door, unadorned as the day she was born.

"Uh-oh," Lottie said. "I see you're out takin' one of *them* walks again, Baby." She reached for a green hospital sheet from a clean stack and tossed it over Baby's shoulders. "Here's you a little painting suit to wear 'til we can finish. Then we'll dress you up in some nice old thing in a better color with maybe some lace. It's too hot to go walkin' around nekked, Honey-Baby. You'll burn that skin and wish you hadn't." She turned back to the cigar box. "Which shade goes best with a dark-complexioned man, do you think? 'Course he's a little paler than usual, I expect, but we'll blush him up and outline his eyes and give him a bright cheery mouth to enter his reward with. I sure hope nobody thinks it was me who colored his hair so black. Looks like shoe polish, don't it? Looks like he's been over to Deal Grimes at the One Call Does All Permanent Rest Center, Heaven forbid. Poor ole Deal just never got the meaning of the word 'natural' . . ." Lottie remarked, discarding a Maybelline labeled "Pink Passion." She picked up a clear red by Revlon called "Paint Me Red."

"Who's that you're talkin' to, Lottie?" Irene called from upstairs. She started down the stairs with her purse, ready to make her noon day trip to the bank, as Baby wandered past the landing, losing her sheet on the banister. "Great stars and little garters!" Irene shouted, heading for the pantry. "Lottie! Lottie-e-e!!!"

"Whatty?" Lottie asked, concentrating fully on the clear red line she was drawing around Wendell Butler's lips.

"I think we've got Baby Flowers out here stark ravin' nekked again!" Irene cried. "Now I am not goin' to take her home again! I've took her home three times this month like that!"

"I give her a sheet," Lottie replied, smoothing out the line.

"Well, she isn't wearin' it!" Irene grumbled. "It's layin' all over the staircase!"

"I told her I'd get her some ole clothes when I finish up these lips," Lottie replied. "I guess she don't like them green sheets. Ever time I put one on her, she throws it off. Probably reminds her of dead people's clothes, since that's what she sees them wearing. She probably don't want to be dressed up like a dead person . . ."

"You give her too much credit for knowin' what she wants, Lottie!" Irene shouted. "She don't know what she wants or much of anything else! Most half-way minded people don't!"

"I don't agree with that a bit," Lottie Shady said. "I think that just about ever half-minded person I know, knows just exactly what they want. It's just smart people who don't have any kind of a idea. And I sure do wish I had her skin and her eyes and hair and figure," Lottie confided, finishing the red bow-like outline around Wendell Butler's lips. "I'm sick of lookin' like Olive Oyl. You look like Garbo and Baby looks like Ava and Mary Jane looks like Mary Jane and I just look like Popeye's ole girlfriend—"

"Let's please don't get off on how you think you look like Olive Oyl right now," Irene snapped impatiently. "Let's concentrate on getting something on that girl before she wanders outside and causes the Grandaddy of Accidents right in the middle of Highway 158!" Irene missed the optimistic glint that flickered across Lottie's face.

Lottie didn't budge. She just kept right on coloring the corpse's lips, as Irene headed for the storeroom in a vain effort to locate a sack of old clothes she'd been saving for the Red Cross.

It wasn't there. Nothing was there but folding chairs, an extra gurney, and several casket crates filled with almost a half century of Christmas tree decorations. The old steel blue 1957 Cadillac hearse with the off-white naugahyde top sat off to itself in the attached garage.

Irene dug around in the closest crate, and was getting ready to try another when the phone started to ring. She grabbed a faded and tattered green Christmas tree skirt with several missing pink sequins that had been trying to spell out "Merry Christmas, Santa!" and hurried inside to answer the phone.

"Couldn't you answer that!" she called out to Lottie, as she hurried up to the front office where she found Baby Flowers rocking in her high back oak desk chair.

"Here!" Irene said to Baby, tying the ragged Christmas tree skirt around her neck like a baby's bib. In her hurry to answer the ringing phone, she tied it on backwards. Baby looked like she was wearing a little green cape.

"Hello!" Irene gasped. "Move, Baby. I gotta sit." She inched in the chair with Baby, who crawled up on her lap. "Oh, Baby, please stand up a minute, Baby. I'm tryin' to talk!" Irene said, attempting to balance Baby and the phone. "Hello! Hello!" she shouted into the phone. "Uncertain Chapel of Memories! Irene Shady on the line!" Irene's painted eyebrows shot upward into two round archs. "I am glad you called, Why-vonne," she said into the phone. "You're just about exactly who I need to talk to . . . " Irene cleared her voice. "Baby's wandered in here nekked again . . . "

"Who?" Yvonne asked innocently.

"Baby! Baby Flowers!" Irene yelled. "You know who!"

"Inn't that awful," Yvonne whined from the other end of the line. "Poor little thang. I don't know why they don't put her away. . . ."

"*They*?" Irene shouted. "How about *you*?"

"*Me?*" Yvonne asked demurely. "Now I didn't call up to talk about *me*. What I'm callin' for is Mary Jane's phone number."

"Whatever for?" Irene asked, her eyes following Baby, who had slipped off her lap and into the vestibule where she stood tracing the lips of a life-sized cardboard Mary Jane Shady.

"It's the Twentieth Year Reunion, Irene! And I'm a volunteer on the Reunion Committee! Now Catsy Ivanhoe and Kay Widders told me that they have been callin' 411 in New York City and Hollywood, California all mornin' long without a bit of luck . . . they are on the Reunion Committee, too . . . but *I* said maybe she moved or maybe she was off vacationin' in Paris, France or somewhere—"

"Oh, she's not listed under her real name, Why-vonne," Irene interrupted, her interest on the rise. "She's too famous and recognizable and somebody's liable to kidnap her or worse. She cain't go in the phone book any more now."

"That is exactly what I tried to tell Catsy Ivanhoe and Kay Widders when they insisted on takin' the 411 route," Yvonne lied. "I said, 'Now let me call up Irene Shady. She's Mary Jane Shady's mother and will know how to get directly in touch with her if anyone will!"

"I'd love to help you out, Why-vonne, but I cannot leave my desk right now to unlock my safe and get that number on a-count of your nekked cousin who is out in my vestibule fingerin' my blow-ups at this very moment!" And with that, Irene slammed down the phone.

Only the length of time it took Yvonne to re-dial passed before the funeral parlor's phone rang again.

"And I am not givin' out any unlisted numbers until a direct Flowers family member comes to get Baby," Irene said without wasting a breath. She hung up again.

The phone rang again.

"I am *not* a direct family member," Yvonne started to protest.

"Oh, stop it, Why-vonne," Irene groaned. "We all have relatives we don't want to claim. At least you're not in business with yours! At least Baby isn't livin' with you day in and day out! At least you don't have to see her first thing in the morning and last thing at night. She don't share no opinions with you, she don't burden you with her thoughts and what color of this or that she likes or any of her wildest desires. You don't have to share the same car and the same check book and the same house with a person, that if things was different, you wouldn't even take out to supper!" Irene grabbed a breath and continued. "I bet she don't take hairnets, pearls, toothbrushes, crochet needles or your last graham cracker while you're not lookin'! I have not gotten to enjoy one last thing to myself since the beginning of my marriage, and including my marriage and don't leave out the death of my late husband, either!"

"No kiddin'?" Yvonne asked sympathetically.

"Why, Robert Shady was not even cold, hadn't even hit the floor before Lottie Shady was all over him like a cheap suit!" Irene screamed.

"I sure am feelin' a lot better," Yvonne offered.

"And that ain't all," Irene went on. "I got years of complaints on you!"

If she'd glanced up a moment sooner, she'd have seen the front door open and Baby go out on the portico. If she'd been paying attention, she could have watched Baby meander down the steps of the portico, passing the sign that warned "BAD INTERSECTION COMING UP RIGHT NOW." If she'd been watching at all, she would have seen Baby start across the intersection, the little green Christmas tree cape flapping back over her shoulders in the breeze, the sun bobbing across the sequined letters on her back.

But she looked out only in time to see the big eighteen-wheeler truck thundering toward the intersection directly toward Baby Flowers.

It had passed Catsy Ivanhoe only a few minutes before. Determined not to be upstaged by Mary Jane Shady's arrival and filled with dressmaking instructions and opportunities for the ex-Hopi Indian to follow, Catsy was preparing to make a left-handed turn off the highway and into the old man's dirt driveway when something flew by her so fast it knocked three gravel niches in her Silver Cloud's windshield.

Down the road, Petunia, Iris, Rose, Daisy, Daffodil, Poppy and Mum hardly had a chance to wave as the truck passed the Flowers' place.

Kay Widders had started out of her driveway on her way to the florist, but thought better of it and put on her brakes when she heard it coming, and she could hear it coming two miles away.

The truck thundered past Catsy, roared past the Flowers and flew by Kay, ready to rocket right through the red light. But just as the driver got even with the fortune teller's tent, he woke up and hit the brakes.

"Fuck a duck!" the driver yelled. "I almost slept right through it!" He blinked his eyes fast, shook his head hard, and slammed on the brakes.

Regaining control, he let out a big sigh of relief.

He had almost come to a full stop when a little green cape floated across the road. A dancing nude figure with long black hair floated along with the cape.

"Oh-h-h-h . . ." the driver sighed, as he watched the girl in the cape. Mesmerized, he stared at the exquisite bare legs, the tiny waist, the perfect breasts, the splendid smiling face.

"I'm dead," the driver said. "And heaven is a centerfold!"

Baby Flowers turned, her buttocks peeking through her long black hair. As Baby moved back up the steps of the Uncertain Chapel of Memories, the driver leaned out and rolled down the window on the passenger's side.

"Wait up, Heaven!" he called out to Baby.

"Look out!" Irene Shady yelled from inside.

But it was too late.

There was a splintering crash as the truck ran right into the sign, somersaulting the driver out the passenger's window.

"I gotta go, Why-vonne!" cried Irene Shady. "I think we got a customer!"

She tossed Baby the phone and ran outside followed by her sister-in-law.

"Wait! Wait!" Yvonne yelled. "You got to give me that number!"

No one answered back, for Baby dropped the phone on the desk and wandered back into the pantry where she picked up a purple eyelining pencil and started drawing dots on Wendell Butler's cheeks.

Irene and Lottie were already out the front door.

"Is anybody dead?" Lottie called out hopefully. "Or are ya'll just hurt?"

"Oh-h-h," came a big moan from the other side of the dented truck and wrecked sign. "I've broke my head, my hand and my heel. . ."

"Lottie and Irene stopped in their tracks and shook their heads in simultaneous disappointment.

"Not dead," they sighed. "Not even bad hurt."

"I'll park that truck along side of the building," Lottie said. She hopped in the driver's seat and shifting into reverse by mistake, she smashed the sign into the gravel as she searched for the right gear to take her forward.

"Okay," Irene told the driver who was still lying in a heap. "Let's get you inside and have a look."

"Oh-h-h, I'm about dyin' . . ." the man groaned.

He was a tall man, over six-feet five-inches, and had the reddest, most wiry hair Irene thought she'd ever seen. His forehead was bleeding, his hand was scratched, and he favored his right foot as Irene helped him inside.

"Where am I?" the man moaned as Irene helped him move up the steps.

"Uncertain, Texas, mister," Irene replied.

"What?"

"You're four hunnerd miles west of Dallas and three hunnerd miles east of El Paso on the southeast border of New Mexico and the northwest border of Texas, and right at the edge of the Permian Basin Area, is where you're at," Irene clarified.

"Uncertain?"

"There used to not be no name for this town and nobody knew if it went to Texas or New Mexico either. That's why they named it what they named it, then flipped a coin to see who got it," Irene explained.

"I used to have a brother who picked him out a wife like that once," the driver whimpered, leaning heavily on Irene.

"He'd understand how this town got its name then," Irene responded, helping the man up the last step.

"What happened?" the driver asked. "I know I hit somethin'. I hope it wasn't something green," he added.

"You run the red light, mister."

"I think I hit somethin'."

"That, too," Irene nodded. "That sign said 'BAD INTERSECTION COMING UP RIGHT NOW. IF YOU MISS IT AND LAND ON THIS PROPERTY, PLEASE KILL YOURSELF,' but you didn't." She opened the front door.

"Is that what that sign said?" The driver couldn't even remember seeing a sign. He wanted to ask her if she'd seen a little fairy wearing something green dancing out on the road, but he didn't.

He followed Irene inside the door and found himself gazing at five big life-sized pictures of a girl he knew from someplace but couldn't remember where.

"She sure looks familiar . . ." he murmured.

"That is Miss Mary Jane Shady," Irene Shady said as she pointed to the blow-ups. "You know her as the Peanut Butter Queen, I'm sure."

"I do?" the driver asked weakly.

"You sure do," Irene told him, lost in her favorite topic. "And isn't that outfit a cute look?" Irene beamed at the blow-ups in undisguised adoration.

Drops of blood trickled down the driver's forehead and slowly dripped onto the tip of his nose.

"Mary Jane Shady has hit the top in Peanut Butter," Irene glowed. "You cain't get a bit further up in it than she has got."

"I'm pleased to hear that," the man offered feebly. He wished she'd ask him to sit down.

"Uh-oh. You're about to drip on the pictures," Irene noticed. She grabbed a handkerchief from her pocket and thrust it toward him. "Hold that over that cut above your eye and follow me."

She turned, walked past the front desk, into the parlor and headed directly for the wall covered with photos of her daughter.

"These are a few career highlights," Irene said to the man who stood weakly, but obediently, at her side. "Go on, sit down."

He did.

"Ever see *Macbeth?*" she asked him. "I saw it on the TV with Orson Welles, I saw it tour through Odessa at the Community Culture Series with Judith Anderson, and I saw it at North Texas State University starring Mary Jane Shady. I am a *Macbeth* expert, Mister, and I am here to tell you that nobody gets a spot out better than Mary Jane Shady did."

The man nodded obligingly.

"Here's *Vanities*. Ever see that one?" Irene asked.

"I haven't seen too many live shows lately," the man confessed.

"Well, then you missed three cheerleaders goin' from high school to college to grown ups with some real bad problems in about ninety-minutes. They aged ten years without ever leavin' the stage. Changed hair and make-up and clothes right before your eyes! Now, that takes talent!"

"Seems like it would," he nodded. He looked at the photo next to it. "I know that blond gal yonder. That's Dove Lightlady."

"Well, she sure wasn't Dove Lightlady when that was taken, though," Irene told him. "She was Earlene Huddleston and nothin' but. Dove Lightlady ain't her real name."

"Naw-w-w . . . ?" He leaned forward in the chair, staring at the photo. "It sure fits her."

"Mary Jane Shady made that name up for her," Irene told him like a teacher about to explain instructions for a final major examination. "When that photo was taken, Earlene Huddleston was nothin' more and nothin' less than a extra!"

"A extra?" he asked. "What's that?"

"A extra is a actor with no words to say. It is the lowest form of show business there is, Mr.—?"

"Diggs. Leo Diggs."

"Well, Mr. Diggs, Mary Jane Shady took one look at a little nobody named Earlene Huddleston and turned that girl's career around by namin' her Dove Lightlady."

"Wonder how she thought it up," he wondered.

"The 'lady' section of 'Lightlady' Mary Jane took from Lady Bird Johnson's first name," Irene replied without losing a beat. "The 'light' section was strictly imagination on Mary Jane's part, but it was inspired by that white skin of Earlene's."

"Pale as pearls . . ." sighed Leo Diggs.

"Oh, she's as white as a sheet!" Irene retorted, exasperated. "If Mary Jane hadn't been so creative, Earlene Huddleston could have just as easily been called Dove Whitesheet or Dove Ghostly!"

Leo Diggs frowned, considering this.

"And Mary Jane insisted that Earlene go ahead and use Dove, even if her bird did have the same name. Now it was a good enough name for a canary, but I think it also turned out real elegant and clean-sounding for a sex symbol."

"A good name for both thangs," Leo sighed.

"And she also got her a built-in theme song," Irene added. Without warning, she squeezed her eyes shut, opened her mouth wide, threw back her head and sang out hoarsely, "On the wings of a snow white dove . . ."

Leo thought she looked like a dying bird begging for food. "I get a real kick when they play that when she comes on them talk shows," he said over her singing.

"Believe me," Irene assured him, abruptly dropping the song, "they wouldn't play that tune for somebody still callin' theirselves *Earlene*!"

"Mary Jane should have probably just kept that name for herself," Lottie said as she came through the front door, slamming it behind her. The jangling bells made the truck driver's head throb.

"It fits Dove, Lottie," Irene replied without looking at her. "It don't fit Mary Jane." Irene pointed at the driver. "This here is Leo Diggs who run into that sign. Mr. Diggs, that's my sister-in-law and business partner, Lottie Shady." She stood up, heading for another photo. "Now look here, Mr. Diggs. Here's Mary Jane Shady in Hollywood with Charlton Heston—"

"Only she don't know him," Lottie added.

Leo Diggs turned in confusion from Irene to Lottie, who came around and extended her hand. "Howdy—" she started, but when she saw him, she could say nothing else.

"They was at a big party together—" Irene tried to continue.

Neither Leo nor Lottie heard a word she said after that.

Seventy-five and never married, never courted and never interested in any man other than her brother, Lottie Shady found herself staring at the reddest hair she'd ever seen.

Leo Diggs stared back at her. Speechless and quivering, he slowly pulled himself to his feet, unfolding his six-foot five-inch frame. Visions of frolicking fairies danced out of his head along with movie stars Dovelight Lady and Charlton Heston and Peanut Butter Queen Mary Jane Shady. He was struck dumb, for standing before him was the spitting image of his all-time heroine: Olive Oyl.

"I'm glad to see you made it, Leo Diggs!" Lottie Shady cried, looking up into his eyes. It was the first time in all her years as an undertaker that she had said that to a survivor and meant it.

The driver, unable to speak, just kept staring down at his heroine's look-alike.

"Believe me, you could have done worse!" Lottie assured him in a rush. His presence was making her talk much faster than usual. "You could have crashed into Deal Grimes' One Call Does All Permanent Rest Center downtown! Over here, we just try to get you to your reward in a form God will recognize. Deal don't do that!"

"Deal just ain't no good deal," Leo Diggs replied, gazing into her eyes.

"Sure ain't!" Lottie beamed. "Now come sit back here at this table and let me look you over." She was dying to touch his bloody face.

As he followed her, he glanced into the slumber room. Seeing the two caskets, Leo stopped in his tracks.

"What kind of a business did you say you're in?" he asked.

"Death," Lottie replied brightly. "And that is my top-of-the-line metallic blue, velvet-lined, seepage, varmit and jewelry-proof coffin you're gazin' in wonder at, and I don't blame you, 'cause it is a bargain at nineteen-ninety-nine seventy-five."

"Whew!" Leo let out a low whistle.

"If you're in the market to shop for your future, I can order one for you," Lottie offered. "That one's probably taken by a stroke victim from Georgia" She glanced at the yellow and cream coffin. "And frankly, I don't think this one suits you."

"I'm not sure I'm ready to pick out a casket," Leo mumbled.

"You can get a package rate," Lottie offered. "See, here at the Uncertain Chapel of Memories, we drain and formaldehyde the body, do the hair, fix the nails, paint the cheeks, mascara the lashes, not to mention performin' horrible accident repairs and offer a fine selection of caskets as well."

"I think I'll just stick to the horrible accident repairs for right now," Leo told her, limping closely behind her.

"We'll see about that," Lottie smiled. She went behind the counter, grabbed a bottle of whiskey and a glass. "First we'll give you a few spirits, then we'll clean you up some."

"If you've got things under control here, I'm goin' on the bank," Irene stated irritably. "I've had about all the interruptions I can take for one day!"

Neither Leo nor Lottie turned to tell Irene Shady good-bye as she stormed through the storeroom and out into the garage.

"Nothin' like some Ole Turkey to get your heart racin'," Lottie said as she poured.

"That and a couple of these ought to fix me up," Leo nodded. He took a crumbled paper bag out of his inside pocket. "Ya'll must have the only red light for a hunnerd miles."

"This same year that red light's caught a hay man, a potato carrier, a livestock hauler and a outfit transportin' sixteen brand new Chevys!" Lottie cried, glad to have a few exciting things to tell the most handsome man she'd ever seen. She took a dishtowel and wet it.

"Quite a record," Leo noted, looking up from his sack.

"Uh-huh," Lottie nodded, putting the towel to his face. "It was round-up time with the cattle truck. We had cow poop on the road for two whole days before they could clean the mess up."

"That light's a hazard," Leo agreed, taking a large yellow pill out of the sack.

Lottie tossed the towel on top of the counter. "That's the biggest yellow asperin I ever seen," she said.

"Percodan," Leo told her. "Asperin gimme a bellyache."

"Me, too," Lottie agreed.

"Want one?" Leo asked. "The sound of that crash probably give you a headache, too."

"It sure did," Lottie nodded. "Irene gives me a headache, too."

"This'll fix that," he promised.

"Then I'll try one," Lottie smiled, taking it. "What are those big black things?" she asked, looking in the bag full of pills.

"They're to perk me up instead of coffee," Leo explained. "Coffee's bad for my stomach." He rubbed the back of his neck tenderly. "Boy, I may have got me another whip lash."

"They's been countless cars and pick-up trucks and six-wheelers previous to you," Lottie told Leo, as she swallowed the yellow pill and washed it down with the Wild Turkey. "Whew! That stuff's nasty!"

"The nastier, the better," the driver grinned. Taking the glass and finishing the drink, he poured more.

"That light's caused four deaths this year alone by fire, flood, plain ole collision and outright shock," Lottie went on.

Leo nodded. "I *know* they's a light there, but by the time I get *here* from clean across the other side of the U.S. of A., I just plum forget about it 'til I'm right on top of it," he confided.

"That's what they all say unless they're too dead to say it," Lottie said.

Leo stared at her in wonder.

She stared back. Then slowly, she started to grin.

"Can I ask you a personal question?" The truck driver reached over and took her hand.

Lottie Shady thought she just might stop breathing for sure. She gave a quick nod.

"Did anyone ever tell you that you look exactly like my all-time heroine, Olive Oyl?"

"Oh, Mr. Diggs," Lottie Shady giggled. "People just tell me that all the time!"

Irene was backing her 1957 midnight-blue Cadillac hearse out of the garage when Yvonne Henderson's limousine pulled up.

"I've come to get Baby!" Yvonne hollered. "Now what's that number?"

"212-265-0060," Irene hollered back. "Ask for Suite 1717."

"I don't think I can remember that," Yvonne called out.

"Of course you cain't," Irene muttered, searching in her glove compartment for a piece of paper and a pen or pencil to write the number on, as Yvonne got out of her limo and headed for the hearse. Finally, Irene cut off her engine as she dug around in her purse. As she did so, she double-checked her mind to make sure this wasn't the first she had heard of Yvonne serving on any kind of Reunion Committee. Yvonne wasn't always reliable, no fault of her own, but Irene seemed to remember Kay Widders telling her that Yvonne had volunteered sometime back.

"I doubt you're goin' to have any more luck than I do even gettin' her on the phone," Irene said, fishing a pencil and an old gas receipt out from between the seats. As she printed the number of the Mayflower Hotel in New York City, she couldn't help but wonder why a person with a choice would deliberately choose to live in a hotel. "Here." She thrust the paper out the window and started her engine. "And don't forget Baby."

"I won't," Yvonne promised as Irene drove off.

But as soon as Irene's hearse disappeared, Yvonne got back in her limousine and drove off without ever going inside the Uncertain Chapel of Memories.

"Hit the gas, José!" she squealed to her driver. "I've all but got Mary Jane Shady back in town!"

MANHATTAN

WISPS OF DAMP CHESTNUT curls clung to her face. Her lips, full and ripe, were slightly parted. Her long dark lashes gave a faint flutter. She moaned and slipped into the song.

> *We were drivin' down the dirt road*
> *After a six-pack picture show . . .*
> *It had just been oiled the day before*

I asked him please drive slow . . .
'Cause if I was gonna put my head down
Underneath that steerin' wheel . . .
I didn't want a broken neck
To interrupt my meal . . .

To the rhythm of the oil pump
My heart was beatin' wild . . .
I felt just like a bluebonnet
Tumbleweed prairie child . . .

When he painted me with his tongue
Like I was a piece of art . . .
That is when my friend
He touched the clitoris of my heart . . .

"Now that is a hit for sure," thought Topsy as the words to her latest career effort floated through her mind. She had already picked out her dress for the Grammys and was ready to compose her acceptance speech when two thoughts hit: This song had no music. And worse, who was this person lying in bed with her? It might be Mary Jane Shady.

"Oh, shit," thought Topsy. "Why does she do that? I haven't even opened my eyes and she's ruined my day."

She squeezed her eyes tight, took a deep breath, and when she opened them she screamed.

Lying beside her was a big black German shepherd.

"Oh, God, don't tell me I fucked another dog and forgot it!" Topsy cried.

The dog, awakened by Topsy's sudden outcry, sat up, looked at her alertly, then nuzzled her gently.

"Is this curiosity or just a low self-image?" Topsy wondered anxiously.

She gave the dog a half-hearted pat and climbed out of the twisted sheets.

"You have to go now," she said, absently noting she had slept in her clothes. "I have a life of my own," she told the big black German shepherd.

She escorted him out of Suite 1717, into the elevator, into the lobby and into the street.

"Boy, do I need a drink," she said to herself, and making an about-face, entered the Conservatory, the bar attached to the Mayflower Hotel. Thank God it opened at eight A.M. Good ole New York.

"Hi, ya," said Topsy to the bartender, who looked amazingly like Bobby Henderson, Mary Jane Shady's old boyfriend from Uncertain, Texas. "Gimme a martini on the rocks with a twist. What time is it anyway?"

"One-thirty P.M.," Bobby-the-Bartender replied.

"Gee," Topsy murmured. "I thought it was early."

"Time flies when you're having fun," Bobby grinned. "Is that your dog? A big black German shepherd just followed you in."

"Well, shit," Topsy sighed with dismay. "I sleep with them once and they think they own me."

Bobby-the-Bartender almost dropped the glass. He did drop the lemon. "You FUCKED that DOG?" Bobby cried. "Do you know what you're saying? Do you know what you did, MARY JANE SHADY?! YOU FUCKED A BIG BLACK GERMAN SHEPHERD!

"Oh, Bobby..." Topsy whispered. "I wouldn't fuck anything else..."

Mary Jane Shady's eyes flew wide open and she shot up in bed like the blast from a cannon, throwing half the pink foam rollers in her hair clear across the mattress.

"Oh, no, no, no, no, no!" she cried to no one, for she was alone in Suite 1717 of the Hotel Mayflower, high above Central Park West.

"Oh, what a nightmare!" she moaned, knocking over the glass of water she was reaching for on the bedside table. "Where did *she* come from?" She held her head in her hands. "Oh, help..."

The phone rang and the alarm went off at the same time. She hit the alarm button and grabbed the phone. "Hello?"

"Is that you, Mary Jane Shady?" a familiar Texas twang sang from a long distance connection.

TOPSY? She was afraid to ask, afraid to say it, afraid to find out she'd lost her mind for sure.

OH, PLEASE DON'T LET ME BE TALKING TO MYSELF OVER THE PHONE NOW, she begged herself.

Carefully, she drew the words out in a whisper. "Who is this, please?"

"Why-vonne!"

Relief! It wasn't Topsy! "Who?"

"Used to be Why-vonne Dee Flowers, but I was adopted and don't let anybody tell you different!" the voice cried. "'Member me? Why-vonne from Uncertain? You remember me, your Aunt Lottie named me after Why-vonne De Carlo!"

"Well, sure," Mary Jane said, immediately visualizing Yvonne's bald spot.

Why-vonne . . . Everyone in Uncertain, Texas, including Yvonne, pronounced her name "Why-vonne." Years ago, when Mary Jane first came to New York, she was introduced to Yvonne De Carlo at a cocktail party. Delighted to tell the star about her namesake back in Uncertain, Texas, Mary Jane had been astonished to learn that everyone, including the star, pronounced "Why-vonne" "Eve-on." Mary Jane had wondered what else she had been mispronouncing all her life and had started diction lessons the very next day.

"I didn't think you'd forget me!" Yvonne shrieked. "You and me have got more than the same birthday in common!"

Yeah, we're both total retards, Mary Jane said to herself. Her Aunt Lottie must have told her the story of the birth of the poor little Flowers girl a million times. "Another low-life delivery," her mother had called it.

"While you went off and got famous, I stayed right here and picked up your pieces!"

"Excuse me?" Mary Jane said with far more control than she felt.

"Why, I married Bobby Henderson, but I bet you already knew that!"

Mary Jane's heart hammered against her chest. Her head pounded. Her throat went dry. Her hands shook.

I DID NOT KNOW THAT! her inside voice screamed.

"Bobby Henderson . . ." her outside voice said, slowly, calmly.

"You and me has got a lot in common!" Yvonne squealed.

"You just got married?" Mary Jane heard herself ask casually.

"Why, we got married the day you left!" Yvonne exclaimed. "And it's been wilder than a rodeo!"

Mary Jane stared at the phone.

"That's not why I called, though . . . " Yvonne's voice droned on.

SINCE THE DAY I LEFT? SINCE THE DAY I LEFT? SINCE THE DAY I LEFT? The words beat against her head like a big bass drum.

"I'll tell you all about it when I see you," Yvonne promised.

"You're coming to New York?" Mary Jane gasped. *WILDER THAN A RODEO?* She felt sick.

"No, silly, I never get past Highway 158! I been tryin' to locate you all day long and finally it occurred to me to get this number from your mother and I sure am glad I did, 'cause I can tell you right now that they do not have a listin' for you in information. How often do people try to kidnap you, anyway? That sure must be some kind of excitin' life!"

Mary Jane laughed hollowly.

"What's New York City like anyway? Looks tall from the pictures. I saw it in that movie *Manhattan* over in Odessa. The Dirt Dauber Drive-In closed, I hate to tell you. It's worse then *The Last Picture Show* here, I'm not kiddin'."

While Yvonne paused for a breath, Mary Jane asked, "When you see me *where*, Yvonne? Are you planning some kind of a trip?"

"No, darlin', I'm all set up in Uncertain. I thought I said that. Listen, I'm richer than God and I *should* take a trip—I'd like to visit Italy, Europe or someplace foreign like that, but I don't have time today! I sure am windy, aren't I?" Yvonne giggled. "I just haven't talked to you in so long and I am so relieved to have finally got you that I almost keep forgettin' to tell you why I'm callin'. Now hold on for the big news!"

Mary Jane squeezed the phone.

"It's twenty years!"

"Twenty years?"

"Since you graduated!"

PLEASE DO NOT SAY THAT, Mary Jane's inside voice snapped sharply. Her left hand automatically reached up to touch the faint new line under her left eye.

"I'm a volunteer on the Reunion Committee and I have got real big plans for your come-back here, and that's why I'm callin', 'cause I know you will just die if you don't get to come!"

HE MARRIED PURE WHITE TRASH. MARRIED IT. WILDER THAN A RODEO . . .

"Starts with the Pep Rally on Friday and that's day after tomorrow," Yvonne stated as if she were reading off a recipe. "I awready talked to your mother who is just waitin' for the word to pick you up at the airport in Midland and drive you on home, so hurry up and call me when you get here and I'll tell you how we're going to have you crown the Homecomin' Queen and ride in the parade and how we're goin' to shine the spotlight all over you!"

"Listen, I'm sick," Mary Jane confided. "It's in my head, my heart and just about everywhere. I can't make it."

"Is it on your face?" Yvonne cried.

Mary Jane giggled in spite of herself. "Well, not yet," she admitted.

"Then hurry up and get here before it reaches your face!" Yvonne told her.

"You sound just like my agent," Mary Jane sighed. "Listen, no kidding, I have to work. I can't come."

"Bein' Miss Peanut Butter Cup?" Yvonne wanted to know. "Well, skip. You been showin' up for years for that job. Won't they let you off for a day?"

"I just can't leave now, Yvonne," Mary Jane said. "I'm shooting a Peanut Butter commercial on Friday. But thanks for asking me."

"But this is *urgent*," Yvonne pleaded. "This is a matter of life and death!"

"I gotta go, Yvonne," Mary Jane said firmly. "I am ten minutes late to the biggest meeting of my life."

"Are you tryin' out for Jack Nicholson?" Yvonne cried.

"How'd you guess?" Mary Jane lied. "I gotta go, Yvonne. I don't like to keep Jack waiting—"

"Bring him with you!" Yvonne squealed.

"Tell everyone I said hi," Mary Jane said quickly. "Tell Bobby. . ." She hesitated a moment, then found her voice. "Congratulations. . ."

She hung up before Yvonne could reply, and stood staring at the phone, as it started ringing again. The ringing became hypnotic, orchestral.

WHEN HE PAINTED ME WITH HIS TONGUE, LIKE I WAS A PIECE OF ART, THAT IS WHEN MY FRIEND, HE TOUCHED THE CLITORIS OF MY HEART. . .

The ringing continued, the song stopped and Mary Jane's heart pounded on.

"Bobby Henderson, you son-of-a-bitch!" she screamed. "How dare you come find me in such a devious underhanded way! You haven't changed a bit! Just get out of my nightmares and off my phone!"

She threw the ringing phone across the room. "Tell Uncertain, Texas that Topsy's dead and neither of us is ever coming back!"

She turned to face herself in the mirror.

"You are dead, Topsy Dingo Wild Dog, do you hear me?" she told her reflection. "Dead, dead, dead."

But like a pregnant woman before any signs of an embryo's life, Mary Jane Shady felt it and knew it and had no idea how to abort it.

PART
ONE

CHAPTER ONE

IRENE SHADY had no sooner parked the hearse in front of the Uncertain State Bank when Kay Widders plunged out of the flower shop next door and waddled toward her as fast as her poundage would allow, waving a gold mum corsage in each hand.

Looks like a baby hippo, Irene said to herself.

"Oh, Irene!" Kay called. "I saw that man wreck your sign! Did he live?"

"Yeah," Irene sighed half-heartedly. "Just some scratches."

"Listen, before you replace that sign, I got a idea!" Kay told her. "Let's get Orville Turner to have the senior art class to write 'WELCOME HOME, MARY JANE SHADY, STAR OF UNCERTAIN,' all over it!"

"Why?" Irene asked, although the idea appealed to her enormously.

"So she can see it when she first drives up and feel real good about herself!"

Irene looked at Kay blankly.

"Listen," Kay went on, "Verona and Morona just about died when I told them Mary Jane Shady was comin' back to crown the Homecomin' Queen! Everybody in town is talkin' about how Why-vonne pulled *this* one off!"

Irene blinked. "Why-vonne sure didn't waste no time!"

Kay nodded. "I am just so proud it was me who had the presence of mind to recruit Why-vonne on the Reunion Committee! Frankly, Mary Jane's returnin' was more that I dared to hope for!"

"Me, too," Irene said, genuinely surprised.

"Verona and Morona saw her on the midnight movie last weekend and have talked about nothin' else ever since. They kept waitin' for her to say somethin', but they enjoyed hearin' her scream."

"That picture was more action-oriented," Irene acknowledged.

"What was the name of it again?" Kay asked. "*Don't Look in the Incinerator*?"

"*A Bullet for Pretty Boy*," Irene corrected.

"That's it!" Kay cried, slapping the flowers on top of the hood of the hearse. "Oh, girl! Verona said when Mary Jane got shot so much blood come out of her left eye she didn't know how in the world Mary Jane would ever be able to wear that nightie again."

"That was a *dress*," Irene replied.

"Blue? Was it blue?" Kay asked.

"Yes, it was," Irene nodded.

"With lace on it, around the arms and the hem?" Kay didn't wait for Irene's answer. "Morona said it was a nightgown, but maybe she thought that since Mary Jane got shot to death in a motel bed."

"But she died *outside*," Irene emphasized. "She had to crawl out the door in twenty-degree weather up there in Montana or Wyoming or someplace to be able to strangle on the barbed-wire fence."

"I thought she died from spider bites," Kay frowned.

Irene shook her head. "You're thinkin' of *Slave of the Scorpions*. That was another picture."

Kay patted Irene's hand. "Movie stars have a rough life, don't they, Irene?"

"That wasn't her dress either," Irene stated.

Kay took her hand back. "No? It looked real good on her from what Morona said. She borrow it from a girlfriend? She may have to buy her a new one when she sees all that blood—"

"That's *play* blood," Irene sighed. "You can buy it over at Wacker's Ten Cent Store if they're not out. You don't think a big movie maker like Zachary Fogleman is goin' to let them ruin a good dress, do you?"

"Was he the director?" Kay asked, wide-eyed.

"Somethin'," Irene replied. "That was a two-hunnerd-dollar dress if it was a dime. Plus, they had *two* of 'em, exactly alike. When they got blood all over one, Mary Jane just took it off and got blood all over the other."

"Why?" Kay asked. "Why'd she mess up two dresses?"

Irene gave Kay Widders a good long stare. "They don't get these things right lickety-split, Kay. Sometimes they're there all day long just tryin' to shoot somebody."

"You're kiddin'," Kay laughed, her fat rolling like ocean waves.

"It is just *grueling*," Irene grimaced. "I don't know how Mary Jane does it. She's worked like a dog to get where she is today."

"What are we goin' to see her in next?" Kay asked. "I sure do love her in those commercials."

"She's goin' to be on a soap opera," Irene announced proudly.

Kay squealed. "Oh! Which one! The twins will probably quit school to watch it unless I buy a VCR!"

Irene was trying to decide which soap opera to name. Mary Jane didn't actually have the job yet, but Irene didn't want to let down

Kay's twins, or Kay either, for that matter, and clearly, news of Mary Jane Shady was the biggest news Uncertain, Texas, ever got. But just as the words *The Young and the Restless*, Irene's favorite, were about to spill out of her mouth, Spider Webb Turner, Uncertain's only policewoman, came running up, yelling, "Irene! Irene! We got a death out on the highway! Ole Mrs. Lester Woolley run the red light again and squished ole Lucie Garden flatter'n a bug!"

"Why do they let ole Mrs. Woolley drive?" Kay wondered. "She's blind. Legally, too."

"Are you sure Lucie Garden's dead, Spider?" Irene asked the six-foot tall woman in freshly pressed khakis. "I've already had one false alarm today."

"If she ain't, she oughter be," Spider replied. "She's *scattered*!"

"Well, make sure and then go on over to the Chapel and tell Lottie. I'm on my break here."

"I done been over to the Uncertain Chapel of Memories and delivered the body! When Miss Lottie saw who it was, she started screamin', screamed right out loud, screamed that she wouldn't touch ole Lucie Garden if she was the last corpse on earth!"

Irene blinked. "She said that?"

Spider nodded. "She screamed it. Said she didn't give a hill of beans if ole Lucie Garden went right over to Miss Deal Grimes' One Call Does All Permanent Rest Center!"

"Naw!" Irene's heart hit a few extra licks at the mention of her competitor. A second later she was back in her hearse.

"You're drivin' off with my flowers!" Kay Widders shouted after her.

But Irene didn't hear her. She was already backing out, her foot full-force on the accelerator, wondering what on earth would cause Lottie to even consider sending business over to the competition.

It took exactly three minutes for Irene to get from the Uncertain State Bank to the Uncertain Chapel of Memories. Later, Sammy Widders told her she almost hit him broadsided as he pulled out from The Hoop and Holler Motel for a Dollar's restaurant, The Hoop It Up Bar and Grill, across the street. Irene never saw him. She only saw the pink two-story stucco building with its neon sign in blue, yellow, green, red and pink steadfastly blinking "Uncertain Chapel of Memories" up on the roof.

"Lottie!" she hollered, going through the door. "How many times have we talked about it bein' your responsibility to turn that sign off durin' the daytime?" Irene slung her keys on the desk and took a deep breath. "LOTTIE!" she yelled.

"Whatty?" Lottie answered, calmly coming into the vestibule from the back of the funeral home, her purse in her hand. "She's in yonder laid out, and ready to be drained and formaldehyded. One arm and half a leg's still in the crash bag. All them Garden's end up in crash bags," she observed, unostentatiously making her way toward the door.

"Where the hell are you going?" Irene demanded. She pushed a strand of auburn hair behind one ear with a jerk and looked down at the person standing in front of her. "I was attemptin' to have a most enlightenin' conversation with Kay Widders, when Spider Webb Turner busted upon us and said Lucie's been dismembered and that you'd lost your mind and was throwin' a conniption fit and yellin' for her to be sent over to Deal Grimes!" Irene cried.

"I ain't touchin' her," Lottie sniffed.

"But *why*?" Irene pleaded. "What'd she ever do to you? You didn't even hardly know her." Irene paced in a little circle around the room. "I never, in all my forty years of workin' here with you, *ever, ever* seen you ready to turn your back on a dead person!"

Lottie squeezed her eyes tight.

"Speak, Sister!" Irene begged, giving Lottie a hard shake.

"She failed me!" Lottie whispered in a high squeaky voice.

"How? How?" Irene asked, her mind trying to recall how and when in Lottie's past, she had been failed by old Lucie Garden. Had Lucie failed to show up for some committee for some fly-by-night idea Lottie often conjured up, like raffling off tickets of ownership for the first Unidentified Flying Object found in Elmer County? Lottie had sold tickets to Gladys Turner's entire fifth grade class and promised the children the winner could take the UFO home with them if they'd just be patient and quiet. It was three weeks before Gladys Turner found out.

Irene sighed. This could be anything, but it was probably nothing as bad as selling non-existent alien outer space objects to little children. "How, Lottie?" she asked.

"She failed me in the second grade!" Lottie cried.

"Failed you in the second grade?" Irene asked incredulously.

"Yes, ma'am, that is right." Lottie stood up, held herself up as tall as she could and pointed at Irene as if she were holding a gun toward her. "Now don't make me say it *again*." Lottie started for the door.

"Hold it!" Irene yelled.

"You hold it!" Lottie yelled back.

"Ya'll both hold it," Leo Diggs pleaded, as he came in the front door. "Please, girls, don't fight." He turned to Irene. "I think Miss Lottie has just got so upset by this second-grade failure of hers that she ain't in no shape to work. I give her a little somethin' to calm her down and promised her a ride out on the highway in my truck."

"If you're plannin' on drivin' how you was drivin' this mornin', you may kill her," Irene snapped.

"If he does, don't send me to Deal Grimes!" Lottie cried.

"You'd send Lucie Garden to Deal Grimes!" Irene yelled.

"That's because I'm hysterical from facin' my second-grade failure!" Lottie screamed. "Now let me go! You been beggin' me to get out of the house for forty years!"

"But why do you have to go on the day I find out Mary Jane Shady's comin' home?" Irene wanted to know.

Lottie gave a big sigh. "Will she be here in the next thirty minutes?" she asked.

"Probably not," Irene admitted.

"Then good-bye for now, we're takin' a ride," Lottie said, as she pulled Leo toward the door.

"Sure your truck will run?" Irene asked Leo.

"Yes, ma'am," he nodded. "I was just out checkin' her. I didn't hurt nothin' but your sign."

"Well, don't worry about it," Irene told him. "Orville Turner is sendin' the seniors over to fix it up for Mary Jane's arrival." She rubbed her eyes. "Wish somebody'd fix *me* up. I feel like *I* been run over."

"Lemme give you a few of these," Leo said, fumbling in his sack for some pills.

"They work!" Lottie sang happily.

"Well, thanks," Irene said, as Leo handed them to her.

She waved half-heartedly as Leo and Lottie went out the door. She watched them drive off in his truck. She stood there alone, and after a moment, she switched off the neon sign. Then she turned and walked back through the parlor, past the caskets and into the saloon. The almost empty bottle of Wild Turkey sat on the table. Irene picked it up and put it behind the counter.

"Okay, Lucie, here I come!" she called, as she found her way back into the embalming room of the Uncertain Chapel of Memories.

A big black plastic crash bag lay in a heap beside the gurney. Irene looked inside. "Lucie Garden!" she cried. "Every bit of you! And Lottie said she had you drained and formaldehyded and ready to go!" Irene looked around in dismay.

Someone had thrown a green sheet over Wendell Butler.

"Why didn't somebody get that extra gurney and put you on it?" she said to Wendell Butler's corpse. "Or move you into the slumber room, one? I need where you are for Lucie!"

She grabbed the sheet and jerked it off.

Baby Flowers lay sprawled under Wendell Butler's gurney, sound asleep.

"Where the hell are them pills!" Irene cried, reaching in her pocket. "And where's that Ole Turkey, too!"

Baby Flowers' eyes fluttered open. She started to smile.

"Oh, don't get up!" Irene cried. "It's my job to keep idiots and dead people as comfortable as possible!"

CHAPTER TWO

"FUCK BOBBY HENDERSON!" Mary Jane Shady muttered as she crossed Columbus Circle in a daze. Cabs and buses whizzed past her. She didn't see them. She just kept moving, weaving crazily through the traffic in her Fendi overcoat, her Reebok aerobic shoes and her Anne Klein sunglasses. A few precariously attached pink foam rollers still clung desperately to her hair.

Miraculously, she cleared the traffic and stomped toward the monument. A break dancer gyrated in front of a squatting bag lady, who obliviously relieved herself. Two pigeons rested on her head.

"Bobby Henderson is a son-of-a-bitch!" Mary Jane Shady screamed hysterically. The pigeons blinked passively.

"Yeah!" the breakdancer shouted back.

"He's an asshole, too!" she cried. Throwing a pack of Kleenex to the bag lady, she marched frantically in circles around the monument.

The old woman stared at the Kleenex in confusion.

"Let's hear it!" the breakdancer yelled.

"Ladies and gentlemen, somebody is an asshole," said a man dressed in a tweed jacket, white shirt, tie and a long black cocktail skirt. He spoke into an imaginary microphone.

"Bobby Henderson!" Mary Jane yelled over her shoulder, pacing wildly.

"Bobby Henderson!" the breakdancer echoed.

"Asshole . . . Asshole . . ." the bag lady muttered.

"Bobby Henderson is an asshole," the man announced over his imaginary microphone.

"You're a asshole!" the bag lady mumbled, wobbling to her feet. "Gimme my skirt!"

"Madame, this is *my* skirt," the man told her indignantly.

"He's wearin' my skirt," the bag lady told Mary Jane.

"Here," Mary Jane Shady hissed. Jerking back her Fendi overcoat, she ripped off her brand new Perry Ellis red wool skirt and tossed it to the bag lady.

"Where's the top?" the bag lady wanted to know, as she climbed into the skirt.

"I gave you everything I could!" Mary Jane screamed. "I have to keep *something* for myself!"

"Why?" the bag lady asked, stepping into the skirt.

"Fuck ole Bobby Henderson!" sang the breakdancer. "Fuck ole Bobby Henderson!"

"Fuck *you*!" Mary Jane shrieked, stomping off. "Fuck *all* of you!"

She stalked across the street toward the Hampshire House, mumbling incoherently ". . . don't appreciate anything! . . . not *one* thing! . . . *nothing, Nothing, NOTHING*! . . ."

Then it started to happen.

The first one she saw was coming out of 240 Central Park South. A cold shiver ran down her spine. She looked straight ahead, but it was no use: the Chihuahua was getting closer. Her hands turned to ice. She walked faster and pulled a hand mirror from her purse. Yes, there it was behind her, bouncing along on the sidewalk! Behind it was a bulldog, followed by some kind of a terrier. In the distance she thought she spotted a Doberman pinscher. Coming toward her were twin Afghans. Trailing them was an Irish setter. She felt herself becoming lightheaded. She gasped. *DON'T FROWN*, she told herself. *SCREAM, BUT DO NOT FROWN*! She pressed two fingers between her eyebrows. With the other hand, she placed her thumb and her index finger at the corners of her lips. She yanked her lips up. *SMILE, JUST SMILE AT THE LITTLE DOGGIES . . . SWEET LITTLE DOGGIES . . . ALL ON LEASHES . . .*

A tiny squeak came out of her mouth.

A big German shepherd came out of the Hampshire House.

"AH-H-H-H-H-H-H!" screamed Mary Jane Shady.

Everything turned black.

"Ladies and Gentlemen of the Academy, I want to thank all of you for this Award. Never in my wildest dreams back in Uncertain did it occur to me I'd get it!" squealed Mary Jane Shady from Hollywood, looking just like Rita Hayworth and Marilyn Monroe and Ava Gardner all rolled into one of Lana Turner's white dresses.

Mary Jane looked sincerely at the audience. "Do you think this will get my mother out of the funeral business? Will it keep my daddy from having another heart attack? Will it help my Aunt Lottie find a husband? Can I skip my piano lesson Tuesday? And—oh, yes—is Bobby Henderson out there looking at me on this show?" Mary Jane peered into the camera and picked up the Oscar. "Look at this, Bobby Henderson," she said. "Now do you love me? 'Cause if you love me it was worth it to win the Academy Award for . . ."

"Mary Jane."

"Huh?"

"Where are you?"

"Here, Bobby. I'm here," Mary Jane Shady said, bringing herself out of her daydreams and back into the back seat of Bobby Henderson's ten-year-old 1954 Ford convertible, parked on an oil road by a well.

"What were you saying? You were mumblin'," Bobby grumbled. " 'I want to thank all of you for this award,' you said."

"Oh, I do!" Mary Jane, quick to the recovery, took Bobby Henderson's high school senior cock in her mouth and mumbled, "I want to thank all of you for this tremendous reward."

Bobby Henderson smiled. Mary Jane knew he was growing more and more attached to her.

So far, Mary Jane had managed to maintain her virginity with Bobby, but it was so exciting to be with him, she found it harder and harder not to go all the way. She loved it when he put his fingers in there and moved them all around. She got the strangest feelings in her stomach. Bobby wasn't the first boy who had put his fingers in there, though. Danny Drinkwater had, but he kissed with his mouth closed and besides, he only used one finger. He certainly did not make Mary Jane's stomach feel strange. Something about Danny Drinkwater made her just want to go home.

Sammy Widders had touched her tits, but that was under duress. They had been at the Yellow Jacket Drive-In and all during the show Sammy Widders had stuck one hand and then another down Mary Jane's blouse to her infinite irritation.

"If you do that one more time, I'm telling your mother, Sammy!" Mary Jane shouted.

Sammy's mother, Scoot Widders, was a longtime friend of Mary Jane's mother. Irene Shady saw her almost everyday, so Mary Jane figured Sammy would stop it.

"You'd let Danny Drinkwater play with them," Sammy said, lighting a cigarette.

Mary Jane looked at the cigarette in horror. "*Please* don't smoke, Sammy," she begged "We'll get killed if anyone finds out you're smoking a cigarette!"

"I like to smoke," Sammy said, puffing away on a Camel.

He's going to be a smoker and a doper and a alcoholic, too, Mary Jane told herself, assessing the teachings of Irene Shady. It occurred to her that Sammy Widders might be well on his way to the sex maniac stage.

"You know what's the best thing about a Camel?" Sammy grinned, taking a puff.

Mary Jane jumped. "What?"

"HUMPS!!!" Sammy laughed as he grabbed both of Mary Jane's tits.

"STOP IT!" Mary Jane Shady yelled into Sammy Widders' blurring face. "GET LOST!"

Sammy's green eyes darkened, his nose became larger, and his light brown hair thinned and blackened as Sammy faded away.

Mary Jane found herself yelling into the most comforting face she'd ever seen.

Herman Top.

He was smiling. "What an entrance," he said, kissing the slight crease between her eyebrows. "My doorman thinks you don't like him."

She sank back into the cushions of the stark white oversized sofa that dominated the penthouse suite of the Hampshire House. The gleaming white marble tiles and Herman's soft dark eyes stared back at her.

"Oh, Herman," she whispered. "I just heard from Uncertain . . ."

CHAPTER THREE

"I CANNOT BELIEVE Mary Jane Shady is comin' home and they have left you and me to get ready for her!" Irene exclaimed to Baby Flowers as she pulled Lottie Shady's best Sunday dress over Baby's head. "You sure look a lot better in it than she does!" Irene told Baby, admiringly. "I hope Mary Jane Shady looks half-way as good as you do when she gets here." Irene reached for a brush to smooth out Baby's long dark hair. "You cain't never tell what changes are goin' to come over a person who's goin' out with such a big-nosed man," Irene sighed. "And I can hardly wait to ask Mary Jane why that Mr. Top don't buy him a hat that fits! Even *you* got more sense than that. Somethin' don't fit you, you just toss it off!" Irene laughed heartily, giving Baby a playful elbow.

"Okay, Beautiful, let's you and me go back downstairs and move Lucie and Wendell around some," Irene told Baby, who followed her, smiling, in Lottie's pale pink silk shirtwaist with the tiny white stars and moons.

Irene stopped in the saloon a moment and poured herself a glass of water and gave Baby a Coke before they commenced to move Wendell Butler, on his gurney, from the pantry and into the slumber room.

"You get his head and I'll get his legs," Irene told Baby. Baby did as Irene told her. "You follow directions real good, Baby Girl," Irene said, automatically arranging the body in the blue coffin. "I wonder if we've probably been underestimatin' you some."

Irene and Baby pulled the empty gurney through the saloon and back into the embalming room.

"Now we got to get Lucie up here," Irene said. "Just the head and torso, though. We'll leave that arm and half-a-leg in the crash bag for now. I'll sew 'em on later." She sighed, pulling a clean sheet over the top of the gurney. "All them Gardens end up in crash bags," Irene told Baby. She put on an apron, then put one on Baby. "Lucie's guaranteed to be a mess," she assured her new assistant, as she reached down for the bag. "Now, listen, if this curls your toenails, don't think nothin' of it. I never have gone through this part yet without feelin' dizzy, nauseated, lightheaded and real, real sick, and I been doin' this for a hunnerd years." She yanked Lucie Garden out of the bag. "Get that leg and swing 'er up!" They pulled Lucie Garden onto the gurney. Irene proceeded to undress her. "Nobody'll get to wear this again," Irene remarked as she removed Lucie's torn, bloody dress.

Baby Flowers stood back and stared. Her smiling mouth quivered, lost its smile, and tears spilled down her cheeks.

"Ma-ma . . ."

Irene Shady looked up sharply. "Did I hear you say 'ma-ma', Baby!?" she gasped. "Honey-Baby!" She took the girl's splendid Ava Gardner face in her hands. "Did you *talk*?" she whispered.

But no other sounds came from Baby, who silently bent down and kissed old Lucie Garden's peaceful, battered face.

"That's not your mama, Sweet Baby," Irene Shady said gently. "But Lucie Garden was a real nice woman. I'll tell you another thing, too. Today is the first I've heard about Lucie Garden failin' Lottie Shady in the second grade! I didn't even know Lucie *knew* Lottie—I mean any better than *me*, and here I find not only did she know her—she failed her!" Irene cast a sharp glance at Baby. "Makes you wonder what else you don't know about a person, don't it? Makes you wonder if maybe they got a whole slew of a secret life tucked away, some kind of a entire hidden past!"

Irene reached for a bottle of germicidal soap and two old rags. "You clean up her face and I'll do the rest of her." She wet the rags with water and applied the soap. "I always have had the feelin' that there's more to Lottie Shady than meets the eye." She glanced up. "You don't have to scrub her hair, Baby. I'll do that."

Baby dropped the rag on the table, turned and opened the pantry doors, searching the shelves until she found the Melba cigar make-up box.

"You want to practice colorin' on Lucie while I drain and fill 'er up?" Irene asked, taking the box from its shelf. "You been such a good help, Baby, I 'spect you won't hurt nothin' by colorin' up ole Lucie. I'll wipe it off and fix her up right later on after we get her formaldehyded and sewed up." She handed Baby the box. "Here you go," she said.

Baby beamed.

"I 'spect Lucie's about to get more color in her death than she ever got in her life!" Irene grinned.

Baby took a stick of clown white and applied it generously all over Lucie's face and neck.

"That's right!" Irene encouraged. "Make her white as a ghost!"

Irene took an ivory-handled pocket knife and made a small incision just below Lucie Garden's right collar bone. "See, we make *two* of these holes," Irene instructed. "Them chemicals goes into the right corroded artery *here* and that pushes the blood right out the jugglin' vein *here*," she told Baby, who was drawing over Lucie's sparse eyebrows with a deep purple pencil.

"Now I'm goin' to hook these tubes in," Irene went on, as if Baby were listening. She reached for a pair of forceps, and holding back the skin, inserted the ends of the tubes into the two incisions. She leaned over to check that the tubes were hooked securely to the rubber hose which attached to the pump, as Baby smudged pink shadows under Lucie's wrinkled eyes, then smoothed gold-flecked eyeshadow over her withered, sunken cheeks. Finding "Paint Me Red," Baby made Lucie a jagged, but bow-like, bright mouth.

"Looks like *The Madwoman of Chaillot*," Irene remarked, pulling the end of one tube into a small toilet hidden away under the sink. "We had to have this installed back in the '40s," she said to Baby. "You need a direct line to the sewer in the funeral business, and I hate a messy sink." She reached for a sixteen-ounce bottle of formaldehyde. "This ain't just pure chemicals we got here," she told Baby. "It's lanolin-based. Says so on the cover." She poured the mixture into the glass cylinder on top of the embalming pump's base and then added water. "One gallon is about exactly right." She glanced at the dials on the pump. "One dial's to show how the fluids flow and one dial tells the pressure," Irene explained. She re-checked the tubes, and satisfied, headed for the crash bag. "After I prepare the rest of the remains, you can flip the switch." She pulled out the arm and the half a leg and threw them into the sink. "I'll just wash these off and get my sewing basket," she said. After drying off the cadaver's parts, she threaded a large-eyed needle with strong plastic thread, pulled her stool up to the gurney, fitted the arm in place and started to sew.

"Ever read *The Madwoman of Chaillot*?" she asked Baby, forgetting herself. "Oh! I guess not!" she replied, pulling the needle and thread through the arm. "I've read ever play Mary Jane Shady ever appeared in startin' with *Anastasia* her freshman year in high school,"

Irene stated as she stitched. "Mary Jane had nothin' but pure-dee problems with her co-stars in that one, on a-count of some real bad casting errors. But then here come *Ondine* her senior year. That was Mary Jane's first major success. She won everything there was to win! Best Actress at District Competition in Odessa, Best Actress at Regional Competition in Lubbock, and Best Actress at State in Austin! And I know you hear people here in Uncertain talkin' about her playin' that mermaid part to this day!" Irene moved her stool around to reach the other side of the arm. "I've read Shakespeare—Baby, I'm a Shakespeare expert— and I don't think much of his plots. Too soap opera. Turn on *Another World*, *As the World Turns*, *General Hospital*—Shakespeare sounds just like 'em! I don't think he likes women neither—never had very many in the shows and was always killin' 'em off! Dez had to die far too soon in my opinion, and the same goes for Lady Mac B! See, he likes the women to die and the men to live—just the *opposite* from real life!"

Baby smiled and drew a green beauty mark on Lucie's right cheek.

"Now I'll tell you who's funny and that is Antonio Chekhov. "*Hilarious*!" Irene threw her head back, guffawed, and laid down the arm. "Well, I wouldn't win a sewing bee, cain't make a straight stitch to save my life, but then, nobody will be able to see this fine piece of work anyhow." She got up and reached for the remains of Lucie's leg. "That Chekhov is *always* funny, unlike Mr. Neil Simon, who sometimes *is* and sometimes is *not*. Neil Simon is just like Tennessee Williams," Irene confided, straightening the leg. "Their tragedies are just a whole lot funnier than their comedies." Irene smiled kindly at Baby. "'Course, I keep up, bein' the mother of a nation-wide famous television commercial celebrity. If you was a famous actress—" She glanced at the grotesque rainbow Baby had made of Lucie Garden's face. "'Course you probably won't be," Irene said sweetly. "You're a beauty, Baby, but you cain't seem to pay any attention to the lines. See how you're out of bounds there?" She pointed to Lucie's face. "Acting is *discipline*. It's hard, hard, hard. Mary Jane Shady never ever, not *once* in her entire life, ever went over the lines in her color book!"

Suddenly a dark look flooded Irene's face and she dropped the leg she was working on. "Oh, Lordy, Baby! I just had a real grim thought! A strange tiny little black hat flashed in my head!" She looked at Baby. Baby stared at her quizzically. "Your head ever do that?" Irene asked.

"Listen, you don't think Mary Jane Shady is plannin' on bringin' that big-nosed man back here to Uncertain, Texas, with her, do you?"

"Maybe," said Baby.

Irene Shady almost fell off her stool.

CHAPTER FOUR

"MARY JANE?" Herman asked softly. "What's wrong?"

She didn't know what to tell him. She had no idea what to say. Her voice was almost inaudible. "They want me to come back." There was a long pause. "To Uncertain."

"Forever?" He was taking the pink foam rollers out of her hair and dropping them gently into the Baccarat "Serpentin" vase she had given him for a birthday present.

"Of course not!" she snapped. Looking up into his eyes, she caught herself.

BE CAREFUL, she warned herself. *CALM DOWN. NOBODY KNOWS. NOBODY KNOWS ANYTHING . . .*

"Oops, sorry," she sighed. "I must have thought I was talking to my mother."

"An easy mistake," He shrugged, dispensing more rollers. "Although, I'm sure she has an inferior mustache."

"It's questionable," Mary Jane replied, reaching up to smooth the dark fringe sprinkled with gray that topped his upper lip. Just touching Herman made her feel safer.

His eyes narrowed. "Your mother really has a mustache?"

RELAX, she told herself. *LIGHTEN UP. NOW*.

"Oh, sure," Mary Jane assured him. "All those old prairie women in West Texas have 'em. Big bushy ones. My mother's is bright gold. She gets it peroxided once a month at Annie Lovejoy's Beauty Shoppe."

"*Really*?" He stared at her intensely. "I want to meet your mother." He pulled the belt of his black silk robe tighter and sat down beside her. "Does she look exactly like you, except for the mustache?"

"She looks exactly like Greta Garbo and I lied about the mustache."

"Asshole." He nuzzled her neck. "You got me all fascinated."

"Aunt Lottie has a mustache."

"I don't believe you." He kissed her earlobe, then behind her ear, then inside her ear.

"I swear," Mary Jane breathed. "Plus, she's the spitting image of Olive Oyl."

"Omagod," Herman groaned sympathetically. "I had an aunt like that. Aunt Ida. Old maid all her life. Not one suitor."

"Aunt Lottie, too," Mary Jane nodded. "Never had a date, said she didn't want one."

Herman licked her neck. "She wanted one ..."

Mary Jane touched his face lightly, like feathers. "She was just waiting for some big Jewish guy to come along and knock her off her—"

"Mustache," Herman giggled.

"You're so silly," Mary Jane smiled, feeling better.

He pulled her close to him. "Aren't you glad I'm so silly, 'cause you're so silly. . . ."

"M-m-m-m . . ." She brought his head down to her chest, between her breasts.

"So where does Aunt Lottie get her mustache—serviced—?" Herman wanted to know. He pushed his tongue toward her right breast. "At Annie Lovejoy's?"

"Annie Lovejoy's Uncertain Beauty Shoppe," she whispered. She could feel her nipples hardening. "Located behind her house, out in the garage, 302 South Maple Avenue, I think . . ." His tongue had found her nipple. "Besides extraordinary teasing . . . great blow-jobs . . . and unique style . . . these operators offer fingernail jobs . . . toe wraps . . . and barbecued ribs on the side . . . "

"How could I pass that up?" Herman wondered, finding her left nipple with his fingers.

"Beats me," she whispered, stroking his head.

He looked up. "So when do we leave?"

"Whenever . . ." she promised. "Don't stop . . . "

"Today?" he asked, sucking on her nipple.

"Huh?"

He looked up at her. "Today? Can we leave today?"

She stared at him, speechless.

"For the barbecue in the beauty shop. To visit Aunt Lottie. To meet your mother."

Her back straightened. "You've got to be kidding!"

"I'm not!" he said, standing up on his knees, "I've never been to Uncertain, Texas. I've been to Dubuque, Tallahassee, Rolling Falls, Salt Lake City, Dayton, Columbus, Cleveland and Cincinnati, but I haven't been to Uncertain."

"And you're not going." She pulled her coat over her breasts.

"Why?"

"Herman, you don't want to be the first Jew to ever enter Uncertain, do you?"

He looked surprised. "I don't think I would be. Surely some Hebrew person has passed through West Texas."

"*Passed though* is a good way of putting it," she said.

"Rack your brain," he told her. "I'll bet you'll come up with *one*."

She sat back and closed her eyes.

"Well?" he asked.

"Okay," she sighed. "I thought of one."

"And?"

She leaned back in the sofa. "My piano teacher's husband. Avram Baum."

Herman looked surprised. "You can play the piano?"

"No," she said.

"But why not?" he asked. "You took lessons."

"Now listen, Herman," she replied. "You asked for a Jew. I thought of one. Avram Baum is a Jew. He lived in Uncertain. He was married to Daisy Baum, my old piano teacher, okay?"

"Was he the first Jew you ever knew?" Herman wanted to know.

"Yes."

"You're sure he was Jewish?"

"That's what Daisy Baum said."

"Why don't you ever play?" Herman asked. "Was she a good teacher?"

"She taught me the basics," Mary Jane sighed. She grimaced as she mimicked Daisy Baum in a deep thundering baritone voice. " 'The white keys are the major, the black keys are the minor, the pedals are on the floor, what they're for don't matter, just don't touch 'em! And middle C divides the keyboard!' "

"So Daisy Baum married a Jew," Herman smiled. "Were they happy?" he asked hopefully.

" 'That goddamned Jew!' Daisy would shout!" shouted Mary Jane Shady. "She'd always shove me off the bench and proceed to play away the last twenty minutes of my thirty-minute lesson! 'Never works, just thinks!' " Mary Jane cried in her Daisy Baum voice. " '*Thinks*! Can't *think* enough money to buy me a new piano though!' she'd yell over her own playing. '*Cheap Jew*!' "

"She doesn't sound like a very good teacher," Herman offered.

"Oh, I watched Daisy Baum's attempts at the keys, totally fascinated!" Mary Jane told him. "I thought she was immensely co-ordinated. Her tits were like two basketballs that just miraculously shifted from side to side with the rest of her very abundant body! I thought Daisy Baum looked exactly like Johann Sebastian Bach, and I just wished that she would not play and yell so loud all at the same time!"

"Poor Avram," Herman sighed.

"Wait a minute!" Mary Jane Shady protested. "I've gone through life never comfortable with the bass clef!"

"Poor Mary Jane," Herman offered sympathetically. Her voice was rising. He could see she was getting upset.

"The first ten minutes of my lesson were always devoted to the treble clef. It took the other twenty minutes for Daisy Baum to assume the bench, arrange her breasts and educate me about the Jews," she explained. "Not only did I receive a total misunderstanding of Bach and Jews, I got a partial musical education at best!"

"Oh, well," Herman said. He didn't know what else to say.

"Daisy Baum robbed me of a possible career in the musical theater," Mary Jane complained. "Admit it!"

"You don't want to do musicals, Mary Jane," Herman consoled. "I don't even want to do musicals, and musicals are what I do."

"You're a star on Broadway, Herman. At least there's some compensation."

"Can I get compensated by going to Uncertain?" he wanted to know.

"Oh, stop it!" she pleaded. "I'm not going." She looked at him tiredly. "You're not going."

"But you're the only other person I know with an aunt who's got a mustache and looks like Olive Oyl," Herman persisted. "I want to meet her."

"She doesn't want to meet you," Mary Jane told him.

"She'll like me when she meets me," Herman said patiently. "I know how to woo old women. I'm a Broadway star."

"You're a baby," she sighed, bending down to kiss his thinning hair.

"I'm a baby," he repeated in a baby voice. "And I wanna go!"

"I have to work," Mary Jane stated. "It's on Friday. You have to work. You're appearing in Chicago. Isn't your first rehearsal tomorrow? I hope you're packed. Your plane leaves in two hours."

"I'll cancel," he said. "Let's both cancel."

"You *never* cancel."

"I'm sick." He coughed. "Flu."

"You're sick all right, but not with the flu." She shook her head in despair.

"It's a benefit in Chicago. They'll have other stars. Herschel Bernardi will be there. They don't need two of us."

"Herman—"

"I WANT TO GO TO YOUR HOMECOMING!" he shouted.

Her eyes grew wide. "How—how'd you know?" she stammered.

"What?"

"That it's my—uh—a Homecoming?"

"Well, what else would it be?" he asked. "Nobody's dead, it's not a funeral, so if they're asking you back, it's probably for a reunion, right?"

She tried to think quickly. "Sort of," she nodded. "I mean, well, it's not *my* reunion. *My* reunion, the ten year one, was two years ago and I didn't even go back for that!" She could feel her heart flutter as she continued the lie. Why had she told *him* she was only twenty-eight? She'd had to lie about her age to get her job in the first place, but she wished she'd at least admitted to Herman that she was "around thirty." In spite of herself, she grabbed a breath and continued. "I graduated from the Class of '73—okay, I *should* have been in the Class of '75, except I skipped two grades—this reunion is for the Class of '65, see, nothing to do with *me*, except they want me to come crown the Homecoming Queen, although I can't imagine why—" She was pacing. Her bare feet hit the marble floor soundlessly. "Anyway, I can't go. I have to work on Friday, there's just *no* way I can make it!"

"So why are you so upset?" he asked.

"Well, I don't want to disappoint my mother, you know. I mean she's so proud of me and everything. She's been hoping I'd come back for—for years." She turned away from him. "I just haven't done what I wanted to do, what I set out to do. Oh, Herman . . ." Her voice was faint. "Here I am . . . *twenty-eight years old* . . ." she said carefully, "And I haven't been on Broadway, I haven't starred in a movie where I didn't die by being strangled with barbed wire or choking to death on glass or being beaten to a pulp with a Raggedy Ann doll or traumatized by insects, rodents or robots!" The tears came full force. "I'm so embarrassed!" She sobbed. "I can't even land a part on a soap opera!"

"That's because it conflicts with your Peanut Butter Cup contract, dummy," he pointed out. "Listen, Mary Jane." He grabbed her by the shoulders. "You make six figures a year. Not many actresses can say that. Not many *people* can say that."

She was shaking. Her chestnut hair, unbrushed, still curled tightly against her perfectly shaped head from having been in the rollers. The curls bounced about her face. She was unable to stop trembling.

"I don't want to disappoint anybody . . ." Her nose was beginning to turn pink.

"Who are you disappointing?" he asked. "You said it's not even your graduating class."

A new avalanche of tears flooded forward.

"Anyway," he said, taking her in his arms. "I think you're a star."

She cried even harder. "I'm nothing but a Peanut Butter Cup!"

Herman held her closer. "There's only one thing to do with Peanut Butter Cup . . ."

"What?" she sniffed.

"Devour it." He threw off his robe and fell to his knees.

"Oh, Herman, *please*!" she protested.

"Aw, shut up," he murmured. "I'll just do this for a little bit . . . and then I promise I'll stop . . ."

"You better not stop," she whispered.

Safe. She was safe with Herman. Safe . . .

CHAPTER FIVE

"BABY FLOWERS, why didn't you tell me you could talk!" Irene Shady cried, jumping off of her stool and knocking it over.

But Baby seemed to have no interest in replying and continued to devote her full attention to the line of blue stars she was drawing across Lucie Garden's forehead.

"Nobody ever tells me a thing!" Irene grumbled. Hearing the front door bells jingle, Irene quickly sat the stool upright. "You just stay here while I see who that is. Maybe it's Mr. Wendell's people and we don't want them to think we don't take ourselves seriously here at the Chapel of Memories," she said, glancing at Lucie's painted face. "They see this mess and they'll think they stumbled into some kind of modern art nightmare, so you and Lucie *stay put*, hear?" She yanked at her skirt to straighten it out. "Better not be any more *new* customers is all I can say, Baby. I don't know about you, but I don't think I can handle another dead body today!"

She pushed the pantry door open and Yvonne Henderson flew in.

"Hi!" Yvonne grinned, directing her salutations to Irene and ignoring Baby. "I think I forgot somethin'!"

"Now listen here, Why-vonne," Irene demanded. "Why didn't you tell me Baby could talk! She let go a blue streak and almost knocked me over!"

"OH, URP!" Yvonne shrieked, seeing Lucie Garden. "What happened to *her*?!" She swung herself into Irene's stool and stared in disbelief at the corpse. "I don't think you're goin' to be able to do a thing for that one, Irene! She better be glad she's *dead*!"

"And furthermore," Irene continued. "Why didn't you tell me straightaway that you'd contacted Mary Jane Shady? I had to find out from Kay Widders!"

"Well, I rushed right over here, Irene," Yvonne protested. "I *wanted* you to be the first to know." She decided it was best not to tell Irene that she had announced Mary Jane's arrival to both Catsy and Kay earlier that morning.

"Frankly, I'm surprised you got a-hold of her," Irene continued. "She stays so dad-blamed busy."

"Oh, she was busy all right," Yvonne nodded, wiggling nervously on Irene's stool and biting on a hangnail with her teeth.

"Please do not gnaw!" Irene pleaded.

Yvonne dropped her hand in her lap and let her shoulders droop.

"Irene, she says she cain't come."

Irene was about to say, "I told you so," when she saw that Yvonne's eyes were welling with tears. Nothing looked more pitiful than Yvonne did when she was sad.

"Aw, don't take it so hard, Why-vonne," Irene offered. "This isn't even your graduatin' class."

"Oh-h-h!" Yvonne cried even harder. "Don't say that! I'll never have a graduatin' class 'cause I didn't ever graduate!"

"Now, now." Irene patted her on the back.

Baby Flowers reached for a Kleenex and timidly offered it to her half-sister-cousin.

"Scat!" Yvonne screamed, grabbing the Kleenex.

Baby gave her a big smile and turned back to her coloring.

"I thought volunteerin' for this would help me kinda fit in," Yvonne sniffed, blowing her nose.

Irene didn't want to tell Yvonne that she viewed her chances of fitting in as somewhat hopeless.

"Why, you don't need to fit into that class, Why-vonne," Irene comforted. "They's not one person in it that's done anything as remarkable as you and Mary Jane Shady!"

Yvonne's head jerked up sharply.

"You got the biggest house in town, Why-vonne," Irene offered quickly. "*That's* quite an accomplishment. There's nothin' to equal it in all of West Texas and nobody, not even Catsy Ivanhoe, can say that. Why, that big magazine even come and took pictures, printed 'em and published 'em," Irene added.

"They just snapped the kitchen," Yvonne complained. "Just ignored the waterfall in the livin' room and I had real live goldfishes put in it, too!"

Irene didn't know what to say.

Yvonne put her hands over her eyes and sighed deeply. "I got a bad image problem around here, Irene, and you know it."

Irene listened silently. She couldn't help but feel sorry for Yvonne.

"I've had nothin' but bad luck since the day I was born," Yvonne moaned.

Irene nodded. "You've had some hard times," she acknowledged.

"I was thinkin' that if I was the one to bring Mary Jane Shady back to Uncertain, maybe I'd get enough credit so that people would forget about . . ." Yvonne glanced at Baby and shuddered. ". . . Maybe they'd forget about . . . about the rest of me . . ." she finished quietly.

Irene nodded sympathetically. "I think I understand what you're sayin'," she said.

"You do?" Yvonne asked hopefully. "Oh, Irene, will you help me to get Mary Jane to come back?"

"I might," Irene replied. She looked at Baby. "But I have got to tell you that you are handlin' the rest of this the wrong way."

"I'll do anything you say!" Yvonne promised. "I'll be eternally indebted to you! I'll work part-time drainin' bodies, you can use my car and driver at funerals, you can hold the services in my livin' room by the waterfall or out by the swimmin' pool or up on the roof top!"

"That's very kind of you," Irene said. "And maybe I'll take you up on it if a governor or somebody important-like passes on and wants somethin' real unique."

"That would be just fine!" Yvonne gushed.

"But that's not what I'm talkin' about," Irene said.

Yvonne looked at her brightly. "Oh. Well. Okay, then, what is it?"

"Baby," Irene said to Baby Flowers, "go in yonder and see how Mr. Wendell Butler's doin' in the blue casket up front."

Baby Flowers obediently picked up her color box and started out the pantry door.

Irene took the box from her gently, selected a brown liner and handed it to her. "Just *very* lightly right *here*," she told Baby, pointing just above her eyelashes. "Just a light touch, please." She handed Baby a Kleenex. "And smooth out those purple dots on his cheeks, too. Make him look like he didn't have the chicken pox."

Baby smiled happily and went out the door.

Irene turned back to Yvonne. "I will help you out here, Why-vonne, on one condition and one condition only."

Yvonne took a deep breath and sighed. "Okay," she said grimly. "What?"

"You are the one makin' yourself look bad," Irene told her. As Yvonne started to protest, Irene cut her off. "*I* know half your life isn't your fault, Why-vonne. We don't always ask for what we get. But I'm goin' to tell you this and you can believe me or not: The only way to make yourself look one bit better in this silly little town is to rise right above *all* of it."

Yvonne's eyes glistened as she listened intensely. "After everything that's happened to me?" she asked. "How? Tell me *how*?"

"Take that Baby in and treat her like she was your very own," Irene Shady said.

"Aw-w-w, Irene," Yvonne moaned. "No, no, no!"

"Yes, yes, yes," chanted Irene. "Believe me, it is the *only* way! You may *think* bringin' Mary Jane Shady back will do it for you, and I will help you out on that if it will help *you* to get started. But bringin' up Baby will do the trick. I guarantee it. That will do the trick."

"Aw, Irene," Yvonne groaned. "Let me just give you a fur coat or somethin'. *Please*."

"Naw." Irene shook her head. "It's Baby or nothin'."

Yvonne sprang out of the stool and paced nervously around Lucie Garden's remains. "I just cain't see Baby livin' with me," she protested.

"I can," Irene said.

"She don't fit into my life-style," Yvonne whined.

"Well, dress her up, curl her hair. Put ribbons in it. Talk to her."

"She cain't talk!" Yvonne pouted.

"Oh, yes she can," Irene grinned. "She said 'mama' and 'maybe' less than a half hour ago."

"I swear I will kill her if she calls me 'mama'!" Yvonne threatened.

Irene looked piercingly at Yvonne. "*Be responsible*. Think of somebody else for a change."

"I don't know how!" Yvonne wailed.

"Practice!" Irene instructed.

Yvonne gulped. "When do I have to start?"

Irene didn't say a word.

"Aw, shee-it!" Yvonne sighed. "And you'll get Mary Jane to come?"

Irene nodded.

"*Shee-it*!" she repeated, starting for the door. Suddenly she turned back. "Wait a minute, Irene!" Yvonne stuck her index finger in Irene's face and shook it as she spoke. "Mary Jane told me she had to work on Friday! She cain't come if she wanted to! Now how are you goin' to get her back?"

"I have my ways," Irene Shady said slyly. "You just keep your end of the promise and I'll keep mine."

"But—" Yvonne started.

"Why-vonne," Irene Shady sighed tiredly. "Trust me." She shrugged her shoulders. "We're just waitin' on you." She yawned. "Whenever you're ready to get out of your own way, we'll get started. But I ain't doin' nothin' 'til I see you make your move."

Yvonne straightened her shoulders, patted her blond wig and shuddered.

"Oh, Bay-be-e-e-e!" she called, going through the pantry door.

CHAPTER SIX

MARY JANE moaned as she felt his tongue. It was hot, wet and he moved it so slowly inside her.

. . . *TO THE RHYTHM OF THE OIL PUMP* . . .

"M-m-m . . ." Herman murmured, lost in her.

But she didn't hear him. She was lost in the song . . .

. . . *MY HEART WAS BEATIN' WILD* . . . lost in memories of Bobby. . .

. . . *FELT JUST LIKE A BLUEBONNET* . . .

"Come on, Mary Jane," Bobby's voice begged. "Just for a minute . . ."

. . . *TUMBLEWEED PRAIRIE CHILD* . . .

"Okay, one minute," he negotiated urgently. "Thirty seconds! I'll take it out! I promise!"

"I don't know, Bobby." Mary Jane's heart was pounding. She was madly in love.

Every time she looked at Bobby, Mary Jane just got wet. She had no idea why this happened and it was downright embarrassing. She could feel her panties get moist with something that was definitely not pee every time she looked at Bobby. She had wanted to let him do "it" for a long time. Never having had anything "in there" but Danny Drinkwater's one finger and several of Bobby's, she was naturally apprehensive, but she felt it was inevitable, after three months of Bobby's fingers, that the real thing was pulled out and put in.

"I just got to get in there, hon," he moaned. "I'm about to pass out!"

"I just cain't!" she whispered loudly. "What if I get pregnant?"

"You *won't*, I promise," Bobby said, taking out a box of rubbers and slipping one on quicker than Mary Jane could say "Jack Robinson." "Come on, baby," he groaned, as he slid his fingers inside her. "I love you, Mary Jane."

"Promise?" Mary Jane just had to be sure.

"I promise," he promised, rapidly removing his hand from Mary Jane's vagina, jerking off his Uncertain Senior High School ring from his finger and thrusting it into Mary Jane's hand. "There. That's yours to wear, and tomorrow I'll give you my last year's football jacket. Now please let me put it in, I'm dyin'!"

Mary Jane's heart was racing. She clutched the ring tightly and thought of the jacket. "Okay, Bobby," she whispered, hoping it wouldn't hurt and that it would be as good as his fingers.

Quickly he slid inside her. She gasped. Oh, it was better! When Bobby rubbed against that wet stuff in there, Mary Jane Shady felt as if she were on a ferris wheel. And then all of a sudden, she felt spasms, like an earthquake. Bobby was shaking like he was having an earthquake, too. And then it happened again and again and again.

Finally, Bobby removed himself from Mary Jane, pulled off the rubber, and throwing it out the window, he called, "Bye, bye, little Bob."

Fifteen years old, a very dazed Mary Jane Shady watched Bobby Henderson throw out the rubber.

"Bye, bye, little Mary Jane," she mumbled to herself.

"Mary Jane?" She heard his voice, but she couldn't seem to focus her eyes. She could feel herself being shaken, but she couldn't seem to wake up. "Mary Jane?" It was Herman's voice. His face became a blur. He was shaking her. Then, slowly, his face took form. He looked very quiet and very serious and very worried.

"Are you all right?" he asked.

She nodded. He was fuzzy.

"I didn't know . . . I thought you went out again."

"Out?"

"Yeah . . . it was . . . unnerving." He shut his eyes and breathed deeply. "You sort of looked like . . . like maybe . . ."

"What?" she whispered.

He opened his eyes and looked at her, disturbed. "Like you were dying."

CHAPTER SEVEN

HIGH IN THE SKY above Madison Avenue, Arabella du Noir viewed all of Manhattan from her vast penthouse offices on the 49th floor of the Hocker-Smockter Building which housed the Hocker-Smockter Agency, one of the most powerful advertising agencies in the world.

"Hello, Miss American Dream," Arabella murmured, admiring her reflection in the handsome bronze Erté mirror she was staring into.

"Black, but not *too* black," Arabella cooed, absorbed in her creamy complexion. "Beautiful . . ." She stepped back to accommodate all six feet of her slender, willowy body. "*Exquisitely* beautiful." She smiled. "Powerful." She laughed. "*Awesomely* powerful."

The mirror was the only new and inexpensive piece she owned. The title, "Narcissism," had appealed to her. She'd bought half of the entire edition in Paris—one hundred and twenty-five mirrors at $3500.00 each—to celebrate the artist's ninety-second birthday. She kept one for herself and gave the others away as Christmas gifts.

The other furnishings—paintings, sofas, chairs, rugs, vases, screens, porcelain, sculptures—she'd inherited from her late husband, Count Roland du Noir. Each piece was listed and catalogued. Each piece was very, very old and very, very expensive and very, very irreplaceable. All had either come from the Count's villa in Sal du Sac de Mer, his home in Paris on Avenue Foch, or the Eaton Place townhouse in London.

When Roland du Noir died in 1974, Arabella sold the villa and the house, kept the London townhouse, and shipped everything she wasn't using there to the United States. She'd been gone twenty years; she'd been a countess ten of them.

The year was 1950 when Arabella had literally walked off the farm just outside of Durham, North Carolina. She was fifteen years old and had been telling her mother for months that she wanted to go to modeling school.

"You too tall and skinny," Axie Max Williams had laughed. "Plus you a nigger."

"I'm goin' to make bein' a tall skinny nigger work for me!" Arabella had promised her mother.

When she'd returned to New York City in 1975, she'd done just that. Her stunning career as Paris' top model during the '50s had introduced her to international society. She'd given up modeling when she'd married Roland du Noir.

"But the Count ain't no count," she'd written home. The Count was "du Noir" of the "House of du Noir," one of the great couture palaces of Paris. Arabella's partnership was splendidly successful. During the twenty years she was married to Roland du Noir, she learned everything there was to know about running one of the most profitable businesses of its kind. she had been blissfully happy. She had also been perfectly prepared for her current position.

When she was offered the job as Vice-President in Charge of Production at Hocker-Smockter, no consideration was given to the color of her skin. She was overwhelmingly the board's first and foremost choice. Arabella du Noir was no token; she was simply the best.

Arabella did not "take" luncheon meetings. Occasionally, she appeared at a benefit or an awards function, and frequently she spoke at these events. She had no time for the three-martini-over-fettucini-affair, however. Almost without exception, the hours from twelve noon until five P.M. were reserved for reviewing accounts.

The videotape sitting on top of her desk this afternoon pertained to the Creamy Crunchy Peanut Butter, Nutty or Smooth account, which five years ago, Hocker-Smockter had won away from J. Walter Thompson.

Arabella didn't care for the name of the product: *too long*. But the product had arrived on the market before she was even born; there was little she could do about renaming it.

Arabella turned her energies toward coming up with a new spokesperson concept. "What is timeless, admired by everyone, and most desirable to be?" she asked herself.

"*White*," she'd responded with a wry smile.

And in the world of advertising it was true. White middle class Americans were *the* consumers. And they responded to purchasing when it was sold to them by someone who looked *very familiar*. It never failed.

It had taken Arabella about ten seconds to come up with a very unoriginal, very workable concept: Miss Peanut Butter Cup. All she'd done was remember what she'd wanted to look like when she was back on the farm in North Carolina milking cows. "I didn't want to look like Wallis Simpson," she told her staff. "I wanted to look like June Allyson."

Arabella listed the qualities she was looking for in Miss Peanut Butter Cup:

Age: 18–23
Height: 5'5"–5'7"
Weight: 110–120 pounds
Waist: 22 inches
Eyes: Blue or Gray (No brown eyes!)

Hair: Blond, brown or reddish brown (No brunettes! No bleached blondes!)
Complexion: Very fair
Overall: *Very pretty*
Then she added an addendum:

MISS PEANUT BUTTER CUP MUST MEET ONE OTHER SPECIFICATION. HER HOMETOWN IS OF UTMOST IMPORTANCE. NEVER WILL A PBC HAIL FROM N.Y.C., L.A. OR CHICAGO. THESE CITIES ARE *URBAN*. I WANT *RURAL*. I AM LOOKING FOR *AUTHENTICITY*, THAT SPECIAL HOMETOWN-PEACHES-AND-CREAM ALL-AMERICAN-PIE-LOOK THAT WILL SELL THIS PEANUT BUTTER! YES, I'M TALKING STEREOTYPE! AND DO NOT EVEN SUBMIT ANYONE WHO COMES FROM A TOWN WITH A POPULATION OVER 1500. (THAT IS ONE THOUSAND FIVE HUNDRED PEOPLE.) P.S. (the memo read) I DO NOT EXPECT MIRACLES. I AM NOT LOOKING FOR A VIRGIN. DO NOT FORGET, THE COUNTESS GREW UP ON A FARM!

Arabella was always amazed at how white Americans confused sexuality and morality.

"I want American men and boys to cream in their jeans when they see her," she instructed her staff. "I want them to *taste* her when they look at her. When they spoon that peanut butter around, I want them to think it's *her* they're spreading . . . "

"What about American women?" a staff member had asked. "What are they responding to?"

"The June Allyson side of her," Arabella had replied.

"How are we supposed to find all that in one person?" another staff member had wondered.

"She's out there," Arabella had assured them. "I'll find her."

She'd looked at thousands of photographs. She'd interviewed hundreds of girls. She knew Mary Jane Shady was her PBC the moment she saw her. She was delighted when Mary Jane told her the population of Uncertain, Texas.

On July 3, 1980, at 3:04 P.M., Mary Jane Shady became Miss Peanut Butter Cup.

Five years had passed. The concept had been exactly what Creamy Crunchy Peanut Butter, Nutty or Smooth, needed to boost their sales, bringing them right back to the top and nose to nose with Peter Pan. Arabella hated Peter Pan. She loathed fairies. "I don't care if they're animated or just your ordinary garden variety New York faggot or something you once read about in the Brothers Grimm," she told her staff. "Don't bring me any fairy concepts. I'd rather be dumped on by dogs and sucked by ducks! Fairies remind me of agents and I hate agents! Believe me, when Peter Pan grows up, he'll become an agent!" She grabbed a breath and continued. "And forget what I said about 'animated fairies.' That's redundant!"

Arabella harbored a very particular disdain for Hollywood agents. Not one of them had been willing to see her in the '50s during her prime as Europe's top model. Arabella especially disliked Ralph Painter, Mary Jane Shady's agent. She called him "The Peter Pan of West L.A." Even though the Painter Perfect Agency maintained offices on West 44th Street, Ralph insisted on handling all of Mary Jane's negotiations and dealings from his Sunset Boulevard headquarters. Arabella was stuck with him. And she didn't like it.

She picked up Mary Jane's videotape, inserted it into the machine and pushed "play."

Mary Jane emerged on the screen in gingham and ribbons, smiling into a gazebo garden setting. She strolled up to a wicker-decorated porch, then into a gingham-curtained kitchen. She reached into a sparkling, newly painted cabinet and brought forth the product: a jar of Creamy Crunchy Peanut Butter, Nutty. Then another: Creamy Crunchy Peanut Butter, Smooth. A miniature picture of Mary Jane, in color, adorned the jar.

"Flawless," Arabella murmured, scanning Mary Jane's face for creases, wrinkles, crow's feet and sagging jowls.

She froze the picture on a close-up and let the image sit there as she stared into Mary Jane Shady's perfect, but immobile smile.

"So what's wrong, I wonder?"she mused. She continued to scrutinize the picture, unable to figure out what was bothering her.

Arabella knew Mary Jane Shady's age. She was twenty-eight now; she'd been pushing the limit of twenty-three when Arabella had hired her. Nonetheless, Arabella reached for the file on top of her desk containing her Peanut Butter Cup's profile.

She flipped it open. It read:

MISS PEANUT BUTTER CUP MARY JANE SHADY

Hometown: Uncertain, Texas (population 1,043 according to 1980 census)
Birthdate: November 9, 1956

Hair: Reddish brown
Eyes: Blue
Complexion: Fair
Height: 5'7"
Weight: 110 lbs.
Waist: 22"
Hat: 7
Glove: 6 1/2
Shoe: 7 1/2 N

DINNER THEATER:
Everybody Loves Opal (tour with Martha Raye) "Gloria"
Play it Again, Sam (tour with Ted Shackelford) "Linda"
Vanities (tour-Cleveland, Detroit, Milwaukee, St. Louis, Kansas City) "Mary"

REGIONAL THEATER:
Resident Member, Theater Three, Dallas, Texas 1977-78
Cohoes Music Hall, New York, 1979
Member of the Wedding "Frankie"
Ondine "Ondine"
Sabrina Fair "Sabrina"
Anastasia "Anastasia"
Blithe Spirit "Elvira"

FILM:
A Bullet for Pretty Boy (starring Fabian) "Fabian's Best Friend's Girlfriend"
Bullet for Baby Doll "Kimberly Nelson"
Keep My Grave Open "Lesley"
Poor White Trash, Part Two "Sarah"
Reckless Return of Baby Doll "Kimberly Nelson"
Slave of the Scorpions "Sylvia James"
Don't Look in the Incinerator "Edna Alcott"

Education:
Graduated Uncertain High School, 1973
Graduated North Texas State University, 1977
Other Special Skills or Training: Some Piano

"Was she lucky I found her. . . " Arabella mused, shutting the file and sitting back in her chair. She stared at the girl on the screen. "You're twenty-eight and perfect, and yet you're looking worked," she told the still locked image. "There's something there I can't see and I don't like it one bit."

Her thoughts were interrupted by a small buzz on her intercom.

Arabella never let her gaze wander from the screen as she answered. "Yes, Pierre?"

"Excusez-moi, s'il vous plaît, Madame," her French secretary offered apologetically. "Claude says there is a very excited sounding lady on the telephone who won't stop calling. She says she is the Peanut Butter Cup's mother—"

Arabella sat up in her chair. "Mary Jane Shady's *mother* is calling? How *bizarre*."

"I know you are reviewing Miss PBC or I would not have interrupted," Pierre explained. "I thought perhaps you were expecting this and I am somehow unaware—"

"No . . ." Arabella told him. "But I will take the call."

"Very well," Pierre responded. "She is line three."

Arabella curled up in her chair. "Hello, Mrs. Shady," she said softly into the telephone.

"Miz Dune-War!" The voice from the other end sounded like an emory board on sandpaper. "Is this Miz Airy-bell-uh Dune-war, Mary Jane Shady's boss-lady and the head of the biggest advertising agency in the whole wide world?"

"That's me," Arabella smiled. Irene Shady sounded exactly like Mrs. Wiggins, who'd owned the farm Arabella grew up on. Arabella *loved* Mrs. Wiggins. Estelline Wiggins had given her enough money to buy a bus ticket to New York when she was fifteen years old, and had talked her mother into letting her use it. "Let the girl try for her dreams," Estelline had told Axie Max. "Otherwise, she'll end up like you working for *me*."

"Are you calling from Uncertain?" Arabella asked.

"You bet your boots I am!" Irene Shady shouted. "Can you hear me?" She was never sure if she could be heard all the way from Uncertain to Manhattan.

"Clear as a bell," Arabella laughed. Her own mother always asked the same thing.

"Listen, honey, I gotta ask a big favor here," Irene Shady said.

Arabella just couldn't stop smiling. If her staff had heard anyone address her as "honey", they would all be mortified.

"Ask away," Arabella invited, somewhat curious.

"I need Mary Jane back here in Uncertain, Texas this Friday," Irene stated. "I know ya'll have got your own plans made for that Peanut Butter deal and all, but cain't you just let her off this once? She's showed up for five years on time for ya'll and this is somethin' real special."

"Oh, I'd like to," Arabella replied patiently, and she meant it. "But we're all set up here, Mrs. Shady. I have a location paid for, permits granted, a cast and crew on call—"

"But it's her Twentieth Reunion!" Irene Shady interrupted.

Arabella blinked and sat up in her chair. "Of what?"

"Of her high school graduating class!" Irene exclaimed.

Arabella du Noir jumped out of her chair.

HOW OLD IS THIS PEANUT BUTTER CUP, ANYWAY? she wanted to shout. *IN HER THIRTIES*?! She figured quickly. *HER LATE THIRTIES*?! She counted again. *SURELY NOT PUSHING—*!

She picked up a Steuben decanter and poured herself a full shot of Courvoisier. She couldn't bring herself to *say* it! She could hardly bring herself to *think* it! And she would never have hired anyone even close to it! *Thirty* was the limit for a PBC. The last moment of twenty-nine was the absolute cut-off. *Thirty* had always been the unspoken age of dissolution. How could she have made such a total mistake in judgment?

The brandy burned as it slid down her throat. "NO!" she cried, finding her voice.

"Yes!" Irene Shady screamed back. "She's awready missed the tenth reunion on account of some job and it'll be ten more years 'til her thirtieth! Now you know what a important event this is in a young woman's life!"

"I know what an important event it is in *mine*," Arabella replied shakily. Her finger found the "play" button and hit it. Mary Jane's soundless image flickered into action and across the screen.

Arabella stared in fascination.

My God, she thought. *I must remember to find out who this surgeon is! Brilliant work, Mary Jane Shady,* she admitted, sipping the brandy. *Really brilliant. You don't look a day over THIRTY. . .*

"It'll be the first time she's ever been back since the day she left and would mean a whole lot to a whole lot of people!" Irene assured Arabella. She had taken the Vice-President's silence to mean 'no.' Nevertheless she was determined to try one last plea. "So why don't ya'll just come out *here* and do that commercial right in the middle of the Pep Rally peppin' and the band playin' and the cheerleaders jumpin' and the Queen gettin' crowned. You won't get nothin' like it in New York City, I guarantee!"

"Now why didn't I think of that," Arabella said half-heartedly.

"Oh, you can take the credit!" Irene offered. But Arabella wasn't listening. She'd flipped open Mary Jane Shady's file and yanked out her contract, scanning it for the "appearance guarantee." Page 13, Section VIII, Paragraph G told her everything.

After the overwhelming success of the initial test spot, Ralph Painter had negotiated for *thirteen guaranteed-to-run* commercials for his client, regardless of her length of tenure. Arabella held her breath as she counted the number of commercials Mary Jane had made since becoming Miss PBC. THIRTEEN. She counted them. Yes. Thirteen! But only twelve had run. She looked again.

Memories of the thirteenth shoot emerged: Mary Jane in yet another gingham-enhanced kitchen with two jars of Peanut Butter and a cocker spaniel for atmosphere.

No one had noticed exactly *when* it had happened, but sometime during the very first take, between "action" and "cut", Miss Peanut Butter Cup had erupted in hives. Mary Jane Shady's face had become a mass of ugly red blotches.

Commercial Thirteen had been scratched. Arabella *had* to use this actress *one more time.*

"You have cheerleaders, a band, a parade, a Homecoming Queen, the works?" she heard herself asking Irene Shady. The new concept was already forming in her head.

"Listen, wait 'til you see Why-vonne Henderson's stretch-out car and Catsy Ivanhoe's Silver-Clouded Rolls coupe!" Irene yelled. "We got it all!"

Arabella heard something clacking in the background. It sounded like a gaggle of geese.

"What's that noise?" she asked Irene.

"Oh, that's Why-vonne," Irene replied. "She's all excited for me to offer ya'll her house to stay in! That'll save you a motel bill! 'Course her house *looks* like a motel—she's tellin me to say *hotel*! And she says if ya'll come by private plane, just use the landin' strip out in her back yard!"

"I will," Arabella promised. Her mind was made up. It was time to retire Mary Jane Shady.

"Whoopee!" Irene yelled.

"We'll be there on Friday," Arabella continued. "Except for Mary Jane. She'll leave now."

"Whoopee!" Irene shouted again.

"Now, listen, Mrs. Shady," Arabella instructed. "I'm doing you a big favor and I want you to do one for me."

"Anything," Irene replied. "Name it."

"Make her get some rest," Arabella demanded. "She's beginning to look almost *thirty*."

"Thirty!" Irene Shady laughed. "Well, that's pretty good for somebody who's just about to turn thirty-six!"

Arabella hung up with number "thirty-six" ringing in her ears like the cry from a bingo barker.

"I cannot get rid of you fast enough!" she said, sending the image on the video player into rewind. "Wind yourself up one more time, Miss Peanut Butter Cup," Arabella told the quickly disappearing celluloid symbol of one of her most popular and successful campaigns. "This is THE END." She pressed "eject" and took out the tape.

She reached for a piece of paper from her memo pad and began to write.

> NEW CAMPAIGN FOR RETIRING PEANUT BUTTER CUPS. LAST LOCATION: PBC'S HOMETOWN. FINAL TRIP ABLAZE GOOD FORMULATED GLORY WILL HOPEFULLY "PERK" AGING PBC FOR HER FINAL APPEARANCE, AS PBC WILL BE WELCOMED SIMILAR TO MISS AMERICA BY HOMETOWN. I'LL GET A GREAT COMMERCIAL: SHE'LL FEEL LIKE A CELEBRITY. CAMPAIGN TO BE USED ONLY AS FINAL PBC APPEARANCE. SCHEDULED TO BE USED FOR FIRST TIME FRIDAY, SEPTEMBER 13, 1985, UNCERTAIN, TEXAS, HOMETOWN OF CURRENT PBC, MARY JANE SHADY, PBC, 1980-1985. *HIGHLY CONFIDENTIAL.*

She buzzed her secretary and handed him the memo. "Better move this from the bottom line to the top," she told Pierre, pointing to the words 'highly confidential.' "I certainly don't want Mary Jane Shady to find out we're canning her before the job. She'll show up looking closer to *FORTY*!"

"Impossible!" Pierre smiled innocently.

"That's what you think," Arabella sighed. She turned and started back into her office.

"We're shooting the commercial in Uncertain, Texas?" Pierre asked, reading the memo.

"That's what *you're* doing," Arabella smiled. "The Countess here hopes to be fucking some cowboy! Now contact Mary Jane Shady and send her home!"

CHAPTER EIGHT

MARY JANE stared at Herman numbly.

I can't tell him about Bobby, she thought. *I can't, I can't, I can't. Nobody, no matter how understanding, is that understanding*!

Herman frowned. Then his eyes widened. "Oh, I see—" he said. Then he started to smile. "That was really good, wasn't it?" He stroked her face.

She wanted to cry.

"That really did it for you, didn't it?" He nodded understandingly, as if answering himself, then shrugged. "Well, what can I say? I was just in top form today."

Mary Jane just couldn't speak. She nodded mutely and closed her eyes.

"You rest," he told her. "I'll make some coffee."

She continued to sit, eyes closed, half-listening as he continued to speak.

"I want to know why you don't want to go to that Homecoming." His voice was far away. She could hear dishes clattering. "I would have gone back to Coney Island . . . except nobody ever asked me."

She smelled the coffee perking. She'd bought it at Zabars. She sat very still, trying not to think.

"Did I ever tell you about the day after I opened on Broadway for the very first time, Mary Jane?" He walked back in the room and nudged her. "Take a listen."

She opened her eyes.

"Okay, I'm a hit, see? *New York Times* says so, *Daily News* says so, the *Herald*, the *Voice*, the Bla-Bla-Bla, they all say so . . . I'm a big, big Broadway hit. My name is all over the marquee, big as the title. Hal Prince has taken out a goddamn billboard that rises all over Times Square with letters as tall as me. 'HERMAN TOP IN *MONSIEUR*!' I'm standing there on 47th and Broadway, looking at the billboard, admiring Mr. Prince, admiring my name, admiring that sign, but mostly admiring *myself*.

"Behind me, someone tugs on my overcoat. I turn around, ready for The People's Praise . . .

" 'Hermie Top from Coney Island High!' this guy says." Herman laughed and shook his head. "Fucker! He don't know I'm a big Broadway star! For all he knows, I never left Coney Island!"

Still laughing, he turned and started back into the kitchen.

Mary Jane looked after him, puzzled. "I don't know if I think that's a very funny story, Herman," she said.

"I been noticing you're losing your sense of humor," he nodded, returning with two cups of coffee. "Listen," he said, handing her one of them. "You don't go back to those things for *them*. You go back for *you*." He settled into a large oversized easy chair. "I'll bet there's all kinds of people you forgot about that you'd get a real kick out of seeing . . . "

Mary Jane put her coffee down on the table before she spilled it.

"See?" Herman smiled. "You already thought of one I betcha. Some old boyfriend, probably six-foot-two, blond hair, blue eyes, captain of the football team, a ten-foot cock, looked like Humphrey Bogart . . . "

The words sounded to Mary Jane like someone else was saying them. Someone far away, someone who'd fallen into a well.

She could see Bobby's steel blue eyes. She'd never forgotten his eyes. One lid drooped slightly lower than the other. This was the fault of the doctor who'd attended Bobby's birth and was careless with the forceps. But Mary Jane thought this accident worked to Bobby's favor and that Bobby Henderson's gotch eye was the sexiest thing she had ever seen, the way one eyelid drooped slightly lower than the other one.

"Did he eat pussy?" Herman wondered, sipping his coffee. He drained the cup and reached for hers. "Most men just don't get into oral sex . . . this is what I *hear*, what I *read* . . . . Somebody should write a book, 'How to Eat It Without Really Touching It.' That would sell!"

"Herman," Mary Jane Shady said, "put a lid on it."

"I'm right!" he laughed. "If Bobby Henderson had only done that *one thing once*, you'd be a miserable, married, matronly mother with five kids, still living in Uncertain, Texas, still hoping to get him to do that *one thing one more time*."

"Bobby Henderson loved oral sex!" Mary Jane shouted. "He was great! He had a tongue the length of my leg! He had a cock as long as your arm and as thick as your head!"

"That's too big," Herman sighed.

"Oh, shut up!" she yelled.

"Where is he?" Herman asked. "In the circus?" He took her in his arms. "Poor Mary Jane," he soothed, holding her. "Her high school boyfriend was a bust." He held on to her as she tried to wriggle away. "C'mere." He kissed her gently. "Did you give that big nimnod your cherry and he didn't know what to do with it?"

Mary Jane started to cry.

"C'mon, sit down and tell Hermie the story," Herman said.

He pulled her into his lap.

She wanted to tell him everything. She'd never told anyone *anything*. She needed to tell him *something*.

Hesitantly, she cleared her throat. Carefully, she chose the safest of two very dangerous topics. "Herman," she said meekly. "How old do you think I really am?"

"Thirty-five," he replied without losing a beat.

"You're kidding," She just stared at him. "Do I *look* thirty-five?" she asked anxiously.

"Nah," Herman said, sipping his coffee. "But you don't look twenty-eight, either."

"How old do I look?" she asked edgily.

He shrugged. "Twenty-nine. Maybe thirty. What's the difference? You look great."

She steeled herself. "What would you say if I told you I *am* thirty-five?" she asked.

He sighed. "I'd say what I *said*. I *know* you're thirty-five. Your agent told me."

"Ralph Painter?" Mary Jane was stunned. "He goes around telling my *age*?"

"He hates you," Herman replied. "He hates all his clients. But don't get excited. He only told *me*. He wouldn't tell an *account*."

"Christ!" She threw herself on the sofa. "I'm going to fire him!"

The intercom buzzed, interrupting them.

"Wait a minute," Herman told her. "Hold the kill. This is my material for Chicago." He buzzed back, instructing the doorman to send up the messenger.

"I'm setting fire to his toupee the next time I'm in L.A.!" she promised furiously as Herman went to answer the door. "Did you know he wears false eyelashes? I'm not kidding! One day I look up and here he is on the set, in *seersucker* and *false eyelashes*! I was so embarrassed I—"

"It's for you," Herman said, returning with an envelope. "From Fucker-Schmucker." He handed it to her. "It must be urgent if they tracked you down."

"For *me*?" Mary Jane Shady stared at the envelope. She was sure it would turn into snakes if she touched it. "You open it," she told Herman. "They've *never* followed me to deliver a work call." She shook her head. "This isn't good, Herman," she whispered. She closed her eyes. "I'm getting fired."

"Don't be paranoid," he replied, ripping it open.

She opened her eyes. "Am I fired?" she asked, anxiously trying to read his face for an answer.

"No. You're not fired," he said. "But you *are* going to Uncertain."

"What!?" She grabbed the message, written on Arabella du Noir's letterhead, and scanned it.

ATTENTION MARY JANE SHADY. RE: WORK CALL FRIDAY, SEPT. 13, 1985. LOCATION CHANGED TO UNCERTAIN HIGH SCHOOL GYMNASIUM, CORNER OF READING AND WRITING AVENUES, UNCERTAIN, TEXAS. 3PM SHARP. USING HOMECOMING FOR COMMERCIAL THEME. AIRLINE TICKET ENCLOSED. TAKE THE FIRST PLANE YOU CAN GET ON. YOUR MOTHER IS EXPECTING YOU. LEAVE NOW. WELCOME HOME, STAR.
ARABELLA DU NOIR

CHAPTER NINE

"WHOOPEE!" Yvonne screamed. "You did it! You did it! You did it! She's comin' back, inn't she?"

"She sure is!" Irene grinned. "Be here anytime now, I 'spect."

"Who else is comin'?" Yvonne cried.

"Ever-body," Irene stated. "The whole shootin' match."

Yvonne's eyes grew wide. "You mean the peanut butter people are really comin' here to Uncertain?"

"That's right," Irene confirmed. "And they're usin' your landin' strip to fly in on and your house to stay in, just like you offered 'em to."

"Oh, good Lord! I may faint!" Yvonne cried. "Wait 'til Catsy Ivanhoe hears about this!" She faced Irene solemnly. "This is the second most important event in my life!"

"At least this is something *good*," Irene assured her.

"You're right," Yvonne nodded. "I just got to get over never ever graduatin' sometime."

Irene blinked. She'd had no idea *that* was what Yvonne considered to be her worst experience.

"Come on, Bay-bee," Yvonne called out. "We got a million thangs to do!" Yvonne turned back to Irene. "You don't know where I can pick up some real good extra Mexskins, do you? That landin' strip needs sweepin', I got to empty and refill my goldfish pond, buy fresh fish and maybe a turtle or somethin' that crawls around and looks inner-estin', fix up all the bedrooms, fill up the icebox. I'm not sure I got enough help."

"You got fifteen or twenty of 'em workin' for you, Why-vonne," Irene said. "That's plenty."

"I sure hope so," Yvonne replied. "Maybe we can get it all done by tomorrow, 'cause I won't be back 'til Friday."

"Back?" Irene cried. "Where are you goin'?"

"Dallas!" Yvonne grinned. "To get my hair fixed!"

"Oh." Irene sighed. She gave Yvonne's blond wig a good long stare and wondered what in the world they did with it off in Dallas, Texas to make it look like a mad hornet's nest. She wondered why Yvonne wanted to travel so far to look so awful.

"They cain't do this at the beauty shop in Uncertain," Yvonne explained.

Irene nodded. "I guess they don't do that style."

"That's right," Yvonne agreed. "And I want somethin' real special to appear in at that Homecomin'. With all those cameras around, somebody's bound to take my picture!"

Irene made a mental note to buy film for her Brownie Kodak. She wanted to be ready to take Yvonne's photo in case no one else showed any interest.

Yvonne lowered her voice. "Now listen. I got so much to do. Don't you think it would be best if Bay-bee just stayed here with you 'til Friday? She's just goin' to get in the way of the servants and all. What if she takes her clothes off again?"

"Why-vonne—" Irene growled.

"You know what happened the last time that happened at my house!" Yvonne shouted.

"Well, *that* won't happen again, now, will it?" Irene responded matter-of-factly.

"Well, no, I guess not," Yvonne conceded.

"And don't go leavin' her with the help, neither," Irene said. "She don't know English, much less Spanish."

"I could use some more Spanish myself," Yvonne replied.

"Take a night class," Irene suggested impatiently.

"And go to *school*?" Yvonne asked incredulously. "What school would take me?"

"Oh, stop that, Why-vonne!" Irene cried. "I'm a split hair away from pickin' up that phone over yonder and tellin' Miz Dune-war to just forget the whole thing! And if I hear one more word out of you, I will!" Irene threatened. "Now you take Baby with you and get her hair fixed as well! And she better come back lookin' real, real special, too!"

As Baby wandered in, Yvonne grabbed her by the arm and yanked her toward the front door. "C'mon, Bay-bee!" Yvonne said. "You and me are about to fly off in my airplane and go get beautified at Odette Lum-year's on Lovers Lane in Dallas, Texas!"

Baby waved happily at the five Mary Jane Shady's smiling silently in the foyer as she followed Yvonne out the door.

Irene watched them get in the limousine.

"A whole overhaul is too much to hope for yet," Irene thought as Yvonne put Baby in the front seat next to the driver.

Irene turned away as Yvonne climbed into the back seat, alone.

"There's a reason why people end up by theirselves," Irene mused as she once more found her way back to the embalming room of the Uncertain Chapel of Memories.

CHAPTER TEN

"How can I leave now?" Mary Jane screamed hysterically. "I don't want to go!"

"Look on the bright side," Herman replied. "You're not fired."

"I might as well be!" she cried. "When Arabella du Noir finds out how old I am, she'll fire me!"

When Arabella du Noir finds out the rest, she'll kill me! her head screamed.

"Nobody's going to announce your age on a loud speaker all over the football field, Mary Jane," Herman sighed. "They won't stick you on a float behind these giant letters that read 'THIRTY-FIVE.' "

"They won't have to, Herman!" Mary Jane spat. "It's *my* home-coming! Arabella thinks I'm *twenty-eight*! I would have been the only eight-year-old senior in the class of '65!" She threw herself back on the sofa. "Of all the horrible things that have ever happened to me, this is the worst! Well, I'm not getting fired *and* going back to Uncer-tain-Fucking-Texas to be publicly humiliated!"

And that's putting it mildly! her head pounded. *That's putting it real, real mildly!*

"I think you're overreacting," he told her. "Arabella du Noir doesn't give a shit if you're fifty as long as you look good."

"Oh, wake up and smell the coffee, Herman!" she screeched. "Don't you think it is just *weird* that Arabella chose Uncertain, Texas? That is not a mere coincidence, old friend! *Somebody* put this fine idea into her head, *somebody* called her—"

"The same person who called you, maybe?" Herman wondered.

" '*Why-vonne*'!" Mary Jane mimicked, raising her voice two oc-taves to imitate Yvonne's pitch.

"Don't," Herman pleaded. "That hurts."

"She doesn't have sense enough to dial long distance!" Mary Jane rattled on. "She couldn't remember the end of the number by the time she got to it—"

"Then maybe that old boyfriend of yours," Herman teased. "Things are probably pretty dull there now. Figured he'd get you back and liven up his life a little." He stuck out his tongue and wiggled it. "Time for a little star sucking—maybe you can teach an old dog some new tricks—"

She slapped him without even knowing what she was doing.

He stopped laughing, shocked.

She stared at him, stunned.

"Hey," he said quietly. "Why don't you tell me what's *really* going on?"

CHAPTER ELEVEN

I'VE GOT A SECRET, fifteen-year-old Mary Jane Shady thought to herself with a smile. *A BIG HUGE DELICIOUS SECRET* . . .

She ran her eyes over Bobby in total, absolute, complete adoration. He had been *inside* her! It was almost unfathomable! She had become so dizzy from the very experience, she could hardly remember anything but that huge, powerful, throbbing release that balleted through her like stallions waltzing in ocean waves.

Oh, Bobby. . . So tall. So blond and tan. His wonderful eyes calm and content, his one lid drooping mystery and intrigue. His smile comfortable and promising.

Her hair blew away from her face in the West Texas fall night. Lit by a zillion stars, she needed not one, her own glow was so strong and bright.

She didn't want to leave him. Not ever. Not even for a minute.

As he drove her back along Highway 158 toward the Uncertain Chapel of Memories, Mary Jane's head filled with their future. And when Bobby Henderson's 1954 Ford convertible approached Mary Jane's favorite street, Melogo Drive, Mary Jane looked at the street with new interest and hope.

Two blocks north of the Chapel of Memories, it was one long, arched block just off the main highway. With only eleven houses on it, it was the most prestigious addition in Uncertain. Each home sat on an acre of land. The eleven families had pooled their resources and brought in oak trees, sycamores, maples, weeping willows, pine trees and poplars from East Texas. Shrubbery, all evergreen, lined their alfalfa-grassed lawns. Assortments of roses, daffodils, irises, petunias, zinnias and daisies, pansies and buttercups preened like princesses from their well-tended beds.

Mary Jane Shady stared at the oasis. Some day she and Bobby would live there, too, right next door to Judge Upchurch, maybe. The

Judge had been the first to build and had afforded himself the privilege of naming the street "Melogo" after his wife and two daughters, Melba, Lois and Golda, using the first two letters of each name.

All of Uncertain's finest lived on Melogo Drive. Perhaps their nearest neighbors would be Dr. Smith and whichever wife he was married to at the moment. Or Mr. Wylie Higginbotham, who was Chief of the Fire Department, Head of the Chamber of Commerce and Mayor of Uncertain, Texas. Maybe Mary Jane and Bobby would move into the house next door to Irene Shady's best friend, Gladys Turner, and her husband, Orville, who was the Superintendent of Schools.

Even Mary Jane's best friend, Milly Rae Waffles lived on Melogo Drive. Milly Rae's mother, Lovely Waffles, had been Mary Jane's first Sunday school teacher. Robert Shady thought Mary Jane was making it up when she had come home several years ago and told him her new Sunday school teacher's name was Lovely Waffles. Mary Jane's eyes twinkled. Soon Lovely Waffles would be her neighbor!

As Bobby Henderson's 1954 Ford convertible passed by the long, arched block that was Melogo Drive, Mary Jane thought of Milly Rae and wondered if she could ever tell even her very best friend about what had just happened with her and Bobby out on the oil road this very night. How could she describe those ferris wheel feelings, the plunge down, the thrust up, overwhelming, full, pulsating, that overcame her when Bobby loved on her? How could she ever explain? And even if she did, how could Milly Rae begin to understand?

As the neon lights of the Uncertain Chapel of Memories splashed across the highway and through her star-studded dreams, Mary Jane looked back longingly toward Melogo Drive.

Oh, how she hated the Uncertain Chapel of Memories. She hated that horrible, embarrassing neon sign that tirelessly blinked its hideous five colors four miles away. She longed for a regular house on a regular street. She longed for a normal car. She'd spent her childhood just wishing she could drive up and get out of a nice green Packard or yellow Studebaker or red Buick or pink Thunderbird instead of that dreadful, foreboding blue-black coffin carrier. How she yearned for a straight concrete driveway to place her feet on, a tar and pebble carpet that led to a regular house, rectangular and white, shuttered and fenced, with trees and grass and flowers on the outside, instead of all over the inside. A house with no carnations . . .

She looked up at the sky and silently prayed for a shooting star so she could make a wish for their new house. Hers and Bobby's. On Melogo Drive.

Connected to the heavens, she gazed in wonder at her sister stars above, and watched, mesmerized, as one began to fall. She laughed gleefully, made her wish, and gazed at the star's quick descent as if observing a Fourth of July sparkler. Never did it enter her mind that the same could happen to *her*. For Mary Jane Shady was too full of her own stars that night, too caught up in her own dazzling light to heed fair warning, even from the heavens.

Just as the star ended its descent, the neon sign on top of the Uncertain Chapel of Memories suddenly went off.

"What's 'at?" Bobby asked, looking ahead at the sign.

Mary Jane tensed abruptly. "That's strange," she said. "That sign's always on at night."

As they drove closer and closer to the Uncertain Chapel of Memories, it took not even a second for her to grasp that something was very, very wrong.

CHAPTER TWELVE

"WELL?" Herman said. He was obviously waiting for some explanation.

She stood in front of him, immobilized.

"I'm sorry," she mumbled, avoiding his eyes. She reached for his cheek.

"Mary Jane," he sighed, pulling away. "When you hit a person, you really want to hit yourself."

She nodded. But it wasn't Herman she was seeing. She was still seeing cars, cars parked all around her house. A crowd of people in the front yard . . .

"So why do you want to hit yourself?" Herman asked.

She shrugged, then shook her head . . . Lovely Waffles was talking to Mayor Higginbotham and the Widders family, who lived in the Uncertain Trailer Court across town. Even Orville Turner, the principal of Uncertain High, was there with Judge Upchurch. Her daddy's sister, Aunt Lottie, was standing with them . . .

"Think," Herman told her.

Mary Jane paled . . . Someone had seen her and Bobby Henderson doing it on the oil road. Now they were in real trouble! The Principal from school was there! She and Bobby were being expelled! Mrs. Waffles was there! She was being kicked out of Sunday school! Mayor Higginbotham and Judge Upchurch were there! Mary Jane prepared herself for juvenile court. It was a CRIME not to be a virgin before you were married. Hadn't her mother told her a thousand times. "Don't ever let one of those boys get in your pants before you get married," Irene Shady had warned. "No man will ever marry a girl who's not a virgin. Never. It's a sin, Mary Jane . . . "

Everyone knew that. How could Mary Jane have let things go beyond fingers and rubbing and into SIN AND CRIME! Why else had Janelle Crowbottom and Sparky Hicks and Linda Lee Lafferty and Tommy Joe Jackson all run off to Juarez, Old Mexico together on the Friday night of last year's prom, gotten married and driven back to Uncertain in time for school the following Monday? They knew the difference between SIN andCRIME and RIGHT and WRONG. They used their heads and *got* married. They hadn't gotten kicked out of Uncertain. She knew Janelle and Linda Lee had been virgins. They'd told her so. Oh, How Mary Jane envied them, even though Linda Lee's parents had made her get her Mexico marriage to Tommy Joe annulled and had then picked up and moved their whole family off to Pecos so Linda Lee would never see Tommy Joe again, and Janelle had been forced to drop out of school because she had gotten pregnant in Juarez and Sparky had had to drop out to support the new family. . .

"Are you thinking yet?" Herman asked.

"I'm trying to."

"You don't want to. You're avoiding thinking."

"I am?"

He groaned. "Give me an answer that doesn't end in a question, okay? Why did you hit me?"

The sight of all those people in front of the Uncertain Chapel of Memories sickened Mary Jane.

"Looks like your folks are havin' a block party," Bobby said. "It's not your birthday, is it?" He winked at her. "How'd you like your present?"

"Shut up, Bobby. You know it's not my birthday and that's no party. Someone saw us out there and told my mother and daddy," she said, anxiously trying to locate her parents in the crowd. "*Oh, no-o-o! Look!* There's *your* mother and daddy! Oh, Bobby, everybody looks like they're crying!" Mary Jane wailed, trying hard not to cry herself.

"There's your preacher comin' out of the house," Bobby said. "Oh, shit. Now look, Mary Jane. I'm already enrolled at Southwestern for next year. I love you more than anything in the world, but I don't want to get married until after college."

"You don't want to die either, do you, Bobby?" Mary Jane hissed. "Don't you dare leave me right now in front of everybody."

"Okay," he said. "But 'member, I'm doin' you a favor . . . "

"I know you're edgy about going back to that reunion," Herman's voice went on. "But you can't be that nervous about losing your job. So you get canned. I've had it happen one zillion times and something better always turns up. Anyway, you've been saying for three years how glad you'll be when your contract is up so you'll be free to do something else. So why are you so upset? I mean, you're speechless. Mary Jane? Mary Jane?" He threw his hands up. "She's mute."

There were so many cars they had to park halfway down the block. With dread Mary Jane had not felt since her last piano recital when, again, the bass clef failed her and she had had to repeat the first four measures of "*Für Elise*" over and over until she finally remembered the last chord and fled from the stage, Mary Jane Shady slowly walked toward the Chapel of Memories with a reluctant Bobby Henderson at her side.

"Okay," Herman's voice said. "Let's take this from the top. We were trying to figure out how Arabella du Noir got the word there was a reunion in the first place . . . "

Her head was splitting. The crowd, seeing Mary Jane and Bobby, abruptly began converging upon them, moaning and crying, and hundreds of arms seemed to be reaching out for them . . .

" . . . and then I made some dumb joke about your old boyfriend and *wham*. You hit me . . . "

Suddenly Mary Jane screamed, "It's not my fault!" The crowd hushed. The preacher spoke. "Of course it's not your fault, Mary Jane. We know you loved him."

"*Loved* him?" fifteen-year-old Mary Jane Shady cried out in thirty-five-year-old Mary Jane Shady's voice. "I STILL LOVE HIM!"

It was at that moment, to her tremendous relief, that Mary Jane Shady learned her father had just died of a heart attack.

"You still love your high school boyfriend?" Herman Top asked incredulously. "Well, *shit*."

CHAPTER THIRTEEN

"HOW'D YOU GET into the death business anyway?" Leo Diggs asked Lottie Shady as she steered his eighteen-wheeler down Highway 115, which intersected with 158 a few miles outside the Uncertain City Limits. She was giving him a sightseeing tour, so she had taken him to see the sandhills, fifteen miles of pure white sand, which lay between Uncertain and Andrews. Said to be an old ocean bed, Lottie was hoping to get Leo Diggs to get out and hunt fossils with her, although most people were more successful in digging up arrowheads and cow bones.

"I was born into it, hon," Lottie said, trying to concentrate on the road ahead of her. The sun hitting the white sand was causing a dazzling reflection. Moreover, she'd never been alone in a moving vehicle with a man she liked before except for her brother Robert, and he hadn't made her heart pound like Leo Diggs did. "My entire family tree is just clogged with undertakers." She looked at Leo Diggs and wondered if he was the kind of man who would enjoy digging.

"I guess most dead people are a lot easier to get along with than live ones." Leo grinned.

"Ain't it the truth," Lottie replied, turning the truck into a road which cut through the sandhills. "I never met a corpse I didn't like."

Leo Diggs looked at Lottie admiringly. "I like a woman who runs her own business," he told her.

"Oh, I do ever-thing myself," Lottie assured him. "Irene's a pretty good assistant, but she's useless in a emergency. Too frail-headed. When Brother was seized, she hit the floor before he did. But I just picked him up, carried him in the back, and give him the same fine service we'd been brought up to deliver for generations—"

"You serviced your *brother*?" Leo reached in his pocket, brought out his paper bag and popped a pill. "Inn't that like a doctor operatin' on his family?"

"That's exactly right," Lottie nodded. "If you cain't trust your own family, who can you trust? He'd a did me, had I been removed first, so why would I send him over to Kermit or Wink or God Save the Queen, Deal Grimes' Permanent Rest Center!"

"That's a good question," Leo nodded, glancing out the window. To his amazement, they were surrounded by nothing but white sand!

"I did a good job, too," Lottie went on. "Put him in his red striped pajamas, 'cause he was happiest asleep, but when Irene come to, she made me change him into his Sunday suit. I put his eyeglasses on his face, 'cause he never had 'em off. Well, she took those away. But I did manage to sneak in his baseball cards and a pack of Camels. Put 'em in the inside packet of that Sunday suit."

"Irene gave you a hard time, huh?" Leo asked sympathetically. He wanted to grab her, but he didn't want to scare her. He was waiting to make his first move.

"She's always givin' me a hard time," Lottie sighed.

"Here," Leo said, offering her his pill bag. "Have one of these . . ."

"What are they for?" Lottie asked.

"For when people give you a hard time," Leo answered vaguely. He looked back out the window. "How long has all this sand been here, anyway?" He just couldn't believe that he had his heroine's lookalike driving his truck. And here they were in the most isolated spot he had ever seen, surrounded by mountains and mountains of pure white sand! He gazed at her romantically and waited.

"Oh, 'bout a million years," Lottie replied, growing more and more excited by Leo's brown eyes and red hair. "Just thinkin' of Irene makes my heart *pound*!" she said, as her heart beat away in her chest.

"Poundin' heart?" Leo asked, opening up his glove compartment. "Here's the only thang for a poundin' heart. Pull over."

She did.

He took a yellow capsule and popped it under Lottie's nose, as she turned off the ignition.

"Oh-h-h," moaned Lottie Shady, as she grew warm, then hot all over. Her eyes widened. "What's *that*?" Tiny yellow dots flickered in front of her.

"Poundin'-heart medicine," Leo murmured softly, sniffing it himself.

"M-m-m . . ." They both inhaled again.

Two slow grins spread over their faces. Leo guided a finger over Lottie Shady's wrinkles.

"My face looks like its wore out thirteen different bodies, don't it?" Lottie grinned.

"I'm hopin' it'll wear out mine," Leo replied, as he leaned closer to give Lottie Shady her very first kiss.

CHAPTER FOURTEEN

"SON OF A BITCH," Herman said. "You're still in love with Bobby Hender-whozitz."

"No, no, that's not it," Mary Jane protested. She knew there was no way to explain.

"Well, that's what you said, Mary Jane," Herman said. " 'I still love him,' you said."

"Herman," she said. "Listen to me." She had no idea what she was going to say. But she knew perfectly well what she wasn't going to say.

"You're in love with a cowpoke quarterback. I heard." He put his hands over his eyes wearily.

Let him think that, she told herself. *Let him.*

"Look, this is not as much of a shock as you might imagine."

She looked up. "What?"

"For one year I've tried to be all those buzz words women read in *Cosmopolitan* they should go looking for in a man—'patient,' 'kind,' 'considerate,' 'understanding.' I understand fear. In fact, *fear* may be the only thing I do understand. She's *afraid* to get married, I say. Well, forget marriage, that's too extreme. Commitment. She's *afraid* of commitment. That's understandable. Everyone is afraid of commitment. Forget commitment. It's too much. How about just spending the night with me? How about that? No, you won't do that. And I think it's your upbringing. Some rural code of backwoods behavior I didn't get over at the Coney Island School of Life. So I finally settle for cocktail hour. That's when I get to see you. Eat fast, talk fast, fuck fast. Why? Because you're in love with someone else, that's why."

"Don't!" She put her arms around him, desperately kissing his face.

"You don't!" he said, brushing her away. "Goddamnit, goddamnit. I am so dumb. No wonder you won't marry me . . . no wonder you never married anyone . . . no wonder you won't live with me . . . or even spend the night with me . . . I am so dumb . . ."

A funny crooked sad smile came over his face, a defeated look Mary Jane had never ever seen before.

"I just need to be in my own bed, with my own things," she protested feebly. "In my own home . . ."

"That's a hotel over there, Mary Jane," Herman said. "That's not a home. It's a hotel."

"I'm used to hotels," she reasoned.

"Then you could have gotten used to *this* hotel," he pointed out flatly.

"That's not the point."

"I don't think I've missed any points," Herman declared.

"You have missed the point entirely," she said, thinking fast. "Here's the point," she explained at the very moment she was creating it. "Remember that pencil audition I had yesterday?"

"Yeah," Herman replied. "You spent the whole day wondering if they wanted a round pencil, a sharp pencil, electronic, octagonal—"

"It isn't funny, Herman," Mary Jane snapped.

"Who's laughing?" Herman asked glumly. "I do this for a living, too, remember."

"Listen to me. Ralph Painter calls long distance from the Hollywood office expressly to tell me to just *try* to look good. And *young*. They want a *new* pencil, he says. He reminds me to attempt to cover up that new line under my left eye. 'This is on-camera,' he says, as if I didn't get it. I may end up being a 'live pencil.' Am I thin enough? They want a *thin* pencil."

"You're thin enough to play a pencil," Herman encouraged. "What's the problem?"

"That new wrinkle under my left eye."

"That same wrinkle is good enough for Miss Peanut Butter Cup," Herman said. "I don't know why it has to be a problem for a pencil for Christsakes. I can't even see the goddamned thing."

"That's the point," Mary Jane sighed. "You're about to miss the point."

"Which is?"

"The camera can see it. It's an overall problem."

Herman peered at her. "And this is why you won't spend the night with me, or live with me, or marry me?"

"I knew you would miss the point," she said. "Don't you understand? I am dependent on a wrinkle-free face! I have to get my rest!"

"Bullshit," he muttered. "*Bad* bullshit."

But she didn't stop. "There were three blondes in that reception room. All waiting to audition. I asked to borrow a brush—I forgot my brush. Why? Because I'd been with you. I was thinking of you. 'Somebody got a brush?' I asked. No one responded! *Can you believe it*?"

"No," he said under his breath. "I can't. And I don't."

" 'Are you auditioning for the part of the pencil?' I asked. No, they're all *erasers*. 'Then someone please lend me a brush! I'm here for the pencil! I'm not up for an eraser! I'm not even a *blonde*!' Those bitches didn't budge! I had to borrow the secretary's goddamned hairbrush!"

"And after a day like that you need to go home and protect yourself from further abuse by *me*," Herman nodded. He picked up her purse and tossed it at her. "Here. You better grab that ticket and fly home to cowboy as fast as you can."

"Herman, you do not understand," she said.

"I understand more than you do," he said. "I understand that this is not about hairbrushes and wrinkles. And I understand that I do not understand why you can't tell me the truth. And I understand that you are about to very nearly exhaust me."

"Herman—"

"Please do not speak to me again unless it is from the absolute most honest, truthful place in you, Mary Jane. I can take anything, really. Don't forget, I was married to Denise La Trelle."

She opened her mouth to speak.

"Be careful. Don't be a liar," he said steadily.

She blinked and said nothing.

"We're as sick as our secrets, M.J. You need to think about that."

"I don't need to think," she said desperately.

"Then don't," he said. "Rest. Rest on the plane."

"Plane?"

"That's how you get to Uncertain, isn't it?"

She reached out for him. "Don't do this, Herman."

"Come on," he said, moving her toward the door. "Let's go. You've got to go home. You've got to find out."

"What?"

"Whatever it is you've been trying to forget."

"Oh . . ." she whispered. "No . . ."

Without another word, she moved through the door. She stood speechless, motionless, in the hall.

Herman locked the door and wandered aimlessly around the room. Staring across the vast garden of the park, the lights of the East Side and West Side seemed sparse and remote.

"This is the hardest thing I've done since opening in *Fountainhead* at the Majestic," he said out loud. He breathed in deeply and fell into a chair. "Ah well," he sighed. "That just wasn't meant to be a musical."

CHAPTER FIFTEEN

MARY JANE had lost Bobby in the crowd in front of her house the night her father died. People had been all over her, making it hard to move as they tried to help her inside.

A Christmas wreath had been placed on the door in the middle of October. Aunt Lottie had brought it from the back of the storage room. Christmas Day was Robert Shady's birthday and Lottie wanted something special hanging on the outside door for her only brother's death.

Irene Shady just about went crazy when Lottie serviced and buried Robert Shady herself. Lottie flatly refused to let anyone else touch him. Lots of people thought it was admirable and lots of people thought it was strange, and Irene thought it was just like Lottie: insane. Just like her to insist on being the last one to handle Robert Shady. When Irene started to scream, everyone, including Lottie, told Mary Jane that it was clear Irene was simply out of her head with grief.

Dr. Smith came with a big hypodermic needle and put Irene right to bed. Then he prescribed special hot toddies four times a day. Mary Jane helped Aunt Lottie crush the Demerol and mix it into the bourbon and tea and honey and milk. Irene Shady did not get up for three days. In fact, Dr. Smith's concoction was why Irene was "resting" and not available to greet the minister from the Assembly of God who had come as a courtesy on behalf of the Henderson family, as they were members of his congregation. He was accompanied by his wife, Myrtle. She stood a respectable two feet behind him, silent and motionless.

"I'm prayin' for your souls," Brother Cleever Hickey solemnly promised Lottie and Mary Jane. "It's too late for your loved one here, bein' as how he never give hisself over to Jesus Christ Our Lord and Saviour through entering salvation by way of the doors of the Assembly of God, the only entrance to Heaven, but you two can get in—"

WHACK.

Irene Shady had appeared out of nowhere and punched the living daylights out of Brother Hickey of the Uncertain Assembly of God, who fell to the floor with two black eyes, a broken nose and a slight concussion.

Mary Jane had been mortified that Mrs. Henderson wouldn't let Bobby see her anymore and Brother Hickey's wife had gone wild with laughter and had to be tranquilized with some of Irene Shady's hot toddy medicine.

Lottie had called the hospital to come get both Hickeys, and then had gone right in her office and made up a sign for the front door that read:

NO HOLY ROLLERS ALLOWED

She quickly changed her mind when she realized what this might do to business; there was an awful big membership in that church. So instead, she put up a sign that read:

PLEASE DON'T SPECULATE ABOUT THE LIFE HEREAFTER INSIDE HERE. FOR FURTHER INFORMATION REGARDING ETERNITY OR WHATEVER, WE RECOMMEND THE FORTUNE LADY CATTY-CORNER ACROSS THE HIGHWAY BY THE PONIES.

Lottie then arranged to get ten cents to every fifty cents that the fortune teller had made off of customers lured over there by the funeral home's sign. Besides, she figured anyone attempting to cross

Highway 158 to find out about "eternity" had a good fifty percent chance of ending up in the Uncertain Chapel of Memories as a permanent customer.

Mary Jane Shady had taken her mother back up to bed.

She half-carried her up the stairs to the top landing. By then Irene was on her hands and knees, crawling toward her bedroom.

Mary Jane was so scared she couldn't think.

"Oh, honey," her mother wept. She grabbed her daughter by the ankles. "Oh, honey, honey, honey..." Mary Jane felt her mother's tears. She felt her mother's grief and it terrified her.

"Mama," she said steadily. "Can I shave my legs?"

She was fifteen years old and a senior in high school and still her daddy had forbidden her to shave her legs. She'd gotten rid of her virginity before she had gotten rid of the hair on her legs. It was a wonder she was still a virgin. Well, he wasn't around to ask anymore, so she'd be told "NO." He wasn't around to be sick all the time so she'd be told to BE QUIET, BE GOOD, BE SMART, BE PERFECT OR YOU'LL UPSET YOUR DADDY AND THAT WOULD JUST KILL HIM...

He'd died all by himself without a bit of help from her.

But she didn't know that.

Irene Shady had fainted, and Mary Jane Shady had shaved her legs and headed right back to the oil pump with Bobby Henderson as fast as she could.

Lit by the stars, she rode him, laughing at the moon...

"Okay, that does it," Mary Jane Shady said, turning away from Herman Top's door. "You've got to stop your mind."

Trembling, she straightened her slip and buttoned her overcoat, concealing her missing skirt.

"There's only one thing I don't have that I need right now. A drink."

A small dry crack of a laugh broke in her throat like splintering glass.

"And a whole new identity..."

CHAPTER SIXTEEN

IRENE SHADY was having a terrible time at her funeral parlor. No sooner had she headed for the switch to start the embalming process on her latest client, Lucie Garden, when the phone started ringing. It seemed to Irene that everyone in Uncertain, Texas wanted to know when her daughter was coming home.

"I don't know!" Irene said to Lucie Garden, as she impatiently tried to wipe Baby Flowers' make-up job off the corpse's face. "I don't know, and we'll never find out, neither, 'cause she's never goin' to have a chance to get through if people don't stop callin'."

Irene felt herself becoming more and more annoyed as she attended to the body. "How could Lottie go and leave me to do everything?" she screamed, as the phone rang one more time. "She's not here!" Irene hollered, attempting to reach over Lucie and grab the phone.

In her haste and frustration, she stepped through the tubes connected to Lucie, entangling the embalming cord with the telephone cord, which wrapped itself clumsily around Lucie Garden's half-stitched leg. As Irene moved around the gurney toward the telephone to lessen the slack, Lucie's detached member inched farther and farther away from the rest of Lucie's body, slowing disengaging itself from Irene's hasty sewing. When Irene finally reached the telephone, Lucie's leg was dangling dangerously over the side of the gurney.

"Uncertain Chapel of Memories. Irene Shady on the line!" Irene cried, fighting the hugging cords.

Mary Jane heard a loud crash at the other end. "Mama?" she said. "Are you okay?"

"Yes, I am," Irene grumbled. "The body I'm workin' on just hit the floor." She stared at Lucie's fallen leg in despair.

"Is *it* okay?"

"What difference does it make, M.J.? It's dead," Irene snapped.

This is not a good time to tell her, Mary Jane Shady thought.

"It is not a good day," Irene went on with a sigh. "They brought ole Lucie Garden in here this mornin' and guess who wouldn't touch her? That's right. Your Aunt Lottie. Said as far as *she* was concerned that ole Mrs. Lucie Garden could just get sent right on over to Miss Deal Grimes' One Call Does All Permanent Rest Center, and off Miss Lottie Shady went on a recreational spree with some wild-haired truck driver who smashed our sign and didn't even have the good grace to die! Left *me* here with Lucie's body and she *knows* I don't like to drain 'em. I don't mind the rest of it, the makeup and all, just the first part. It's complicated. You have to be *real* careful, sometimes they twitch and even after a hunnerd years of this I'm still not used to *that*. Lottie can do it all with her eyes closed, but no, no, no, she wouldn't touch Mrs. Lucie Garden who she still holds accountable for failin' her in the second grade. You wouldn't think that would be a sorespot for a seventy-five-year-old woman, would you, but apparently that aunt of yours has got a long memory. Did you know Lottie failed the second grade, Mary Jane?"

"No," Mary Jane said despondently. "I didn't know that." *I don't know anything*, she added to herself. *Except I'm not coming back to Uncertain . . .*

"Well, neither did I and I find it a little strange that nobody told me this bit of family history 'til today and here I've had my whole mornin' halfway ruined on account of it, and I am of the opinion that this is just another addition to a long list of inconsiderations your daddy's sister has pulled on me. I'd hold it against her except I don't think she knows what she's doin'."

Maybe I'm just like Aunt Lottie, Mary Jane thought somewhat hopefully. *Maybe this runs in the family . . .*

"Never go into business with friends or in-laws. It's bad business and leads to pure-dee heartache." Irene noticed to her chagrin that one of Lucie's eyelids had flown open. "What are *you* doin'?" She reached down and shut the lid and continued. "I wished you'd a-gotten a soap opera before you got home. You could replace 'Faren' on *Y&R*. They could put you in all those binds and messes and scrapes. You could pretend you lost your memory and didn't remember nothin' that happened in your former life as good as anybody. Hadn't that show gone down since her and Andy left? I may turn over to *Another World*—"

"Mama—"

"It don't matter to ever-body here, though. They're all actin' like Katharine Hepburn is about to descend—"

"Mama—"

"Where are you anyway? At the airport? Ready to leave New York?"

"No."

Irene let out a yell.

"Don't get so excited, Mama. I—I had to pack." *Why can't I just say I'm not coming*? Mary Jane asked herself. *Why can't I just say it*?

"Lucie Garden's good leg just flew right up in the air and nearly kicked me over!" Irene screamed into the phone. "I dearly hate it when these dead people just come alive and nearly drive you crazy!"

This is the first thing you've said that makes one bit of sense to me, Mary Jane thought.

"Get lots of rest on the plane so you'll look your best when you get here, hon," Irene advised. "I knew you'd miss ever single flight out today, but I guess you had to take a minute to pack, didn't you? I got you booked on the first flight out tomorrow. American Airlines. Seven A.M. You can make that if you go to bed early. I'll be there to meet you at the Midland-Odessa Airport if I can find my way out of here. Lottie has got all the Christmas decorations stacked back in the casket storeroom. Six big bells four feet high and wide as Kay Widders. I've never seen so many fat women in one little town in my life. Why do you think that is? A lot of them are young, too. Beats me." She grabbed a breath. "Well, bye bye and have a good trip," she said. "And don't forget your Peanut Butter Cup dress."

She hung up.

Mary Jane Shady stood staring at the pay phone in the bar of the Hampshire House Hotel.

"I'm not coming," she announced out loud into the dead phone. "I'M NOT GOING ANYWHERE."

CHAPTER SEVENTEEN

IRENE HUNG UP THE PHONE, called New York, repeated her daughter's flight schedule to Pierre, Arabella du Noir's secretary for good measure, and turned back to her task in dismay.

She was genuinely annoyed with her sister-in-law. Lottie was getting more and more strange by the minute, and she had never been like anyone Irene had ever known before to start with. It occurred to Irene that if Lottie had not confided in her about failing the second grade, what else had she held back or left out? And more importantly, who knew who else Lottie was going to refuse to work on and for what reason? Sixty-nine years was a long time to hold a grudge.

She gave an impatient sigh. Apparently, Baby Flowers had gone through her sewing box, for three new spools of thread had been unwound all the way and cut into tiny pieces which now lay in a heap at the top of the box.

"This could be one big mess," Irene mumbled as she picked the threads out of the box. "I hope she didn't run off with my needles. I don't know how I'm goin' to sew that leg back on without any thread or any needles. I don't know how I'm goin' to have time to even think about it and get to the beauty shop and Gladys Turner's sister's funeral, neither."

Irene's eyes narrowed as she thought of Gladys Turner. Gladys was supposed to be her best friend, but it hadn't surprised Irene Shady one bit when Gladys had taken Evelyn's body over to Deal Grimes instead.

Irene was glad she'd lost the job anyway. She didn't want to do Gladys' sister or any of her relatives because she knew that Gladys would be hovering all over her, telling her what to do and how to do it. Gladys Turner considered herself an authority on every little thing. Irene Shady could not recall ever having met one fifth grade school teacher who did not have this quality, and Gladys Turner was no different. In Irene's opinion, Gladys Turner thought she knew too much, and there was hardly a thing the two of them agreed on.

Gladys claimed it was her *sister's* desire to be sent to the Permanent Rest Center, that Deal and Evelyn had been the best of friends. Furthermore, Gladys promised Irene that whenever she herself died or any member of her *immediate* family, Irene could undertake all of them, but this time Gladys just could not give Irene the business, being obligated as she was by Evelyn's dying wishes.

Irene knew this was a lie, but she expected it. Almost everyone she knew in Uncertain bent the truth here and there to suit their own purposes. It was a pastime, like Canasta, bingo or dominoes. Gladys Turner just happened to be a real poor player.

A totally vindictive idea materialized in Mary Jane's mother's head. Suddenly she knew how she could get the best of Gladys Turner and Lottie Shady, both at the same time.

She picked up the phone and dialed the Uncertain Chapel of Memories' only competitor, Miss Deal Grimes at Deal's One Call Does All Permanent Rest Center.

"Deal, it's Irene on the line. I'm kind of in a emergency here," she explained, carefully stretching the truth. "Now I know you got Gladys Turner's sister's funeral in a little while. I'm goin', but I won't be able to stay for the whole thing because of what just come up. I guess you heard Mary Jane's comin' home for the first time in twenty years. Lottie's become unexpectedly unavailable—got somethin' wrong with her head. I got to go get beautified, make that funeral and then head right for the Midland-Odessa Airport, and that's why I want to know if you can work Lucie Garden in and finish her up for me? I got her drained and formaldehyded and ready to go. I'll leave the back door open, so you can just come on in and get her. Don't forget the crash bag. Her left leg'll be in it. Just watch your step when you pass through the casket boxes. We're rearrangin' and redecoratin' here and you'll break your neck on a Christmas bell if you're not careful and I'll have me a new customer. You!" Irene laughed heartily and hung up. Then she immediately redialed Deal's number. "We got a Mr. Butler up front in the slumber room. Take him, too!"

Irene slammed down the phone triumphantly and let out a wild chortle. She was delighted with herself. Her sister-in-law was going to be furious. She knew Lottie never dreamed she would really give Deal any bodies.

"Lottie just hates the competition," Irene said, dumping Lucie Garden's leg in the plastic bag. "Look at how she handled the second grade!"

She laughed gleefully as she climbed the stairs, imagining the look on Lottie's face when she discovered the bodies were missing. No one was going to be there to tell Lottie where they were either.

"I'm gettin' me a room at the Nite Flight Motel next to that airport," Irene said, as she opened her closet and took out her overnight bag. "I'm gettin' me a good night's sleep so I can be the first one at the airport the first thing in the mornin'. I don't want to be late when Mary Jane walks down the ramp. What if I had a flat in the mornin' on the way over? This way if I have a flat, I'll have plenty of time to get it fixed. I cain't afford to turn up late. She don't come home that often."

She packed her toothbrush, a set of pink nylon pajamas, a matching pink nylon robe and a pair of pink slippers into the suitcase.

She carefully selected a gray cotton-knit three-piece suit, a string of pearls, matching earrings and a small white pillbox hat to wear to the airport.

"It's too hot for gloves," she said, unfolding a pair from a plastic sandwich bag, "but I'll carry 'em anyway."

She put on her ensemble, picked up her overnight case, and stopped to give herself a final once-over in the full length mirror at the top of the stairs.

"This looks okay for the funeral, too," she said.

She decided not to even leave a note telling Lottie she was spending the night sixty miles away. Let her sister-in-law wonder where she was and what she was doing. Let her wonder what had happened to those bodies. Let her wonder, wonder, wonder what was going on.

And as for Gladys Turner, it would serve her right that Irene had to leave in the middle of her sister's service. She was lucky Irene was coming at all!

Irene took a compact out of her purse and ran the powder puff over her nose. Looking at her face in the mirror, Irene suddenly grinned.

Mary Jane Shady was on her way home and that precious child only had one mother in this whole world and that was her.

Irene tossed the compact in her purse, picked up the funeral parlor keys, walked down the stairs and locked the door.

"Okay, Turkey Neck," she said. "Let's go paint the town red."

CHAPTER EIGHTEEN

MARY JANE took a pink-colored cigarette from the silver Tiffany case Herman had given her last spring, an engraved memento to mark their first anniversary. Inside, cut in clear straight letters, were the words: *OUVRE TON COEUR*

She snapped the case shut.

Silently, she lit the cigarette, the first of many, and watched the amber bubbles dive into the stem of the champagne glass, resurfacing to the top in effervescent invitation.

The glass almost seemed to smile.

Louis Roederer Cristal, 1979. Only in a fine walnut-paneled, leather-encased New York bar. No imports in Uncertain.

She dragged luxuriously on her slender Nat Sherman pastel Jubilee Light, sensing the bar without looking around. Low murmuring voices, smiling strangers, friends for the half-hour, rubbing silk and cashmere, exchanging capsulized versions of today's *Wall Street Journal, Variety, New York Times*.

Long past were the days of non-filtered Camels, Thunderbird wine, Coors beer and Bobby Henderson's old convertible Ford. Long past love-making out on the oil roads, car lights flashing in three close sets, signaling other parkers to seek another well pump to homestead for the evening. Long past the urgency, the need to get there, turn off the engine, throw back the top, let the pump set the rhythm while the stars fell in . . .

She put out her cigarette and lit another. She finished the bottle of wine and asked for another. She watched Herman pass through the lobby with his luggage, ready to leave for Chicago. He didn't see her in the bar and she did not seek his attention.

Silently, she waved after him. Her hand gave a small, mothlike flutter and lit on the silver cigarette case.

"I'd open it," she murmured, looking at the inscription. "If I had it . . . "

CHAPTER NINETEEN

"GET ON TOP," Bobby Henderson had said the night of the day Mary Jane Shady had shaved her legs, right after her daddy died.

"Huh?" She'd been lying contentedly in the backseat of Bobby Henderson's Ford convertible, facing the heavens, her ceiling the Milky Way.

"C'mon, M.J.," Bobby said. "Git up here."

Eagerly, she slid out from under him, as he rolled over. Gladly, she climbed on top. Whatever would make Bobby happy is what she wanted to do . . .

"C'mon, Topsy," Bobby breathed, as he balanced her, gripping her ankles with his quarterback hands.

TOPSY. Mary Jane smiled. *WHAT A CUTE LITTLE NAME*.

"Now, ride me," Bobby told her. "Go on."

Slowly, she began to move, rocking back and forth.

"Git me." Bobby Henderson moaned. "Ride me 'til you git me, Topsy . . ."

TOPSY. She liked that little name a lot. She liked it when Bobby talked low like that to her in sort of a growl and kind of a whisper.

"Faster," Bobby said.

She moved faster, her newly hairless legs gleaming in the moonlight.

"Slower." She slowed down.

Guided by the pump, she rode him, lit by the stars.

Thrusting herself against him, bearing back, she sat on top, moving up, then down, as gradually that funny feeling inside her started again, up and down her entire insides.

"Oh, Bobby," she moaned. "Oh, Bobby... it's that ferris wheel feelin' comin' all over me . . . ."

"Oh, yeah-h-h . . . ." Bobby Henderson grinned, moonlight dancing on his soft draped lid. "I'm just a one-man amusement park . . . "

She forgot her daddy lying dead in the living room. She forgot her mother in bed upstairs. She forgot Aunt Lottie, hitting preachers, making up highway signs, hanging up Christmas wreaths in October, sorting out dump cakes, ice box cakes, date cakes, fruit cakes. She forgot the sympathetic visitors who brought them.

She forgot herself.

She went to Bobby and her oil pump and all the stars she knew. That's where she stayed and would have stayed forever.

But then, something else unexpected happened, something she just never would have anticipated: shortly after her daddy was buried, Bobby Henderson started acting like someone she hardly even knew.

They'd pulled up beside the pump. She'd jumped out of the car and thrown the top down on the Ford. Then she'd jumped back in, pulled all her clothes off and thrown them in a pile. She threw her arms around Bobby and climbed right on top.

A funny look came over his face. Then he abruptly sat up. Then he started reaching for his clothes. Then he said, "Let's go."

She backed off momentarily. Why was he wanting to go?

"Just lemme git on top for a minute, Bobby," Mary Jane said. She knew he liked *that*. He'd call her 'Topsy', she'd start to ride him, she'd get him in the mood.

"Huh?" Bobby mumbled, buttoning his shirt.

"Lemme git up there," Mary Jane repeated. "You look at the stars. Let Topsy ride you."

"Ride me?" Bobby Henderson pulled back. "I'm not a horse," he stated flatly. "Let's go."

She ignored the panic she inwardly felt.

"Yes, you are," she giggled, nervously pressing on, kissing his face. *What in the world was the matter with him*? "You're my Bobby Horse," she told him, licking his ear.

"Quit. That tickles," he said.

Still, she didn't stop. And Bobby Henderson was not smiling as Mary Jane Shady heedlessly climbed on top.

"It's almost 10:30," Bobby said, as Mary Jane ran her hands all over him.

Did I lose my touch? Where did it go? She rubbed harder, licked faster, pushed deeper.

"We been out here forever," he said.

"No, no, it's not even nine," Mary Jane corrected. "We just got here."

"Nine!" Bobby bolted straight up. "I gotta go! I got football practice, don't forget. I got homework."

"You got me," she breathed. She was on top of him now, looking down at him, one hand fondling him, balancing with the other arm. "Just wait a minute . . ."

Forlornly, he slumped back on the seat and closed his eyes.

Slowly, she moved against him, waiting for him to get ready again. "Call me 'Topsy'," she said. "Say it . . ."

"Ow!" Bobby muttered, reaching for his withered cock. "C'mon. Git off."

"Just five more minutes," she pleaded. "*Please.*"

"You are remindin' me of football practice," Bobby said quietly. He was buttoning his shirt. He gave her a little shove and reached for his Levis. "Aw, shit. You wrinkled my pants."

Mary Jane was flabbergasted. She stared at him incredulously. She could hardly even speak.

"Football practice?" Mary Jane stammered. That sounded bad. "What do you mean?"

His eyes softened momentarily. "I don't know, M.J.," he said. "I'm just not feelin' too good."

Relief! *He's sick, getting a cold, not feeling well, that's all . . .*

"Well, why didn't you say so?" she asked sympathetically. Quickly she moved off of him and showered him with hugs. "You just relax." She jumped out of the car and jerked up the top. "Too much fresh air!" she gushed.

She heard the car start. Was he about to pull away? Without her? She jumped in, grabbed her clothes and was still trying to find her bra as they drove off.

"I was really worried there for a minute," she said, determined to sound light and carefree. *Okay, now laugh, ha-ha-ha. Make a joke, ha-ha-ha . . .*

She heard herself laugh. "I thought you were about to leave me!" That was the joke! She heard herself laughing harder.

He didn't answer. She stopped laughing. They drove silently down the oil road, then through town. She felt her throat start to close, but made herself speak anyway. "I thought for a minute something else was wrong—"

Still, he didn't speak.

"Bobby?" Melogo Drive was whizzing by. She wasn't paying attention. She missed it.

Before she could gather her feelings into a sentence, they were sitting in front of the Chapel of Memories.

"Here you are." Bobby Henderson smiled, suddenly looking to her just exactly like the healthiest person alive. "You're home, Topsy."

Mary Jane Shady told her mouth to turn right up into a nice bright smile. "Well, thanks!"

"Sorry I'm sick," he grinned sheepishly.

"Oh, that's okay!" she sang in a cheerful, happy tone. And bouncing out of his car, she turned to wave. But Bobby Henderson was already pulling away. And that was just the beginning . . .

CHAPTER TWENTY

"HOME AGIN, home agin, jiggidy-jog," Lottie Shady sang out to Leo Diggs as she attempted to stick her key in the front door lock of the Uncertain Chapel of Memories. Her head was still buzzing from sniffing that yellow capsule. She'd also consumed half a beer between Frying Pan Handle Road and Highway 158. But it was Leo Diggs's first kiss that had made her truly dizzy.

"Home is where the heart is," Leo smiled. He just couldn't take his eyes off Lottie Shady. "Uh-oh," he said as Lottie dropped the keys. He watched her lean down to pick them up.

"Here, lemme do that," Leo offered. Gallantly, he bent over her and placed a sprawling palm across her slight, birdlike fingers.

"Oh-h-h," Lottie sighed. His frame practically covered her small figure. Even though she was on all fours, she wasn't sure she wanted to get up.

"Here go," Leo said. With astonishing ease, he pulled her toward him, with quick sure grace, he turned the lock with the key.

"Oh-h-h-h, my!" Lottie exclaimed admiringly. She focused on the lock as if it had never before been opened. She peeked in the door as if it held some secret kingdom. She looked at Leo for further direction, as if she had never entered this place every day of her life for the past forty years.

"After you," Leo said, swinging open the door.

Lottie smiled up at Leo and floated through the door. More and more he was reminding her of a sort of cross between Houdini and Valentino.

"Looks like there's nobody here but us chickens," Leo observed, nodding playfully at the five Mary Jane Shadys as they moved into the foyer.

"Did I ever tell you Mary Jane Shady was born in a casket?" Lottie asked, flipping on the foyer light.

"My ex-sister-in-law had her baby up in the air," Leo said. "Now she gets free air travel. Anywhere in the world. For the rest of her life."

"The mother or the daughter?" Lottie wanted to know.

"The daughter," Leo replied.

"That figgers," Lottie sighed. "Mothers don't get nothin' but kids." She shook her head sadly, taking the opportunity to appear sympathetic. "Pore ole Irene." She didn't want Leo to think she was hard-hearted. "She's off scramblin' around to get ready for Miss Somebody who hadn't even come back for a visit since the day she left. Pore ole Irene."

"I don't have no family," Leo Diggs said. "But if I did, I sure wouldn't be drivin' all over tarnation in a truck."

"You don't have *nobody nowhere* at all?" Lottie asked, trying not to sound all that happy about it.

"Just me," Leo answered, as Lottie made every effort not to smile. "This sure is a *interestin'* house," he commented, passing on through the foyer and into the office.

Lottie wanted to tell him it would be a lot more 'interesting' with a man like him around. But she was afraid to say anything that might sound too forward.

"We hadn't had a man around full-time since Brother's fatal attack," Lottie explained. "Mary Jane was never the same after that."

Leo looked sympathetically at the wall full of horror movie posters.

"She flat-out disappeared the day after her high school graduation. Left home and never come back. You'd think somethin' horrible had happened to her."

Somethin' horrible did happen to her, Leo Diggs thought, as he stared in wonder at a poster of a girl being thrown into a giant oven. *DON'T LOOK IN THE INCINERATOR* was written in bold red letters across the picture.

"Maybe her daddy dyin' is what did it," Leo offered. "I know I was never the same after my daddy went."

Lottie seized the moment to take his arm in her arms. "When did he go, Leo?" she asked. "When did he go?"

"I don't know," Leo said. "I was so little I never even got to remember him."

"Oh, good Lord!" Lottie Shady was afraid she might be about to cry. She decided the best thing to do was keep talking and turning on lights. "I think it had somethin' to do with that Henderson boy," she told Leo, as she moved around the parlor, pulling cords and flipping switches. "The one Why-vonne ended up married to." She headed toward the saloon. "What a couple!" She clicked on more lights.

"Who are they?" Leo asked eagerly. He didn't have a clue who she was talking about and he didn't care. He just wanted to hear Lottie Shady talk. "I'll fix us a drink and you tell me the story."

"Fix us a big tall one," Lottie told him, going to the pantry. "This story is goin' to take some time." The pantry door swung shut behind her. Lottie raised her voice and shouted out. "See, for starters, Why-vonne's *mother* was buried in the same coffin Mary Jane was *born* in."

"Well, there's more than one use for ever-thang," Leo observed, grabbing two glasses.

But no sooner had he found the Wild Turkey and filled the glasses than Lottie Shady started to scream.

"What is it!" Leo hollered, as she rushed out of the pantry.

"She's gone!" Lottie screamed. "Gone! Gone! Gone!"

"Don't git so upset," Leo cooed, taking her his arms. "Ever-body dies sometime. Life is for the livin.' Let's you and me live it now."

"Oh! Oh! Oh!" Lottie screamed wildly, and darting around him, she flew through the parlor and into the slumber room. "Great stars and little garters! He's been stolen away!"

"He was your only brother," Leo offered sympathetically. "And Mary Jane's only daddy. I know I could never take his place . . ."

"Oh, yes, you could!" Lottie Shady cried out. "But that's not what I'm talkin' about. I'm talkin' about a Mr. Butler and a Mrs. Lucie Garden! 'Member them?"

"Mr. Butler? Lucie Garden?" Leo repeated. "I'm searchin' my memory, now. It's the one thang I cain't count on."

"The bodies!" Lottie cried.

"The bodies?"

"The *corpses*!" Lottie hollered. "My *corpses* are missin'!"

"Oh. *Them*."

Leo just stood there and smiled. Lottie Shady had told him he could take her brother's place. And he wasn't about to let her forget it.

CHAPTER TWENTY-ONE

" 'Git topsy' is what Bobby Henderson said . . . 'Git Topsy' . . . " Mary Jane Shady told Eddie, the bartender at the White Horse Tavern on Hudson at West 11th. She was drinking her way across Manhattan bar by bar. "Then he got her . . . then he didn't want her . . . didn't want her on top, that's for sure, that much is for sure . . ."

"You mentioned that," Eddie nodded politely. He refilled her tequila and replaced her beer. He eased away, turning his attention to a customer at the far end of the bar.

" . . . didn't want her at all, but he didn't say that . . ." Mary Jane told the bottle of beer sitting beside the Cuervo in front of her " . . . nothing so clear as 'I'm bored,' 'you're boring' . . . no sir . . . didn't say he was ready for someone new . . . " She slowly navigated her hand toward the beer, picked it up and drank. Finishing the beer, she called out to Eddie, "You know he married *Why*-vonne Flowers . . . "

"I know," Eddie replied, as if he were well acquainted with these people. And after hearing about them for the past hour, he could have almost pictured them. But Eddie was a bartender. His job was to look like he was listening. As soon as she left, he would forget. Someone else would take her stool and her place and his attention. But for now, he knew Yvonne. He knew Bobby. He knew everyone she was talking about.

"Trash," Mary Jane said, knocking over the bottle of beer by mistake. "Pure white trash." She reached for the bottle. "He married it."

Eddie picked up the empty and wiped up the foam.

"See, he didn't say to Topsy, 'I lost interest.' Didn't say *that* . . . nothing as clear as *that* . . . he said . . . he said . . . what *did* he say? . . . see what he wanted was . . . I don't know . . . what he wanted . . . what did he *want*? . . . why didn't he just say *something* I could've understood? . . . 'cause, see, then I could've . . . but what happened was . . . oh, I don't know what happened, why can't I figure out what happened? . . . all I know is . . . nope . . . uh-uh . . . didn't get rid of her like that . . . no, no, he wasn't through . . . *he wasn't through* . . . he wanted to play . . . he still wanted to *play* . . . " Mary Jane looked around. "Where's my beer? Who took my beer?"

Eddie placed another beer in front of her. "Want to order a bite now?" he asked. "You could use something to eat."

"Not while I'm thinking," Mary Jane murmured. "I'll take a beer, though . . ."

"You got a beer, honey."

"Oh." She looked at the beer. "I need a Lone Star beer."

"That's what you got." It was a Bud, but she wouldn't know it.

"Oh." Mary Jane moved her hand slowly toward the beer. "I hate him."

Eddie looked at her sympathetically. He had heard it a million times. He nodded. "Yeah." He gave her hand an affectionate pat. "Order a cheeseburger. A plate of fries. Stop thinking."

But she didn't.

Mary Jane hadn't seen Bobby the day after he took her home early. He didn't come to school at all. She'd tried to call him on the phone, but his mother had answered. She'd said he wasn't able to come to the phone. He hadn't called her back either. But the next day, Bobby stopped Mary Jane in the hall between classes. He looked very serious and spoke in a whisper.

"Got bad news, honey," he said. "I been to the doctor and he says I cain't see you no more."

"Why, Bobby?" Mary Jane's eyes opened wide.

"Allergic."

"What?"

"Allergic. I'm allergic to you."

Mary Jane just stood there speechless.

"Sorry, babe. Doc's orders. Breakin' up is hard to do, but that's the prescription."

"We're breakin' up?" Mary Jane whispered.

"That's right, sugar. Meet me at lunch and we'll settle up."

He walked off without another word.

Mary Jane was mortified. What could she possibly have that would make Bobby *allergic* to her? Mary Jane suddenly felt sick with fear. She felt as if she were going to faint. *A social disease*. She had a social disease. Sudden visions of her body rotting away flashed into her mind. It caused blindness, too. She vividly remembered this from a movie they had seen in P.E. You could get it from other ways than just love-making. Toilet seats she knew about for sure. That hadn't been in the film, but Sue Higgley had a cousin in Quail, Texas, who had gotten the clap from a toilet seat at the drive-in there. She didn't go blind, though. Sue said the doctor had given her some shots and she got over it just in time.

Shots. Mary Jane would have to get shots. But where? She couldn't go to Dr. Smith who lived across the street. He would tell her mother and that would kill her mother. Irene Shady would never be able to live through the death of her husband and Mary Jane's social disease all in the same semester.

Thank goodness band was the only class left before lunch. Mary Jane told her instructor, Mr. Justice, that she was a little under the weather and sat alone on the bleachers as the Uncertain High School band marched through their formations on the football field.

It was almost time for Homecoming and for Uncertain High to elect the Homecoming Queen and her court. Mary Jane hoped she would at least be elected to the court, but she had never really been a favorite among her peers. Her mother hadn't seen any need for her daughter to attend the first grade since she herself had already taught Mary Jane to read the funny papers, count to a hundred and write her name. After three days, Mary Jane had been promoted to the second grade. Later, Irene insisted she be allowed to skip the fifth grade. Irene explained to Mary Jane that Gladys Turner, the fifth grade teacher, didn't know one thing more than Irene knew, and in fact, knew a lot less. Mary Jane's grades continued to soar, although her popularity had been permanently diminished. But this year, she had sympathy on her side since her daddy had just died, plus Bobby's enormous popularity with the student body.

She imagined herself in a beautiful new evening dress special ordered from Neiman-Marcus in Dallas. She would be riding in the backseat of a convertible loaned to the school from McGarity's Chevrolet. The convertibles filled with the three nominees dressed in their new Neiman-Marcus ordered gowns would circle the football field with all the girls waving to the excited crowd.

All three girls would be escorted from their cars by their chosen escorts from the A football team of Uncertain High, dressed in their football uniforms.

As the name of each girl was announced, her football hero would present her with a bouquet of flowers. The third and final girl to be announced was the Homecoming Queen.

Mary Jane was overcome with joy to find the last bouquet was hers! As Bobby Henderson placed a dozen red roses in her arms and the Principal of Uncertain High placed a crown of papier-mâché and rhinestones on her head, she heard the voice of the Principal magnified over the entire football field.

"Ladies and Gentlemen of Uncertain, Texas. This year's Homecoming Queen is Miss Mary Jane Shady. She has distinguished herself in many ways, but never more so than now. Friends, Miss Mary Jane Shady is the only Homecoming Queen Uncertain, Texas, has ever had who has a SOCIAL DISEASE. I'm sure you will all agree that this is not a fitting characteristic for anybody's Homecoming Queen, so, Miss Mary Jane Shady, instead of the usual kiss, I, the Principal of Uncertain High, usually bestow upon the Homecoming Queen, I will not even shake your hand. Instead, Dr. Smith is going to give you a shot."

Dr. Smith appeared before Mary Jane with his black bag. Opening it quietly and efficiently, he took out his equipment—a double barreled shotgun—and pointed it between Mary Jane Shady's eyes.

BANG!

Mary Jane Shady fainted right in the middle of the bleachers. When she came to, Mr. Justice, the band director, was standing over her. He immediately wanted to send her home and call her mother.

"It's okay, Mr. Justice," Mary Jane mumbled, struggling to her feet and grateful beyond belief not to have received any of Dr. Smith's shots. "I really don't need a doctor. I think I'll be okay if I have some lunch."

Mary Jane was desperate to meet Bobby Henderson and get more information.

Bobby Henderson did not prove to be very informative.

"That's all he said, Mary Jane," Bobby told her as they sat in his car parked across the street from the school. "Said I was, *repeat*, allergic to you and for health reasons I cain't see you no more. So gimme back my ring and my jacket and a little kiss for ole times sake."

"Have they done all the tests?" Mary Jane asked.

"All but one," Bobby said.

Tears started to fall down Mary Jane's cheeks. He didn't even know the worst yet. He didn't even know she had given him a social disease.

Mary Jane began to sob uncontrollably as she tried to unwrap the tape from Bobby's senior high school ring.

"I don't have your jacket on me," she stammered through hot tears and a runny nose. Bubbles foamed from her mouth everytime she tried to speak. Her body wracked with spasms and the ring fell from her hands.

"Here, lemme do that," Bobby offered. After a couple of clumsy tries, he looked at Mary Jane hopelessly. "Aw, what the hell. Give it to me tomorrow, M.J. And try to get yourself together. Don't you have a history test this afternoon?"

The bell rang for the afternoon classes to begin. Bobby hopped out of the car.

"You can give me my jacket later, too," he called, leaving Mary Jane sitting in the car staring numbly at his ring covered with half a wad of rumpled tape.

Her shaky fingers slowly wound the tape back around the ring. It no longer fit nice and tight and neat. In fact, she couldn't even get it back on her index finger, so she put it on her pinkie and walked home.

Mr. Justice would confirm that she had fainted at band practice.

And Bobby. They had been in love until today or yesterday or whenever he got that allergy or whenever she got the social disease.

Mary Jane Shady went home to the Uncertain Chapel of Memories and went straight to bed.

"If I'm lucky," she thought, "I'll just die in my sleep."

CHAPTER TWENTY-TWO

MARY JANE SHADY'S head was lying in a puddle of tears. Someone was shaking her.

"C'mon, honey, you gotta get up."

Two Eddie the Bartenders stood in front of her, their images intermingling. They wiped her face with a soft warm rag.

"My tears," she mumbled. "You're taking away my tears . . ."

"You spilled your beer," the two Eddies said.

She put her head back down on the bar.

"No, no," said the Eddies. "It's time to go home."

She looked at the double image hopefully. "Oh, yes," she nodded. "If I'm lucky, I'll just die in my sleep . ."

"You're not gonna die," the Eddies assured her. "But you may not feel so hot tomorrow."

"I'm going to die," she promised. "I want to . . ."

Eddie looked at her sharply. He did not like this kind of talk at all.

"Do you know how many times he took back that ring and that jacket?" she asked, suddenly indignant.

Eddie shook his head. He didn't ask, "What ring?" "What jacket?" He wanted her to leave.

"Hundreds. All the rest of the year. Back and forth, forth and back. It was too big—it had tape around it—the ring, not the jacket—the jacket was too big, too—" She stopped talking for a moment to reflect on this.

Thinking that she was lost in a daze, the bartender started to move away. She pulled him back.

"I didn't ever have a social disease . . . ." she whispered. "It was a lie . . . he wasn't allergic to me . . . see what I mean? . . . ."

Then she grew silent again. Her eyes once more became cloudy. If she squinted, she could almost merge him into one image. "Wouldn't you?"

"Wouldn't I what?"

"Wouldn't you just die in your sleep?"

"I'd go home first," Eddie sighed.

"It's too late," she told him. "I'm fired. Did I tell you they fired me?"

"You lost your job?" he asked. This was serious. An old boyfriend was one thing. Losing a job was another. And she wasn't taking it well at all. What if she did try to kill herself? Dylan Thomas had consumed thirty-seven brandies at the table by the window in the next room and dropped dead on the steps outside. He knew it could happen. Some depressed manic or another was always coming here to drink themselves to death. "Do you have a shrink?" he asked. "Call your shrink, first thing, right now. Go home. Get on the phone. Call for help." God, he hated the '80s. Before, in the '60s, you just served them, listened to them ramble, and let them stumble on home. If they were held up, robbed, slit their wrists or jumped out a window, it was their problem. Even when Dylan Thomas died, no one had blamed the bartender. He shook his head. Not today, not in the '80s. Today, the law said *he* could be held responsible. Today, he took away their booze, ordered them a cab and told them to call their shrinks. "I'll order you a cab," he said.

"I wanted a house . . . a house with no carnations . . . "

"Who's your shrink? What's his number?" They all had shrinks. It was disgusting. They made him want to quit his job, but what would he do? Drive a cab? Then he'd have to drive them home. The shrinks were the only ones who came out on top. They got paid for listening to this drivel.

"I'm too stupid to live," she mumbled. "I'm gonna end up playing eraser heads and tomatoes . . . I'm too old to be a pencil . . . not thin enough . . . got a new line under my left eye . . . see? . . ." She tried to raise her head.

"What do you do?" he asked, wondering what was the difference between a shrink and a bartender. Ask questions. Listen. Ask questions. Listen. A shrink got paid more. A lot more. And he didn't have to fix any drinks or clean up any messes. A shrink didn't even have to call a goddamned cab. And if a patient committed suicide after a visit, the surviving family had to pay the fucking bill!

"I was Miss Peanut Butter Cup." She'd managed to raise her head up and was looking at him apologetically.

"Oh. Yeah. Right." He looked at her. Her raincoat was half buttoned, revealing a slip. Her hair was a mess, frizzy and tangled. One lone pink roller trailed down the back. "How old do I look to you?" she asked. "See this line?" She pointed under her left eye.

Looking closer, he began to recognize the delicate features, the flawless skin, the perfect blue eyes. She looked to him like a broken china doll.

"Listen," he said with new determination. "I'm putting you in a cab." He felt sorry for her. He couldn't help it. "You're going home. Now." That's why he was a bartender. He had too much fucking sympathy!

Mary Jane heard a voice, but it was not Eddie's. She heard Herman. "*Go home, Mary Jane Shady,*" Herman's voice said. "*You've got to find out . . . whatever it is you're trying to forget . . .* "

CHAPTER TWENTY-THREE

LEO DIGGS walked over to Lottie Shady and stood before her. But he was so tall and she was so small, he decided to sit down.

"Lottie," he said. "Forget them corpses. They're dead and gone and wherever they are is fine with them. Let's don't let death ruin our good time."

This was a whole new way of thinking for Lottie. She was not accustomed to having a lackadaisical attitude when it came to her business. "I've had a lot of strange things happen here at the Uncertain Chapel of Memories," she replied. "But I never had no dead bodies walk out on me."

Leo gently pushed her hair away from her face. "Let's devote ourselves to *our* bodies," he said. "Them's the only bodies let's concern ourselves with tonight."

This appealed to Lottie so much her knees started to shake. "Wonder if Irene had somethin' to do with this?" she wondered. "Wonder if this is some kind of underhanded trick she's playin' to get back at me for goin' off with you and takin' our ride? Wonder if she stooped so low and slunk so far that she up and give them bodies over to Deal Grimes at the One Call Does All? Wonder if she went that crazy?"

"While you're wonderin', I'll get our drinks," Leo said. He moved into the saloon where he added another ice cube and an extra jigger to the bourbon he had already poured.

"She's went crazy before," Lottie told him, as she got up and followed him. "She danged near permanently damaged Brother Cleever Hickey of the Uncertain Church of Christ onct. Flat-out busted him up!"

"How come?" Leo asked, handing her the drink.

"Aw, he assured us all we was goin' to hell. But he's a preacher, you know. That's his business. He didn't mean nothin' personal."

Leo nodded. "Seems like somebody is always tellin' me I'm goin' to hell," he said. "But then, I always 'spected to."

Lottie let out a little groan. She couldn't bear to think of Leo so far away. "Oh-h-h-h," she moaned. "That makes my head throb."

"Drink this," Leo said, handing her the drink. "And chew up one of these." He pulled his sack from his pocket and selected a big white pill.

"What is it?" Lottie asked. "What's it for?"

"Throbbin'-head medicine," Leo told her. "It's for when thangs make your head throb."

He bit the pill in two, swallowed half, and handed her the other.

"Okay," Lottie said, washing the pill down with the bourbon. "Thanks." She had never met a man so prepared to deal with headaches.

She felt herself relax some; the tension just seemed to pour out. And now that she thought of it, she didn't really care where those bodies were. If Irene had done something with them to get back at her, it certainly wasn't working, because more and more she was caring less and less.

Lottie Shady looked up at Leo Diggs and smiled.

"Feelin' better?" Leo asked.

"I sure am," Lottie nodded. "To heck with them corpses. I'm just as glad to get rid of 'em anyhow."

"Didn't they ever give you the heebeejeebies?" Leo asked, taking a long steady drink. "I think they'd give me the heebeejeebies. I mean, don't you *know* most of 'em? Aren't they personal friends of yours?"

"Oh, I know most of 'em," Lottie nodded. She looked at Leo. Something was telling her not to tell him it never bothered her one bit to drain every ounce of blood out of people she knew. She decided to skip explaining that after they stopped breathing and the light went from their eyes, they bore no resemblance to anyone she had known before anyway.

Leo Diggs was waiting to hear how awful and horrible her whole life had been before him and Lottie Shady knew it. Some inner instinct was directing her. She followed its call.

"I told you I grew up in a funeral parlor, didn't I?" she began, attempting to sound sad.

"You sure did," Leo said. He took her hand and held it.

"Oh-h-h." Lottie shook her head in despair. "All them strange corpses!" To her delight, Leo nodded sympathetically. "And even worse was them familiar..." She loved how he was stroking her hand. "One day, there they'd be, smilin', drivin', shoppin', frownin', gettin' sick, recoverin', goin' to school or church or work or someone else's funeral. Next day, here they'd be, laid out practically in the middle of this livin' room . . . "

"Dead," Leo Diggs sighed.

"That's right," Lottie nodded, trying out a little sob. "Dead . . . "

"Want another drink?" Leo asked. "Want another pill?"

"I sure do," Lottie moaned. "Grief..." she continued as he refilled their glasses. "I seen grief I never even wanted to know about. Weepin' and wailin' and heartbroken families . . . "

Leo poured the last of the bourbon from the bottle and divided it between their glasses. He bit another white pill in half.

"Laughter..." She took a slug of her drink and washed down the pill before he'd added the ice cubes. "Sometimes the dead ones would be all but forgotten, lost in a party of reunited relatives, just tickled pink to be still alive and kickin'. Reassured as they was by their own buzzin' voices and blood-pumped frames, they'd be just happy as clams to forget their loved one's last remains . . . "

Leo nodded understandingly.

"Surprises . . ." she continued. "Who could ever forget the day Le Grand Council come in from Hazelhurst, Mississippi, buried her mother and married her step-father two hours later?"

"I couldn't," Leo Diggs murmured. "I could never forget a thang like that."

"Bizarre . . ." Lottie went on. "The things people put inside the caskets to go to the grave with their loved one's last remains . . . "

"What?" Leo wanted to know. His hand was on her knee. He was moving his fingers over her kneecap in slow circular motions. "What kinds of thangs?"

Lottie Shady continued, hypnotically. "Underwear, hairpieces, Rudyard Kipling poetry... that case of Jax beer Wilmer Posey put under his daddy, Wilson Posey's feet... Summer Poole requested for her dead cat's bones to be dug up out of her backyard and placed in her silverware box and put under her head for a pillow . . . Autumn Poole, Summer's baby sister, took all the silverware to the grave with *her*. Ozella Wade took her collection of clay birds. Junior Boy Mackey took his shotgun and was buried with his boots on. Somebody put pictures of nekked little boys all tied up inside his boots . . . Lady Poole, niece of Summer and Autumn, was buried with her flute . . . "

Leo's hand was moving up and down Lottie's leg.

"Oree Brockley took her green stamps. One hunnerd and twenty-seven books."

Leo's other hand moved up and down Lottie's other leg.

Lottie felt herself quiver. "Secrets . . ." she said. "Angry explosions, wild accusations, mean rebuttals, desperate defense tactics, weepy admissions, hasty reunions . . . I know all the secrets . . . "

"I got a secret," Leo Diggs confided in a low whisper. "You want in on my secret?"

Lottie's eyes grew wide. She wasn't sure she was ready for Leo Diggs' secret.

"You got any secrets?" Leo asked softly. She could feel his warm breath up against her ear.

"Can you keep a promise?" Lottie whispered back. "You got to promise you won't never repeat what I'm about to say."

"I promise," Leo Diggs promised. "And you can count on that."

Lottie Shady took a deep breath, shut her eyes and said it. She said what she'd always been afraid to say. "I took Oree Brockley's green stamps," she confessed in a quick quiet whisper.

Leo Diggs' mouth turned into a big amused smile. He just loved how unpredictable she was. He had no idea that was what she was going to say.

"Now that's the only time in my life I ever took a thing out of a coffin, but I swear, I couldn't bear to see somethin' that had never met its full potential go and get buried in the ground that way."

"That's exactly how I feel," Leo assured her. "I feel exactly the same way."

"I didn't use 'em yet neither," Lottie confided. "They're up yonder in the safe, hidden under papers. I felt so bad about takin' 'em, I couldn't enjoy usin' 'em. Besides, I was afraid if I used them right after Oree went, somebody would find out."

"You could have used 'em book by book." Leo mused.

"I could have," Lottie agreed. "But I didn't."

"But you didn't," Leo whispered. "You was savin' it all for somethin' real, real special, wasn't you?"

"Yes, I was," Lottie whispered back, practically in a trance. Leo Diggs' face was moving closer and closer. "I was savin' the whole collection . . . "

"For me . . ." Leo said.
"For you . . ."

CHAPTER TWENTY-FOUR

MARY JANE SHADY touched the buzzer in the basement entry of her psychiatrist's Horatio Street brownstone, turned her back to it and waited nervously for some response. She buzzed again. Then she knocked. Then she pounded. Then she kicked.

When the door finally opened, Dr. Goldman wasn't standing in it. And when the door closed, it wasn't Mary Jane Shady who went in.

"Good evening, Topsy. I'm Dr. Blank," said Dr. Blank. "Come in."

Topsy looked at Dr. Blank, who looked like somebody's shadow.

"Sit. Sit."

Topsy sat. Somewhere a clock ticked loudly, like the metronome Daisy Baum, Mary Jane's old piano teacher back in Uncertain, had kept on top of her piano.

"Well? Well?"

The quietness of the room and the ticking were making Topsy perspire.

"I think I might have possibly done something real, real bad," Topsy began tentatively.

"That's pathetic," Dr. Blank replied. "Like what?"

"I think I might have dreamed I did something with uh—uh—"

"A big black German shepherd," stated Dr. Blank.

"I don't want to talk about *that*!" Topsy cried. "I want to ask you about Bobby Henderson! Can't we talk about him?"

Dr. Blank looked really disgusted. "Look," said the doctor. "I am not here to answer your questions, so don't try to change the subject. How was the dog?"

"What?" Topsy tried to think of what other questions she had asked Dr. Blank that Dr. Blank had answered.

"How was he? I assume it was a *he*?"

Topsy nodded.

Dr. Blank sighed. "Thank God. I don't see any more homosexuals until tomorrow morning. Homosexuals with dog fetishes are Friday afternoons only, so you can keep your appointment. Continue."

"Huh?"

"*Proceed*. How was the dog? Fair, good, excellent? On a scale of one to ten."

"Could you explain the grading system in more detail, please?" Topsy asked Dr. Blank.

"No." Dr. Blank glared at the patient.

"Then ask me a specific question," Topsy pleaded.

"Oh, all right!" Dr. Blank snapped. "Christ, why do I always have to do all the work! Did he lick you?"

Topsy gulped.

"Well, did he?"

"Yes."

"Oh, for God's sake! That dog *licked* you?"

"It was on my—"

"*Don't* say it!" Dr. Blank threatened. "I don't want any details!"

"Then how are you going to—"

"All right, that's it. If you ask me one more question we are just going to drop this dog matter for the rest of your life."

"That's fine with me," Topsy nodded.

"And I think you can do better than that," Dr. Blank said.

"I beg your pardon?"

"I think we have a little apology coming to us. Wouldn't you say so? You might as well learn a few manners while you're here."

"I apologize," Topsy offered.

"For what?" Dr. Blank asked.

"You asked for an apology and I apologized," Topsy said helplessly.

Dr. Blank nodded silently. "For what are you apologizing?"

"For asking questions—"

"And interrupting," Dr. Blank threatened.

"You sound like my mother," Topsy said.

"We are not here to talk about your mother," Dr. Blank said. "Unless you dreamt you slept with her."

Topsy's mouth fell open.

"We'll talk about her next week," Dr. Blank said. "Now you've insisted that we talk this dog thing through, so why don't you tell me how you feel about the dog. I know you're going to anyway."

"Guilty."

"Well, you certainly should," Dr. Blank acknowledged. "You should feel *very* guilty. The worse, the better. How could you have taken advantage of a poor animal?"

Topsy stared at Dr. Blank in disbelief. "Wait a minute. You don't know what happened."

"And I don't want to know."

"But, please, let me explain what happened—"

"It just doesn't matter," Dr. Blank said flatly.

"You mean no matter what happened to make me so distraught that I somehow ended up engaged in a dog entanglement, no matter what, you would still, always, give first consideration to the *dog*?"

"You're supposed to know what you're doing," Dr. Blank replied. "A dog just obeys."

"But what if I *didn't* know what I was doing?" Topsy cried.

"Then you should have thought about that," Dr. Blank responded. "Did you ask for help? Did you go to your mother? In any case, you should have first considered the position of the dog."

Topsy's head pounded in frustration. Then she heard the sound of her own voice. The words coming out of her mouth in slow, defiant sentences were formed and spinning forth all on their own.

"The first position was on my back and him on top," she heard herself say. "Then I turned over. I decided I'd see what kind of instincts these animals really have. I let him make his way down between my oh-so-heavenly thighs . . ." She could see the blood drain from Dr. Blank's face, and before Dr. Blank could speak, Topsy leaned forward and whispered conspiratorially, as she extemporized. "I moaned as he sniffed my pussy and began taking ravenous, hungry laps—"

"That's *sick*!" Dr. Blank snapped.

" 'Fuck me, you beast!' I cried as I turned over on my tummy, raising my ass a little so the humping German shepherd could get inside me—"

"Stop!" cried Dr. Blank.

" 'His enthusiasm makes up for his size,' I told myself," Topsy went on. " 'Bang it, Blackie, you dog, you animal, you beast!' "

"Pervert!" screamed Dr. Blank.

Topsy stopped. " 'Wait a minute,' I said," Topsy said. " 'Maybe that's the wrong approach,' I told myself. 'Wonder if he's into humiliation and likes to be called a cat or a bird or a rat. Maybe he's just a normal dog, though and I should just keep telling him what a big black hairy beast he is!' "

"Oh-h-h-h-h . . ." Dr. Blank moaned. Her head was in her lap. Her hands covered her ears.

Topsy leaned closer to Dr. Blank and raised her voice. "I turned over on my back. I lifted my legs into the air. I threw them around that animal and I screamed, '*FUCK IT, YOU BIG BLACK HAIRY BEAST*!' " She paused. Her voice softened. "But he didn't. He waited until I got still and quiet and gentle . . . that's what he wanted . . ."

Dr. Blank was sobbing now.

"He liked it," Topsy continued in a whisper. "He didn't want to be whipped or talked dirty to or peed on. He didn't want to try on my underwear. He didn't want me to pull his tail. And he didn't care if I got on top. He's just a regular dog. Just me, all by myself, was exciting enough, not too wild and wild enough . . . *I was enough*." She looked at the doctor. "What do you think of that?"

Dr. Blank's voice sliced through her head like a knife. "I *cannot* answer your questions."

"Oh," Topsy moaned, looking for the door. "This isn't right . . . "

"Right, right, right," mimicked Dr. Blank. "You'll never get it right!"

"I don't think you've got much of a future with me," Topsy offered frantically. "Have you ever considered suicide?"

"ARE YOU CRAZY?" screamed Dr. Blank. "How many times do I have to tell you not to ask me any more of your goddamned questions! You know, you're fucking rude! That's your problem! All you ever think about is yourself. All you ever talk about is yourself. Every question you ask *begs* for an answer that relates directly to you, YOURSELF. But do you want a straight answer? NO!" Dr. Blank's voice was thundering. "You think you can drag yourself in here, hopscotch around your worst transgressions, things, that in your next life, are going to bring you back as a *slug* at best, and find some kind of absolution just because you *showed up*?!" Dr. Blank screeched. "You have a tricky mind, Topsy, but I didn't stick with you for nothing! I've spent years preparing for you, you devious little dog-snatching pervert deviate! Yes. Yes. Yes. I have considered suicide. Everyone has considered suicide. BUT I WILL NEVER KILL MYSELF UNTIL THE DAY YOU REVEAL YOURSELF! AND I KNOW YOU! YOU WON'T DO IT!"

Dr. Blank threw open the door of her inner office and shoved Topsy into the outer office.

"YOU'RE AS SICK AS YOUR SECRETS, SISTER!" she screamed, throwing open the door to her outer office and kicking Topsy into the hall. "AND YOU'RE GOING TO STAY THAT WAY!!"

Topsy fell backwards, colliding with Mary Jane Shady, who was screaming, "I'll never reveal myself! Never! Never! Never!"

Topsy hit her so hard that Mary Jane Shady suddenly stopped banging and kicking Dr. Goldman's door.

"Cut it out, lady," yelled a voice two stories above. "They're not here nights. Go home."

"But I'm in a crisis!" cried Mary Jane Shady.

"We're all in a crisis," the voice called back. "Come back tomorrow like the rest of us!"

CHAPTER TWENTY-FIVE

MARY JANE SHADY tumbled back from the brownstone's doorway, tripped across the narrow brick entry, stumbled up the stone steps and careened into the street.

" 'You're mine, Topsy,' " she muttered bitterly. "That's what he said. '*You're mine*!' "

HA, HA, HA, TOPSY.

"I did it . . . " The tears would not stop. "I did it . . . I did it . . . "

COME ON, TOPSY. COME ON . . .

She weaved down Horatio Street.

"C'mon, Mary Jane," Bobby Henderson pleaded. "C'mon, c'mon, c'mon."

"Okay, okay, just five more minutes." She licked her lips and stuck her pink second-chair piccolo tongue in Bobby's ear.

"No, no, no," Bobby begged, wiping his ear. "Stop that."

"Hush, Bobby, hush. The whole town will hear you," Mary Jane said.

"It's gonna take the whole county to satisfy you," Bobby snapped. "Goddamn. Ow! Quit it!"

She spoke before she could stop herself. "This is what you wanted!" she cried. "This is what you begged me for night and day, day and night, isn't it?"

He said nothing.

"You better be glad I like it!" she exploded. "Some people would say there might be somethin' the matter with you!"

"Bull-shee-it!" he yelled. "Bull-shee-it, horse-manure and donkey dicks! I'm a fuckin' Sampson!" Bobby Henderson shouted. "Hercules and Goliath got nothin' on me, babe! You wonder where to find me, check out the Fuck Book of Records in the libery. I'll be in it! Look me up!"

He started the car.

She jerked the keys out of the ignition and threw them out the window.

"You promised me the stars," she cried desperately. "What's the matter with you?"

Bobby Henderson looked at her evenly. His eyes cut through her like steel.

"Nothin's the matter with *me*, M.J. Somethin's the matter with you."

"What?" she gasped anxiously. "What? What? What?"

"You don't want to know," Bobby told her.

"Tell me," she begged. "Please say it."

"Okay. . ." he sighed. "You just don't git me hot no more."

Her heart pounded. Her body trembled. She felt as if she were growing large, like Alice in Wonderland. Bobby suddenly seemed very, very small. And she felt very, very tall. Any moment, she expected her head to collide with the stars.

HOW CAN I GET HIM HOT? her head screamed. *I KNOW I CAN DO IT IF I CAN JUST FIND OUT HOW*!

"I can be exciting," she heard herself tell Bobby Henderson in a bold voice that seemed to belong to someone else.

Bobby looked at her doubtfully.

"I mean, I *was*, I was before . . . wasn't I?"

Bobby gave a short nod.

"Okay, then," she said eagerly. "If somethin's wrong, I'll fix it."

He looked at her hopelessly.

It never occurred to her not to try to keep him. "Just tell me what to do."

He stared at her. "That's just it," he mumbled.

"What? What's it? What *is* it?"

"Well. Look." He shuffled from one foot to the other. "I have to tell you what to do."

"No, you don't," she protested. "You don't have to tell me what to do. I know what to do. I'll do it!"

"Wait."

She waited.

"I mean, that's it. That is just it. You're takin' off all by yourself, like somethin' wild, like a animal or somethin.' "

She stared at him in confusion. "Isn't that what you wanted? Somethin' wild? And free?"

"Well, yeah," he admitted. "Sort of . . ."

"Some kind of a wild animal is what I thought you wanted me to be like."

He looked at the ground. "In the circus," he said, "tigers have trainers."

"Huh?"

He sighed. "Why do I have to repeat ever-thang twice?"

"I'm sorry," she whispered. "I just don't understand."

"Okay." He sucked in his breath. "*I* have to tell *you* what to do. Understand?"

Her eyes grew wide.

"Don't just go takin' off on your own," he told her.

"Oh," she said. "I see. You want to tell me what to do."

"That's right," he said. "You're on the right track."

"Why didn't you say so?" she asked.

"Why do I have to?" he retorted.

"Well, that's okay," she said quickly. "That would be okay. I like it when you tell me what to do."

"No, you don't," he said. "You're not listenin' anymore. You're not listenin' when I tell you what to do."

"I'm not?"

He shook his head. "You never even give me a chance to tell you what to do."

She reached out desperately. "Don't leave me!"

For one quick second his look reminded her of her mother's face. Serious and quiet and very disappointed.

"See there!" he hollered. "Stop tellin' me what to do!"

"What?" she cried. "What?" What had she told him?

He shook his head. "See? See? You don't get it."

"Explain!" she pleaded. "Please, explain!"

He stared at her silently.

A house with no carnations, shuttered and white, fenced and lawned, rectangular and neat, flashed through her mind and right out of her head.

She grabbed him fiercely. "I will do anything for you," she promised.

He seemed to be looking through her.

"Anything," she repeated. "Anything you say."

Bobby nodded solemnly. "Okay," he said, considering her willingness. "I'll think about it."

And then she made a fatal mistake. She couldn't help it.

"While you're thinkin' about it," she said. "Can I just get back on top?"

"Oh, I shouldn't have done it!" Mary Jane Shady screamed up and down Horatio Street. "I should have known I wasn't going to the top!"

"Go to hell!" someone yelled out from a window.

"Go get laid," came a voice from a bum by a trash can.

"Go shopping," advised an old woman pushing a wire cart. "You look terrible."

"Go get your hair done," said a yuppie crossing the street.

"Go purple," advised a punk coming around the corner.

GO WILD, said Topsy into Mary Jane Shady's ear.

CHAPTER TWENTY-SIX

LEO DIGGS kissed Lottie Shady long and deep. Then he kissed her some more. He wanted to do some other things, too.

"Boy," he said, rubbing the back of his neck tenderly. "I better take another ole yaller. I may have me a whip lash."

"Aw-w-w-w." Lottie grinned slowly. "I sure hope you don't."

She couldn't figure out for the life of her why she was grinning about a thing like that, but she knew she was and couldn't quit.

"Look at your purty smile," Leo said. "Look at your purty white teeth."

"Dr. Watson over in Odessa put 'em in for me," Lottie giggled. "I used to have longer ones with a little gap in the middle."

"We talkin' teeth or tits!" Leo guffawed.

Lottie hee-hawed.

They weaved and swayed, laughing dizzily, lightly, as Leo pulled her down on his lap.

"I'd wreck fifteen more trucks to have you on my knee," he told her.

"Oh, Leo," Lottie gurgled, bouncing against the rhythm of his knees. "Oh-h-h-h-h-h-h, Le-o-o-o-o-o-o-o . . ."

"Oh, Lottie-e-e-e-e-e-e," Leo murmured. "Oh-h-h-h-h, Lottie-e-e-e-e-e-e . . ."

He stopped bouncing, his head resting on the back of the chair, both hands on each of Lottie's knees. "Oh," he moaned. "My headache is comin' back."

"Mine, too," Lottie groaned.

"Alcohol'd help," Leo swooned. He picked up the bottle of bourbon and turned it upside down. It was empty. "Oh, no," he said. And fumbling for more pills, he took one, while Lottie crawled off his lap and on her hands and knees, made it to her purse, slithering back with a bottle of cooking sherry she had just picked up at the grocery store that morning.

"Good, good," Leo whispered. "I'm sick, girl. Real sick. That wreck 'bout done me in. I think I maybe better lie down."

"Me, too," Lottie said. "Me, too."

"We better get me in a bed," Leo groaned, as they pulled one another up.

Stumbling from the parlor, they turned in circles toward the slumber room, where Lottie guided Leo right over to her finest and most expensive navy blue casket.

"Don't leave me!" Leo cried, taking another slug of cooking sherry. "My! What a sweet drink."

Lottie took the bottle and swallowed some. "M-m-m," she echoed. "What a sweet drink . . . " Her head was swimming like a whirlpool. "Uh-oh. I think I feel faint."

"Here, hon," Leo moaned. He snapped something under Lottie's nose.

"What's that?" Lottie asked, weaving and swaying. It smelled like the hospital vapors. "What's that?"

"Feelin'-faint medicine," Leo murmured. "It's for when you're feelin' faint . . . "

She breathed and sniffed, and sniffed and breathed, as she heard another yellow capsule pop and then another as Leo Diggs pulled Lottie Shady into her very best navy blue casket with him.

Lottie and Leo sniffed and sniffed. They twisted and writhed. And then Lottie felt her clothes coming off, felt hands and tongues all over her. She was wet inside and out. Then she felt something hard enter her. A thousand stars blinked in her brain, leaving one yellow blazing ball bouncing between her eyes and the inside of her head, as her pelvis thrust against that hardness again and again, and again, and the blazing yellow ball became a tiny yellow dot.

Dot. Dot. Dot. Dot...
dot ....dot ....dot ....d ....o ....t ....
..........................d..........................o...........................t
....

Ecstasy is the last thing she remembered.

"Now you're mine," said Leo Diggs. "My own Olive Oyl Lady. Mine forever." He gave Lottie Shady's still lips one last kiss. "And that's my secret."

CHAPTER TWENTY-SEVEN

SHE DIDN'T REMEMBER how she got there. She didn't remember walking the street. Mary Jane Shady didn't remember a thing. But by the time she walked into Cleo Nebraska's All Nite Shave and Cut on West 4th Street, Topsy certainly thought she knew exactly what *she* was doing.

"So how's the Peanut Butter Cup?" Cleo smiled. "You look shot, girl. Let me get you some tea."

Mary Jane Shady fell into a 1930s wicker chaise lounge. Topsy drank the tea.

It wasn't the first time Mary Jane had come to Cleo's in the middle of the night. Celebrities often frequented the salon in the wee odd hours. They came like night owls when no one else was there to bother them, when they couldn't sleep, had no place to go. Celebrities, hookers, nuns, painters, movie stars, soap queens, society ladies on the prowl, Broadway stars after a show.

Arabella du Noir had sent her to Cleo's years ago. Cleo and Arabella had modeled together in Paris. In the middle of the night, Cleo's was the place to go.

"Purple," said Topsy, pointing to Mary Jane's hair. "Purple."

"I don't think so," Cleo grinned.

"White-blond, then," Topsy told her. "Like Kim Novak." Bobby's favorite.

"White-blond!" Cleo shrieked, shaking her head. "Take a nap, girl. Cleo's not going to do nothin' crazy with your hair." She knew she'd have to answer to Arabella du Noir.

"Wild . . ." Topsy breathed. "Do something wild . . ."

"Let me wash it first," Cleo said. "C'mon back to the bowl." She led Mary Jane back, practically holding her up.

"Wild," Topsy pleaded. "Please make me wild . . ."

"Okay," Bobby promised. "*I'll* make you wild."

It was the evening of their high school graduation. Midnight and the moon was full. Close by she heard a dog bark. The words to the song drifted through her head.

> *Drivin' down the dirt road after a six-pack picture show . . .*
> *It had just been oiled the day before,*
> *I asked him please drive slow . . .*

She hoped she could be just exactly wild enough for him. She knew she could, if he'd just tell her how.

"You got to prove it," Bobby said. "You gotta prove to be how wild I tell you to be."

"I will," she vowed solemnly. "I will prove I can be as wild as you tell me to be."

"Will you do anything I tell you to?" he asked.

"Anything."

"Okay," Bobby said. "And no more."

"And no more."

"And no less."

"And no less."

"You're sure?"

"I promise, I swear."

"And you'll never ever tell what happened this night, now or ever after. Amen."

"Now or ever after. Amen."

"Okay." He opened the car door. "Get out."

She got out, pulling the tulle of her green formal with her.

Alone, by the oil pump, lit by the stars, highlighted by the moon, she stood. Waiting. Her heart pounded in counter syncopation with the oil pump nearby.

He took a bottle of Thunderbird wine he'd been drinking all night and offered it to her. She drank from it and coughed. It tasted terrible. Her throat stung. But she didn't complain. Soon she started feeling mild.

"Okay," he breathed. "Pull down your panties."

She did.

"Lift up your evenin' dress."

She did.

"Close your eyes."

She closed them.

She heard Bobby whistle softly, twice. "C'mon, boy," he hissed.

"Who's that?" she asked.

"Nobody," he told her. "Don't ask questions. You don't git to ask questions."

"Then why did you whistle?" she wanted to know.

"Shut up and bend over. Keep your eyes closed. You're goin' to break the spell," he warned. "C'mon. Put your elbows against the fender. You can lean against the car."

She could sense his excitement, even with her eyes closed.

She could almost feel his quivering, even though he wasn't even touching her.

"Now hold on there," he instructed, "while I pause for a cause."

She knew he was drinking more Thunderbird.

"Want some juice?" he asked.

"Uh-huh."

"Hold your head back."

She did.

"Feelin' good?" he asked.

She was wondering how good she felt, all bent over the car fender. Her formal was scratching her legs.

"Sit," Bobby said.

She started to sit.

"Not you," he told her.

"Huh?"

"I'm not talkin' to you."

"Oh." This time she didn't ask who he was talking to. She stood up, pushing all speculation out of her head. She was determined to do whatever he said. She'd prove to him she could be everything he wanted her to be. And no more. And no less. She'd prove she could be just exactly wild, but not too wild, just exactly exciting, but not too exciting. Just exactly perfect.

She felt his fingers touch her from behind. Quickly, easily, they slid inside her. Oh, she was wet. She waited in anticipation. Then she felt his tongue. Licking her, lapping her. His tongue was rough. She swooned. He'd never done that before. This *was* exciting!

New words spilled into her head.

To the rhythm of the oil pump,
My heart was beatin' wild . . .
I felt just like a bluebonnet
Tumbleweed prairie child . . .
When he painted me with his tongue
Like I was a piece of art . . .
That is when my friend
He touched the clitoris of my heart . . .

She felt herself pulsate and quiver, waves of ecstasy pumping through her.

"Oh, git me!" she cried, forgetting herself. "C'mon and git me!"

"I'll git you, Topsy," he promised. "Bend down on the ground. On your hands and knees."

She did.

"I'm gonna ride you this time," he said. "Hold still. I'm gonna break you like a bronco buster."

He moved fast and quick. His panting came hard and deep. And then, he began to moan, low and deep.

Oh, the waves going through her. Oh, the pulsating. Huge, liquid ecstasy, mounting, expanding, releasing, again and again, and again.

She laughed when she heard him howl. She threw her head back and howled with him. She laughed at the moon and howled at the stars above. She turned to laugh with Bobby.

But it wasn't Bobby Henderson she'd been laughing with. It wasn't Bobby she'd heard howling. And it wasn't him that she'd made love to.

Mary Jane Shady fell back onto the ground in sheer stark horror. She stared into something so black and huge and hairy, she could hardly tell what it was. She hovered, shivering, her mind reeling like a roller coaster.

She hoped it was a Negro. She prayed it was. She hoped it was the Loch Ness monster, the West Texas killer, the Silent Stalker, all rolled into one. But it wasn't. And she knew it.

"Bobby?" she whispered feebly. "Is that some kind of a dog?"

"That's ole Dingo Humpfuck!" Bobby Henderson guffawed.

"You fucked ole Dingo Humpfuck!"

She felt the wine, hot, like sour blood, coming up in her throat.

"Now that was just too wild!" Bobby Henderson sniggered nastily.

Her face was in the sand. West Texas dirt, in her mouth, mingled with the wine. She was afraid she might vomit. Her long green dress was tangled in a tumbleweed, hooked on a cactus.

Suddenly she wondered if it were possible to get pregnant from a *dog*!

"I think we better get married," she gasped. She could hear her dress rip as she tried to move toward him.

"I cain't marry *you*!" Bobby Henderson said in mock incredulity. "Now, I was *goin'* to, Topsy. I was *plannin'* to. But it looks like you just eloped with ole Dingo here!"

"What-t-t?" she stammered. The blood rushed from her head. She knew she was going to vomit.

"Whenever a human bein' fucks a dog, that dog becomes part human, and the human gets to be part dog." Bobby Henderson kneeled down beside her on his knees. "You should have taken Latin and you would know this."

She was gagging. Sticky, foamy goo was bubbling out of her mouth. She tried to choke it back, but it kept surging forth, like a stopped up toilet. The dog was trying to lick her face. She was trying not to scream. "What are you talking about?" she shrieked, pushing the dog away.

"I cain't marry a dog-woman," Bobby explained patiently. "And I cain't compete with my best friend, ole Dingo, here. And I can tell from watchin', you'd a-rather fuck that dog than *me*."

Mary Jane screamed.

Dingo barked.

Bobby Henderson giggled.

"Lovers' quarrel!" he tittered. "Lovers' quarrel!"

He stood up, towering above her, and staggered toward the car.

"We are gettin' married!" Mary Jane Shady screeched hysterically. "I mean it!"

Bobby turned abruptly. His voice was hard and low. "Nobody tells me what to do," he said. "And nobody tells me when to do it. Now shut up. I'm not marryin' any dog fucker. You are a sex maniac, pure and simple. You'd fuck anythang in sight. You just did. And if you don't keep your mouth shut, I'll tell ever last soul in Uncertain, Texas what you did to this pore ole dog here, and how you took advantage of a pore ole animal and degraded *me*," he threatened. "Now git in. You're lucky I'm givin' you a ride home."

She started to howl. She howled all the way home.

"Good-bye, Mary Jane Shady!" Bobby Henderson hollered, pushing her out of the car and into the shadows of the Uncertain Chapel of Memories. "Hello, Mrs. Topsy Dingo Wild Dog!"

CHAPTER TWENTY-EIGHT

MARY JANE SHADY jumped out of Cleo Nebraska's shampoo bowl.

Topsy Dingo Wild Dog let out a long crazed howl.

"Jesus Christ! Hold on here!" Cleo said, jumping back.

Topsy's teeth bared back and she started to growl.

"Goddamned drug addicts," Cleo muttered, turning the spray on her. She'd seen customers go mad in the middle of the night before.

Topsy flung herself through the spray and out the door.

Cleo watched her running wildly down the street. She saw her cross 4th Street and go into a place with a neon sign. She knew the place. It was a tattoo parlor.

Cleo went to the phone and dialed Arabella du Noir.

"For God's sake," Arabella said. "It's three o'clock in the morning."

"I'm sorry," Cleo apologized. "But you got problems."

"I sure do," Arabella replied. "I can't get a decent night's sleep."

"Listen, Belle," Cleo said. "I hope this is important enough to wake you up. But your Miss Peanut Butter Cup came in here tonight and just now went stark raving mad."

"Goddamnit," Arabella said, sitting up. "She's supposed to be in Uncertain, Texas."

"I don't know where that is," Cleo responded. "But she ain't there."

"Is she with you now?" Arabella asked.

"No, she isn't. The last I saw of her, she was going into a tattoo parlor down the block."

"All right," Arabella sighed. "I'll send my car."

"Send a big strong man," Cleo advised. "She tried to bite me."

"Well, what do you expect?" Arabella asked wearily. "She's an actress."

Arabella hung up the phone and dialed her secretary, Pierre. She instructed him to take her car and driver, pick up Mary Jane Shady, take her by her apartment, get her luggage, and see that she was buckled into the first plane that left for West Texas.

"And notify her mother," Arabella told him. "So she can meet the plane."

"Her mother called after you had gone," Pierre explained. "She is expecting the Peanut Butter Cup in the morning." He paused, puzzled. "What is the problem? Doesn't Miss Peanut Butter Cup want to go?"

"Doesn't look like it," Arabella replied. "But it doesn't matter. She's going. I told her mother she'd be there and I intend to keep my word. My car should be arriving for you in about two minutes, so get over to that tattoo parlor and pick her up. And Pierre—"

"Yes, Madame du Noir?"

"Don't forget her Peanut Butter Cup dress."

Arabella du Noir hung up and went back to sleep.

CHAPTER TWENTY-NINE

THE NEON LIGHTS blinked red, yellow, blue, pink and green.

She looked for the cactus on the sign, but could not find it. She went inside quietly, hoping no one would still be up. She tiptoed through the door, hoping they wouldn't notice her torn dress, the sand in her hair. She wondered if they would be able to tell what had happened by just looking at her. The sand felt wet. How had her hair gotten wet?

She heard someone say, "Yes?"

She tensed. Her eyes darted to the side. She moved back against the wall.

"Heart," she whispered.

"Okay," the voice replied. "You want a heart?"

She nodded.

"On your arm?"

She shook her head.

"Your ankle? Shoulder?"

She shook her head again. She pointed between her breasts.

"Oh. You want a heart *on* your heart. Over *your* heart. Well. Sit down."

Mary Jane Shady felt nothing. The needles darted through her skin, but she felt nothing. She heard nothing.

When the two men came through the door, pulled her out of the chair, and put her into the car waiting outside, she never even knew it.

Mary Jane Shady did not scream. And Mary Jane Shady did not hurt. For Mary Jane Shady was no longer there.

Topsy Dingo Wild Dog, lying dormant for twenty years, had crawled out of Mary Jane Shady's soul and into Arabella du Noir's car.

"Wait!" yelled the engraver as he ran out of the tattoo parlor. "You can't take her home with half a heart!"

PART
TWO

CHAPTER THIRTY

ANYONE DRIVING east or west down Highway 158 through Uncertain, Texas, on Thursday, September 12, 1985, would not have seen Baby Flowers out taking her walk that day. For the first time in nineteen years, Baby did not wake up with her six sisters and one brother-maybe-daddy poking and dressing her. For the first time in nineteen years, Baby did not eat Crackerjacks for breakfast or get left without a rocking chair to sit in. For the first time in nineteen years, Baby Flowers did not walk down the highway to stare at the sun. She didn't have to. For Baby was no longer in Uncertain; she was above it. And from where she now sat, which was next to her half-sister-cousin, in Yvonne's twin engine Cessna, Baby Flowers had never, in nineteen years, had a better view of the sun.

The first thing she did was the first thing she always did. She stared into the sun as long as she could without blinking. She couldn't manage as long a stare as she was used to, for the sun was much closer. But Baby didn't mind. She was just thrilled to be right in the light. When everything got bright and hot inside her eyes, she squeezed them as tight as she could. Then, instead of turning in circles like she usually did, Baby rolled her head around on her neck, giggling with each rotation.

"Is she going to do that all the way to Dallas?" the pilot asked Yvonne.

"Don't ask me!" Yvonne snapped impatiently. "I don't even know her! I'm just doin' somebody a big, big favor!" She flipped open the top of a canned marguerita mixed drink and downed half of it in one long gulp. "I don't know why I had to bring her anyway. This is a real, real important shoppin' trip I'm goin' on!"

Far above Uncertain, Texas, Baby pressed her face against the window of the Cessna and looked toward the ground below.

To her utter delight, the whole world was miniature! Everything was smaller than she was! It looked so neat and tiny and manageable. Baby waved to all the little people, cars and buildings she usually passed on her daily walk. How she would love to move them all around, put the fortune teller's tent where the high school was, place the Uncertain Chapel of Memories across the street from the Permanent Rest Center, move Yvonne Henderson right next door to Catsy

Ivanhoe! Place her own Flowers family, tin cans, rotten tires and all, smack in the middle of both of them!

Baby stretched her neck so she could peer out the window. The last thing she saw before turning back into the sun was a row of seven rocking, waving figures, out by the highway.

"Parts Unknown!" Baby whispered through cupped fingers toward the little figures. They looked like eyelashes, waving off the face of the earth. She unclasped her fingers, kissed each fingertip, and blew the kisses toward her rocking relatives below. "We're off to Parts Unknown!"

The next thing she knew, Uncertain seemed to just disappear off the ground.

"Would you please be still, Baby?" Yvonne frowned, as she flipped through the latest issue of *Soap Opera Digest*. "I'm tryin' to relax."

But Baby paid no attention. She was looking at a big bird coming toward them in the sky. As the bird got closer, Baby gleefully saw that it was another airplane. She squealed at the magic occurring right before her eyes. She laughed until she could not stop, as the wings of the bird became the wings of the plane. She clapped her hands over and over as the nose of the bird turned into the nose of the plane.

Yvonne looked at Baby and snorted with impatience. She finished her canned marguerita, pushed a black-out mask over her eyes and pulled a set of headphones over her ears. Yvonne Henderson was so covered up with gadgets that she missed the big American 727 enroute to the Midland-Odessa Airport from New York City. But Baby Flowers didn't miss it. Baby Flowers did not miss a thing. She waved to the aircraft and blew kisses to every passenger on it.

"Parts Unknown!" Baby cried as plane passed plane. "Ever-body's goin' off to Parts Unknown!"

It had still been dark outside when Irene Shady woke up in her rented single bed at the Fly By Nite Motel five miles west of the Midland-Odessa Airport, sixty miles east of Uncertain, Texas. She had tugged on the shower cap that had served as a hairnet, straightened her pearls, fluffed up her pillow, turned over, and for thirty minutes had tried to go back to sleep. Finally, at 5:30 A.M., she dropped off and dreamed about Gladys Turner's sister's funeral over and over and over until a woman at the front desk called her and told her it was way past time for her wake-up call.

"You mean it's after 8:30 A.M. already?" Irene had shouted.

"Yeah," the woman replied. "It's 10:30. I would have called you at 8:30 like you ast, but one of my kids was sick and I had to take 'em to the doctor."

"Well, it's a good thing I'm as organized as I am!" Irene cried. She cradled the phone to her ear with her shoulder as she hurriedly made up the motel room's bed. "Otherwise *your* sick child could have been *my* flat tire!"

She tucked the sheets tightly, flipped a quarter on the bedspread to check her work and hopped in the shower.

"I'll make this quick," she told herself. "I don't have time to get *Psychoed* today!"

She jumped out of the shower, took off the shower cap, kept on the pearls, put on her suit, hat and gloves, climbed in her hearse and headed for the airport.

Later, when the motel's maid opened the door to clean Irene's vacated room, she looked around, then simply shut the door. It didn't seem to her as if anyone had used the room at all.

It was 11:10 when Irene arrived at the airport.

"I'm here!" she announced to the first person she saw sitting behind a desk. "I'm here to meet Miss Mary Jane Shady who's arrivin' on a jet plane from New York City at 11:51! Now where's that gate?"

"I don't know," the man sitting behind the desk replied. "I'm the car rental service."

"This is exactly why I arrived forty-one minutes early," Irene told the man. And turning on her heels, she redirected herself.

By 11:22, she had found the gate, found a seat and found a stranger willing to listen to every word she had to say about Mary Jane Shady's imminent arrival and current career as Miss Peanut Butter Cup.

Irene's only problem after that was how to say everything she had to say about Mary Jane Shady in a mere twenty-nine minutes. She looked at this as a challenge and talked on.

It was almost 11:30 A.M. when Lottie Shady awakened from what she would henceforth refer to as her "coma."

"That is the best night's rest I ever had in my life," Lottie thought to herself as she slowly opened her eyes.

As her pupils began to focus, Lottie could see she was not in her own bed at all, but lying in something that felt like a sea full of satin.

"Uh-oh," Lottie said. And that is as long as it took for her to recognize the inside covering of her very best and most expensive navy blue coffin. "Wonder if I'm still alive?" she asked herself.

"I have a suspicion that we have been spared," came Leo Diggs' weak reply.

Lottie felt her heart kick up at the sound of his voice. She tingled all over. Goosebumps played hopscotch up and down her body, tumbling all over her skin like a bunch of Mexican jumping beans. She raised up a bit and looked right into the soles of Leo Diggs' boots, which were hanging over the end of the pale yellow coffin Irene had been paying out on layaway, but insisted on keeping in the vestibule as a demonstrator.

Lottie Shady grinned so hard she almost lost her teeth plates. *Now don't get over-anxious,* she told herself. *And get that silly grin off your face. Better play this helpless angle up some more.*

"Have we been doped and drugged?" she asked, making her voice sound groggy.

"Doped and drugged and maybe even robbed," Leo lamented.

"ROBBED!" Lottie forgot her act and sat straight up in her coffin. "What'd they take?"

"Don't you 'member?" Leo asked. "Lucie Garden and Wendell Butler was stolen yesterday?" He swung his legs over Irene's coffin, pulled himself over the side, and ambled over to Lottie.

"Oh, them." Lottie stared in wonder at Leo Diggs. His shirt was open and across his chest was a tattoo of Garfield the Cat. Enclosed in a black ring that pointed to the cat's mouth were the words: I AM LAZY, SLOTHFUL AND FAT. I LIKE THAT IN A CAT.

I like that in a cat, too, Lottie thought.

"'Member?" Leo asked, quietly running his hand through Lottie's hair. "We decided it was for the best them corpses was taken so our bodies could *live*?"

"Listen, Leo." Lottie's back was as straight as a stick, her stare as direct as a daggar. "Forget them bodies. What I want to know is, if you're seventy-five years old and still a virgin and just lost you cherry, but don't hardly remember it, does it count?"

Leo gave a soft sigh. "No," he said. "If you don't remember, then it don't count."

Lottie Shady was suddenly so overwhelmed with embarrassment that she didn't know what to do. She could feel her face flush as red as a gobbler's comb. Never in her life had she felt so completely, absolutely and positively out of control.

"Oh, Lord!" Lottie cried, throwing her legs over the metallic siding of the casket. "It's 11:30 the next morning!" She glanced frantically at the clock. "I'm three hours and a quarter late for number two!" She jumped out of the Uncertain Chapel of Memories' most expensive item and ran right toward the downstairs bathroom where she intended to lock herself behind the door and stay for the rest of her life.

"I'll be right here waitin'," came Leo Diggs' voice behind her.

Lottie slowly turned around and brought her eyes up from the floor. How unlike her to be looking at a floor! All of a sudden she was feeling things she had never felt before. Her eyes were flying off to strange places. Her feet and legs were taking off on their own volition. Her head was struggling to keep up with every part of her that suddenly and singularly seemed to take on desires individual to arms or eyes or feet. All of her parts seemed strangely disconnected from working like any kind of a body tuned to function as a whole. In short, she was a wreck. In fact, Lottie Shady found herself so completely discombobulated, that what came out of her mouth next was the result of pure instinct. In her confusion, she reverted to her inner truth: she said exactly what was on her mind.

"Aw, Leo," Lottie whispered. "I couldn't never forget."

"You sure couldn't," Leo agreed, stooping to fit the bathroom's doorway. "'Cause you're not never goin' to get the chanct."

Lottie gulped. She was afraid her eyes were about to dart back down to that linoleum again. She stole one quick glance at it. Then, like a pilot struggling to command the aircraft, she pulled her eyes from the floor (which she noticed could use a waxing), to the door. Finally, her orbs felt like a couple of marbles rolling around a pin ball machine, so she just let her head fall back toward her backbone. That way she knew she'd be looking straight up into Leo's eyes.

"Are you tryin' to tell me somethin'?" she mumbled.

"Let's you and me take a ride and talk it over," Leo suggested. "'Cause what I have in mind inn't exactly stayin' and inn't exactly leavin', but I don't want to be explainin' any of it when Sister comes back."

Leo's calling Irene "Sister" made Lottie blink. Then abruptly, as she was blinking, her eyes took off on their own again. They darted around the room like a couple of freed flies.

Circling through the parlor, Lottie realized that she had no idea if Irene was upstairs, downstairs or heading sixty miles east for the Midland-Odessa Airport. Then abruptly her eyes, head and feet came together all at once.

"I don't know where she is and I don't care to find out," Lottie told Leo. She was so relieved to sound like herself that she threw her arms around Leo Diggs, opened up his shirt and kissed Garfield the Cat right on his mouth. "Come on," she said, feeling better and better. She picked up her purse and pulled Leo toward the door.

"M-m-m. He likes to be kissed like that," Leo grinned.

"He ain't seen nothin' yet," Lottie grinned back. "I'm kissin' ever part of that animal I can find."

Leo Diggs counted his blessings. "You goin' to let Sister know you're goin'?" Leo asked, shutting the front door of the Uncertain Chapel of Memories.

"I'm not even leavin' a note," Lottie Shady told Leo Diggs. As he inserted the key in the lock, Lottie put her hand over his hand. "Wait a minute, honey." She stepped back inside and flipped a switch. "Just for pure-dee meaness, I'm lightin' up this neon sign!"

CHAPTER THIRTY-ONE

TOPSY WAS SITTING on a silver-plated throne donated by the Uncertain Jaycees. The throne was resting on top of "The Queen of the EX's Float." Gliding through the main street of Uncertain, the float sat on top of Sammy Widders' daddy's four-wheel drive pickup, which was concealed by billions of real silver roses imported from Tyler, Texas.

Topsy was wearing her Valentino suede pants, a Victorian Oscar de la Renta blouse and a full-length coat made of lavender turkey feathers, trimmed in purple ostrich and lined in antique Chinese silk. She'd gotten it on sale, but the thing had still cost a fortune on Madison Avenue. Herman had been with her when she bought it.

"Are you sure you want to buy that, M.J.?" Herman had asked. "Where on earth would you wear it?"

The crowd was cheering! Thank God she'd bought the coat! The street was lined with people waiting to see *her*—THE QUEEN OF THE EX-STUDENTS!—floating by on a silver-plated throne, dripping in purple feathers! At every stop light a banner ran across the sky proclaiming "WELCOME HOME, STAR!", "MARY JANE SHADY DAY!", "OUR COMMERCIAL QUEEN!", and "TOPSY IS TOPS!"

Topsy's head was spinning. This is what she had LIVED for—this moment—when all of Uncertain lined up to pay her homage, respect, adoration—to WORSHIP her. And why not? What other face from Uncertain, Texas, had graced the screen of every TV set in the land? Who else had put Uncertain, Texas, on the map! Why, if it hadn't been for her, not one psychiatrist in New York City or Los Angeles, California, would even know there *was* such a place as Uncertain, Texas! She goddamned well deserved this fucking parade!

Topsy rose as the crowd cheered and applauded and the float slowly came to a halt at the courthouse square.

"Speech!" they cried. "Speech!"

Topsy smiled graciously. "Ladies and Gentlemen of Uncertain," she began. "You have overwhelmed me with this most recent honor. My Grammy for the song I never ever finished, my Academy Award for the movie I haven't even made, my Tony Award for the Broadway play I never got cast in, even the Shiksa of the Year Award Herman said I am sure to get because I have this perfect nose—none of these can begin to compare to the pleasure you have given me by—"

Topsy felt something tugging her feathers.

Ignore that tugging, she said to herself. *I should have known these goddamned feathers would give me a problem.*

She pursued, and smiling at the crowd, continued . . . "by honoring me with . . ."

"Give her the Old Age Trophy!" three voices cried out in a simultaneous squeal.

Topsy looked sharply toward the sidelines. Standing ahead, and just to her right were a group of three cheerleaders. Topsy gasped. They looked exactly like some girls she'd known in high school— only *they* hadn't changed at all! They were still teenagers!

Fifteen-year-old Yvonne Dee Flowers, Catsy Shoemaker and Kay Hobbs stepped out from the crowd and moved into a V formation.

"GIVE HER AN *'O'*!" yelled Yvonne.

"GIVE HER AN *'L'*!" yelled Catsy.

"GIVE HER A *'D'*!" yelled Kay.

"WHADDAYAGOT?" they cried out in unison.

"*Old*," sighed Arabella du Noir, who materialized within the crowd and stood opposite the three cheerleaders. "Give her the Liar's Award," Arabella instructed. "That's what she does best."

"No, it inn't," said Bobby Henderson, who emerged and stood, snickering, next to Arabella du Noir. "Give her The Dog Award! *That's* what she does *best*!"

Suddenly purple feathers were flying everywhere. Someone was bumping into her. She attempted to keep her composure, but the crowd had stopped cheering and had started to titter. She tried to turn around, but whoever it was had their hands on her shoulders. My God, they were HUMPING her! And those weren't hands! They were PAWS!

Uproarious laughter erupted from the crowd. Over her shoulder she saw Dingo Humpfuck as he pushed her over on her hands and knees and thrust against her again and again.

"WELCOME HOME, TOPSY!" yelled the entire crowd. "WE ALWAYS KNEW YOU'D GO TO THE DOGS!"

Topsy screamed.

Dingo barked.

The float flew through the air.

As if by magic, it bumped through the clouds, careening wildly through the sky. Flailing frantically for something to hold onto, she struggled for balance to no avail. Her arms and legs drifted through clouds and more clouds as she rolled through eternity, endlessly tossing and turning, never stopping, flung forever through the sky.

Her head rolled, her stomach churned. Would this never stop? Was she destined to spin endlessly through space?

A voice from beyond sliced through her head like a cold steel knife. "Ladies and Gentlemen, the Captain has just turned on the seat belt sign." The voice was one of clarity, authority, and finally, of specificity. "We will be arriving in Midland-Odessa as scheduled . . ."

Topsy Dingo Wild Dog opened Mary Jane Shady's eyes.

A plane. She was on an *airplane*.

"Thank you for joining us today on American's Special Service to the Permian Basin Area . . ."

She was on her way back to *Uncertain*.

"We hope you have had a pleasant journey, and we look forward to seeing you again soon . . ."

Pleasant? She didn't even know how she had gotten on the plane. And she didn't care. She didn't remember getting to the airport. And she didn't want to. She had no idea who had dressed her in her Peanut

Butter Cup outfit. And it could matter less to her if she ever found out.

Only one thing mattered: *She was going home.*

Her hands curled into fists. Her shoulders knotted in tension. A grim smile cut through her lips.

Had it been only yesterday when her greatest problem was how to wrangle a hairbrush out of three competitive actresses at an audition? Had it been only yesterday when the worst possibility confronting her was coming up with a voice for a *pencil*?

She rasped. The feeble half-laugh departed her throat like the sound from a dying dove.

Oh, how she longed for Mary Jane Shady! Removed from Uncertain, Texas, she had known what she was doing! Compelling, confident, beautiful Mary Jane Shady had dazzled Herman Top. Secure, talented, multi-dimensional Mary Jane Shady had charmed Arabella du Noir. Warm, winsome, flawless Mary Jane Shady had won the hearts of Peanut Butter eaters all over America.

But as the wheels of the plane hit the West Texas ground, there was not a trace of this Mary Jane Shady anywhere.

Separated from herself and abandoned by herself, there was only Topsy Dingo Wild Dog. Mary Jane Shady had deserted her. Topsy was on her own. Lying, loathsome, spineless Topsy Dingo Wild Dog was going home.

Nobody cares how many Peanut Butter eaters you've charmed, Topsy's head said over and over and over. *They don't care how many Broadway stars are in love with you. Arabella du Noir isn't going to care how old you are, either. They're only going to care about one thing.*

The plane stood still. People around her were standing up, reaching over and under her for their luggage.

Once they know you fucked that dog, nothing else is going to matter.

She stood up.

She sat down.

She could feel every organ inside of her struggling to operate. Her heart heaved heavily in erratic clumsy beats. She could almost see her liver, plump, raw, red and screaming. Her legs felt like two rubber floats filled half-way with water. Beads of sweat popped out of her forehead, dripping onto her nose. Her breathing was short and shallow, her esophagus dry and brittle. He entire nervous system felt like the string section of an orchestra where every instrument had snapped simultaneously. Undone.

Just lie, she wearily instructed whoever she was, the part of herself that was left. *And no matter what, do not ask one question or answer one question about Bobby Henderson. Whatsoever. Do not even mention his name*.

She stood up carefully.

She moved slowly down the aisle until finally, she stood at the threshold of the portal. All that was left was to descend.

Where was she going and where was she coming from? She took one last breath and grappled for some source of inner strength, for it suddenly seemed that she had never even left in the first place. She felt like she had never been away at all. Everything that had happened to her in the last twenty years seemed, at best, a mere trifling diversion, and at worst, a total figment of her imagination. It was as if she had completely imagined the last twenty years of her life. Only Uncertain was real.

She heard Herman's voice. "*You've got to go back,*" Herman had said. "*You've got to find out* . . . whatever it is you're trying to forget . . ."

"Did you forget something, Miss?" the stewardess asked.

"No," said Topsy Dingo Wild Dog. "I did not forget a thing."

She stepped forward and moved right back into the middle of her past.

CHAPTER THIRTY-TWO

TOPSY CLIMBED GINGERLY down the ramp of the airplane at the Midland-Odessa airport, hanging on to the railing for support. Usually a plane just sidled up along a building here, digesting a convenient breezeway for passengers to simply step from the plane and into the airport attractively intact. But today, the plane had stopped three hundred feet from a chain link fence surrounding the airport and let its passengers make their way down the narrow steps of the plane as best they could, as the wild winds of the West Texas plains hurled against them.

A big banner hanging across the airport terminal proclaimed:

EXCUSE US WHILE WE ARE GETTING OUR FACE-LIFT.

Topsy didn't see the sign. She didn't look up until she had gotten down the steps, and when she did, there among the ten or twelve greeters, weaving this way and that in the wind, was Irene Shady, swaying along among the others. It looked like everyone was standing on a wind machine in a fun house, clothes flying, the people holding on to each other for support, and laughing. Almost everything about Topsy's mother was moving—her body was swaying, both hands were waving—her hat and scarf blew away and two men ran to catch them. Both were returned, but it didn't matter. Not a hair on Irene Shady's head had moved one bit.

"Here, hon!" Irene screamed, as if her daughter might have trouble locating her.

A hug and a kiss later, Irene Shady grabbed the pilot as he climbed down the ramp. "I'm so glad to see my little girl and you would be too if yours was a television commercial star like Miss Creamy Crunchy Peanut Butter, Nutty or Smooth!"

Without waiting for the pilot's reply or to hear if he even had one, she put a strong arm around her daughter's shoulder and guided her into the airport building.

"Construction and reconstruction," Irene explained, motioning toward the renovation site. She smiled and nodded and waved at each and every passing stranger.

I wish I was that building, Topsy thought forlornly. *I need someone to tear me down and build me over . . .*

From the back of her head came a remote and peculiar voice. *All you ever think about is yourself. . . All you ever talk about is yourself . . . Every question you ask begs for an answer that relates directly to you, YOURSELF*!

Who is that? Topsy wondered. *Who said that*? *Did someone say that to me*?

"How'd you like a coke, hon?" Irene Shady was saying, as she headed them into the coffee shop. "Was it a good trip?" Finally undistracted, she looked at her daughter closely for the first time. A line as straight as a West Texas highway plowed right through the middle of her face. "You look like you maybe didn't get enough rest," Irene observed, scowling at such a disheveled appearance.

"How are you?" Topsy asked carefully. Then she smiled carefully. "I am fine." *Run Jane run. See Jane run. Sit Spot sit . . . Spot?!!* She giggled hysterically. *Oh, no, NOT SPOT!*

"You don't look fine," Irene said doubtfully. "You don't sound so fine, either. You go too hard. Rush, rush, rush. Here." She reached into her purse and pulled out a brush. "Here's a brush, baby. You just about blew away."

But I didn't, Topsy thought. *I did not blow away*.

Irene had reached further into her purse and was handing her daughter a mirror.

Like a vampire caught in the light, Topsy pulled away.

"See?" Irene said, thrusting the mirror in front of her daughter.

Topsy stared into bloodshot eyes and a mop of still damp hair. The line under her left eye was matched in size and definition only by the line under her right eye. Her lids were red and puffy.

Irene made another trip into her purse and produced a can of Aqua Net. "Here, sugar. 'Member where the bathroom is? Go comb your hair before it's so tangled it'll never come out." Irene sat down at the table and stood up again immediately. "Want me to come with you? I will. Want me to order the cokes? What do you want?"

"Diet 7-Up's okay," Topsy said. *With arsenic*.

"You don't need a Diet 7-Up. You're skin and bones. Get a regular 7-Up. Somethin' with some pep in it. You want me to come comb your hair? Did I give you a brush?"

"I've got my own brush," Topsy said, sliding her mother's hair apparatus toward her. She wondered if she had remembered to give the secretary's brush back to her yesterday. She wondered who had gotten the part of the pencil. A brush wouldn't help. Nothing would help.

"Well, take the spray or you'll blow away all over again. Wind's just as bad in the front of the building as it is in the back."

Topsy disappeared with the can of spray net into the ladies' room. She carefully avoided looking in the mirror. She splashed her face with water, stuck her head under the soap dispenser and ran the pink grainy soap into her mouth, pushing it across her gums and teeth with her fingers. She longed to throw up. She yearned for a Valium. She went back into the coffee shop and handed her mother the spray net.

"You need a new brush, M.J.," Irene Shady said. "Your hair is still a mess, baby." She started for her purse again. "Now here—"

"Perm . . ." Topsy mumbled.

"Huh?" Irene pulled out a handful of clothes pins. "Oh, shoot. I meant to take these to the line." Back into the bag went her hand which pulled out a box of Saltines. "Now *that's* not what I want. Wouldn't be polite to eat your own food in a place where someone else is tryin' to make a livin' at it, would it?" she said, stuffing the clothespins and crackers back in the bag and coming up with the brush. "Here it is."

"Permanent," Topsy said.

Irene looked at her daughter intensely. "You mean you did that on purpose?"

Topsy nodded. It was such a little lie.

Irene regarded her silently for a few moments. She picked up the brush and put it back in her purse.

"You are takin' a big chance, Mary Jane," she said seriously.

"What do you mean?" Topsy whispered. A sudden vision of the one time she had failed to produce an A plus during all her years in the Uncertain schools suddenly came to her mind. She had felt an obligation to give back the five dollars her mother had given her in advance, assuming, as always, that she would never make less than an A plus in anything whether she understood it or not. "What kind of a chance?"

Irene Shady looked at her daughter. "Well, don't be an infantile idiot. After goin' to all that trouble to become Miss Creamy Crunchy Peanut Butter, Nutty or Smooth, you are takin' a big chance that there are some people in Uncertain, Texas, with you wearin' hair that looks like it was fried along with yesterday's eggs, who may just not recognize you."

Topsy took a deep breath. It was too much to hope for.

"Life is a series of results, Mary Jane," Irene went on, picking up her purse and motioning for her daughter to follow. "You have to be prepared to reap what you have sown."

"I know . . . I remember . . . you taught me that a long time ago," Topsy said with some surprise. Why hadn't she remembered? How had she forgotten? How could she forget a thing like that?

"I know I tried, Mary Jane, but sometimes when you come up with things like a Jew boyfriend and a fried egg hair-do, I wonder if you learned anything at all."

I didn't learn anything at all, Topsy acknowledged. *How could I just go through life not learning anything at all?*

"And whoever did that to your hair ought to be hog-tied," Irene continued.

Wonder who it was? Topsy wondered. *Wonder who did this to me*?

"Now let's get that luggage," Irene went on. "I hope you didn't bring fourteen suitcases."

"Suitcases?"

"Clothes. You brought some rags to wear, didn't you?" Herman Top and his little bitty hat had materialized in Irene's mind and she was mad and didn't know it.

"Clothes?" Topsy asked dumbly.

"Well, for God's sake!" Irene cried. "Did they give you a lobotomy or what? Didn't you bring some luggage with some things to wear in 'em?

"I don't think so," Topsy said uncertainly.

"Well, for-ever-more!" Irene stared her daughter in amazement.

Topsy just looked at her, bewildered.

"Well, forevermore," Irene repeated. "Anyway. You got here."

Topsy nodded. "I got here," she repeated. *Someway*.

Irene shook her head and frowned. "Are you awright?" she asked.

Topsy nodded. She could still taste the pink soap.

"You don't seem awright," Irene said.

"I'm all right," Topsy said. *Turn your face up in a nice bright smile and smile! smile! smile!*

Her lips turned up, her eyes shined, too brightly. But Topsy Dingo Wild Dog just smiled and smiled and smiled. "I'm here!" she announced in a happy, happy voice. "I'm here, and so is my Peanut Butter Cup dress!"

"Well," Irene Shady grinned, relieved to see some life creep into her daughter. "I guess we'll head home with ever-thing that counts!"

THIRTY-THREE

TOPSY STARED AHEAD, mesmerized by the sea of oil wells that constantly emerged, never ending. She looked behind her. There they were. Endless. Like the sky.

The sky. She had forgotten the sky.

In New York, the sky had always been hidden by the Chrysler Building, the Empire State Building, the World Trade Center, or had just simply been upstaged. In New York, it wasn't the sky—it was the *skyline*. And if not the skyline, then Central Park or the Museum of

Modern Art or the Hudson River, Rockefeller Center, Lincoln Center, Shubert Alley—hell, the Russian Tea Room.

The sky was definitely not a priority in New York.

And in Los Angeles, the only time Mary Jane Shady had even thought about the sky was the first time she wanted to take a look at the Hollywood sign and could barely decipher the letters because of the huge yellow haze that engulfed it and everything else. She thought it was beautiful—like a halo around the sign. But the halo made her eyes water and made her sneeze, sort of taking away from the mystical experience. Later, she found out the halo was something called "smog" and that it would probably kill everyone in L.A. and that no one should go outside when it was there, which was always.

One day, after she had been in L.A. for some time, she noticed while driving along the Hollywood Freeway, that what had first appeared to be a halo around the sign *was* just yellow green yuck, and the letters on the sign were crooked. And one was missing. She simply didn't look at the sign again—even after it had been replaced—or the sky, which only got worse.

She hadn't gone to L.A. or New York to see any more sky anyway; she had gone to get away from the goddamn sky. And in that respect, her departure from Uncertain had been a success.

But now here that sky was again. And after twenty years it was exactly the same. The way it looked, anyway—and the way it mysteriously changed. Only a few moments before it was blue, with huge billowing clouds like ballerinas in slow motion floating through one another, inexplicably disappearing into nowhere, and now the blue was framed with violet and gold and pink, so distinct that no earthly painter would have dared to leave a work so unblended.

Nothing touched it. Not the mesquite bushes, nor the Indian blankets that covered the land, nor the oil pumps. And that's all there was.

"Gladys Turner's sister died," Irene said, interrupting the silence.

"Oh."

"Funeral was yesterday."

She made herself talk. "Did you go?"

Irene gave her daughter a "are-you-crazy-of-course-I-went" look. "I sent flowers from both of us. Pink carnations. Guess why?"

"Because her sister died." Topsy ventured.

"Of course because her sister died, but why else?"

"Why else?"

Irene Shady often ended her statements in questions, and Topsy knew that the most simple way to get along was just to *answer*. Her response, not her reply, was the important thing. No matter what she said, her mother had more to add.

"Well, I don't care much for Gladys, between you and me, and I didn't even know her sister, but to top it off, Gladys, my *supposedly* best friend, sent her *only* sister over to my *only* competitor, Miss Good-Deal Grimes. So I sent carnations since they're the cheapest pink flower you can buy. And pink was the theme of the funeral, so there was no choice about that. And Mary Jane, hon, it was the *pinkest* funeral you ever have set eyes on. I saw right off the bat that Gladys and the rest of them kin didn't give a thought to that dead woman or what *she* would have liked, 'cause, honey, they buried her in a robe the poor ole thing had never ever *seen*, much less *wore* before a day in her life. Went out and took it upon theirselves to pick out and buy her a brand new pink robe, and not even from a decent foundation department. They got it from that discount collection Deal keeps over at her One Call Does All Permanent Rest Center. I got to feelin' so bad about sendin' them pink carnations when I saw that poor ole woman all laid out in a shocking pink eight-hunnerd-dollar casket—bottom of the line, I can assure you—lying there in that spanking new silly, frilly pink robe that surely she wouldn't be caught dead in if she was alive, wearin' them pink lips and pink cheeks that Deal had painted on. I swear, the only other color on the woman was a black wig Deal had slapped on her head. Deal says it is too much for her to do hair, make-up *and* embalm, but I know it's because she saw money in the wig business, and now everyone who goes to her is forced to buy wigs for their dead because she won't do *hair*. Her wig selection is limited, though. The woman don't have the sense God give a black-eyed pea, so if you don't die at the right time, you might be buried a redhead after you lived your whole life a dishwater blonde! Oh, that Miss Good-Deal has got a real lively sideline business out of dead people. Three of 'em . . . caskets, wigs and discount lingerie." Irene Shady continued. "I know I wouldn't recognize my own self after Deal got through. I tell you what, you can put me in my aqua suit—the two-piece Butterick pattern number fourteen-seventy-two when I go—"

"Mama, please," Topsy protested.

"Now this is important," Irene continued, overriding her. "And don't you tell a soul what I'm about to tell you 'cause I don't want any hard feelings on Deal's part. She took over Lucie Garden for me yesterday when your Aunt Lottie ran out on me, and I appreciate that. And speakin' of Lottie, please *do* send me to Deal when I expire. At least she's dependable. What I was goin' to tell you is this: The last time I was in Lubbock, I went over to Hemphill-Wells' Department Store to their wig section and got me one that comes the closest to resemblin' my own head of hair that you're lookin' at right this minute, and you can slap that aqua suit on me and that Hemphill-Wells' wig and tell Deal just to change my fluids and *forget* the make-up job. And don't let her sell you a casket, neither. Mine's on layaway down in the slumber room. I'm keepin' it on display 'til I need it. Now listen. No tellin' what she'll come up with since the wig and the outfit won't come from her, as well as the casket. So keep an eye on her, M.J., when the *time arrives*. I do not want her gettin' *creative* on my face, especially if she was really and truly tryin' to do a commendable job on Gladys' sister." Irene started to laugh. "Oh, boy, was that woman pink!"

"Poor woman," Topsy sighed. She was looking out the window, fascinated with the flatness of the land that stretched endlessly in front of her.

"Oh, I forgot to tell you what I did on my way out of town," Irene continued. "I felt so bad about the woman and how I had just given her those cheap ole carnations and no one had given her a thought, I went back to the flower shop to get somethin' better. But bein' right before Homecomin', they were preparin' for all you ex-students and makin' hunnerds and hunnerds of those Homecomin' corsages. So I got me one of them. I took it out and put it next to where her grave was goin' to be. It was real pretty—a big gold mum with a whole bunch of ribbon streamers runnin' down and blowin' in the wind like a lot of little flags. And over the mum made out of pipe cleaners it had the word 'EX' spelled out. They had made 'em up that way at the flower shop for all of ya'll ex-students that was comin' home to wear to the game, but it seemed to me they couldn't have made a more fittin' arrangement for me to put on Gladys's sister's grave if they had tried."

"That was real sweet of you, Mama," Topsy murmured.

"Oh, hon," Irene Shady sighed. "I should have gotten one for you."

They drove on in silence.

Topsy looked once more out the window. The quietness and stillness and vastness remained overwhelming and uninterrupted, until the Uncertain Chapel of Memories' neon sign, like an arrow, pierced the horizon and Topsy's heart, for she realized that in a few minutes she would be home.

Mary Jane Shady had received her summons to appear in Uncertain, Texas around four P.M. on Wednesday, September 11th. At four A.M., on Thursday September 12th, Topsy Dingo Wild Dog had been picked up by Arabella du Noir's chauffeur and secretary in the West Village at the corner where 4th crosses 12th. They had reached the Mayflower Hotel by four-fifteen. Bathing her had been easy; getting her to eat something was another matter. In her condition, it simply had not worked out. Nor had she been of any use in getting into her Peanut Butter Cup dress. It took the embarrassed chauffeur and the resigned secretary exactly one hour to bathe her, dress her, and attempt to feed her. By five-thirty A.M., they were back in the limousine, heading for La Guardia. They arrived before six, but it took half an hour to get her inside. Finally, the men had carried her by her elbows in a standing position, balancing and supporting her between them. The chauffeur requested a wheelchair, but the last one had just been stolen by an Iranian cab driver. She was on the plane and strapped into a seat belt by six forty-five. By seven-fifteen, she was in the air. Two hours and forty minutes later, the plane stopped over in Dallas. An hour after that it was back in the air. It took sixty minutes to get to West Texas. Half an hour to get off the plane, greet her mother, drink a coke, comb her hair and try to explain why she had no luggage. And one more hour to get to Uncertain.

She didn't remember enough to figure it up. But it had taken her twenty-two hours, twelve minutes and twenty years to get back home.

CHAPTER THIRTY-FOUR

SHE WAS STARING into the distance at the only neon in Uncertain. There it was. Red, yellow, blue, pink and green. One limb of the cactus had burned out. Only two arms were glowing in the bright afternoon sun.

"It'll all go out at this rate!" Irene cried as she stepped down hard on the accelerator. "Why, why, why Lottie Shady cain't turn that thing off, off, off, is what I wonder, wonder, wonder!"

They had just passed Catsy Ivanhoe's gate and private road.

"I cain't wait to see what Catsy Ivanhoe cooks up for this Homecomin'," Irene mused as they sped on toward Uncertain. "She's so competitive with Why-vonne it is pathetic."

"Competitive? With Yvonne?" Topsy was wondering what it would be like to compete with only one person. And only on a personal level. No hairbrushes. No Peanut Butter Cup parts. "What are they competing over?" she asked.

"Well, Why-vonne has got more money than Judas, Mary Jane."

Topsy blinked. Yvonne had made some reference to something like that on the phone, but she'd paid little attention. She wondered if that was why Bobby had married her? She wondered just how rich Yvonne was.

"How rich?" she asked, before she could stop herself. "How'd she get rich?"

"You know," Irene replied. "I wrote you all about it."

Stacks of mail she'd hurriedly scanned, piled up and sometimes never even opened at all, materialized in her head. Twenty years of details were just sitting in storage somewhere.

They were still two miles from the Chapel. On their right, the Flowers' shack came into view.

Yvonne's old home place looked worse than ever to Topsy. Heap after heap of tin cans surrounded the decrepit wooden shack like red ant mounds. The huge, towering oak tree had died. Only a stump marked its former existence. Beside the stump sat the disemboweled leftovers of some kind of a truck. Both the passenger compartment and the pickup bed were stuffed with stack after stack of old Crackerjack boxes. Two of the truck's flat tires had been placed under the porch to brace the steps. Endless litters of wild kittens lived in them. Mum Flowers used the third tire to pee through whenever he got tired of hitting his tin cans. The fourth tire was still on the truck.

In the middle of stickers, weeds, flat tires, broken hoses, abandoned machinery, tin cans, thirteen suspicious wildcats, and an endless supply of Crackerjacks, seven rocking chairs rocked, fourteen hands waved and each Flowers cried out as they recognized the midnight-blue 1957 Cadillac hearse riding down the road.

"Hidy, Irene!" yelled Petunia.

"Hidy, Irene!" shrieked Iris.

"Hidy, Irene!" shouted Rose.

"Hidy, Irene!" hollered Daisy.

"Hidy, Irene!" squealed Daffodil.

"Hidy, Irene!" screamed Poppy.

"Hidy, Irene!" gurgled Mum.

"Hidy, morons!" Irene called back, waving. She turned to Mary Jane and grinned. "They cain't hear me." She waved again. "Pore ole morons."

Why'd he marry a moron? Topsy's head cried. *Why, why, why did he marry a moron*?!

"I guess Why-vonne and Baby'll be back from Dallas tomorrow," Irene remarked.

They were heading toward the red light, past the Widders' trailer-made-house, past the fortune teller's tent, past the pony man's ponies.

"Baby?" Topsy asked. "Who's that?"

Irene gave her daughter a sharp look.

"Who's *Baby*?" she mocked. "You know who *Baby* is, Mary Jane. I wrote you all about *Baby*," she added pointedly.

"Oh," Topsy mumbled, digging her memory. She vaguely remembered something about a baby named Baby whose mother was probably one of her sisters. Hadn't she mated with the only Flowers male, like Yvonne's mother? "So what's Baby like?" she asked.

Irene looked at her daughter shrewdly. *I bet she's sittin' there visualizin' some sort of a pathetic, malformed, mongoloid idiot,* Irene thought to herself. For if Mary Jane Shady was seriously asking this question, it meant only one thing: her daughter had not read any of the letters Irene had written her. Their visits had been infrequent, their telephone conversations short, but Irene had consistently written Mary Jane long, detailed letters, none any less than twenty-five pages, at least twice a week for the past twenty years. She recalled the care she had taken detailing Baby's perfect, exquisite beauty. "Think of Ava Gardner playing Helen of Troy," is how Irene had put it in one of her missives.

"Oh, you remember Baby," Irene repeated, smiling sweetly. "I wrote you all about her." *And about nothin' else for the last several months*! Irene thought to herself.

Fake it, fake it, fake it, thought Topsy Dingo Wild Dog. "She just didn't sound that interesting," she heard herself say out loud.

"Mary Jane Shady!" Irene Shady cried, "Los Angeles, California and New York City have demented you!"

They screeched to a halt at the red light.

And there it was before her, the Uncertain Chapel of Memories, just as it was the day she left. The paint was still peeling. The stucco was still a faded, dusty pink. And it reminded her more than ever of the Alamo.

Irene Shady glared at the neon sign. She was mad as an old wet hen at her sister-in-law. She glared at her daughter. She was mad at her, too. *That little twit*, she said to herself. *Hightailin' off to parts unknown and never ever readin' my letters! And then when she finally shows up, here she comes lookin' like somethin' that just dropped out of a tree*! She turned back to glare at the light. *Well, that does it*! she promised herself. *I'll be durned tootin' if I'm tellin' Little Miss Thing sittin' next to me one more fascinatin' detail about what's been goin' on around here for the last twenty years*!

Topsy closed her eyes, bit her lip and cursed. Weak. She was weak. She'd already been on the verge of trying to find out more about Yvonne, more about Bobby, more about Baby. Why hadn't she read those damned letters! But they were so long, pages and pages of endless details. What they had for breakfast. What they ate for dinner. What they had for supper. Recipes and ingredients, and substitutions if you were out of something and didn't have time to go the store. And the funerals. Details of funerals and more funerals. Who came, who stayed longest, who stayed shortest, who never showed up at all. Who cried hardest, who didn't cry, who looked like they wanted to cry. Who sent flowers. What the arrangements looked like. How long the arrangements lasted. Lists of bizarre personal articles the bereaved tucked away in their loved ones' caskets. And so on and so forth and so forth and so on. And that's what she'd stored. That's what she thought she'd stored.

Not one single question, she promised herself. *You're not going to ask one single question that even remotely relates to Bobby Henderson. Ever.*

The light changed.

She took a deep breath. In another moment, she'd be standing exactly where Bobby Henderson had left her.

She closed her eyes.

But Irene Shady did not pull into the Uncertain Chapel of Memories. She made a sharp right when the light turned green and headed north on Farm to Market 18 toward town.

Topsy opened her eyes. On her left, they were passing Melogo Drive. House after house appeared before her, rectangular and fenced, shuttered and white.

. . . houses with no carnations . . .

Dream after dream reappeared and disappeared.

At the end of the block, she saw it. It moved slowly and deliberately toward her. To her horror it seemed to smile. And then, with a growl, it lunged for her window.

Topsy screamed.

The dog barked.

Irene Shady yelled.

"Good God, Mary Jane Shady," Irene Shady cried, pulling the car off the main road and careening onto a side street. "Annie Lovejoy is as good a hair setter as you'll find anywhere in Winkler County, and a danged sight better than whoever burned your tresses." She was parking the car in front of a white frame house with a sign which read:

> ANNIE LOVEJOY'S BEAUTY SHOPPE. SPECIALIZING IN COLORS, PERMS, SETS, SHAMPOOS, BLOW-DRYS, BAR-BE-QUE RIBS TO GO AND MANICURES BY APPOINTMENT ONLY. P.S. (the sign said in very small letters) *we don't do feet.*

"That dog almost got us!" Topsy cried. "Didn't you see that dog?"

"What dog?" Irene scoffed.

Topsy thought her heart would stop. "That dog that almost got us," she whispered.

"What dog? What dog? There wasn't any dog," Irene snapped impatiently. "Are you in the middle of some kind of a nervous breakdown or are you just tryin' to get out of doin' this?"

Topsy was shaking. She was shaking all over. "Didn't you see it?" she gasped. "You didn't see it?"

"Now, I'm sorry you're not takin' to this idea," Irene said, getting out of the hearse and slamming the door, "but I sure didn't think you'd scream at me about it and start makin' things up like a little baby." By now she was at the other side of the car and opening her daughter's door. "And you can stop carryin' on, too, and get out and come on and see if Annie can work you in."

Still shaking, Topsy got out of the car. Any moment, she expected the huge dark creature to come jumping out at her again. Exhausted, she slumped against the door of the hearse. Her eyes lit on Annie Lovejoy's sign. She shook her head in disbelief. Day before yesterday she had been in Elizabeth Arden's on Fifth Avenue. Today her mother was dragging her into Annie Lovejoy's garage.

People she knew would be inside. People who knew her. . . .

WELCOME HOME, TOPSY! She could hear them when they saw her. *WE ALWAYS KNEW YOU'D GO TO THE DOGS*!!!

CHAPTER THIRTY-FIVE

ANNIE LOVEJOY'S shop was bustling with activity. It was so crowded that Irene Shady could hardly open the screen door to pull Topsy inside. All five dryers were filled and blowing. Two black assistants were washing heads of hair in the back. A fat woman was getting a manicure over to the side. Behind the fat woman and the manicurist was a huge rotisserie with barbecued ribs revolving on it. The smell mixed with spray net and fingernail polish remover and hair coloring intermingled with an overwhelming aroma that Topsy immediately identified as "Jungle Gardenia" perfume. The sweet, heavy scent seemed to be coming from the fat lady's direction.

Dizzily, she heard voices humming the news of her arrival, as one by one each customer whispered and poked the person sitting next to her. One by one the plastic dryers flew back and shut off as the ladies in Annie Lovejoy's beauty shop leaned closer to get a better look. One shampoo girl haphazardly sprayed her client's face with cold water, while the other assistant vigorously applied a handful of Jergen's lotion into her customer's hair. Far in the back, two heads wheeled around at the exact same moment, and Annie Lovejoy gave a groan as her tray of clips and rollers hit the floor.

"Hidy, Irene!" bellowed the fat lady, waving two handfuls of wet magenta fingernails in the air. "Who's that stranger you got with you!"

"See?" Irene hissed under her breath to her daughter. "Even Kay Widders don't recognize you!"

"Oh, praise Sweet Baby Jesus you're here, Mary Jane!" squealed the fat lady. "I just don't believe it!"

I just don't believe it either. Topsy's head started to grind. She was seeing things for sure. Hallucinating. First the dog, now *this*. For sitting there in that fat lady's disguise was her old high school classmate, Kay Hobbs.

"Finally got her home," Irene smiled back at the fat lady. "She was so durned busy gettin' out of town, she didn't have time to get all fixed up. Hardly had time to get on her dress. It got all wrinkled on the flight. That's why she looks such a wreck. It's worse than goin' to China and back to get from there to here. We're goin' to get her all fixed up in no time—"

How did she fit herself into that little chair? wondered Topsy as she tried not to stare at the fat lady. *And how is she going to ever get out of it again*?

"Well, she's here and that's what counts!" the fat lady declared. "Don't worry about your hair," she told Topsy. "Annie Lovejoy does *wonders* with hair. In sixty minutes you'll be a different person!"

"That's what we're hopin'!" Irene assured Kay. "What a *horrible* trip! Plus, she hasn't stopped workin' since the day she left!"

Topsy squinted. Could it really be *Kay* behind those folds of flesh, that fluorescent eyeshadow, the purplish blush? Had Kay spent the past twenty years wrestling with chairs?

"Now listen, Mary Jane," the fat lady said. "Did Why-vonne get a-hold of you yet? It was *my* idea for you to crown the Queen and it was *her* idea for you to ride in the losers car in the parade—"

Losers car? Topsy nodded. *Okay*. She held herself erect and poised. *Here it comes . . .*

"Losers car?" Irene snorted. "She's not ridin' in any losers car."

"I mean the runners-up car!" Kay corrected excitedly. "For ever-body who didn't get to be Queen! You know, the attendants! We thought if Mary Jane rode in there with 'em maybe they'd forget about losin'! Havin' a Hollywood personality in the back seat is bound to cheer them up!"

"She's not ridin' in any losers car, I can tell you that right now," Irene Shady stated flatly. "She didn't fly ten thousand miles and change planes in Dallas and risk her life gettin' out of New York City to ride in on anything less than her very own float."

Change planes in Dallas? A new wave of anxiety swept over Topsy. *Did I change planes in Dallas*?

"New York City?" Kay asked, stunned. "You told me she lived in Hollywood!"

"No, I didn't," Irene replied. "I never said she lived in Hollywood. And I hope you arranged for a float."

Kay Widders stared at Topsy, puzzled. "Somebody led me to believe you live in Hollywood, Mary Jane." She turned to Irene. "I recommended that you get Orville Turner to put up that welcome home sign, Irene. And you know good and well I'm in no position to promise any kind of a float." She looked back at Topsy, perplexed. "Do you really live in New York City?"

"Maybe Why-vonne told you she lived in Hollywood," Irene replied irritably. "But she lives in Santa Monica when she lives in Los Angeles. Now it's too late for a welcome home sign, but this isn't the end of that float—"

"Santa Monica?" Kay frowned, growing more and more disappointed. "Where's *that*?"

Topsy's head reeled back, remembering when she had first decided to move to L.A. and become an actress all those years ago. At the time, she was reading *Berlin Stories* by Christopher Isherwood. She thought it was just about the finest book she had ever read. On the back flap of the book there was a picture of Mr. Isherwood and underneath it, it said that he lived in Santa Monica, California. Topsy remembered how reassuring that was at the time. Why, if Christopher Isherwood lived in California, then it couldn't be all that bad. She had wondered if Santa Monica was anywhere near Los Angeles and had hoped and prayed that it was.

She smiled wanly. For years now, she had kept a guest house in Santa Monica's Rustic Canyon. Christopher Isherwood had been her neighbor. They had taken walks together on the beach. She remembered the very first time she'd recognized him. He was leaning over the cookie counter at the Brentwood Mart. "Oh, Mr. Isherwood!" she had cried, "I just knew if you lived in California and Santa Monica was close to L.A., everything would be all right!"

She would never forget how he'd laughed. How she missed that laughter. *Wonder what he would have made of all this*? she wondered. "*Not even a paragraph*." She could almost hear him say it.

She giggled.

"What's so funny?" Kay asked, hurt. "Surely I'm not the only one who ever wondered where Santa Monica was."

"Mary Jane, *tell* Kay where Hollywood is," Irene Shady said.

"You said she lived *in* Hollywood, Irene," Kay Widders insisted, attempting to shift in her chair.

The theme song of the Class of 1965 had been "The Blob." Kay Hobbs had nominated it as a joke. And now look what had happened.

"No, I did not," Irene repeated. "I said she was *out* in Hollywood. She's got a little house by the ocean in Santa Monica and a hotel apartment in New York City across from that big park."

"You live in a hotel?" Kay shook her head, bewildered. "Why do you live in two places? Why don't you just move to Hollywood?" she asked innocently. "You might get better parts."

Topsy thought she heard her mother gasp.

"Oh, we just think the world of Miss Peanut Butter Cup!" Kay exclaimed effusively. "If only it just wasn't so short!"

"All commercials are short, Kay," Irene Shady said. "Anything longer wouldn't be a commercial—"

"And we just saw that picture you made where you died in a nightie in the hotel room bed last week on the midnight show," Kay babbled. "I told your mother how much we enjoyed hearin' you scream. Why didn't they let you *talk*?"

Chocolate and whipped cream, Topsy thought sadly. *This woman is the victim of chocolate and ice cream . . .*

"I told you that was an action picture, Kay," Irene Shady sighed. "Shot on location way up North."

Cake, pie, mashed potatoes, bread, M&M's . . .

"Didn't they make *that* in Hollywood?" Kay asked. "That picture with you and Dove Lightlady," Kay said. "I believe *she* got to talk."

Donuts. Chicken fried steak. Ice cream. Looking at Kay Widders was mesmerizing. *French toast. Gravy. Pecan pie.* She watched Kay's three chins, fascinated.

"Where'd they make it, Mary Jane?" Irene asked.

"What?"

"What?!" Irene echoed in frustration. "That show where you named Dove Lightlady? What in the world do you think we're talkin' about?"

"Burbank," Topsy murmured. *Dove Lightlady . . .* She wished she were Dove Lightlady. *Everybody loves Dove . . .*

"That's where Johnny Carson lives," Kay nodded. "Where *is* Burbank, anyway?" She looked around as if she might find it over her left shoulder.

"Mary Jane, tell Kay where Burbank is, for heaven's sakes!" Irene cried.

"Well, you don't have to say it like I'm some kind of a imbecile, Irene," Kay pouted, looking like a great big baby doll. She turned to Topsy and explained, "I have things to do right here in Uncertain, Texas that prevent me from keepin' up on the geographic location of each and every township in Southern California. Anyway, it's beginnin' to sound like a mess to me out there, is what it's beginnin' to sound like."

Kay. Kay. What happened, Kay? Topsy was thinking hard. The fat lady gave the manicurist her other hand and Topsy felt another claustrophobic wave of Jungle Gardenia. Or was it the repetition of the conversation? Or was it her hangover? She tried not to stare, but she could hardly help it. There was Kay, imprisoned in layer upon layer of fat. Little, lithe Kay, who had been a twirler three years in a row, then a cheerleader. Pretty pert Kay that all the boys had chased after. Silly, fun-loving Kay. She'd picked out "The Blob" and lived to define it.

"Mary Jane, tell Kay where Santa Monica is," Irene Shady was saying tiredly.

"I thought Hollywood was Hollywood," Kay sighed. "Excuse me for livin'."

Topsy wished her head were more clear. She wasn't up to explaining Los Angeles and when it was the City of Los Angeles or the County or something else. Marina Del Rey, Mar Vista, Pacific Palisades, Playa Del Ray, Topanga, Venice, Santa Monica, Brentwood, Westwood, Bel Air, Beverly Hills, Century City, West Hollywood, Hollywood Hills, Hollywood, L.A . . . .L.A. county or L.A.-L.A.? Toluca Lake, North Hollywood, Studio City, Encino, Sherman Oaks, Thousand Oaks, forget the Valley. Los Feliz, Silverlake, forget East L.A. Forget Inglewood, forget Hawthorne, forget Long Beach. Who cared? Forget La Mirada. She wanted to give her old chum a diet and wash her face. She wanted to hand her a head of lettuce, a copy of *Fit for Life*, a jar of Max Factor cold cream and the name of a good therapist.

Therapist? She rubbed her eyes, alarmed. She seemed to sort of vaguely remember stumbling around the Village and going over to Dr. Goldman's. But she couldn't remember seeing Dr. Goldman. She had a sickening suspicion that she'd seen *someone, confided* in someone and whoever it was had reacted with frightening and intense hostility. But she couldn't remember. She could not remember.

"Are you goin' to tell me where Burbank is now?" Kay was asking patiently.

An outbreak of recall plummeted through her head.

"*You mean no matter what happened to make me so distraught that I somehow ended up engaged in a dog entanglement, no matter what, you would still, always, give first consideration to the dog?*"

"*You're supposed to know what you're doing. A dog just obeys.*" *Who was that?*

"But what if I didn't KNOW *what I was doing?"*

"Then you should have thought about that! Did you go to your mother? Did you ask for help?" Who? Who? Who was that?

"Are you goin' to tell her where Burbank is?" Irene Shady demanded.

"I don't *know*!" Topsy snapped.

She looked into her mother's face. She shut her eyes. She thought she was going to faint.

"Mary Jane Shady, what in the world is goin' on with you?" Irene asked, giving her daughter a shake. "Of course you *know*!"

"I'm thinking," Topsy said. *Don't think*, she told herself. *Do not think*.

"She thinks too much," Irene told Kay Widders.

Topsy took a deep breath and told herself to get hold of herself. *You know what to do*. And, giving Kay that dazzling smile that made peanut butter eaters all over America love her, she proceeded to explain the entire structure of L.A. from Pasadena to Malibu in one and half minutes.

"Well," Kay nodded amiably as Topsy finished. "I'd have to get a map."

Irene Shady turned her back on the subject and picked up a copy of *Mademoiselle* magazine. It opened right up to a two-page layout of Dove Lightlady. She slammed the magazine shut and threw it back where she'd found it.

"Now listen, Mary Jane. I hope you intend to go ahead and crown the Queen, no matter what kind of vehicle you ride in on is all I can say," Kay said, concerned. "I wasn't countin' on any more problems. I got my hands full of problems as it is. If Catsy and Why-vonne wasn't so all-fired determined to outdo each other, I'd resign. But I feel like I have a obligation since I'm the only one on the whole entire committee who really and truly even graduated. Somebody responsible has got to see that some care is taken in the matter of the transportation. Your mother may want you to ride in on a float, but how she thinks you are goin' to do that when they cain't make paper flowers, is beyond me."

"Paper flowers?" Topsy repeated. "They can't make them?"

"No, they cannot," Kay said, shaking her head and her chins. "Irene, didn't you *tell* her about the paper flower ordeal?" Kay asked, flabbergasted. She turned to Irene's daughter, overwhelmed. "It's been a nightmare."

"I wrote her," Irene replied pointedly. "I wrote her all about the flowers and all the extra-curricular activities bein' cut back on account of overall bad grades in the State of Texas school system. But frankly, I expected an exception for Mary Jane."

"Well, it is just horrible, but I cain't do a thing about it," Kay said, attempting to cross one leg over another one.

Don't try that, Topsy wanted to say.

"School inn't like what it used to be like, Mary Jane," Kay explained.

She's going to pull that leg off, trying to cross it, Topsy worried.

"What does Sammy think?" Irene asked.

"Sammy?" Kay snorted. "Sammy don't think!"

Good, Topsy thought. *My kind of guy*. She looked at Kay and smiled. "You married Sammy—"

"You didn't know I married Sammy?" Kay asked surprised.

"Yvonne told me—" Topsy tried again.

"I wrote you," Irene chimed.

"I got my hands full, too," Kay continued.

"Really?" Topsy wondered if Sammy Widders was somehow responsible for all this weight. She wondered if he still smoked Camels. The son-of-a-bitch. She wondered if he had changed as much as Kay. She wondered if she would recognize him. She wondered if she had had a session with Dr. Goldman. She wondered who was the craziest person in the beauty shop right this minute.

"Well, sure, with the twins and all," Kay went on.

"Twins!" Topsy exclaimed. She didn't know much about kids. "How lovely!" *Are they fat, too? Is Sammy fat? Did you all get fat together*?

"Didn't you tell her I had twins?" Kay asked Irene.

"I wrote her," Irene said tightly.

"We're real proud of 'em." Kay smiled. "Well, one of 'em anyway. Morona is runnin' for Homecomin' Queen this year."

"That's wonderful," Topsy bubbled. *Well, one twin's thin. No such thing as a fat Homecoming Queen*.

"Not for Verona," Kay confided.

"Oh." *The fat twin*. "Sibling rivalry." Topsy nodded understandingly.

Kay frowned, confused. "I don't think they've had that yet."

Topsy was feeling worse and worse for the whole bunch. *Get off your judgmental, perfectionist highhorse,* she reprimanded herself. *They're just fat. There's nothing wrong with being fat. A lot of things are worse than being fat. And one of those twins is thin. Probably looks like Kay used to look. It could be a lot worse. Looks aren't everything, as you well know*!

"Well," Irene Shady said. "Won't Verona at least be an attendant?"

"Oh, sure," Kay nodded. "That's them over yonder that Annie Lovejoy is combin' out," Kay said to Topsy. "The one on the left is Morona and the one on the right is Verona. Looks just alike, don't they?"

Topsy directed her attention to where Kay indicated.

"Come on," Kay said. "They're dyin' to meet you." The manicure table wobbled precariously as she balanced her palms on top of it. She emerged like a whale surfacing water. The floor shook as she stood. The little chair hugged onto her bottom for a moment before crashing to the floor. She stepped right around it. "I'll innerduce you. You go first."

Topsy moved obediently and carefully in front of her.

"Naw, naw, naw," Verona and Morona Widders were saying to Annie Lovejoy simultaneously.

Topsy's eyes grew wide. She just stood there and stared.

"That hair," Verona instructed, drawing a random, imaginary line across the extended and uninterrupted stem that connected her head to her sister's, "*that hair*," she repeated, pointing to the far side of the line, "is *her* hair."

"And *this* hair," Morona said, pointing to the side nearest her, "is *my* hair."

"They're Uncertain's only Siamese twins," Kay Widders declared proudly.

"You know *her* hair from *my* hair, Annie Lovejoy," Verona went on. "Cain't you even make a part right?"

"Well, it's hard to do two heads at once with ya'll wigglin' around like you do," Annie mumbled, looking up. "Hidy, Kay. Your nails dry?" Annie asked, trying to work her way in between the twins' heads. "I'll be through with 'em in about twenty minutes. How you doin', Mary Jane?"

"Jesus Christ," Topsy whispered.

"Well, what's the matter?" Irene Shady whispered into her daughter's ear. "Don't they have Siamese twins in New York City?"

Two sets of eyes gazed at Miss Peanut Butter Cup in star-struck awe.

"Looks like Sammy, don't they?" Kay Widders stated.

"Hold still," said Annie Lovejoy.

"Ouch!" whined Morona.

"Ow!" griped Verona.

"Well, you just ruined the part, Verona," Kay said to her daughter, "jerking ya'll's heads like that."

"I don't yank *your* head, Verona," Morona sniveled.

"I want to look at that movie star!" Verona swatted at her sister as if she were a fly. "Move!"

"This here is an ole friend of mine and Daddy's, girls," Kay said. "Miss Mary Jane Shady—"

"— known all over America as the Peanut Butter Queen," Irene interrupted proudly.

"Well," Verona declared flatly, as she and her twin ran up and down Topsy with their eyes, "you sure don't look like her. But I recognize the dress."

"Verona!" Morona squealed. "Sh-h-h-h!"

"See?" Irene said to her daughter. "That's the second person who didn't know you. You cain't get under that wash bowl a minute too soon!"

"I recognize you," Morona giggled. "From hanging off that barbed wire and gettin' stung by them scorpions and beaten up by that big ole giant baby doll."

"Oh, yeah," Verona nodded. Morona's head nodded with her twin's. "I recognize her from *that*. But that's not Butter Cup's hair-do. Butter Cup would never wear her hair like *that*—"

"Whatever," Kay said "Anyway, Mary Jane, the one with the comb is Annie Lovejoy, the beauty operator, and—"

"—the one with two heads is us!" Verona growled.

"Don't mind her," Kay explained tiredly. "She just does that for attention."

"I do not," Verona countered. "I get all the attention I need, thanks to *her*." She poked Morona in the ribs.

"Ow! Mama, make her stop!" Morona howled.

"Ya'll be still," Annie Lovejoy pleaded.

"Yeah, ya'll be still," Kay repeated. "Is this any way to act in front of a movie star?" She shook her finger into their faces. "I'll be back in twenty minutes and ya'll better be ready." She turned to Topsy. "I got to go to the cleaners before it closes. We cain't wait 'til the last minute to make sure they altered them dresses right for tomorrow's crowning."

The crowning? Topsy considered this vision with dismay.

"Believe me, alterations is just one problem," Kay Widders said.

Topsy certainly was glad she hadn't gotten serious with Sammy Widders. Or maybe it was Kay's side. She shuddered and giggled all at the same time. *Feeling superior*? a little voice asked. *Laugh on, dog fucker*.

"She wouldn't know anyway, Kay," Irene Shady remarked, giving her daughter a sharp look. "She don't have no kids."

"You got time," Annie Lovejoy said as she studied the part in Verona and Morona Widders' hair. "Anyway, you got a boyfriend. Your mama told me that. Said you was goin' with Herman Top. Maybe he'll turn out to be a husband, even if he is a Jew."

The entire beauty shop fell silent.

Kay Widders stopped dead in her tracks, sending rolls of fat cascading like a landslide.

There it goes, thought Topsy. *The San Andreas Fault*. She watched Kay ripple. *Banana pudding? Rice pudding? Pork chops? Fried okra, fried potatoes, fried pie?*

"You're goin' with a *Jew*?" Kay was asking incredulously. "God will put you in hell for that, Mary Jane. You will burn right up forever."

Casseroles! thought Topsy Dingo Wild Dog. *Two sticks of butter, a can of cream of mushroom soup—*

Verona and Morona turned their heads around and stared at Topsy. "What's a *Jew*, Mama?" they asked.

"Christ-killers, girls," Kay Widders replied. "Don't they teach ya'll nothin' at Sunday School? I always told ya'll there's worse things in this world than bein' hooked together at the head, and bein' responsible for the death of Jesus Christ Our Lord is one of 'em. I don't know how you can live with yourself, Mary Jane. Whatever possessed you to put your eternity in such a fatal position?"

Cream. Ice cream. Whipped cream. Everything but cold cream—

Without waiting further for an answer, Kay went out the door.

"Does that mean you won't fix her hair, Annie?" Morona asked Annie Lovejoy curiously.

Irene frowned at Annie irritably. She could have bitten Annie's tongue off for letting that information out.

"Naw. I'm not religious," Annie replied without looking up. "Ya'll turn ya'll's heads back around," she said to the twins, "and I'm goin' to step up on this little stool here and try this from a different angle."

"Mary Jane Shady?" asked Verona Widders. "What *color* is a Jew?"

"Well," Irene Shady said to Topsy Dingo Wild Dog, "you may have just knocked yourself out of ridin' in on a float."

"*Well,*" said a voice to Topsy that sounded like Christopher Isherwood's. "*Still wondering who's the craziest person in this little room*?"

CHAPTER THIRTY-SIX

"IT'S JUST UNREAL," Topsy said to her mother as they got into the hearse and drove away from the beauty shop. She shook her head in disbelief. She thought how she was just sitting there in that car, shaking *one* head. *Her* head. Those twins would always be nodding together, shaking together. The words of that song, "Together, Forever, Forever, Together" drifted through her mind. *Oh it's just awful*! she thought. *Wonder what in the world Kay thought when they presented her with Siamese twins? No, WONDER she's so fat. I would never let another man touch me as long as I lived if that was the result! Poor Kay. Poor Sammy. Poor twins . . .* She sighed. "I just don't believe it. It's unreal—"

Topsy's mother glared ahead as they approached the Uncertain Chapel of Memories and its still lit neon sign. She was mad at Annie Lovejoy and mad at Kay Widders and now she was working herself into a dither, getting ready to face off with her sister-in-law. "If you want reality, then go to a movie!" Irene spat. She hurled the steering wheel to the right and pulled into the funeral parlor's driveway. "We are goin' to have an electric bill to beat the band!" she complained, glaring up at the neon sign. "Would you look at that cactus arm? The whole limb is dead. And who do you think is responsible for that, I wonder?"

Mary Jane shook her head again. *My head . . . One head . . .* "I guess it just wasn't possible to separate them at birth—"

"Separate them at birth?!" Irene cried. "Why in the world would they do *that*? Why, those twins have an annuity for life!"

"What?" Topsy blinked.

"Well, look on the bright side, Mary Jane," Irene admonished. "This way they can go join a circus and maybe get their own private tent. They can spend the winter in Florida with Ringling, Bailey and

Barnum, and have all those animals and little midgets to play with. They got it made! If they'd a-been cut up, they couldn't do that! There's just not much of a life for a ex-Siamese twin, any way you look at it. This way they can go on the road for life and always be in the company of *interesting and unusual* people that they have lots of things in common with. Now what more could anybody want!" She turned off the engine, slammed the door and stormed into the funeral parlor.

Topsy watched her mother disappear.

She got out of the car. She shut the door. She walked toward the portico. She stopped. Her head felt like a bucket of worms, crawly and slimy. She was sure if her head opened up, jillions of watery worms would spew out. She started to shake, wet with icy sweat. She couldn't breathe. She couldn't move. She looked down.

She was standing on the spot.

She stared at the spot where Bobby Henderson had left her. She looked around.

"I'd say it's about fifty yards to the highway, seventy-five to the red light," she said softly to no one. "A quarter of a mile to the ponyman, maybe." She glanced at the portico. "Seven steps and a front door home."

She stared at the spot once more. *I never left this spot.* She looked up at the sky. The sun was setting in the west and the moon was rising in the east. *I've been standing in the same place for twenty fucking years*! She looked at the highway beyond. *I thought I went somewhere and I didn't even budge.*

The comprehension of what had not happened was overwhelming, the delusion that she had left all this behind her, devastating.

She wanted to curse Bobby Henderson, but she didn't. She wanted to hate Bobby Henderson, but she couldn't. And as that started to sink in, something really strange happened. A feeling so bizarre began to emerge that her only wish was not to define it. But still, it came, and she could not hold it back.

What is this I'm feeling? she wondered anxiously, looking back and forth from the sun to the moon. *And why are they both up there at the same time*? She wanted to shake them down like a bunch of old cobwebs.

And then it hit her. She knew it when she felt it and she was feeling it all over.

"Oh-h-h-h . . ." she moaned. "God help me . . ." She started to laugh and she started to cry. She stood on the spot, giggling at the sun, bawling at the moon. "I haven't changed a bit!" she told the mellow, golden ball. "I haven't changed at *all*!" she cried out to the silver shining slice. "Oh-h-h-h!" she hollered as the neon sign suddenly went completely out. "I AM CRAZY!" She stomped the ground she was standing on and kicked the hearse. "I AM CRAZY, NUTS, INSANE, MAD AND PERMANENTLY DERANGED!" She gave a cheerleader leap, flew into the air, and landed in a heap, clawing the spot where he'd dumped her.

"I've missed him!" It came out of her like vomit. She pounded her fists until they were bleeding. "I can't wait to see him!" She kissed the ground fervidly. "I can't wait, you son-of-a-bitch! I want you so bad I don't know what to do!" Rocks, dirt, weeds received her savage embrace.

The words to the song plummeted through her brain:

We were ridin' down the dirt road
After a six-pack picture show . . .
It had just been oiled the day before
I asked him please drive slow . . .
'Cause if I was gonna put my head down
Underneath that steerin' wheel . . .
I didn't want a broken neck to interrupt my meal . . .
To the rhythm of the oil pump
My heart was beatin' wild . . .
I felt just like a bluebonnet
Tumbleweed prairie child . . .
When he painted me with his tongue
Like I was a piece of art . . .
That is when my friend
He touched the clitoris of my heart . . .

"H-E-A-A-A-A-A-R-R-R-T-T-T!" screamed Topsy Dingo Wild Dog, throwing her arms up to the sun, the moon and out toward the Texas highway. "I miss having a heart! I want some heart!" She shot up from the spot and stomped wildly around the hearse. She was burning up all over. Bolt after bolt of electrical bright hot heat shot through her.

"Goddamn you, Bobby! Goddamn you!"

She jerked the dickey off of her Peanut Butter Cup dress and threw it into the air. "Take it!" she cried. "Take it, you bastard! Come here and get it!"

Breathless and panting, grinning deliriously, she collapsed against the hearse. *Oh, boy, I'm nuts . . . I'm really raving . . . I've gone over the edge, no kidding, oh, my God, I can't wait to see him . . . I can't, I can't, I can't . . .*

She grabbed the dickey and tried to attach it, not noticing she'd jerked off some snaps when she'd thrown it in the air. Fumbling, she looked down at the dickey she was holding against her throat. Part of the fabric fell through her fingers.

"Oh, well," she sighed, intending to thrust the dickey into her pocket. "I'm just as crazy as can be, crazy, crazy, crazy . . ." Something crimson caught her eye. A rash. She pulled back her neckline.

"Oh, *shit*," she gasped. The dickey fell from her hands.

She stared at her chest in wonder. Half a heart stared back at her.

"I've been *branded*!" she whispered, in shock.

"Mary Jane!" called Irene Shady from the front door. "Are you goin' to come in or what? We've got company in here. Somebody's come to visit you and they're in here waitin', and wonderin' if you're ever goin' to come home."

Bobby! He was waiting for her inside! She knew it!

Frantically, she snatched the dickey from the ground, hastily attached it to the remaining snaps, tucked the fabric inside her neckline and ran up the steps. She hurled into the foyer where she found herself face to face with five cardboard blown-up versions of who she was supposed to be. A burst of hysterical laughter erupted from her throat like lava from a volcano.

"Oh, goody!" she cried, maniacally kissing each perfect, smiling trouble-free face. "My better halves!"

She spun around, tingling with frenzied anticipation.

"Here she is!" Irene Shady announced proudly. "The real thing!"

CHAPTER THIRTY-SEVEN

"OH, I wish I'd had a camera!" Gladys Turner cooed, approaching Topsy open armed and smiling. "I'd have loved to have snapped her up when she first stepped in the house, the minute she walked in the door, the exact second she appeared and kissed all five blown-up versions of herself first thing!"

Topsy glanced around, agitated. *Idiot. Fool. Jerk. Perversion junkie.* How had she let herself get all caught up in a setting sun and half a mooned beam? She anxiously fingered her crumpled dickey and nervously rubbed her half-hearted heart. *A tattoo*?! She sure didn't want to remember where that had come from. She didn't want to know where that sudden, overwhelming, intense *longing* for Bobby Henderson had come from either. She was in the midst of a really serious hangover, that was for sure. The kind where bad things look good and good things look bad. She could feel Gladys Turner's fifth-grade-teacher eyes all over her, inspecting her from tip to toe. She felt dizzy and nauseated, depressed and exhausted, confused and angry. She needed a bath and something to eat. She needed to sleep. She wanted to see him.

"But no!" Gladys beamed, advancing. "I unfortunately have no camera on me and now Mary Jane's re-entry into Uncertain will be lost except in my memory bank, and hers and in her mother's!"

What lives in my head lives forever, Topsy thought forlornly. She watched Gladys move in on her helplessly. She could smell Gladys' damp, faint body odor, the slight sharp smell that cut right through every effort of Ban, Mitchum's, Roll-Aid and starch, Ivory soap and Lysol room deodorizer. Gladys had a problem even greater than being a fifth grade school teacher. She changed clothes three times a day and more if she had a chance, but still, she smelled like old clothes that had been left out in the rain and mildewed.

Turning her head to avoid Gladys' fleshy lips, Topsy stared at the room in shock. Every picture frame and available wall space was filled with one horrible memento after another of her pathetic and failed career. She turned her back on *Slave of the Scorpions* only to face *Reckless Return of Baby Doll.* The titles seemed prophetic. Her life was turning into one great big grade B nightmare.

Topsy caught her breath as Gladys' musty arms enfolded her.

"Ow-w-w-w, look at that hair!" Gladys observed, as if admiring a painting. "Isn't it shiny and pretty and *thick*!" she exclaimed, and like a child in a museum, who just has to reach out and feel what it's drawn to, Gladys dug her fingers into Topsy's hair and ran her fingers right through it, pulling on the sprayed strands with a hearty tug. "Would you look at that thick, thick hair, Irene," Gladys directed. "Now she didn't get that from you—"

Topsy winced with pain.

"Well, for God's sakes, Gladys, don't pull it out!" Irene cried, giving Gladys' fingers a smart slap. "I paid seven-fifty for that coiffure, not exactly a bargain! 'Course Annie earns her money. She had her work cut out for her. I don't know what they think they're doin' with *hair* up in New York City, but I'm never gettin' a permanent there, is all I can say! Now listen, Gladys, about these floats—"

"Just as perfect as her pictures," Gladys smiled, patting Topsy's cheeks.

Topsy felt her cheeks smarting.

"Quit that, Gladys," Irene said. "Stop pawing on her."

"Just as young and unlined and *white.*" Gladys sat down in the closest chair and began to make herself comfortable. "Why-vonne Henderson called long distance for you from some dressing room in Dallas, Mary Jane, where she was tryin' on clothes. She said she wanted to make sure you got here all right—"

"Did she say M.J.'s riding in the losers car, Gladys?" Irene interrupted.

"Well, I just let myself in the back door like I always do when nobody is here, and I knew nobody was here, because the sign was on in the daytime," Gladys continued. "But I saw ya'll pull in just as Why-vonne called, so I assured her that you had arrived. She says she's starting back just as soon as they unroll her hair. You know she wears *wigs,*" Gladys confided in a whisper. "To cover up that *bald* spot," she added, nodding.

"Gladys," Irene said. "Did Why-vonne mention any float?"

"Let me think . . ." said Gladys.

"I'll watch you try," muttered Irene Shady.

Topsy looked at Gladys' hair and wondered if Yvonne's hair could possibly be thinner than her mother's best friend's. What was left of Gladys Turner's hair lay in gray flat strands which she combed across her head like a disguise. Balding antique dealers, old actors, vain ministers, fading politicians and Gladys Turner all combed their last strands this way.

"Oh!" Gladys beamed, remembering. "She says she'll come right over the minute she lands!" Then she added, "She didn't mention a float, Irene."

"Did she buy anything for Baby?" Irene asked.

"Baby?" Gladys repeated, surprised. "Is she talking to Baby?" She was taking off her shoes.

"Never mind, Gladys. And put your shoes back on. It's not time to relax yet. I need you to help me empty out the car."

"Oh, I'm not supposed to *lift,*" Gladys protested. "It's my calloused fingers," she explained to Topsy. "From grading papers." She shook her head emphatically. "I just couldn't lift a thing. Besides," she reminded Irene Shady sweetly, "Please don't forget I'm in *mourning.* I shouldn't even be here. I'm supposed to be *grieving.*"

"I'm sorry about your sister," Topsy said quickly. A confrontation was coming. Topsy could see it coming. It made her skin itch. She longed to undress and lie down. She wanted a closer look at that heart. Maybe it was just red ink. Surely she would have remembered getting a *tattoo.* She rubbed her throbbing head. It had hurt when Gladys pulled on her hair. It had hurt before Gladys even touched her.

"Wasn't that something?" Gladys asked, eagerly responding to the sympathy. "That's what a death wish will do for you."

"I didn't know that's what she died of," Irene remarked, motioning for Topsy to follow her to the hearse. "I thought she died of cancer."

She marched out to the driveway where she opened the end of the hearse and loaded two sacks of groceries into her daughter's arms.

Gladys traipsed behind them and watched. "A tumor in her breast that spread up and down her arms and into her head," Gladys explained, observing Topsy balance the bags.

"That's cancer," Irene said, shoving her overnight case and a hanging garment bag into her daughter's arms.

"Well, it didn't have to be," Gladys continued. "What happened was —"

"What happened to the 'Welcome Home, Mary Jane Shady' sign, Gladys?" Irene asked. "I thought Kay said Orville was sending some kids over to make up a sign out front."

"Orville is in *mourning,* Irene. He didn't even go to work today. Our whole *family* is *grieving.* You know that," Gladys retorted emphatically as she turned to go inside. "Death is the only thing that could keep Orville Turner out of his office, especially with this Homecoming upon us, and if God had ever been the Superintendent of the Uncertain Public School System in the State of Texas, I'm sure He would have taken her *another time,* but God's God and Orville's Orville, and today Orville is *struck numb with grief, sadness and mourn-*

ing, just like me." Daintily, she took the hanging bag, as Topsy struggled with the groceries and overnight case.

"I hope he recovers by tomorrow," Irene mused drily.

"You went to the store?" Gladys asked Irene, ignoring her last remark. "When did you go to the store? I thought you said you went with her to the beauty shop."

"While she was under the dryer," Irene replied, watching Gladys poke around in one of the grocery sacks her daughter was holding. "I figgered eventually *somebody* would get hungry."

"Oh, I haven't eaten for two days," Gladys nodded pitifully. "I hope you got something good. I think maybe I could finally use something to eat right about now. Did you get anything sweet?"

Irene rolled her eyes and handed Gladys the only thing her daughter had arrived with: her purse. "Here. Work up your appetite on the way upstairs and take this to the south room." She slammed the rear door of the hearse.

"The south room?" Topsy asked. "But my room's the north room."

"Not anymore. I switched."

"What?" Topsy followed her mother inside like a puppy. "You switched my room?" Now that she was back, it seemed important.

"'Bout ten years ago. Stop followin' so close, M.J. You're about to step on my heels."

"She was just wanting to die—" Gladys said, empty-handed from the doorway. She had hung the garment bag and the purse on the cardboard hands of the first two life-sized figures in the foyer.

"Excuse me," said Topsy Dingo Wild Dog to the life-sized Mary Jane Shadys as she retrieved the garment bag and purse.

"Excuse me," said Irene Shady to Gladys Turner. She swiftly shoved both sacks into the school teacher's arms.

"Irene, this is about to kill my fingers!" Gladys protested.

"You better hurry to the kitchen, then," Irene said.

Gladys hastily disappeared, talking all the way. "She had a clear-cut choice. She could have had just the tumor—they said they could have frozen it and given her chemotherapy and maybe it would have shrunk even—"

"Leave it to God to strike Gladys numb but not dumb," Irene muttered, starting up the stairs.

"Why did you change my room?" Topsy demanded, following her mother past stills of *Don't Look in the Incinerator.* "You didn't say a word to me about changing my room." She tried not to look at the posters and photos, but Irene Shady stopped right in front of a color shot of her in *Poor White Trash, Part II.* She was dead in the picture. Hanging from a tree.

"Your old room is easier to move supplies into. That's why I changed. It was nothin' personal. I wasn't creatin' a vendetta, if that's what you think." Irene took the garment bag and overnight case from her daughter and left her standing with her purse. "Anyway, fifteen years ago I wrote you and wrote you repeatedly about it and you never answered, even when I asked you on the phone—you just lit off into another subject, like your ole room was bottom slot on the totem pole, so I gave it another five years and just did what I wanted to do. You never came back here anyway." She turned and disappeared into the Uncertain Chapel of Memories' frontview honeymoon suite.

Topsy walked slowly down the hall. The door to the north room was shut, but the door to her new room stood open. She walked into the south room.

Her mother had meticulously placed everything in the exact same way. Instead of facing Melogo Drive, she now looked out over the old Farm to Market Highway, but her four poster bed still wore the same eyelet covering. Her daddy's little oak radio still sat on the bedside table. A copy of her high school annual, *The Yellow Jacket,* from her senior year, still sat beside it. A locked diary, a small white Bible, (the King James version with "Mary Jane Shady" engraved in gold letters), and her favorite book from childhood, *The Velveteen Rabbit,* the one her father had read to her over and over, were still stacked neatly to the side. On her dresser was a mirrored tray containing a set of tortoise haircombs. They had belonged to Aunt Lottie, and before that, to her father's mother. She had pleaded for those combs her entire childhood. Aunt Lottie had finally given them to her for graduation. And she hadn't thought of them since. She had just gone off and left them and never given them or anything else in this room another thought. Until now.

She picked up the combs and started to draw one through her hair, which was stuck, brittle and dried together with spray net. She looked into the dresser's oval mirror and stared at the bizarre image confronting her. Her hair was shaped like a cone. She hadn't even looked when Annie Lovejoy had finished with her, or if she had she didn't remember. Kay Widders and those twins had completely distracted her. She pressed down on the cone and it sprang right back.

Her reflection was shocking.

She looked old, as old as somebody's mother. Depressed, she knew that she *was* old enough to be somebody's mother. She could be those twins' mother. She could have had a whole family. But no, what had she done? Arranged her life so that twenty years later here she was, jumping up and down out in the driveway like *she* was still some teenager. Eating dirt. *Don't let anyone see you acting like that, asshole,* she told herself. *It's bad enough that you're here at all, wearing this shitty Peanut Butter Cup garb and a stupid cone hairdo and trying to act like you're only twenty-eight and never fucked a dog and don't have a tattoo . . .*

"They said they could have shrunk it!" Gladys hollered as she climbed up the stairs. "But Evelyn was the type never could make up her mind about anything or not—" She stopped halfway up to catch her breath.

"What are you sayin', Gladys?" Irene screeched. "Cain't you *wait* one minute please? Are you tryin' to tell us she didn't know if she wanted it shrunk or what?"

"Well, that wasn't it exactly. . . " Gladys huffed and puffed as she came up the steps.

"Oh, let's go downstairs!" Irene cried wickedly as Gladys finally reached the top.

"I will in a minute," Gladys panted. "I just want to tell you how Gladys got cancer. . . "

"She's already dead. Cain't it wait 'til we've had a cup of coffee?" Irene asked. Over and over again it hit her how mad she was at Gladys for sending her sister to Deal Grimes. She had no interest in a corpse she hadn't serviced. And here Gladys was literally following her up the stairs to tell her more about her dead sister than any uninvolved undertaker would ever want to know. "Where are you, Mary Jane?" Irene called out. "I don't want to have to hear this twice!" Irene wished someone would ask her about *her* problems. Mary Jane didn't even have a welcoming home sign, much less a float!

Topsy walked into her mother's room and stared out the windows. She was very, very tired. "Does that palm reader still live over there?" she asked, looking past the pony man's pony, to the fortune teller's tent.

"Oh, yeah. Nothin' changed, hon." Irene folded up the garment bag she'd removed from her clothes.

"You changed *her* room," Gladys pointed out.

"Just from one side to another. No one knocked down walls or leveled the place like the doctor's current wife over on Melogo."

"Leveled it . . . " Topsy repeated wearily. She wished she were interested.

"Total," said Gladys. "The first wife had built it. Then the second wife repainted it. The third wife remodeled it, but number four just got a bulldozer, plowed it down and started from scratch from the ground up. Said she wasn't about to live in a house that four other women had called 'home' before her. Moved her and Doctor over to the Hoop and Holler Motel until the job was complete."

"I wrote you that," said Irene.

"Oh," said Topsy. Her head felt sluggish and heavy. She made herself try to listen. She wished she knew how anyone just tore down something worn out, but familiar, and simply started all over from scratch.

"She's an ex-show girl from Las Vegas and she's got her own ideas about style," Gladys said emphatically, plopping down on Irene's bed and gazing out the window.

"You're givin' her too much credit, Gladys." Irene frowned as she watched Gladys rumple her covers.

"Oh, no," Gladys moaned, peering outside. "Scoot's car just pulled up over at the Widders' place. She'll be over here next."

"Good," Irene declared. "I just love Scoot Widders."

"I don't know how we're goin' to live with her if those twins get to be Homecomin' Queen," Gladys fussed.

"I think those twins are the greatest thing that could happen to a Homecomin'," Irene replied. "I wish we had a set runnin' ever year."

"It's embarrassing me half to death," Gladys complained. "I don't care what they say, this is one case where two heads are *not* better than one!" Gladys turned to Topsy for sympathy. "Poor Orville has enough troubles running Uncertain High School as it is. He's been worried for days what he's going to say in his speech if those Siamese twins are named Homecoming Queen. In thirty years as Superintendent of Schools, my husband has never had a problem like this one, believe you me."

"I hope he's savin' some of his speech for *Mary Jane,*" Irene stated emphatically. "She hadn't come here and dragged half of New York City with her to be ignored, Gladys."

"Ignored!" Gladys cried. "Of course not! And if I hadn't had a woman with a death wish and a funeral as a result of it, you would have seen a welcoming home sign as big as life out in your front yard, Mary Jane! I came over here myself, mourning state that I'm in aside, just to let you know that we're planning to display you prominently in the festivities!"

"Well, you better display her on her own float, is all I can say," Irene said.

"Oh, Irene, please!" Gladys cried. "I hardly got to enjoy my own sister's funeral with you running down the aisle and whispering in my ear all through the service to get Mary Jane a welcome home sign and get Mary Jane a great big float! You know we can't have floats! The State of Texas is responsible for the paper flower ordeal, not me!"

Topsy gazed across the highway. It was beginning to get dark. She wondered if she had married Bobby, would they have children now?

Irene Shady glared at Gladys Turner. "Maybe if we had better *teachers,* our kids would make their grades and then we'd have our floats."

A nurse in a starched white uniform walked into Topsy's head. In her arms was a blanketed bundle. Cries and whimpers and little moans and groans exuded from the bundle . . .

"When's the last time you taught school, Irene?" Gladys replied sarcastically.

Topsy reached out for the bundle . . .

"I can handle heathens," Irene claimed.

"What is it?" she asked the nurse. "What did I have? I didn't have Siamese twins, did I?" . . .

"Sure! Dead ones!" Gladys cried. "You work on dead people all day long! Who's going to give you any problems if they're dead?"

The nurse handed over the bundle. Hundreds of puppies slithered out toward her, black and shiny and wet. They crawled upon the bed beside her, circling her, pawing her, licking her wrists and neck and breasts . . .

"Relatives!" Irene hollered.

"Look at that!" the nurse observed. "*You have birthed a litter of puppies! . . .*"

"Now wait a minute," Gladys interrupted. "Are you trying to change the subject or what? I was going to tell you about Evelyn's death wish, and somehow you have yanked this whole thing around to criticize me and my job. Orville and I work like dogs, I'll have you to know!"

Horrified, Topsy cringed. Puppies . . .

"Dogs . . . ." shuddered Topsy Dingo Wild Dog.

"That's right," Gladys nodded. "We work like two dogs! You have no idea the things Orville and I have missed out on in life by just working as hard as we do."

"Gladys, the only thing that's missin' is a big pot of coffee and if you'll just follow me downstairs, I'll put it on and we will all devote ourselves to your sister's demise. Okay?" Gladys Turner was about to wear Irene Shady out.

Let's drink to my litter, thought Topsy grimly. *I'll drink to that.*

"Oh, the coffee's made," Gladys smiled, standing up, victorious. "That's why I came on over. I thought I'd have it ready for you when you got home. It's not every day that Mary Jane Shady comes back to Uncertain, Texas!" she sang as she disappeared down the stairs and into the kitchen.

"Well, you're actin' like it is!" Irene called after her.

She watched Gladys' head and thinning hair vanish through the bannister. "She just walks in and takes over, just like it was her own home," Irene muttered as she straightened up her bed and smoothed out the covers.

"She's your best friend and has been for thirty years," Topsy Dingo Wild Dog said, exhausted.

Irene puffed up her pillows and hurled them on the bed. "That don't mean I like her!" Irene retorted as she stomped down the stairs.

CHAPTER THIRTY-EIGHT

IT HAD BEEN just past noon when the white limousine Yvonne Henderson had hired to meet her at Love Field in Dallas, Texas, pulled up in front of Odette Lumière's, Yvonne's favorite store in the world.

The driver had anxiously jumped out and hurriedly opened the limousine's door for Yvonne. He needn't have rushed. As intent as Yvonne was on getting inside to shop, she certainly didn't want to make an appearance at Odette Lumière's without a fresh face of make-up, so as they pulled up, Yvonne reached for her Carlos Falchi rainbow-pasteled leather and canvas tote, brought forth a cache of cosmetics, and for five minutes, proceeded to groom herself with various and sundry powder puffs, lipstick brushes and mascara wands.

Baby Flowers stared in wonder through the limousine's tinted glass windows at the store's soaring double gold doors implanted with towering, sparkling, beveled, etched glass. Fascinated, Baby gazed into the shining sundrenched windows running on either side of the doors. Like Christmas boxes opened at one end to invite glimpses of promised magic, each window was filled with groups of splendidly attired ladies, each silent and attentive, gracefully posed in delicious expectation, each serenely waiting, all calm in their assurance that some wonderful exquisite thing was about to happen. Not one lady moved. Not one lady spoke. Each looked like an angel on top of a Christmas tree.

Baby stared and stared, taking no notice of Yvonne, who chattered away to the driver as she dumped her make-up back into her tote bag.

"I'll be ready when you see me," Yvonne told the driver. She extended her hand and cueing him to help her, grabbed his arm and wiggled out of the car.

Baby followed, moving trancelike toward the windows, toward the quiet luscious ladies, toward the mystery and magic. She didn't stop moving until her nose was pressed flat against the glass.

"Bay-beee!" Yvonne screeched, yanking her half-sister-cousin away from the window, "Get your snotty nose off that window and listen to me!" She wheeled Baby around toward her. "If you don't act right I'm sendin' you back to the car, hear? I mean if you touch *one* thing, you are out of here, hear? This is a classy place inside there! They're used to people like me, so just act like *I* do, only don't *touch* nothin' and don't say nothin'! And don't you dare do anything to *embarrass* me neither, and I'm talkin' about like takin' all your clothes off! If I catch you nekked, I'll send you to Sing Sing and throw away the key, do you understand, you retarded moron white trash idiot?!"

Baby's large emerald eyes gazed back at Yvonne in silent obedience. She sure didn't want to sit in the car. She wanted to see what was inside those gold doors. She wanted to look at more of those splendidly decorated, peacefully still, Christmas angel ladies who lived in the Christmas boxes.

A tall black man in a tall black suit thrust open the doors with an encouraging warm smile. "Good afternoon, ladies," he said, stepping aside so they could enter.

Baby Flowers followed her half-sister-cousin through the magic gold doors and gasped in delight.

Flowers, real flowers in magnificent crystal vases sat everywhere. Woven carpets covered the floor. Thickly textured with pale pink, soft red and muted yellow roses, the flowers on the carpets matched the real ones in the vases. Baby would have been on her hands and knees trying to smell the petals if she hadn't been totally consumed in taking in the walls.

Flying clothes leapt from the walls. Bejeweled and feathered, knitted and woven, spun and fringed, garments flew through the air like splendid goddesses sweeping over the moon.

Mesmerized, Baby glided through the salon, transported by the fragrance and richness and beauty of haute couture.

"Parts Unknown," murmured Baby Flowers. "It's Parts Unknown . . ."

"C'mon, Baby," Baby heard Yvonne say in a strange soft sweet voice she had never heard before. "We don't want me to be late for my beauty shop appointment, now, do we?"

Like a child in a magic castle, Baby Flowers followed her half-sister-cousin into heaven and through rooms filled with treasures beyond her wildest imagination. Cases of gold and silver bracelets, necklaces, earrings and rings, encrusted with rubies, diamonds, pearls, and emeralds, sparkled in their majestic settings as if winking hello.

Baby smiled and winked back at each sparkling jewel. She waved at the hats, blue-plumed, ostrich-feathered, cardinal-gilded, veiled, sabled, ribboned, and pearled. She recognized the handbags and thought of lizards, snakes, alligators, pythons, crocodiles, and Catsy Ivanhoe.

Shoes. Flat, high, pumped, in satins, suedes, linens, fur skins, leathers, tapestries, with organdy trims, diamond bows, and ribboned ankle-straps filled one room.

Nightgowns. Sheer and billowy, luscious and fluid as soft summer rain filled another room.

Frames. Zillions of twinkling delicate, ornately etched and molded silver frames kept company with ebony, inlaid walnut and mother-of-pearl frames, velvet frames, satin frames, lace frames, fur-skinned frames. Hand-painted porcelain frames. Hand-painted enamel frames. Rare tree-bark frames. A frame of marble from an ancient Irish castle. A frame that had belonged to one of Eleanor Roosevelt's mother's sister. A collection of African native pygmy-teeth frames. Antique pavé bejeweled frames.

Baby winked and blinked. Baby waved.

A Christmas angel waved back to her.

"Oh-h-h . . ." Baby cooed as she saw the angel move.

"Oh-h-h . . ." cooed the Christmas angel.

Baby smiled that smile. The Christmas angel smiled back. Baby stared at the angel's hair, her thick, long, black hair. The angel stared back. Baby moved closer, timidly, toward the angel. The angel moved closer, shyly to Baby. The angel was still smiling. Baby was still smiling. Baby stood an inch away from the angel, who stood an inch away from her.

"Parts Unknown . . ." Baby whispered to the most beautiful creature she had ever seen.

"Parts Unknown . . ." said the Christmas angel at the very same time.

Baby's heart leaped! She had never met anyone who had ever understood her, much less said what she was thinking at the exact same time before in her whole life!

Baby giggled. The Christmas angel giggled. Baby reached out to touch her. The angel reached forward toward Baby.

"Bay-bee!" screamed Yvonne. "Don't you touch that mirror! You put your dirty little fingers in those pockets and get in this beauty shop this minute or I'll lock you up in the limo!"

Baby waved to the Christmas angel, blew her a kiss and danced past a cubicle of belts, gloves and scarfs. She was almost inside the beauty shop when a tiny thought entered her sweet small mind: That exquisite Christmas fairy had been wearing a dress *exactly* like *hers*!

Awed, Baby turned back for one last glimpse. But the Christmas angel had disappeared.

"Here," Yvonne was saying as she pulled a wig out of her tote and handed it to Colin, Catsy Ivanhoe's hairdresser, who five years ago had also become her hairdresser. "I hope you got those orders ready that I called in long distance." She handed over a long brownish colored wig. "And I want you to make this one look exactly like Miss Peanut Butter Cup's hair does on TV."

The hairdresser stared at the wig dubiously, but without surprise. This customer was always wanting him to conjure up an identity for her unlike her own. Never mind that he had worked until one in the morning and gotten up at five to complete Yvonne Henderson's wigs for today's appointment. And he had long since given up on trying to improve Yvonne's color sense. He could make the wig chestnut brown with red highlights, no problem. But Yvonne Henderson was never going to look like a Peanut Butter Cup celebrity any more than she looked like Kim Novak or Farrah Fawcett or Dove Lightlady. No,

Yvonne Henderson in long chestnut brown hair was going to look more like someone's old worn-out shoe.

"Well, all right," he said patiently, "peanut butter brown."

"Great!" squealed Yvonne. "I want to look just like her!"

Colin was about to advise his customer against becoming too hopeful about this transformation when Baby Flowers wandered in. The hairdresser almost dropped his brush.

Standing before him was the most glorious head of hair he had ever seen in his entire career.

"Who," he whispered, "is *this*?"

"Oh, that's some charity work I'm involved in named Baby Flowers," Yvonne replied. "And while those wigs are settin', you can cut all that hair off for her before she gets it caught in a door or somethin' and yanks her head off and I get the blame!"

"I believe this hair is long enough to sit on," Colin observed, reverently running his hands through Baby's luxurious, raven locks.

"And that's exactly what she does with it, too," Yvonne replied. "She's goin' to wear the ends off with her butt, sittin' around all the time like she does. Whenever she's walkin', she's just lookin' for a place to be sittin'. I sure hope you can do somethin' with her to make her look less white trash."

Colin nodded, looked at Yvonne, smiled serenely and made a decision. His coloring mixtures were going to be all wrong today. It would take him all day long to color Yvonne's wig. His time would be so eaten up trying to correct his "mistake" that he would not have time to cut Baby's hair. Oh, he would shampoo it, set it and comb it with pleasure. But Baby Flowers would leave with every lock intact.

"Please make yourself at home in the store," he said politely to Yvonne Henderson. "And while you're shopping, we will make your wig chestnut hued."

"You better mind him," Yvonne threatened Baby. "I'm goin' back yonder and try to find somethin' to wear and I expect you to be-have!" Over her shoulder she called back to Colin, "If you have any trouble, I'll be in Dressing Room One!"

Colin turned to Baby, escorted her to a wrought iron garden chair under a gazebo in the beauty shop's garden setting and handed her a magazine.

"You won't find anyone as beautiful as you in these," he smiled, "but I hope you enjoy looking at pictures because it's going to take forever to shampoo, condition and set your hair." He looked softly into Baby's docile eyes. "Now tell me. How would *you* like your hair?"

Baby Flowers' long black eyelashes fluttered like butterfly's wings as she smiled that Baby smile.

"I see," Colin said kindly. "Well, listen. When you leave here, you'll think your hair has been cut ten inches, but when the ribbons loosen and the flowers fall, you'll find that nothing, but nothing has changed at all."

Baby Flowers smiled and nodded and nodded and smiled.

Colin smiled back. "I wouldn't cut your hair for all the oil wells in Texas," he promised.

"Parts Unknown," smiled Baby Flowers. "I got me Parts Unknown . . ."

"Oh, I agree entirely," Colin nodded gently. "Ribbons and roses, it is then . . ."

Lottie Shady and Leo Diggs stood before Judge Sarah Lou Alexander Gurnsey in the judicial chamber of the Loving County Courthouse, in Mentone, Texas, forty miles southwest of Uncertain and just east of the Pecos River. Lottie had insisted on a quiet ceremony in Loving County.

Judge Gurnsey had been just about to lock her door and leave for the day when this couple from Uncertain had detained her. She rushed through the ceremony. She was wearing a new pair of shoes that were killing her and she was anxious to get home and soak her feet in Epsom Salts.

"Leo Langford Diggs, do you take this woman, Lottine Jewel Shady to be your lawful wedded wife?" Judge Gurnsey asked from memory. "Do you promise to love her, keep her, honor and cherish her above all others in sickness or in health, for richer or poorer, 'til death do you part, so help you God?"

"I do," smiled Leo Diggs.

"Me, too!" grinned Lottie Shady.

"Well, fine then," said Judge Gurnsey. "I pronounce you man and wife."

Leo Diggs picked Lottie Shady Diggs up in his arms and smothered her in kisses.

"Well," laughed Judge Sarah Lou Alexander Gurnsey. "Nobody's goin' to have to tell *you* when to kiss the bride!"

* * *

Yvonne Henderson stood in her favorite dressing room, extra-spacious Number One, examining herself in four pink-tinted, beveled-mirrored walls. Champagne in a Steuben glass stood on top of a silver Victorian tray which sat on a hand-hammered iron and marble-topped French Art Deco table. A small silver telephone from an old Parisian hotel was placed next to the tray. A Baccarat ashtray waited next to the telephone, accompanied by a Russian red Cartier cigarette lighter. A towering array of fresh fruit rested in an exquisite Lalique crystal bowl. Across the room, an 18th century Chinese dressing table supported a collection of brilliant old cosmetic jars with tortoise-shell tops, several Waterford atomizers and a cluster of antique cologne bottles. A box of Europa chocolates perched on the dressing table's stool.

Yvonne's saleslady, Lee Jennings, waited patiently as Yvonne turned and fussed, preened and posed. Lee had been zipping and unzipping Yvonne, buttoning and unbuttoning her all afternoon long and was glad to do so. For the past five years, Yvonne Henderson had been Lee Jennings's best customer. Lee Jennings had no earthly idea where Mrs. Robert Otis Henderson went to wear her choices and as glad as she was to sell them to her, she sincerely hoped that Mrs. Henderson would not tell anyone that she, Lee, was responsible for recommending certain combinations. For as hard as she had delicately attempted to persuade her customer to wear only one designer outfit at a time, Yvonne Henderson had insisted, for the past five years, on mixing Givenchy suit tops with Oscar de la Renta cocktail skirts, Claude Montana jackets with Coco Chanel blouses, Cardin with Chloé, Lavin with St. Laurent, Narakas with Ungaro, Herrera with Blass, Adolpho with Valentino, and so on with so forth.

For the past three years, the store's present owner, and Odette Lumière's son, Oscar, had simply taken the day off when Mrs. Robert O. Henderson appeared. It just made him sick to see so many designers crowded onto and hanging off of one woman. He had been trained since childhood to regard with the utmost reverence the finest fabrics known to man, the most fluid and precise designs ever created. He had been bred from the cradle to select for only the most appreciative, therefore the most deserving. Oscar Lumière's sensibilities were utterly offended by Mrs. Robert O. Henderson. But since 1980, who had come to his shop with more money than God? Yvonne Henderson, a hick from Uncertain, Texas, who wanted twelve of everything, at least. Cashmere sweaters, leather skirts, suede blouses, crocheted dresses, embroidered vests, creweled bodices, silk pantsuits, brocaded jackets, paisley shawls, ermine earmuffs. Organdy, taffeta, silk organza ballgowns. Velvets, satins, linens, wools, flannels, and cottons, trimmed in lace, pearls, sequins, sable, fitch, fox, chinchilla, spangles, dangles . . .

"Everything but Bojangles," Mr. Lumière complained. "Each piece *alone* a masterpiece! But *all together*?! A hodgepodge! a Balenciaga nightmare!"

Yvonne Henderson could not have been happier. The minute she had gotten rich, she got on the first plane to Dallas, hired a white limousine and headed right for Lovers Lane. She knew Odette Lumière's was where Catsy Ivanhoe shopped and where she got her hair done and she couldn't wait to have her hair fixed fancier and spend more money and buy more clothes than Catsy. The store's refined, and truly wealthy regular local customers, as well as the genuinely international patrons, escaped Yvonne's notice completely. Catsy Ivanhoe was her standard. And she was determined to outdo it. Yvonne's personal slogan was "More Is Never Enough."

Yvonne had insisted on Catsy's own personal saleswoman, as well as her hairdresser. Colin McCabe never said a word to anyone about anyone's business and his bank account reflected his integrity. Lee Jennings could not resist having a fine giggle recounting Yvonne Henderson's purchases to Catsy Ivanhoe, although the truth was, she found Catsy almost as laughable as Yvonne.

"At least she doesn't wear them in *Dallas,*" Catsy would drawl, feeling completely and orgasmically superior, unaware that she was part of the joke. "I have to go *home* and look at genius utterly *destroyed* on the streets of Uncertain, Texas everytime I run into Whyvonne Henderson!"

Catsy had almost stopped shopping at Odette Lumière's after one season when Lee Jennings was bored and had cunningly sold her the tops and bottoms to some of the outfits Yvonne Henderson had discarded while mixing and matching. She knew it was breaking a cardinal rule to sell pieces of an ensemble, but she had not been able to resist. Catsy Ivanhoe threw a fit, Yvonne Henderson returned her entire season's wardrobe, and Oscar Lumière had fired Lee Jennings on the spot. Lee laughed herself silly and took a six-month trip to Paris. When she returned, Yvonne Henderson and Catsy Ivanhoe had insisted that Oscar Lumière hire her back.

Catsy Ivanhoe limited her wardrobe selections to the colors red, black, brown, beige and white after that. She said she wouldn't be caught dead before five in a sequin or a rhinestone. She wore only black or white at night. Her furs and accessories remained exotic and provocative, however, for she adored wearing animal skins. Catsy could never resist her furs.

Yvonne had never tried to look *exactly* like Catsy in the first place. She chose any color for her clothing except black, white, red, beige or brown. She liked aquas, peaches, lemon yellows, lime greens, sapphire blues, hot pinks, festive purples and screaming oranges—all at the same time. The only thing that matched were Yvonne's shoes.

After her hair was finally combed and set, Baby Flowers had spent the past half hour on the floor of an adjoining, but more modest dressing room. Her new playmate, the Christmas fairy, had appeared out of nowhere to keep Baby company. To her delight, her angelic friend had put ribbons and flowers into her hair, too!

Baby waved. The Christmas fairy waved. Baby raised her eyebrows. The angel raised her eyebrows. Even when Baby squeezed her eyes shut and held them closed for as long as she could, when she opened them, the Christmas angel was still there with her, giggling with her, blinking and winking.

Baby shook her head. The angel shook her head. Petals drifted to the floor, ribbons danced off their shoulders. Baby blew the angel kisses. The angel blew kisses back.

Baby had never had so much fun in her life. She had never had a friend before, someone to play with, who liked to do what she liked to do, who actually did everything she did.

Baby gazed at her new friend worshipfully and devotedly.

"Parts Unknown . . ." Baby lovingly told her Christmas angel. "*You're* Parts Unknown . . . "

"Parts Unknown . . ." whispered the Christmas fairy back. "*You're* Parts Unknown . . . "

Baby Flowers didn't know much, but she knew a thing of beauty and gentleness when she saw it. And so far, this Christmas angel was the most beautiful, gentle creature she had ever seen. Baby Flowers loved her angel. She wanted to be exactly like her in every way. Oh, how glad she was that nice man with the shampoo and rollers had given her both roses and ribbons for a start!

Baby shushed her angel and the Christmas fairy shushed Baby as Yvonne's voice carried over the partition from the adjoining dressing room.

"I don't like this either!" Yvonne told Lee Jennings. "Don't you have somethin' more—?"

"*Vivid*?" Lee Jennings asked, concealing a smirk.

"Well, yes!" Yvonne cried. She stepped over a pile of clothes, tossing them out the door. "These are just not me!"

"I have been saving something very, very special," Lee Jennings revealed. "It's a splendid one-of-a-kind piece by a new French designer. I think you will love it."

"Why'd I have to wait all afternoon to see it?" Yvonne grumbled.

Because you wouldn't have liked it five hours ago, Lee Jennings said to herself.

"Well, bring it here then," Yvonne sighed. "I got to leave here with somethin' on my back!"

Lee Jennings returned holding a strapless maroon and gold sequined *bustier* attached to a short fluttery silk organza maroon-colored skirt. The skirt gathered in ruffles from top to bottom. Suspended from a neck band of maroon and gold jewels, was a choker of arch-bowed, golden and maroon-tipped exotic feathers.

"Maroon and gold!" screamed Yvonne Henderson gleefully. "Them's my school colors!"

"It's *you*," smiled Lee Jennings, as she draped a solid gold breastplate around Yvonne's bosom. From curved and sculpted spiky gold nipples, dangled two pavé-jeweled yellow jackets encrusted by yellow diamonds and deep red rubies.

"Oh-h-h-h!" swooned Yvonne. "It's *me*!"

"But, wait," crooned Lee Jennings, who had commissioned the outfit herself several weeks ago from the as yet undiscovered designer, whom she had met while vacationing in Paris. She placed a golden crown shaped like a small nest on top of Yvonne's head. From the diamond-studded gold netting, which coiled up the crowned nest in the shape of a beehive, flew five matching pavé-jeweled yellow jackets dangling from five-inch golden rodded stems.

"You've done it this time!" Yvonne squealed, crawling into ruffles, sequins, coils, breastplates, dangling bugs and huge stiff feathers.

"Oh, don't forget the wings!" Lee Jennings, said, stifling a threatening guffaw, as she produced a set of gigantic gold mesh wings.

"Great!" cried Yvonne, as Lee Jennings slapped the wings on her back. "Now let me grab a Sandy Rhodes for a cape and use your phone, and I'm outta here!"

Lee Jennings didn't bat an eye. She had already pulled and had waiting at her fingertips three Zandra Rhodes for Yvonne to choose from.

"It's like the actor who goes out the stage door for a cigarette, hears his cue, and walks back into the wrong theater," Oscar Lumière often mourned. "Two shows destroyed at once. Two designers annihilated."

"I sold our first Lacroix today," Lee Jennings beamed.

Oscar Lumière's eyebrows shot up, impressed. Although overwhelmingly unique, the new designer's special creation had been *very expensive*, even for Yvonne Henderson.

"And that's not all."

"More?" Oscar Lumière asked, "She bought *more*?"

"Oh, yes," smiled Lee Jennings. "She purchased a *most* unusual wardrobe for a strange beautiful creature named Baby. . ."

Oscar Lumière's eyes grew wide. "You mean Yvonne Henderson's got a *girlfriend*?"

Lee Jennings laughed. "I don't know, but if she does, her girlfriend's a hell of a looker! I haven't seen a face like that since Ava Gardner's!"

"Money," signed Oscar Lumière. "People like that can buy anything in the world once they've got enough green stuff. . . ."

Kay Widders slammed the aluminum door of her trailer-made-house in her mother-in-law's face, furiously watched Scoot Widders drive off toward the Uncertain Chapel of Memories and waddled straight to her telephone.

"I should have known better than to expect a sympathetic ear or even a good piece of advice from your daddy's demented, star-struck mother!" Kay Widders barked, dialing the phone.

The twins trailed behind her, each still carrying a plastic bag containing their formals, which Kay had picked up at the cleaners earlier.

"Catsy!" Kay screamed into the telephone. "Mary Jane Shady's back and we've been deceived! She's not pure as Peanut Butter at all!"

The twins exchanged anxious sideways looks.

"She's livin' in some ho-tel up there in New York City where she's fallen into and gotten tarnished up by a *Jew*!"

The twins moved closer, trying to hear what Catsy Ivanhoe had to say.

"That is right! You heard me all right!" Kay spelled it out. "A J-E-W! Can you believe it?! She paused for a moment to savor Catsy's response. "Oh, I got this first hand from Annie Lovejoy who announced it for the whole entire beauty shop to hear right in front of that little tart and her mother, who's got one foot in hell herself, as far as I'm concerned. Irene Shady knew what that Butter Cup was up to and didn't do a thing to stop it! I've heard of movie stars actin' like this, I wasn't born yesterday you know! But what I cain't understand is how Mary Jane Shady could even walk the streets of Uncertain, Texas, with that piece of bad news hangin' off her back! How could she come back here after cavortin' in Sodom and Gomorrah in some ho-tel room and datin' the Jew-Devil hisself! And furthermore, how am I goin' to replace her from crownin' the Homecomin' Queen and ridin' in the losers car by tomorrow afternoon is what I want to know! I will burn myself up in the bonfire in the middle of Uncertain Field before I allow that prostitute of Satan's to place a crown on Verona and Morona's heads!"

Catsy Ivanhoe smiled into the telephone.

"Don't worry," Catsy Ivanhoe purred into Kay Widders' ear. "Don't you worry about a thing . . ."

CHAPTER THIRTY-NINE

GLADYS TURNER'S voice hit Irene and Topsy before they even reached the bottom landing. "Do you take cream and sugar, Mary Jane?"

She didn't want coffee. She wanted a drink. "Sweet and Low."

Irene picked up her cigarettes and lighter and sat down at the round oak table in the saloon. She sat where she always sat, next to the window. Gladys carried in the coffee and sat where she always sat, with her back to the bar. Topsy sat facing the pantry. Her Aunt Lottie always faced the front door.

"Where's Aunt Lottie?" Topsy asked.

"God knows," Irene said tightly. She rose in martyred glory, went into the kitchen and brought back a package of Oreo cookies. She was beginning to wonder where Lottie was herself.

"Sweet and Low causes cancer in rats," Gladys remarked to Topsy as she filled her coffee half full of cream and added three heaping spoonfuls of sugar.

"Is that what caused your sister's death?" Irene asked, sitting back down and ripping open the Oreos.

Topsy looked at the two women. They had been sitting at this table together for as long as she could remember with hardly a kind word passing between them.

Gladys shook her head. "No. It was that faith healer from Nacogdoches."

"I thought you said it was a tumor." Irene offered Gladys a cookie.

"He promoted it," Gladys replied, ignoring her. "He whipped through the door of that hospital looking just like Liberace, with his hair all piled up pompadour-style and wearing a rhinestone jumpsuit just a-glittering and a-jangling to beat the band. He put his hands on her breasts and started talking in the unknown tongue. Then he told her, 'Get up, get up, if you love Jesus. Go on home and pray and have faith in Jesus and you will get well.' "

"And she did?" Topsy asked.

"That's right. She just got up and went on home. Told the doctors she couldn't make up her mind to let them do anything to her 'til she had talked it over with Christ."

"How long did she talk to Him?" Irene wanted to know. "I'd think that situation would call for the hot-line to heaven."

"Months. She was real long-winded. And all that time that cancer from the tumor was spreading like a spider web," Gladys replied.

Spider webs in her head. Gladys Turner's sister died from spider webs in her head!

"Anyway, she was talking to Him in that unknown tongue," Gladys continued. "She should have just spoken to Him in plain English, because by the time it went from what *she* was sayin', to that faith healer, and from the faith healer to Christ, I'm sure God in Heaven didn't understand a word either one of them was talking about! *Nobody got the message*! And that's when she died!"

"How in the world did a man like that faith healer get his hands on her?" Irene asked.

"He was her boyfriend," Gladys sighed.

"I didn't know she had a boyfriend," Irene remarked, lighting another cigarette and starting on another cookie.

"Well, he wasn't much of one. Didn't even appear at the funeral." Gladys poured herself more coffee and reached for the cream and sugar. "Talked her right out of that operation and right into the grave, and that's why I say she died of a death wish—*his*. And he got all her jewelry, too."

"What did he leave you?" Irene asked. "Anything?"

"Yeah. All the bills for that durned funeral," Gladys replied.

"Well, I was remarking to Mary Jane on the drive from the airport what a *spectacular* job Deal Grimes did," Irene said, hoping to end the subject once and for all.

Topsy looked at her mother in amazement. *Lies.* Her mother was sitting there telling lies.

"Is that so?" Gladys smiled demurely. "Oh, I'm so glad you thought so, because I did try to make it real special, especially without your help, Irene. I had to pay for it every bit myself, too. She didn't have a penny left after the faith healer finished with her. Said she'd given it all to Jesus—"

"What a shame," Irene consoled, looking as sincere as could be.

What is she up to? Topsy wondered irritably. *Why doesn't she just tell Gladys she deserved to get ripped off if she's not going to be loyal*?

Her thoughts were interrupted by the bells jingling on the front door.

"Yoo-hoo!" Scoot Widders called, letting herself in. She walked right past the five cardboard blow-ups of Mary Jane Shady as if they didn't exist, kicking the door shut with her boot.

"I knew it," Gladys hissed under her breath. "She's followed me to torment me, wait and see."

"Well, hello, hello, hello, Mary Jane Shady!" Scoot hollered.

As Scoot strode through the parlor in her faded Levis and well-worn work shirt, Topsy could see that Sammy Widders' mother hadn't changed a bit. Scoot Widders had been a roper, a wrestler and for the past twenty years, the foreman of one of the largest cattle ranches in West Texas. And she still looked like a porcupine gone mad.

"The grandbabies told me they run into you over at Annie Lovejoy's and I thought I'd just come on over and see for myself what a real live movie star looks like!" Scoot tore a red bandana off her head, letting loose a wild headful of salt and pepper hair. She threw the bandana on top of the table, where it landed with acute precision squarely on top of Gladys Turner's coffee cup. With arms akimbo, she marched over to Topsy, and giving her cone hairdo several staccato pats, Scoot jerked her head back and forth in perpetual vehement approval. "Well, you look real Hollywood to me!" she cried, slapping Topsy on the back.

Topsy hung onto her chair for support.

"Did Kay say anything about runnin' into Mary Jane?" Irene asked carefully.

"Ain't Kay a caution?" Scoot winked. "Fat girls have the slipperiest personalities, don't they? One minute chipper as chipmunks, next minute crawly as snakes. Kay's just too big to get over herself, is her problem." She grabbed the bandana from off Gladys' coffee cup, tossed it around her neck, stepped over Lottie Shady's chair, sat down in it, and leaned forward, grinning into Gladys Turner's face. "And here's Gladys Turner! Drinkin' coffee with a star!"

Gladys' lips pursed as if she'd been sucking a lemon.

"Hidy there, Scoot," said Gladys. "We missed you at the funeral yesterday."

"Well, I didn't come 'cause I didn't know her," Scoot said.

"Got any more coffee, Irene?" She turned to Topsy. "What's goin' on in Tinseltown, M.J.? Does Robin Williams think up his own jokes? He's the cutest thing I ever saw walkin' around on two legs. I could eat him up with a spoon and let him melt!"

"Irene came to the funeral and she didn't know Evelyn," Gladys continued, as Irene got up and poured Scoot's coffee.

"She don't have two Siamese twin grandbabies runnin' for Homecomin' Queen tomorrow neither," Scoot told Gladys. "What are we goin' to see you in next, M.J.? I just live to see how they're goin' to kill you off!" She turned back to Gladys. "I hope Orville's got the concrete ready, Gladys! Let's pour Mary Jane's feet 'n fingers out in front of the schoolhouse while she's here!"

"Only one of those twins is running," Gladys corrected.

"Don't matter," said Scoot. "They both have to be there. And Kay always dresses 'em identical, so they might as well both be runnin'. Anyway, they're a handful. You know these high school girls." Scoot smiled at Topsy. "Is Robin Williams *married*? You and him ought to star in somethin' together—"

"Well, it was a real fine funeral," Gladys stated. "That Deal Grimes is just amazing at putting these events together—"

"'Scuse me, but a funeral is not an event," Scoot corrected. "Now the Homecomin' tomorrow is an *event,* but a funeral is what you would call an *occasion.*"

"This funeral was an event," Irene sighed.

"It was something," Gladys nodded. "I was just telling Irene and Mary Jane here that I had to do the whole thing myself, and believe me, Homecoming, floats and all cannot begin to compare with what goes into getting a body into the ground."

"It's all in a day's work to me," Irene sniffed. She thought Gladys was being especially insensitive to just keep talking about it.

"Just hold on a minute and I'll get my purse. I got the Polaroids with me and I'll show you what I mean—" Gladys pulled herself up from her chair and headed for the living room.

"Why didn't she give *you* the business?" Scoot asked in a loud whisper.

"I was too busy," Irene fibbed. "Had to get ready for *M.J.*"

More lies, Topsy thought in amazement.

Scoot turned to Topsy. "What did you think of my girls? Did you ever see anybody look so much like each other in your life?"

"I don't think so," Topsy answered carefully, and felt an immediate stab of resentment. *I sound just like her,* she thought, glancing at her mother. *Why didn't I just say, "No. I have NEVER run into a set of Siamese twins. Even outside the Safeway on Sunset Boulevard in Hollywood at seven o'clock in the morning!"*

"Well, it was somewhat startling at first when they appeared out of the womb like that," Scoot said.

"I'll bet," Topsy heard herself whisper understandingly.

"Now *that* was an *event,*" Scoot nodded. She glanced over her shoulder at Gladys, who was still digging in her purse. "Her ole sister's funeral was just an *occasion.*" Scoot helped herself to an Oreo. "What are the Academy Awards like, Mary Jane? See? Now, *there's* an *event*! *BOY-HI-DEE*! I'll tell you what, if Robin Williams needs a date, tell him I am sure dyin' to go!"

"I'd be glad to," Topsy told Scoot. "Except, listen, Scoot, I don't know Robin Williams—"

"You don't?" Scoot smiled optimistically. "Who *do* you know?"

"Here they are!" Gladys cried, reappearing with a handful of Polaroids.

Topsy wondered if her mother had any gin or vodka around. She was desperate for a drink.

"The closeups are the best," Gladys announced, "but you can kind of get the full effect from a couple that was taken from further back in the pews. I told Orville to take the overall views only during the singing. I just think it's tacky for a flash to go popping off while people are trying to *pray.*"

"Sometimes it's the only time to get the shot, Gladys," Irene explained wearily.

"Everything looks pink," Scoot said, peering at the photos.

"He took some with the instamatic, too, but they haven't been developed yet," Gladys told Scoot.

"Everything *was* pink," Irene informed Scoot. "It was the theme."

"Well, that's just not my color," Scoot said flatly, shuffling the photos like a deck of cards and dealing them out on the table. "Don't ever bury me in pink, Irene. It is definitely not for me."

"I can see that," Gladys nodded. "Your skin's got a tinge of yellow to it, so you're right to stay away from pink."

"I don't have yellow skin," Scoot said, examining her arms.

"My skin got yellow when I got hepatitis that time," Irene offered. "My eyeballs, too."

"Is this her real hair?" Scoot asked, picking up a close-up.

"Naw. It fell out, so I bought her a new wig. Everything was new. New wig, new dress—"

"Why'd you get such a black one?" Scoot wanted to know.

"I told you I paid for everything myself. I was on a limited budget and Deal let me have it at a discount since it had been there awhile," Gladys explained. "Do you know how expensive it is for a loved one to die?"

"You're with pros here, Gladys." Irene had just about had it.

"I think you got took on the wig, Gladys," Scoot offered.

"Now hold on here," Irene interrupted. "Why'd her hair fall out?"

Topsy looked behind the bar. Nothing. She went into the kitchen and looked in the refrigerator. Nothing. She opened the freezer. Nothing. She looked under the sink. Nothing.

"The chemotherapy made it fall out. It does that," Gladys told Irene.

Topsy closed her eyes and tried to put her mind in her mother's mind. Where would her mother keep an extra bottle of liquor? She knew Irene kept something hidden away somewhere for customers who needed it.

"But you said she said she couldn't make up her mind whether to let them give it to her or operate or not or anything. Isn't that what you said?" Irene asked.

Topsy walked up front to the little office. She opened the safe and felt around toward the back. The first thing she pulled out was her picture with Herman on their very first date. She'd gone with him to a United Jewish Appeal benefit in Cincinnati. It had to be the only picture of her that was not hanging up in this room somewhere. She slipped it in her pocket, felt far in the back of the safe and pulled out stack after stack of green stamp books. Buried under them was a bottle of vodka. She opened the top and drank from the bottle. There might be Siamese twins running for Homecoming Queen in Uncertain, Texas, but she'd bet her life that there wasn't a Jew.

"I meant give it to her *anymore,*" Gladys emphasized. "She was on it and then got off of it. It made her sick to her stomach. And do you know what this one doctor from Dallas told her to do about it? He told her—and I swear this on the Bible—he told her if she would smoke a *marijuana cigarette* before the treatments she wouldn't get so sick."

Topsy leaned back in her mother's office chair and took a another long slow swallow. It tasted bitter and it stung. It felt good.

"Can you beat that?" Gladys went on. "A doctor prescribing illegal *dope*? I'd rather die."

"I wouldn't," said Scoot. "I'd take the dope."

"Me, too," Irene nodded.

Me, too, nodded Topsy. *Shoot me up . . .*

"But if I do die, don't put me in pink, Irene," Scoot cautioned.

Don't put me in my Peanut Butter Cup Dress, Topsy giggled.

"I wouldn't dream of it," Irene promised.

"They ought to lock him up," Gladys exclaimed.

"Who?" asked Irene and Scoot.

"Why, that doctor from Dallas. He was the one who drove her right into the arms and influence of that Brother Ewell Crownover—"

"Brother Crownover!" Scoot yelled, banging her knee on the table as she hopped up.

"Careful. You're going to spill coffee on the pictures," Irene said, stacking them neatly to one side.

"O-W-W-W! I'm crazy about Brother Crownover!" Scoot screamed. "Don't you ever watch him, Irene? He's gettin' his very own syndicated show on TV! Corinda Cassy and The Cowgirls for

Christ are scheduled as his first special guests! It's goin' to play all over East Texas and part of Louisiana!"

"Over my dead body," Gladys muttered.

" 'The Lame Will Walk, The Blind Will See, The Deaf Will Speak If They Come To Me,' " Scoot recited. "That's his motto. And by golly, it works!"

"Well, it didn't work for my sister," Gladys replied crossly.

"Then she probably didn't try hard enough," Scoot said, "'cause that man knows his business or he wouldn't be gettin' him his own syndicated TV show and Corinda Cassy sure wouldn't show up for it!"

"Are you telling me my sister died because she didn't try hard enough?" Gladys yelled.

"Probably had a death wish," Irene laughed.

"That's not funny, Irene Shady, even if I think it's true," Gladys snapped.

"So I was right!" Scoot cried gleefully.

Topsy wandered out of the office, through the parlor, up the stairs, past the women's voices. She thought of Bobby and smiled. She thought of Herman and smiled. She climbed the stairs, listening to her mother and Irene's two best friends and smiled some more. She took another drink. It wasn't so bad being home. She was actually beginning to feel better. She sat on the top of the stairs and gazed at the posters, benevolently. Making horror movies hadn't been so horrible. They had paid her insurance, they had paid her rent. Jack Nicholson made *The Shining*. Faye Dunaway had done *Mommie Dearest,* Bette Davis, *Hush, Hush Sweet Charlotte* . . . Robin Williams would probably make one any day now . . .

"I believe in Jesus, but not in that faith healer, and I certainly do not put my faith in a lunatic that goes around speaking in the unknown tongue and dressing like Liberace and taking advantage of dead women's jewelry!" Gladys exploded.

"I'm real sorry about your sister's jewelry," Irene offered to Gladys. "It seems this Crownover man you're so intrigued with got off with Evelyn's jewelry," Irene informed Scoot.

"Now, hold on!" Scoot said emphatically. "My sister Winkie Kermit talks in the unknown tongue all the time!"

Gladys began to cry. "I love Jesus," she wept, "and I know if He knew what I just went through, He'd take that man off the air!"

"God knows best!" Scoot hollered. "And He's givin' Crownover his own TV show!"

"You are flat-out crazy, Scoot Widders! And so is your sister! There is no way you can redeem that man to me, impressed as you are by him being on TV." Gladys stood up. She took the Polaroid pictures and put them in her purse, I'm leaving," she announced, going toward the door. Turning around, she said to Scoot with a pointed finger, "I'm going to pray for your whole family when I get home!"

"Why wait?" Scoot yelled after her. "Why not start prayin' right now?"

Gladys slammed the door, got in her car and drove off in a frenzy.

"Never would occur to old Glad-Ass that she could have offended *me,*" Scoot muttered, taking one of Irene's cigarettes. "My sister, Winkie Kermit, talks in the unknown tongue the better part of the time, and so does her intended, Mr. Horatio Ravenhill and there ain't a thing wrong with *them*! 'Course I cain't understand what neither of 'em is sayin', but that don't bother me. In fact, I think the thing I like the best about the unknown tongue is that I cain't understand a word of it. Winkie and Horatio together sound like some kind of a foreign music band. They're just mindin' their own business, drivin' the Born Again Independent Bus Company all over West Texas, transportin' cripples to Judson so they can see Jesus in that screen door and get well! One look at that image and they heal up left and right! There's worse things to do with your time, you know!"

A born again bus! Topsy weaved. *Throw me on the bus! Show me to the door*!

"Now, listen, Scoot," Topsy heard her mother say. "As soon as Brother Crownover gets his new show set up, you ought to get Verona and Morona on it. I think they'd be a real extra attraction. Especially televised."

"Really?" Scoot cried excitedly. "I never thought of that! I don't know a thing about show business!"

"Well, I know all about show business," Irene Shady beamed. "And I think this idea is a winner. You ought to listen to me, Scoot. I been havin' one big brainstorm after another lately."

"But what would they *do*?" Scoot asked. "I mean, who knows if they are even *talented*?"

"Scoot," Irene replied. "Siamese twins don't have to be talented. All they have to do is show up."

Scoot stood up. "Well, bless my soul, Irene Shady. This is the best idea you ever had in your life!"

"It's one of 'em," Irene agreed. "Now the first thing to do is to win that Homecomin' Queen crown tomorrow. That kind of publicity money cain't buy."

Scoot held up both hands with fingers crossed.

Irene grinned. "That's the spirit." She hugged Scoot and walked her to the front door. "We've got big time people comin' in tomorrow, people with influence. Those girls won't go unnoticed, mark my words."

"You really think a big shot like Crownover might be interested?" Scoot asked.

"There's a untapped market for Siamese twins, Scoot," Irene promised. "Show business religion is like everything else—supply and demand. That's all it is. Supply and demand."

Topsy Dingo Wild Dog pulled herself to her feet with her head reeling and slowly climbed the stairs. Her mother was up to something and she very much didn't want to hear what it was.

She passed herself being icepicked. She passed herself being strangled with barbed wire. She passed herself being attacked by scorpions. She stood still and listened.

Just inside the foyer of the Chapel of Memories, Scoot turned to give Irene a hug. "I just love this idea, Irene!" she said. "At this rate, my girls could end up in Hollywood with Mary Jane and Robin! If there's ever anything I can do for you, just let me know!"

"Well . . ." Irene confided, "there *is* one thing I'm concerned about . . ."

"Shoot!" cried Scoot.

Here it comes, thought Topsy Dingo Wild Dog.

" . . . and that's when Mary Jane rides in on her float . . . "

"What float?" asked Scoot Widders.

"That's just it," said Irene Shady. "Mary Jane don't have a float!"

"Forget the fucking float!" muttered Topsy.

"Oh, listen!" Scoot Widders said quickly. "You innerduce my twins to all the right people, and Mary Jane Shady will have her own float!"

"Done!" cried Irene Shady.

"All but done!" grinned Scoot Widders.

"Done in," groaned Topsy Dingo Wild Dog.

She reeled toward her room, stumbling into her own screaming face. *KEEP MY GRAVE OPEN*! cried the blood red letters running across her ravaged image.

"Oh, fuck off and die," she said to the poster.

Irene walked Scoot to her car and waved triumphantly as she drove away. It was dark now and time to turn on the sign. Irritably, Irene thought of Lottie and wondered what in hell had happened to her sister-in-law. She sure never expected Lottie to stay gone all day. She walked back inside, locked the door, and looked around for her daughter. "I hope she's gone off to bed," she said to the five Mary Jane Shadys in the foyer. "Because in less than a few hours she's goin' to have to look exactly like *you*."

Upstairs, Topsy Dingo Wild Dog opened the door to her room without turning on the light. She slipped off her clothes, longing to fall into bed. She was too exhausted to even pull back the covers. Wearily, she remembered that the dark room she was standing in was the north room—her old room. She stared out the window. Melogo Drive, though visible, seemed as distant and unreachable as the Land of Oz. She stood there, peering nakedly toward her street of lost dreams. Far away, a dog barked. A lone tumbleweed rolled down the highway and Scoot Widders drove right over it.

Suddenly a blast of red, pink, blue, yellow and green tornadoed through the window and ripped through her face. Startled, she jumped back, bumping into something large and metallic and cold. Another spasmodic burst of light hurled through the window. Rivers of color splashed across her half-hearted heart.

Spikes of light cascaded on the dozens of caskets that encircled her. Her old room was a neon lit tomb.

Wilted and bent, she tore herself from the room like some sweet half-dead rose saved from an old funeral bouquet.

If I'm lucky, she thought as she stumbled across the hall, *I'll just die in my sleep.*

She got in bed, crawled under the covers, and waited.

Her half-hearted heart pounded on.

CHAPTER FORTY

TOPSY heard a faint tapping at the window by her bed.

"Who's out there?" she whispered.

"I'm your welcome home committee," a familiar voice answered back. "I come to welcome you back home."

"Who are you?" she whispered. "Who are you?"

"Just an old admirer," the familiar voice answered.

It was Bobby. She knew it. "What do you want?" She tried to keep her voice steady.

"What do you think?" the familiar voice replied.

"Well, go away. My mama will get real mad if she knows you're out there." *Feeble.*

"C'mon, M.J. Open the window and let me in."

She was shaking. Her heart flogged her chest. "I don't want to see you."

"You will when you open the goddamn window."

"You're going to get me in trouble, Bobby."

"I sure hope so," he said. She could almost feel his smile. "You're a grown woman. I'm a grown man. Open the window, M.J." His voice was low and firm.

"I can't," she stammered. *Lame.* Oh, God, there was that feeling. That merry-go-round feeling.

"Why not?"

"You're married . . . "

"Not from midnight 'til three A.M.," he laughed.

"I can't," she repeated. *Helpless.*

"Open it," he said.

"I won't," she vowed. *Weak.*

"You better."

"No." *Yes.*

"Want me to break the fuckin' window in?"

"I don't want to see you or talk to you, Bobby. Go away." Topsy said. God, how she wanted him. It was awful.

"Oh, I know that, Mary Jane. You *never* wanted just to see me or talk to me. People never really change. I didn't expect *you* to. Just open the window, hon. I know what you want."

She hesitated. "Are you *alone,* Bobby?"

"Huh?"

"Are you *by yourself*?"

"'Course, I'm by myself," He laughed softly. "Open up this window, baby."

She sat up slowly. She knew she was going to open it.

It was dark outside. No one had seen Bobby climb up the portico. No one would see him climb in the window. She could barely distinguish his presence herself. She raised the glass and unlatched the screen.

"I'm going to lock my door," she whispered.

"Good idea, baby. You do that. Just like old times."

Rising from the bed, she felt her way across the room to the door. "Just like old times," she murmured, turning the lock.

"Come here, honey. Hold me."

"Where are you? I can't see." She could barely speak. Oh, this was bad. Deliciously bad. Exquisitely horrible. Why did she still want him? She didn't care. She couldn't wait.

As if reading her thoughts, he interrupted her, saying, "Don't worry, hon. I'm ready for you this time."

She reached out for him in the dark. There he was. Her hands were on his head. It was smooth. She felt a twinge of sadness when she realized Bobby was bald. Oh, well. She ran her fingers down his smooth, smooth face. She wanted to kiss his eyes, but where were they? She felt awkward and a little silly. She giggled.

"Turn around," she said.

It was so dark he probably couldn't see her either. She touched his cheeks. They were wet. Was Bobby crying? Had he come to tell her he was sorry, he'd been wrong, his life without her had been a mistake and that he regretted every bit of hurt and pain he had ever caused her? Sympathy surged through her. Moved, she moaned, putting her arms around him. His body was hot and pulsating. She waited for him to hold her, but he didn't. She reached up to kiss him, but again felt the smoothness of the back of his head.

"Stop turning around," she said a bit impatiently. She was almost annoyed, until again, she remembered he might be afraid of apologizing. It might be hard for him to say he was sorry.

"It's okay," she whispered. "Really. I forgive you." She tried to brush the tears away. "I'm just so glad you came, Bobby..." Her hands were sticking to his tears. They were hot and sticky. She paused, puzzled. In fact, these tears weren't really like tears and he wasn't sobbing at all. Quickly, Topsy ran her fingers all over his head. The wetness was coming from the top of his head.

"I think you're bleeding," she said. "You must have cut your head coming in the window."

He laughed. The laugh was dark and low. "That's not blood," he said.

She did not like the sound of that laugh. She filled with anxiety. He still hadn't said a word about being sorry, about wishing he'd never left her. He hadn't said a word to indicate that his entire life had been a mistake from top to bottom without her.

Why is he here? What does he want? Fear. She felt fear.

Frantically, she switched on the night light beside her bed. When she turned to face him, her heart almost stopped.

A man-sized purplish-pink penis with white liquid oozing from the top was the ONLY thing in the middle of the bedroom.

"This is all you want," it said in Bobby Henderson's voice. "This is all you ever wanted, and this is all there is."

She staggered backwards, falling against the bed.

The penis grew larger and larger, engulfing the entire room. Then, like a huge pink rocket, it crashed through the ceiling and shot off in the sky, every burst filling the heavens with trillions and billions of twinkling cosmic sperm, which separated and formed a semened continuous sign across the sky:

> GOOD-BYE MARY JANE SHADY!!! HELLO MRS. TOPSY DINGO WILD DOG!!! HELLO MRS. TOPSY DINGO WILD DOG!!! GOOD-BYE MARY JANE SHADY!!! GOOD-BYE MARY JANE SHADY!!! HELLO MRS. TOPSY DINGO WILD DOG!!!

"NO-O-O-O-O-O-O-O!" screamed Topsy Dingo Wild Dog. "What is *this*?" she shrieked, as her name collapsed in the stars and dripped across the sky. "What is happening!?"

"There's your welcome home sign!" his voice thundered. "It's the Milky Way! It's the Fourth of July! It's Heaven!"

"No, it's not!" she shouted. "It is not heaven! Don't do that! COME BACK DOWN HERE TO EARTH AND APOLOGIZE!!!"

"Are you kidding?" his voice bellowed. "For *what*!?"

She collapsed in a riot of self-pity, exploding with what she didn't want to know. "WHY DON'T YOU WANT ME?!"

"Because you're a schemer and a dreamer and a liar, you dog fucker!" Bobby's disappearing voice told her. "And you don't get me hot!"

She wept. "I don't understand . . ."

"BECAUSE YOU'RE A SCHEMER AND A DREAMER AND A LIAR, YOU DOG FUCKER!" Bobby's voice roared. "AND YOU DON'T GET ME HOT! YOU DON'T GET ME HOT! YOU DON'T GET ME HOT! YOU DON'T GET ME HOT! . . . you don't get me hot . . . you don't get me hot . . . you don't get me . . . you don't get me . . . you don't . . . you don't . . . you don't . . . don't . . . don't . . . don't . . . don't . . . don't . . . don't . . ."

The sky turned black. The room turned black. Everything was black. Snap. The blackness snapped to blazing light. Topsy covered her eyes with her hands, groping for the covers, a pillow, something to keep out that blazing light and Bobby's voice.

"Are you goin' to sleep through the entire mornin'?" Irene Shady asked, trying to adjust the window shade that had flown to the top with a crack. She opened the closet and pulled out a robe. "Here, Miss Highness. Put this on." She tossed Topsy the robe and walked out the door.

Haggard, Topsy opened her eyes and slowly looked up at the ceiling. It was intact. She looked at the window. It wasn't even raised. The door didn't have a lock on it. Never had.

And she hadn't seen Bobby Hendersen in twenty years.

CHAPTER FORTY-ONE

"WE'VE HAD NO less than forty-two phone calls during the time you have been in yonder gettin' your beauty rest!" Irene Shady told her daughter, as Topsy wandered into the kitchen. Although the announcement sounded like a complaint, Topsy knew her mother could not be more pleased.

Irene had unfolded the ironing board next to the stove and was pressing Topsy's freshly laundered Peanut Butter Cup dress with one hand and scrambling eggs with the other.

Topsy pulled her old pink chenille robe around her. She had hidden what was left of the vodka from the night before in the pocket. "I'll finish ironing that," she told her mother.

"Uh-uh." Irene shook her head. "This is 'Mary Jane Shady Day.' All you have to do is sit down and eat, get dressed and look pretty, show up and smile. At this very minute, ever-body is Uncertain, Texas is gettin' ready to come see you crown the Queen!" She reached over the ironing board and flipped the bacon which she had fried to a crisp. "What else would Your Highness like?"

"Just a couple of aspirin," Topsy murmured.

"You cain't eat aspirin on a empty stomach. It rots your insides out. Have a cup of coffee first." She dumped the bacon on the plate, bowed deeply, and handed it to her daughter with a flourish.

Topsy looked at the eggs swimming in margarine, the bacon floating in its own grease and two perfectly flat homemade biscuits. She took the food into the saloon and sat in her regular place, facing the pantry.

"There it goes!" cried Irene as the telephone rang. "We've had calls from people *I* thought were dead!" She came out of the kitchen door and circled into the pantry toward the ringing extension. "Hello? . . . What? . . . Stop talkin' so fast! . . . Quit yellin'! . . . Well, hang on to your horses and I will!" Irene dragged the phone out of the embalming room and placed it next to her daughter at the table. "No 'hello' or nothin'. Just kept sayin', 'Put her on, put her on,' in some kind of a foreign accent. If that's that boyfriend of yours, you can tell him to send off for some manners!"

Topsy grabbed the phone. "Herman!"

"It's Ralph, Mary Jane!" Topsy heard her agent yell. "Ralph Painter of the Painter Perfect Agency, 9200 Sunset Boulevard, Los Angeles, California, U.S.A., North American Continent, Planet Earth, the Universe, phone number 213-737-3328 and that spells '*perfect*' in numbers. I know where the fuck I am. Now where the fuck are you?!"

"Uncertain . . . "

"No, shit!" Ralph growled. "Why the fuck didn't anybody tell me where the fuck you were going?"

"I don't know what happened," Topsy said quietly. "I didn't know I was coming—"

"Ha, ha, very funny," Ralph Painter spat. "You're going to be the cause of my stroke, Mary Jane. I'm having a fucking major stroke this very minute. Arabella du Noir tells me that she's arriving in Uncertain, Texas, at three o'clock this afternoon! What does this mean, please? Can you tell me what this means? No! Of course not! You can't talk! If it doesn't come in a script, you don't know what to *say*! You know why you're there! Stop trying to make a fool out of me! How dare you impose your silly requests on Arabella du Noir so you could go back to your high school reunion! What do you think we're running here, kindergarten? Well, she's not happy, I can tell you that! And neither am I! But she's on her way! And so am I!"

"*Here*?" Topsy whispered. "*You're* coming *here*?"

"That's right, Mary Jane. Congratulations. You're getting it. You'll work up to a point two IQ yet! Now how long does it take to get there? Don't exert yourself, don't get a headache thinking!"

"It takes all day—"

"I mean *flying,* you stupid cunt!" Ralph screamed.

"I mean flying, too," Topsy said. "And I really wish you wouldn't call me a cunt."

"I don't like that kind of language one bit," Irene snapped. "I don't appreciate that one bit." She turned on her heel and headed for her office.

The bells rang on the front door as Ralph continued to holler in Topsy's ear.

"I'm moving rapidly into paralysis, Mary Jane. And your six-figure salary is diminishing to two cents right before my very eyes. Is it possible for you to comprehend or even begin to imagine the value of *two cents* these days? You're a mathematic moron, you know that? And you're not getting any younger either. I don't know what Arabella has in mind, but it does not look good, let me assure you, your future is not looking too bright. Those new headshots that Marty took last week came back and what do you think came out in every single shot? A *line,* just under your left eye. A line, Mary Jane, as in *wrinkle, crow's foot, AGE*. Get the picture? Looks like Arabella du Noir did. I told you six months ago to take care of those lines and now you've pushed her—"

Someone put their arms around Topsy's waist and gave her a big kiss on her cheek from behind.

"Hi! Hi! It's *me*! Why-vonne!" Yvonne's high-pitched voice sang. "Oh, gosh, I got lipstick all over you! Here, let me get it off!" She rubbed Topsy's cheek vigorously with her fingers.

Topsy turned around to see Mrs. Bobby Henderson, who, at ten o'clock in the morning, was dressed in a strapless maroon and gold sequined top with a maroon ruffle-duster mini skirt, wearing a carrot red wig and looking just like a drag queen out of some bar in New Orleans.

"Oh, my God," gasped Topsy.

"Now you're getting the picture," Ralph hissed. "So how long is it going to take me to get there? And I mean fucking realistically?"

"Don't let me interrupt your call, Mary Jane," Yvonne gushed, patting her red wig and continuing to rub Topsy's cheek.

"Don't worry about it," Topsy said to Yvonne.

"Worry about it! I'm having a fucking heart attack!" Ralph screamed. "I have *meetings*, I'll miss *lunch*! I told you NEVER, NEVER, NEVER make a direct request! Let me do that! That's my job!"

"Is that your Jew boyfriend?" Yvonne whispered.

"Agent, agent," Topsy told Yvonne.

"Don't call me names!" Ralph bellowed.

"I'm not talking to you, Ralph," Topsy said.

"Fine. Don't talk. Who cares. If you've blown this Creamy Crunchy Peanut Butter, Creamy or Smooth job—"

"Nutty or Smooth," Topsy corrected.

"You're fucking rude, you know that? All you ever think about is yourself! All you ever talk about is yourself! Every question you ask just begs for an answer that relates directly to you. YOURSELF—!"

Why do I bring this out in people? Topsy wondered, confused. *What am I doing wrong—*?

"Did you think throwing the entire Hocker-Smockter Corporation into a tizzy wasn't going to have dire consequences? I've spent years dealing with you devious little undermining glutton-driven day-players, and I'm going to tell you something it may be too late for you to remember! You are in no position to request fringes, Mary Jane Shady! A trip like this is called a 'perk' and you don't get one, dear. *Why*? Do you want to know *why*? Let me tell you why, Miss Peanut Butter Cup! For one reason and one reason only: YOU ARE NOT A STAR!" He hung up.

"Oh, I hope I didn't interrupt your call," Yvonne said. "Was it important? Was it from *Hollywood?!*" She extended her arms and took a presentational stance on the word "Hollywood."

"*. . . you are not a star . . . you are not a star . . .* "

"Was it important?"

Topsy looked at Yvonne and thought of Bobby.

"*. . . you don't get me hot . . . you don't get me hot . . .* "

She looked at Yvonne's wig. She stared at the dress. Yvonne's excited grin bled across her face like candlelight through a jack-o'-lantern's mouth.

"Would you like something to drink, Yvonne?"

"Oh, I already had about fourteen cups of coffee I was so excited to see you. I tried to call back last night, but the line was tied up. Then it got too late, and I know that's a long trip from where you come from, so I waited this mornin' 'til I couldn't stand it any longer."

"Yvonne. Would you like a drink?" Topsy repeated. *Don't ask about Bobby,* she told herself. *Don't bring him up. Don't start thinking* . . . Her hand was rubbing her face, right under her left eye. *This is what he married. This is what looked better than me* . . . She jerked her hand away from her face. Yvonne was staring at her. Does she know? Topsy wondered frantically. Does she know about me? Her hand was scratching her face again. *All you ever think about is YOURSELF*! She yanked her hand away. *Quit it! Stop scratching! Stop thinking! Don't think* . . . "I think I'll have a little drink . . ."

Yvonne looked a little blank. "You mean a *drink-drink*?"

Topsy smiled a Mary Jane Shady smile for Yvonne and headed for the kitchen.

Yvonne grinned. "Why not!" she squealed, following her. "We'll just Hollywood-it-up right here in ole Uncertain!"

Topsy reached into the robe's deep pocket, pulled out what was left of the vodka, filled up two ice tea glasses halfway, threw in some ice and added tomato juice. She was about to add Tobasco and pepper when her mother appeared.

"What in the world are ya'll doin'?" Irene Shady wanted to know.

"We're gettin' ready to Hollywood-it-up!" Yvonne giggled, as Topsy handed Yvonne her drink.

Irene took Topsy's Bloody Mary and threw it down the sink. "I need that worse than you do, but we got to have our heads clear," she told her daughter, handing her her Peanut Butter Cup outfit.

I don't want a clear head! screamed Topsy's head. *I don't want to remember this*!

"Now go start gettin' yourself ready. You got to be prepared by the time the Pep Rally starts."

"Why'd you throw my drink out?" Topsy asked, harassed. "Why did you do that?"

"Because ever-time anybody in this family takes a drink, they do somethin' crazy," Irene Shady said. "The last time I took a sip of somethin', I ended up in West Texas runnin' this funeral parlor. That stuff clouds up your brain waves. And you're goin' to need ever bit of yourself you can pull together to deal with that agent of yours. How could you let anybody talk to you like that!"

"What?" Topsy asked, distracted. The last of the vodka was at the bottom of her mother's kitchen sink.

"Now listen," Irene snapped. "I hate to admit to what I done, but I didn't like the tone of that man when I answered the phone. I figgered he meant trouble. So I picked up the extension in my office up front and listened in. Mary Jane, I know I promised I wouldn't do that no more, but I couldn't help myself and let me tell you somethin' else: I won't stand for the way that man talked to you so I had to put a stop to it."

"What? What?" Topsy said frantically. "You didn't call him back or anything did you?"

"Course not," Irene shot back. "I don't mess with inferiors."

Topsy looked at her mother sharply. "What did you do?"

"I picked up the phone just now and called the Smocker-Hocker Agency in New York City, got my best new friend, head honcho Airy-bell-uh Dune-war back on the line, told her that this agent Ralph Painter from the Painter Perfect Agency in Hollywood, California, who claims he is from the Planet Earth, is less than perfect, not to mention human, and had spoke to you like you wasn't neither, and in short had to be put in line and put there quick!"

"You spoke to Arabella du Noir?!" Topsy gasped.

"Stars are my business and fame is my game!" Irene Shady proclaimed.

"They been on the phone non-stop for two whole days!" Yvonne grinned.

"No!" Topsy whispered, traumatized. "No, no, no . . ."

"Yep," Irene smiled. "I just called up yesterday and told 'em that I was Miss Peanut Butter Cup's mother and they put me right through to Miz Dune-war. I explained how it was your twentieth reunion and that you needed to come home and see all your friends and celebrate your success and attend your high school reunion and crown the Queen—"

"*Ladies and Gentlemen of Uncertain, Texas, here to crown this year's Homecoming Queen is Miss Mary Jane Shady. She has distinguished herself in many ways, but never more so than now. Friends, Miss Mary Jane Shady is an aging dog fucker. You will recognize her by the line under her left eye, the tattoo over her heart and the tail growing beneath her Peanut Butter Cup skirt—"*

"In a crisis, go right to the top!" Irene stated. "That Miz Dune-war is a reasonable woman. I'm lookin' forward to her acquaintance."

"Me, too," Yvonne grinned.

A river of rage, followed by an avalanche of fear burst through Topsy. She reached for the empty vodka bottle without thinking. "They're coming," she whispered. "This is it."

"That's right, and that's why you cain't drink that stuff," Irene said, tossing the bottle into the trash. "Yvonne here can get drunk as a skunk, but you got to be sober and perfect for all the Peanut Butter people from coast-to-coast and all their TV outfit which is on their way in a couple of Smocker-Hockter Lear Jets—"

PERFECT. PERFECT. PERFECT. She looked around desperately. *How am I going to be perfect perfect perfect?*

"One jet's comin' from New York City and Miz Dune-war is sendin' another with that agent of yours in it. She says she'll straighten him out first thing—"

"*. . . you're not a star, you're not a star, you're not a star. . .* "

"I told her to get ever-body here before the Pep Rally and maybe they could use it as background. She says that's the most 'creative'—yessiree, that's the word she used—'creative'—idea she has heard of in about the last ten or fifteen years—"

"*. . . YOU JUST DON'T GET ME HOT. . . YOU JUST DON'T GET ME HOT . . . YOU'RE NOT PERFECT. . . YOU'RE NOT A STAR. . . YOU'RE NOT HOT. . . YOU'RE NOT PERFECT. . . YOU'RE NOT. . . YOU'RE NOT. . . YOU'RE NOT HOT . . . .*"

"—I told her I would tell them cheerleaders to just keep cheerin' over and over 'til her Peanut Butter people arrive. Now I got to get the Superintendent of Schools on the line and see if he's out of bereavement and anywhere near prepared for all this."

"*. . . DOG FUCKER! DOG FUCKER! DOG FUCKER!. . .* "

"Find me the phone book, somebody."

"NO!" Topsy screamed, backing away. She banged into the table, sending her plate to the floor and slices of bacon and fragments of eggs into the air. She saw her mother and Yvonne staring at her, concerned. "They can't get here that fast!" she stammered desperately. "They'll never make it! They'll have to land in Midland and unload and drive all the way over and everything! They'll never make it!" She thought she was going to pass out. "Tell them not to come!" she shouted. "You pick up that phone and tell them just don't bother! TELL THEM IT WILL ALL BE OVER BY THE TIME THEY GET HERE!"

"No, no!" Yvonne cried. "They're landin' on my landin' strip out in the backyard!"

Topsy closed her eyes. Scrambled eggs clung to her toes. *A direct flight from L.A. or New York to Uncertain in a Lear Jet? Three hours, four.* She looked at the clock. It was ten-fifteen in the morning.

"That's what I told 'em and that's what they're goin' to do!" Irene announced triumphantly.

Yvonne handed Irene the Uncertain telephone book. "I sure am glad you thought to call that head honcho up in New York City," she said excitedly. "I sure would have never thought of doin' that!"

Topsy rose slowly and moved with fixed determination toward the bar. Two bullet holes smashed through her image in the mirror where, long ago, someone had shot a gun off in a bar fight. The crazed markings on the mirror ricocheted across her forehead. She didn't notice. She was staring just beneath her left eye. There it was. The line. She gazed at it, spellbound. The harder she looked, the larger it grew.

Irene flipped through the pages of the phone book, chanting, "Stars are my business and fame is my game!" She found the number she wanted and dialed. "Hello. This is Irene Shady over at the Uncertain Chapel of Memories. I need to speak to the Superintendent of Schools—" She grinned at Yvonne and winked. "Well, get Mr. Orville Turner fast and tell him to call me back quick! . . . Do I have to talk to him now? Hon, I needed to talk to him *yesterday*!" She hung up and said, "How's that for puttin' it to 'em?"

Irene stood up, put the phone book down and walked over to her daughter. Slowly, she turned Topsy around, looked at her carefully and took her face in her hands.

"Hand me my glasses, Why-vonne."

Yvonne got them from the table, Irene put them on and peered at Topsy's face. "That's just a little tiny line under your left eye, hon," she said finally. "I'll ask Miz Dune-war where to get that fixed."

Her big strong arms wrapped themselves around Topsy, and she held her daughter for a long, long time. "There's just about nothin' in life that cain't be put right one way or another," she told her daughter.

Tears filled Topsy's eyes, then they streamed down her face, and finally she wept, long deep racking sobs.

"Go get a wet rag and those eyedrops out of the medicine cabinet in the bathroom," Irene instructed Yvonne as she rocked Topsy back and forth in her arms. "You got to make yourself stop cryin' now, hon, so your eyes won't be red for the Peanut Butter people. You don't want to have driven yourself crazy for nothin'."

"I drove myself crazy for nothin'," Yvonne confided. "And I'm still not sure it was worth it."

Topsy Dingo Wild Dog looked up at Yvonne. Had he broken her heart, too? What had he done? It didn't matter. She wanted to kill Bobby Henderson. She wanted to kill somebody.

The phone started ringing and Irene reached out to answer it. She sat down in a chair. "Hello? Oh, hidy, Orville." Irene pulled her daughter down in her lap and held the phone between her head and her shoulder, put one arm around Topsy, and took her glasses off with her other hand. "Well, what I'm callin' to tell you is this: we're about ready here to Hollywood-it-up in ole Uncertain!"

CHAPTER FORTY-TWO

TOPSY DINGO WILD DOG watched Yvonne Henderson walking toward her carrying a bottle of Visine.

"Okay," grinned Yvonne. "Now lean your head back."

I don't think she'd be putting eyedrops in my eyes if she knew anything... Topsy tried to reassure herself.

"Now open *wide,*" grinned Yvonne.

But what if she's being nice to me because she KNOWS what happened? Topsy looked up at Yvonne, studying her hard. *What if I'm the first person Yvonne ever met that she can look down on*?

A big drop of Visine hit her left eye. Another hit her right eye. Yvonne blurred.

Paranoid, Topsy's head said. *You're paranoid....*

"Okay," said Yvonne. "Let's give 'em another squirt!"

Two more drops landed in her eyes.

She wondered what Yvonne's life was like... did she live on Melogo Drive in a big rectangular house, fenced and white, shuttered and lawned with sprinkler systems and disposals, dishwashers and electric can openers, central heat and air? Did a maid come twice a week or did Yvonne do everything herself? Was she just the perfect little woman? Did she and Bobby have children? How many? What gender?

Were they happy? How old? How tall? How small? Did they have little bald spots? Did they have little close-set eyes? Or were they blond and sweet laughing angels? Did Bobby tell them bedtime stories, campfire stories, war stories? Did he tell them about her? Did they know *The Tale of Topsy Dingo Wild Dog*? Did they all sit around, laughing, giggling at the plight of Mary Jane Shady, The Quintessential Victim, that stupid airhead who had fled from the horror of one night with a dog only to be pitted against one monster after another in one horror film after another, to finally, finally, finally get a decent job where people actually even asked for her autograph sometimes, where she was sometimes treated with a modicum of respectability, where she was at least able to make a living and not wait in unemployment lines or wait tables or have to be kept or have to write home for money, only to come back and lose everything she'd worked for, to be publicly humiliated and permanently destroyed. Would all of Uncertain be at the Pep Rally, laughing together, pointing at her, tittering, like he had . . . like Bobby had . . . were they all just waiting for her to fall?

"Okay," said Yvonne. "Let's give 'em another squirt!"

Don't ask . . . sighed Topsy Dingo Wild Dog, surrendering to Yvonne Henderson and the Visine bottle. *Do not ask* . . .

She fell back into the chair.

"While your eyes are shut," she heard Yvonne say, "I want to hear how you got to the top."

Topsy Dingo Wild Dog opened her eyes and looked up at Yvonne suspiciously. She peered at Yvonne, standing there gazing adoringly at her with two brown beady eyes and a wig that was supposed to help Yvonne resemble Miss Peanut Butter Cup.

Oh, shit, I'm losing it . . . *Yvonne is so innocent it's pathetic* . . .

"I'm listenin'," Yvonne said patiently. "I'm listenin' to hear how you got to the top . . . "

Topsy Dingo Wild Dog started to laugh softly. *This isn't funny,* she told herself. *Really. It isn't. It isn't funny at all* . . .

"Yvonne," Topsy sighed, "I don't know. Believe me, if I knew how to get to the top, I'd be there. *Right now.*"

Irene had just finished talking to Gladys' husband, Orville Turner. She was now on long distance in her office, trying to describe Yvonne's house to the pilot in New York, who promised to describe it to the pilot in Los Angeles, when Gladys Turner hurried in the front door carrying a black and white kitten.

"It's the biggest house in town, hon," Irene was saying, "and the only one with a landin' strip out in the backyard . . . "

"Irene!" Gladys interrupted, as the kitty wiggled through her fingers and scurried into the parlor. "I got to talk to you!"

Irene waved Gladys away and put a finger in her ear. "How long is it? . . . Oh, a couple of miles, I 'spect. You think that ought to do it? . . ."

"Mary Jane!" Gladys Turner called, hurrying toward a lamp the kitten was about to leap on. "The most awful thing has happened!" Gladys caught the little black and white animal right in midair.

"She cain't talk now, Gladys!" said Yvonne Henderson, as she put Visine into Topsy's eyes. "She's got eyedrops in her eyes!"

"Good morning, Why-vonne," Gladys said primly, holding the kitten tightly. "What a shiny dress." She absolutely hated Yvonne Henderson for being so rich and especially for getting so rich the way she had.

"Thanks!" Yvonne said cheerfully. "Wait 'til you see the *rest* of it!" She dabbed at Topsy's eyes with a Kleenex. "Just let that set now." She looked at Gladys and grinned. "Where'd you get that cat?"

"Would you look at this, Mary Jane?" Gladys asked, ignoring Yvonne and thrusting the wiggling kitten toward Topsy. "Why did this have to happen to me?"

"She cain't, Gladys. She's gettin' her eyes ready for the Peanut Butter people," Yvonne said. "Don't open up your eyes, Mary Jane."

"This is just awful," Gladys complained, as the cat crawled over her shoulders. "I don't know what on earth I'm going to do with it—"

"Can you believe they're comin' all the way from Los Angeles, California and New York City to make a picture show starrin' Mary Jane Shady at our Homecomin'!" Yvonne squealed, squeezing another drop of Visine in Topsy's left eye.

Oh, dear God in heaven, Topsy groaned. *Why is this happening*?

"My daughter-in-law gave it to me," Gladys sighed. She caught the kitten by the tail and it tumbled over her breasts. "And I just can't keep it. It's already climbed all over my little dish collection. I don't know why on earth Darnelle didn't think of that—"

"It's not a movie, Yvonne," Topsy said, holding her head back with her eyes closed. "It's just a commercial." She tried to sound casual. "Where's the little cat?"

"—and I'd die if one got broken! She knows that!" Gladys continued, dropping the kitten into Topsy's lap and heading into the kitchen toward the percolator.

The kitten snuggled up close to Topsy. It's rough little tongue licked her hand. Topsy opened one eye slightly. *That's all it is. Just a little black and white kitty. With a harmless little pink tongue . . .*

"Yippee!" Yvonne cried. "Hollywood is about to appear right here!"

Don't scream. It's a cat. It's not a dog. It's a little tiny cat . . .

"They're not going to get much of a Pep Rally show unless I get this cat dilemma settled," Gladys called out. She stared at the empty coffee pot, stunned. "There's not any coffee. How could that be?"

You don't have problems with cats. Not that you know many cats . . .

"Well, the pilot's set," Irene announced, hanging up the phone in her office. "What is it, Gladys?" she called as she walked through the parlor and the saloon toward the kitchen. "What's wrong?"

"Is it broken?" Gladys asked, fiddling with the stove. "You always use the percolator anyway. Why isn't it plugged in and perking?"

"We've got hotter things cookin', Gladys," Irene stated from the doorway. "Bigger fish to fry. I just spoke to Orville and he's ready to go. Miz Dune-war from New York City will take care of ever-thing else—"

Wait until Arabella sees Gladys . . . Topsy sighed. She sat straight up in her chair. *Wait until Gladys sees Arabella du Noir*! Before her she envisioned Arabella, tall and dark, in Galanos and pearls. *Oh, no*! she gasped. *Arabella du Noir can't come to Uncertain, Texas! This town is not ready for her! This town will NEVER be ready for her! Oh, my God, this is horrible, horrible, horrible! Terrible, terrible, terrible! How can a disaster get worse*?! She wondered if Arabella du Noir knew anything about West Texas. She wondered if she had any idea whatsoever what she was getting into. She wondered how on earth her mother had talked her into coming to Uncertain, Texas in the first place. *Try to sound sane. Try to sound calm. Try to sound like somebody would listen to and take seriously. Try to sound like Helen Hayes. Pretend you're Helen Hayes.* "Have they left New York yet?" she asked her mother anxiously. "Did they leave? Have they left?"

"Is she going to take care of this cat?" Gladys asked, moving out of the kitchen, past Irene and into the saloon. She picked the kitten up from Topsy's lap and put it on top of the table, where it wobbled right over to the cream pitcher. "Somebody better do something about this cat. Darnelle gave it to me to help me through the grieving process, but I'm afraid it's going to break my little cups and saucers if I leave it at home by itself—"

Gladys Turner is dangerous, Topsy thought. *Gladys Turner is just to the right of Attila the Hun . . . She's going to think Arabella du Noir is Little Black Sambo's Mother. . .* "Mother!" she cried. "Did they leave New York?"

"Why didn't she just send flowers?" Yvonne wondered. "I never heard of sendin' cats—"

Oh, my God, Topsy's head banged away. *What on earth is going to happen when these primitives are confronted with a—dark person . . . a colored person? a black person? Out here there's no difference! They're going to treat her like a NIGGER*!

"I'm goin' to take it outside and put it under the red light if you don't get it off my table!" Irene told Gladys.

"Don't get so upset, Irene," Gladys said, reaching for the cat. "I'm the one who's supposed to be upset!"

"Mournin's over, Gladys!" Irene Shady said. "Your sister's *buried*! This is '*Mary Jane Shady Day*'! And she's not sharin' it with a cat!"

Topsy dizzily looked at her watch. Were they in the air? Had Arabella du Noir left Madison Avenue? Had Ralph Painter left Sunset Boulevard? "Where's Arabella du Noir, Mother? Where is she? You better call her. I need to talk to her. You better get her on the phone. *I mean it*!"

"Oh, settle down!" Irene snapped. "You don't need to talk to her. Anyway, she's up in the air. Stop worryin'. Me and Miz Dune-war know what we're doin'!"

Topsy fell back into the chair. She liked Arabella du Noir. She admired her. And she did not want to see this powerful, handsome woman insulted. But there was nothing she could do about it now. Nothing. *You were thinking about yourself. You were all involved with yourself. Now look what's going to happen because you were SELF-INVOLVED WITH YOUR SELF!*

"That's easy for you to say, Irene," Gladys sniffed. "But I don't want to hurt Darnelle's feelings—"

Ralph Painter. That scum heap. That rat. That vermin. That hickey sucker. How he's going to love to watch a bunch of heathens work over the Countess du Noir. She's too rich, too powerful, too female, too royal, too black. He hates her. She's where the top stops . . . .

"We established that, Gladys. Let me ask you a simple question: what-do-you-want-to-do-with-that-cat? What will make you stop talkin' about it *right now*?"

"I don't know," Gladys replied, steeling the kitten on her lap. "Do you think the coffee's done? I just can't hurt Darnelle's feelings. You know how *sensitive* she is. I don't want her to think I don't appreciate the little cat or anything, but—"

Topsy closed her eyes. *Arabella du Noir is going to be insulted. Ralph Painter is going to get the laugh of his life. And I'm going to end up exactly where I started: IN UNCERTAIN-FUCKING-TEXAS WITH NOTHING, NOTHING, NOTHING!*

"So what's it goin' to be?" Irene questioned flatly.

"Well, I don't know—" The kitten slid through Gladys' fingers and hopped back upon the table.

"Here's the options!" Irene was gritting her teeth. "We can take it in yonder and drown it in the tub, or we can let the dogs eat it up or you could give it away or you could keep it!"

Dogs! Topsy Dingo Wild Dog thought she would scream. "What dogs?" she yelped. *YOU ASKED A QUESTION*! her inner voice thundered. *YOU FORGOT AND ASKED A QUESTION! BAD, BAD, BAD, BAD, BAD . . .*

"I couldn't drown a cat!" Gladys looked appalled. "Look at how little it is!"

"I could!" Irene said, going for the kitten, whose head had disappeared into her cream pitcher. "Give it here!"

"No!" Gladys screamed, lunging across the table.

"Then keep it!" Irene shouted, as the cat leapt through both of them.

"I can't! I can't! I can't!" Gladys cried, as the cat jumped into Topsy's lap.

Topsy opened her eyes. She grabbed the cat. "I'll take it!" she shrieked.

They all looked at her.

"I don't have any pets," she cried. *I've got to get over this dog thing . . . I'll start slow and work up . . . I'll get a litter box and give it a name and get it some tags and shots and Purina and yarn! I'LL BE FINE!* "I'll take it back to New York with me."

"New York?" Gladys said dubiously. "New York? How's it going to get there?"

"With the Peanut Butter people," Irene offered quickly. "I'll fix it so it can ride back with Miz Dune-war."

"Are they nice people?" Gladys wanted to know. "I'm responsible for this kitty, you know. How long have you known Mrs. Dune-war, Mary Jane? How many people will be on that plane?"

Topsy took a deep breath. "I think we should discuss Ms. du Noir, *no kidding—*"

Irene's face looked like the beginnings of a Wichita Falls tornado. "Why? Is she allergic to cats?"

Gladys was waiting to be placated when the phone rang.

Yvonne grabbed it. "Hello? Hello? Hello? . . . The prettiest girl in the world? Why, that's *me*! . . . Oh, *her*!" She giggled. "It's for you, M.J. It's a *man*."

"If that's that agent, give me the phone!" Irene yelled.

Topsy took the phone in one hand. She was still holding the cat. "Herman . . ." she whispered.

Yvonne was bouncing on her toes. "It's Herman Top, inn't it!" She turned to Gladys, grinning. "I heard her say 'Hi, Herman!' "

Gladys Turner was asking, "The Jew? Is she talking to the Jew?"

Topsy stopped listening. She looked up. She stopped talking. She stopped thinking.

Irene was frowning at Gladys. Gladys was scowling at Yvonne. Yvonne's eyes were opened wide. She hadn't looked away from Topsy for a minute.

"Herman. Listen to me," Topsy said urgently. "Herman. Don't you dare come here. I mean it. Do *not* come. I'm hanging up now. *Don't come here*! I have to go. To the Pep Rally. I have to, Herman. Because! I *have* to! I've got to crown those Siamese twins!" She hung up.

"Was that Herman Top?" Yvonne squealed. "The one I see on the Tonight Show and in the Woody Allen movies? The one who sings those little foreign songs!" Yvonne gushed. "Oh, I *love* him! Why'd you tell him not to come? We could have had us *two* stars!"

"I am not a star, Yvonne," Topsy said violently. "I am *not* a star."

"Oh, yes, you are!" cried Irene Shady. "You are, too, a star! This is 'Mary Jane Shady Day' and you're the *star*!"

"The one who's a Jew?" whispered Gladys Turner. "If my cat goes to New York, will it get petted by a *Jew*?"

"What about it?" Topsy snapped.

Irene Shady's face started to storm over again. "What's wrong with that?" she asked Gladys sharply.

"Well," Gladys said hesitantly. "I just didn't know if he knew anything about animals or not . . . "

"Noah was a Jew, Gladys!" Irene Shady shouted. "And he brung 'em in two by two! I guess if Noah could manage a zoo on a boat, Herman Top can take care of that little black and white kitty!"

Irene Shady never failed to amaze Topsy.

"Tell Herman Top when he gets tired of pettin' that little pussy, he can come pet mine!" Yvonne Henderson giggled.

Appalled, Gladys put her coffee cup down on the table and got up.

A squall of laughter flew through Topsy Dingo Wild Dog. It spiralled up through her stomach, careened through her throat and exploded like broken coils.

Gladys took her purse, the kitten and started for the front door. "Well, I'll just keep it at my house 'til the Pep Rally's over . . . I'll put it in the birdcage . . . Orville's parakeet died and that cage is just sitting there . . ."

"Good-bye, Gladys," scowled Irene Shady.

"Good-bye, Gladys," grinned Yvonne Henderson.

"Good-bye, Gladys," howled Topsy Dingo Wild Dog.

"I got drunk, sober and a hangover all in ten minutes!" Yvonne giggled. "Welcome back to Uncertain, Mary Jane!"

Topsy laughed harder. *I'M LAUGHING*! Topsy thought, startled. *Ha-ha-ha is coming out of my mouth*!

"And did you hear what she said about my dress?" Yvonne fell into a chair. "Said it was *shiny! Shiny*! That's what she said! Wait 'til she sees what I'm puttin' on for the Pep Rally! She ain't seen nothin' yet!"

Topsy looked at Yvonne enviously. She wiped her eyes, wished she were a moron and decided she was acting like one anyway. She wondered what was the difference in being a born moron or just acquiring moronic behavioral skills. She decided to think of nothing except what Yvonne was going to wear. *What if I've overestimated myself? What if I'm the moron and Yvonne is just a brilliant, fucking genius and I'm nothing but a born, doomed FOOL*? . . . This thought literally took her breath away. Don't think about that, she told herself. *You're better off thinking about Arabella du Noir and Ralph Painter and Herman and Bobby and Siamese twins and German shepherds,* she told herself. *You're better off to think about three o'clock this afternoon and losing your job and Arabella getting insulted and Ralph laughing and Herman not understanding and what Bobby Henderson looks like and if he's missed you or not and what he's going to say or not and if he's changed or not and if—*"

Yvonne turned to Topsy. "Nothin's changed around here, Mary Jane, and nothin' ever will. People will talk about you no matter what you do, so I just try to give 'em somethin' interestin' to talk *about*!"

Irene Shady's eyebrows shot straight up.

Topsy looked at Yvonne and laughed tiredly. "Well, everybody is going to have plenty to talk about after this afternoon," she said.

"I hope nobody laughs at my wig," Yvonne said quietly. She paused for a minute. "It just inn't right, is it? I don't know what got into Colin yesterday. I told him I wanted to look just like *you*!"

"You didn't get that from Deal Grimes?" Irene asked.

"No, I did not!" Yvonne laughed. "I flew all the way to Dallas, Texas to get this hair fixed up just like *hers,* but somethin' didn't come out right."

"Well, it looks cute and colorful," Irene said encouragingly. She didn't want Yvonne to suddenly turn sad, as she had sometimes seen her do.

"Oh, I got tons of 'em in every color, Mary Jane," Yvonne told Topsy. "'Cause ever-time I go to church, those kids at Sunday School yank 'em off my head to play touch football with. Got to where I finally carry a spare in the car so I can go on into the service. I tell you, those little Holy Rollers play rough."

Oh, that bald spot, Topsy thought sympathetically. *She wears those wigs to cover up that bald spot.*

"I thought you grew up Baptist," Irene remarked.

"I did!" Yvonne replied, "even though I was born a Methodist. Then when I married Bobby, I had to change to Assembly of God to keep from hearin' his mama tell me I was goin' to go to hell day in and day out if I didn't—"

Bobby. There. Finally. His name. Finally. Out loud . . . .

"—so then, ole Catsy Ivanhoe said, 'You was a lousy Methodist and a rotten Baptist, now what makes you think you're goin' to be a good Holy Roller?' And I said, 'I don't expect to be, but ole Mrs. Henderson won't know it!' "

Yvonne and Irene laughed and laughed, while Topsy wearily remembered how Mrs. Henderson had said the same thing to her so many years ago.

Bobby. She didn't want to think about him. She wasn't going to think about him. She wanted to sit here with Yvonne and not think.

"Oh, gosh! I got to go home and finish gettin' dressed!" Yvonne cried. "Come on and go with me, Mary Jane. I promise I won't take long!"

Startled, Topsy hesitated.

"Go on, hon, you got time," Irene nodded. "And anyhow, you ought to see Why-vonne's house."

Topsy stared at Yvonne. Was she wrong about Yvonne?

"Aw, throw some water on your face and come with me," Yvonne pleaded.

She tried to clear her head. *Stop . . . stop being paranoid . . . Yvonne's no actress . . . she doesn't know . . . if she knew, I'd know . . .*

Topsy nodded slowly. Maybe it was better to see him now and just get it over with. Maybe he had asked Yvonne to bring her over. Maybe he hadn't told anyone. Maybe he wasn't going to say anything. Maybe he wasn't even home . . . .

"I laid one of your skirt and sweater sets out on your bed," Irene said. "I don't want you messin' up your Peanut Butter outfit yet." She turned to Yvonne. "All her luggage was lost in midair! She got here with nothin' to wear but her Peanut Butter dress! I don't know what we'd do if she hadn't had it on!"

Lies, thought Topsy Dingo Wild Dog. *All lies . . .* She looked at Yvonne carefully. *She doesn't act like she knows . . .*

"I'll just take a quick shower," Topsy said slowly.

"Hurry!" Yvonne hollered as Topsy disappeared up the landing. "I cain't wait to show you how things have changed for me since you left!"

"Don't get your hair wet!" Irene called out after her.

As soon as they were alone, Irene turned to Yvonne. "So how's Baby?"

"Oh, fine!" Yvonne answered enthusiastically.

Irene Shady looked at Yvonne Henderson shrewdly. "Things are workin' out then?"

"Why, sure!" Yvonne grinned, eyes twinkling. "And, yes! I got her hair fixed and I bought her a brand new dress!"

Topsy hardly remembered stepping in or out of the shower. She didn't even look at her chest. She was wondering what to expect, how to prepare. How could she balance herself for the moment when she drove up with Yvonne to her house on Melogo Drive. *Her* house with no carnations . . . Numbly, she stepped into the old matching green skirt and sweater set. She did not put on any make-up. She did not look in the mirror.

I'm not dressing up for Bobby, she determined. *I'm not doing one thing special for him . . . .*

As she walked down the stairs, Irene Shady beamed proudly. "Honey," she said. "You look exactly like you're fifteen years old again!"

Yvonne Henderson shook her head. "I could never get the feel of a co-ordinated outfit," she confessed. "Things that match just make me *nervous*!"

Is she mocking me? Topsy wondered. *Is she*?

"And a-course, ole Bobby, he made me wear those co-ordinated mix and match sets for years and years and years," Yvonne went on. "Listen! The reason I'm wearin' this look-a-like wig today in your honor is because you're *here*! Believe me, Mary Jane," said Yvonne Henderson, "it took me years to finally get my own style!" She got up from the table, moved toward Topsy and pulled her out the door. "Come on Mary Jane Shady!" grinned Yvonne Dee Flowers Henderson. "Let's go look at my look! I guess you could say I drive like I dress and I dress like I drive and I live like look!"

Irene Shady followed Yvonne with her eyes as she pranced down the steps of the portico. "You dress like a mess! And you *live* like you dress!" Irene said as she closed the front door of the Uncertain Chapel of Memories.

CHAPTER FORTY-THREE

THE FIRST THING Topsy wanted to know when she saw Yvonne's convertible limousine was the name of the drug the designer of this vehicle had been on at the time of its creation. But she didn't have to ask.

"This design is all my own, see," Yvonne explained, as she circled Topsy around the car. "Got it put together in Midland by this guy who specializes in dune buggies and helicopters. It's the only convertible limousine in the State of Texas. The front part's Chrysler, the back's Cadillac, it's got a Chevrolet engine—I could have had a whole Rolls Royce but everybody in the Permian Basin with half a pump has got one of those and I didn't want to be runnin' into myself all over creation and I didn't want anything foreign or unoriginal either. Now as you'll see, those are real black and white cow skins we're about to sit down on and this here's a coyote skull head on top of the hood. I don't believe you'll ever see another car like it anywhere, do you?"

"No," said Topsy evenly. "I don't expect to."

"Well, good!" Yvonne cried. "I worry constantly that somebody or another is goin' to come along and steal this design. Or the color. I stood in that shop and mixed it myself. It's red paint and blue paint. Together they turned purple—just like in art class! Then I added a bunch of metallic to get this permanent glow. The whole thing come to me in a dream!"

"It looks like a cross between a Maud Frizon shoe, a Fellini movie and a Carlos Falchi handbag," Topsy observed.

"A purse, a shoe and a picture show!" Yvonne cried. "Yeah! And a big ole fur coat!" Yvonne laughed. "It looks like a car ought to look!" Giving the glass on the driver's side a sharp rap, Yvonne hollered, "Hey, James!" She turned to Topsy and confided, "His real name's José, but I call him James so he'll feel more American!" She rapped on the glass again. "Wake up and open the doors!"

A tall, young Mexican in full evening attire emerged from behind the dark tinted glass, silently opening the doors as Topsy and Yvonne slid into the Holstein covered upholstery.

"That's the only English he knows," Yvonne said. " 'Open the door,' 'shut the door,' 'turn on the TV. . . .' " She pushed a button and the glass dividing the driver and the passengers slid open. "Hey, turn on the TV, James." She looked at Topsy and explained, "I could do it myself, but I'm tryin' to educate him. Don't ask me why. Soon as they learn how to drive and talk they leave and I have to start all over. It's hard to find good servants, Mary Jane."

Servants?

"I bet you have a great big staff up in New York City and out in Hollywood," Yvonne grinned. "How many servants *do* you have, anyway?"

I could count the doorman, Topsy thought. *And the entire housekeeping staff in New York. The restaurant, the bar, and the parking garage attendants . . .* She looked at Yvonne. "Yvonne," she said, "I live in a hotel, remember. All that sort of comes with it . . . "

"What about a secretary? Don't you have a secretary?" Yvonne persisted. "Who helps you go through your fan mail? The *doorman*?" Yvonne found this wildly funny.

"I have this service," Topsy explained. "I give them the letters and they answer them."

"A fan mail service?" Yvonne was stunned. "You don't answer your own fan mail?"

Topsy shook her head.

"You ought to get a good secretary, Mary Jane," Yvonne recommended. "And make sure they can type. Then ya'll can answer your fan mail!"

Yvonne hit a control and the volume on the TV brought with it a voice and face all too familiar.

"Oh, look! It's *you*!" Yvonne squealed. "Here you are in the back seat of my car and there you are on my TV set!"

Yvonne sat back, held up an imaginary jar of peanut butter and cooed along with Topsy's TV image: "'For energy . . . health . . . and pure rich taste . . . it's Creamy Crunchy Peanut Butter—Nutty or Smooth.' " She pantomimed dipping her finger into the jar and licking it. " '*Yummie-e-e-e-e*!' " Delighted with herself, she burst into giggles. "See! I can do that!"

"Sure," Topsy sighed. "Anybody can . . . ."

Yvonne shook her head solemnly. "You sell yourself short, Mary Jane." She pointed toward the front seat. "*He* couldn't. At least not until he learns to speak English!"

Topsy fell back against the cowskin upholstery. She reached in her purse and put on her Anne Klein sunglasses.

"What kind of a car do *you* have, Mary Jane?" Yvonne wanted to know.

"I don't have a car," Topsy replied.

Yvonne looked at her confused. "Well, how do you get anywhere?"

"I take the subway," Topsy told her. "Or a cab. In L.A. I rent a car."

Yvonne looked at her sympathetically. "You have to *rent* a car?"

Topsy nodded. "In New York, I mostly walk."

Yvonne stared at her. "*Walk*?"

"That's right," said Topsy. "I don't have a limo. I don't have any servants. I don't really have much fan mail. And I really like to walk."

"You don't want to walk *now,* though, do you?" Yvonne asked anxiously.

"No," Topsy said. "I've never ridden in a car like this before . . ."

"Oh, *good*!" Yvonne leaned back and sighed. "I just cain't believe you don't own a car . . ."

They were passing the Uncertain City Park and Swimming Pool. The pool's large oval, aqua-painted basin had been drained for the fall and winter. The yellow railings, faded from the summer sun, waited for their annual coat of paint. A small wooden building, built along with the pool in 1935, had been painted yellow to match the railing. Twenty years ago Bobby Henderson had helped repaint the pool house.

Bobby had been a lifeguard there every summer when he was in high school. Sometimes, before she had ever let him do anything but fondle her, she'd gone to the swimming pool at night when he was locking up. They'd take off all their clothes, jump in the water, hot from the West Texas heat, and slowly he would track her in the pool, two lovely lean bodies playing chase, alone in their very own love pond, swimming in exquisite anticipation of what was yet to come. They'd never gone back there once she'd gone to the oil well with him.

She looked at the old swimming pool. She hadn't liked to swim much anyway. Her skin was too fair to stay out in the sun and her mother had always been afraid if she went swimming in a public pool, she might catch polio. Mary Jane Shady hadn't been in a swimming pool since the summer of 1961.

The Uncertain City Swimming Pool was the largest and cleanest in West Texas. Not one person had ever gotten polio in the Uncertain City Swimming Pool. Five people had come down with polio, but each one, it turned out, had been off visiting friends or relatives in neighboring communities like Balmorhea or Wink, had taken their lives in their hands and gone swimming there, and low and behold, had come down with paralysis. Polio victims were automatically prohibited use of the Uncertain City Swimming Pool. They were not allowed to try out for drum major or twirler in the band, or for cheerleader at school. They could, however, try out for the class plays, provided the part did not call for much movement.

Lillian Crow, the first victim, was eighty-seven years old, denied ever having been *in* a swimming pool or *out* of the Uncertain City Limits for that matter, and made it clear from her iron lung in the hospital, that she had no interest whatsoever in becoming a cheerleader or handling a baton or acting in any kind of a stage show at school.

Wilmer Wiggins, the second victim, was a six-month-old baby, so nobody asked him.

Two other victims died.

That left only Harla Elaine Lewis, the fifth victim, with any interest in extra-curricular school activities, and that is how Mary Jane Shady ended up with Harla Elaine as an acting partner her freshman year in high school.

Mrs. Jones, their drama teacher, decided on "The Recognition Scene" from *Anastasia* for District Competition. Harla Elaine was cast as the Dowager Empress. That way, Judy Jones figured it would be logical and creative all at the same time if she staged the part of the grandmother in a wheelchair. Mrs. Jones' husband, Tolbert Jones, who was the high school head football coach, Economics I, Sociology II, Drivers' Education and shop teacher, suggested adding a character to the scene, sort of a servant type, to push around the wheelchair. Coach Jones had recently caught Sammy Widders, his second-string halfback, smoking cigarettes in the school parking lot, and as punishment for this forbidden act and heinous offense, had his wife cast Sammy as the wheelchair pusher in her play.

Sammy wasn't any happier about being the second-string halfback than he was about pushing Harla Elaine Lewis around in a wheelchair in a play, and when he realized Mrs. Jones had every intention of making him wear old-timey dress-up clothes and stand on a stage with lights so bright the whole world could see he had on a face full of make-up, Sammy Widders considered this the ultimate insult.

For two weeks every afternoon after school, Sammy, Harla Elaine and Mary Jane went over and over and over the same words and movement.

Harla Elaine came from a family of thirteen children, was the oldest and considered her malady a gift from God. Now that she couldn't walk, she didn't have to, and even though she had the full use of her body from the waist up, she had no choice but to sit down, which made it impossible for her to reach a sink, wash clothes, change diapers or run a household, but very possible because of Mrs. Jones' ingenuity, to be a lead in the Freshman Class Drama Selection for District Competition. Being from a family of thirteen children, competition was nothing new to Harla Elaine. She told Mrs. Jones that she was tickled pink to have polio and intended to make the most of it.

Mary Jane had been devastated at Mrs. Jones' choice. Why did Mrs. Jones have to be humane at a time like this? She knew she would be upstaged by a polio victim playing the Dowager. It was the best part anyway and the role she had wanted in the first place.

"Now, Mary Jane," Irene Shady said. "You'll have plenty of opportunities, and this will probably be *it* for Harla Elaine Lewis. Polio limits actresses, you know, so be a little more charitable."

"But how can I do my best with her and Sammy Widders?" Mary Jane had squealed. "His cigarette smoking and her infantile paralysis are ruining my entire life!"

Nonetheless, rehearsals continued, and finally the day arrived when Mrs. Jones, Mary Jane Shady, Harla Elaine Lewis and Sammy Widders drove forty miles east to the Odessa Texas Permian High School Auditorium for District Competition.

Mary Jane had been somewhat cheered by her costume. Old Mayor Bowles' cousin had been a real Broadway actress, and Mrs. Bowles had rummaged around and found some of Brenda Bowles' old clothes in a trunk. She loaned these to Mary Jane for the occasion, and Mary Jane felt confident that she looked beautiful and played her part brilliantly, but even so, who was going to pay any attention to her with a partially paralyzed Harla Elaine valiantly emoting under a white wig from that wheelchair?

With only half an hour before their time to perform, Mary Jane grabbed Sammy Widders in the hall by the dressing rooms.

"Listen here, Sammy Widders," Mary Jane said. "I know this competition doesn't mean a hill of beans to you, but it does to me because I'm going to be a real actress when I grow up, so every appearance I make counts. I don't know if you understand the term 'upstaged' or not, but just by the very nature of Harla Elaine's *condition,* that audience is going to pay more attention to her than they are to me and it's not fair!"

"So what do you want me to do about it, Miss Shady?" Sammy drawled. "I'm just the chair pusher."

"I want you to move that chair down to the *end* of the stage and turn it *up* toward me, so all the audience can see of Miss Harla Elaine Lewis is her back."

Sammy looked at Mary Jane Shady steadily. "What's in it for me?"

"What's the best thing about a Camel?" Mary Jane Shady smiled seductively.

Sammy grinned, staring into Mary Jane's chest. "HUMPS!"

"Well, keep that in mind when we go out there."

Mary Jane turned on her heels and swung lightly out of the room, confident that she would, two hours hence, receive her first acting award for Outstanding Actress in Freshman Class District Permian Basin Dramatic Competition.

The competitors were the neighboring towns of Notrees and Wink. Notrees did a scene from *Our Town* which their freshman class performed each and every year, and which was no more impressive this year than it had been in the past. It did occur to Mary Jane that she would have far preferred Harla Elaine dead in their play than alive in hers.

But Wink did a scene from *Hamlet* between Hamlet and Ophelia. Both Sammy and Mary Jane were stunned. Mary Jane was horrified that the competing school had chosen such difficult material. It was impressive, and that little girl from Wink, Texas could easily win for just memorizing all those words, even though it was plain enough it was clearly difficult for the girl to remember them. She had a whiny, high-pitched voice and spoke with a dreadful West Texas drawl, but so did everyone in West Texas, including the judges; that wasn't going to hurt the girl a bit.

Mary Jane Shady was shaking.

Sammy Widders was fascinated. His mouth had literally fallen open when he recognized Wink's first-string quarterback, Quintin Davis, walk on stage in bloomers, a fancy blouse and dancing tights. *Quintin must have done somethin' totally horrible,* Sammy thought to himself and proceeded to wonder what it could have been.

But as he watched Quintin, even Sammy realized that the quarterback was good. The girl playing the girl sucked eggs, but ole Quintin was walking around, thinking, saying his part just like he was another person from another time and place. It flew thorough his mind that James Dean had done play-acting for a living. And "Jimmy" had been Sammy's hero.

A curious thing happened to Sammy. The same feeling he got when playing football suddenly began to get all over him. HE WANTED TO BE ON THE WINNING TEAM. *Our Town* was out. It was overdone; Mrs. Jones and Mary Jane said so. *Hamlet* was their only competition.

Anastasia had Mary Jane and Harla Elaine in the wheelchair going for it. Sammy decided to go for broke.

Mrs. Jones, watching from the audience, was spellbound. Mary Jane Shady was a good little actress for a freshman student. And her commitment was almost maniacal. Judy Jones congratulated herself on her choice of Harla Elaine. Certainly no one could fail to be impressed with Harla Elaine's efforts.

But it was Sammy Widders who was astounding her. Whatever had come over him? In rehearsal, he had plodded through the part, reluctantly shuffling here and there, and even though he didn't have anything to say, he had said plenty by his lack of interest and obvious resentment.

And now, as Judy Jones watched her group perform, she marveled at the way Sammy poured the tea with flourish and gracefully maneuvered Harla Elaine's wheelchair, gallantly stepping behind the chair, as he carefully stationed it in a position where Harla Elaine could be seen by everyone. Judy thought that Mary Jane seemed a little more tense than usual, but that was good. Anastasia wasn't supposed to be relaxed here. Mary Jane was making more eye contact with Sammy, too, in a very pleading way. Good. That way it would look even more like Sammy was supposed to be in the scene all along.

Now they were getting to the end.

For the past fifteen minutes, Mary Jane's Anastasia had been trying to convince Harla Elaine's Dowager Empress that she was really her granddaughter.

Harla Elaine took the pause just as they had rehearsed it. Mary Jane fell to Harla Elaine's feet just as they had rehearsed it. And as Harla Elaine cried, "Anastasia, Anastasia, is it really you!" Sammy Widders gave a light, unnoticeable tilt to the wheelchair and Harla Elaine Lewis sprawled all over the stage floor, wracking with sobs from embarrassment and humiliation, right on top of Mary Jane Shady, who screamed in pain from the dead weight of the metal braces that had knocked her off her feet and were now crushing into her.

Not knowing what else to do, the two girls frantically threw their arms around each other and wailed and wailed and moaned and moaned.

Sammy Widders was so proud of himself he was about to pee in his pants. The way Mary Jane and Harla Elaine were carrying on down there on the floor looked just like an average Pentacostal Revival.

Sammy could no longer contain himself. He laughed until tears rolled down his cheeks.

"How inspired!" the Judges screamed to each other. "Look at those girls, hugging and weeping on the floor, and that boy so glad for their reunion, so moved that real tears are coming down his face!"

The Uncertain Freshman Entry won District Competition that year.

Harla Elaine Lewis won Best Actress.

Quintin Davis won Best Actor.

The girl who played Ophelia won Best Supporting Actress.

Sammy Widders won Best Supporting Actor.

Mary Jane Shady didn't win a thing.

CHAPTER FORTY-FOUR

"HERE WE ARE!" Yvonne cried. "Home again, home again, jiggety-jig!"

As the limousine bumped across the cattle guard beneath a double-gated entry, Topsy realized they were not approaching Melogo Drive at all.

The gates closed smoothly and silently behind them. Topsy stared behind her at the big wooden sign over the gates. Two letters stared back: the bottom of an R's right leg mated and became the left branch of a capital Y.

"Okay!" Yvonne announced. "Git ready!"

As the limousine glided into a circular driveway, Topsy found herself staring at an architectural nightmare of monumental proportions. This time there was no question in her mind regarding the origin of the design.

"It's a mini-version of the Anatole Hotel in Dallas," Yvonne explained.

Topsy peered at the square, redbrick, casement-windowed five-story structure in amazement, as the driver braked to a stop in front of two thirty-foot Mexican carved double doors. The insignia on the cattle guard's gates had been implanted upon these, as well.

"— but I just copied the outside of that," Yvonne continued. "The inside I used the general layout of the hotel, but added a color scheme that was inspired by Kim Novak. You'll see!"

Kim Novak. Bobby's favorite . . . Topsy looked down at her old green skirt. She thought of all her clothes in all of her closets in New York and California. She wished she'd put on make-up. She wished she'd brought that damned purple-feathered coat. She longed for Max Factor, false eyelashes, red lipstick.

Yvonne pressed the intercom. "Hey, James! Open up the door!" Yvonne turned back to Topsy. "I haven't had time to landscape the front yard yet," Yvonne apologized. "I can either go with trees, grass or pebble it. What do you think?"

Good God, Topsy thought, dizzily. *I don't own a car . . . I don't own a house . . . I don't even own a plant!*

She made herself look at what Yvonne was referring to as the "front yard." It was flat and sandy and untended. It went as far as the eye could see.

"Have you considered a moat?" Topsy asked. She was beginning to feel very, very large.

"What's that?"

"It's a big wide trench filled with water that goes all around the house. Like knights used to build around castles to keep out dragons." *Keep talking,* she told herself. *Keep talking.* Her head felt like it was filling with water. She felt bloated and huge, as if she were a float.

"Oh, like Playmobile!" Yvonne's eyes grew wide. "I could build a little drawbridge right there!"

Topsy looked back towards the road where Yvonne was pointing. The road swayed back and forth. "You could."

"I could push ever-body I don't like off the drawbridge and they could drown in the moat!" Yvonne giggled. She looked up at Topsy and grinned. "Don't you sometimes just want to get rid of every-body who ever bothered you for even a minute?"

"Yes . . ." Topsy looked away from Yvonne. She wished she didn't feel so big and watery. She wished her head would stop swimming. *Is he in there? Is Bobby inside?* She shut her eyes. *What do I do when I meet him? What do I say? Should I just hit him, just flatten him, just kill him . . .*

"C'mon!" Yvonne cried as the chauffeur opened the limousine's door and then moved to open the door of the house. She jumped out and hurried inside.

I could leave right now, thought Topsy. *I could jump in the front seat and drive off in her car. I could drive all the way to Midland, get on a plane and get out of here. I could drive to Mexico . . .*

"Come on, Mary Jane!" Yvonne stood in the doorway, waving. "Ever-body's waitin' for you to come on in!"

Topsy Dingo Wild Dog floated out of the limousine, her head a maelstrom of emotional upheaval, wondering what he would look like, wondering if he had changed, wondering what to say. *"Hello, Bobby." (congenial?) "Hi, Bobby." (perky?) "How've you been, Bobby?" (friendly?) . . . Then him: (brooding? mysterious? sexy?) "How ya doin', M.J.? Fucked any dogs lately?" . . . A pause, (knowing the value of a beat) Finally: (deadly, eyes locked, a short harsh laugh . . .) "I fucked you, didn't I?"*

Topsy Dingo Wild Dog walked through the huge double doors, teeth clenched, fists knotted, shoulders tensed, eyes squinted. She almost forgot to smile.

"Here she is!" cried Yvonne Henderson. "Uncertain's only star is standin' right here!"

"Bienvenidos!" cried a chorus of voices. "Bienvenidos, Mary Jane Shady!"

A dozen Mexicans, all dressed in starched white uniforms stood in a line, dutifully waving in front of a gigantic planter filled with gigantic plastic flowers. An array of colorful stuffed birds swung from various perches. Topsy peered at the birds. Had they been alive? They looked pretty real. It was quite a collection. Orioles, bluejays, redbirds. Her eyes widened. There was a *mockingbird,* the State Bird of Texas!

"Yvonne," she said without thinking, "it's illegal to kill a *mocking-bird . . .* "

"I know," Yvonne smiled sweetly. "But I just had to have that bird." She pulled on Topsy's sleeve. "C'mon!"

Topsy turned and followed Yvonne past the greeting committee. At the end of the line stood the most beautiful girl Topsy had ever seen in her life. The girl's beauty was so rare it was overwhelming. Translucent skin, clear green eyes, a Valentine face wrapped in ribbons and roses which adorned her magnificent raven hair. Topsy looked at the girl's outfit. Although it was white and gave the appearance of a uniform, the fabric and cut were expensive. Topsy could swear she'd seen it in someone's collection. *Pauline Trigère? Yves St. Laurent*? The simplicity of the outfit only served to show off the perfection of the girl herself. And she was simply breathtaking. Topsy gazed at nature's gift, truly awed. *This is a star. . .* she thought. *This is a star. . .*

Standing next to such perfection in her twenty-year-old matching sweater set, she felt more awkward and taller than ever. And old. She felt old. *Why did I put on this stupid outfit*! she thought in despair. *I must look like an old, old woman trying to be a young, young girl . . .*

"They're my servants!" Yvonne announced joyfully to Topsy. She clapped her hands to dismiss them. "Ya'll go on now! Vamoose! Work! Work! Rub! Scrub!"

What if he thinks I wore this for him? she suddenly wondered. *What if he thinks I've been dressing like this for twenty years*!

The line of helpers filed past Topsy, nodding and waving. The beautiful young woman passed slowly. She smiled and smiled and moved closer. She stood in front of Topsy and stared into her eyes. Then, slowly, she raised her hand and shyly waved.

"Parts Unknown . . ." whispered the splendid looking creature.

"What? What?" whispered Topsy, startled.

"Look here, Mary Jane!" cried Yvonne, pulling Topsy through the entry and past the planter.

Topsy moved toward Yvonne, distracted. What was that person trying to tell her? Was Bobby sending her a message? And if he was, what did he mean by *"parts unknown"*?

She pulled away from Yvonne and looked around, but the beautiful young woman was gone.

"Okay," Yvonne said, grabbing her by the arm. "Tell me the truth? What do you think?"

Don't start thinking, Topsy told herself harshly. *That's exactly what you're doing again! Thinking! For God's sakes, this is no time to think . . .*

Her eyes widened as she turned her attention to the interior. She could imagine the effect Yvonne had aimed for. But the limitations of size here made the symmetry seem as ridiculous as the limitless use of space in the real model itself.

The marble fountain placed smack in the middle of the living room and gushing a good thirty-five feet in the air, was simply scary. The open-ceilinged room was large—two hundred feet by two hundred feet. And tall. Fifty feet tall. Two clear plexiglas, oval-cut elevators rotated up and down the five-storied formation. Exposed hallways wrapped around three sides of each floor, offering views of numbered rooms, exactly like in a hotel.

Sleek, modern velvet-covered sofas, curving U shapes, were dispersed intermittently throughout the lower floor.

Every wall, every door, every sofa, table, chair and vase were some variation of the color purple. Pale lavender walls, eggplant-colored elevators and steel railings, fuschia sofas.

"Now look up at the very top," Yvonne directed.

A huge, purple stained-glass dome consisting of one big circle surrounded by one dozen solid stripes, obviously meant to depict sunrays, dominated the ceiling.

"Mary Jane," Yvonne said. "Do you think Kim Novak would like this?"

"I don't know," Topsy mumbled. "Ask her the next time she's in town." She was amazed at how the space had been made to look so small.

"Oh, Mary Jane, you're so silly!" Yvonne giggled. "Kim Novak isn't ever really goin' to come to Uncertain, Texas! She don't know a soul here! But if she *did* come, do you think she could just move right in and feel right at home?" Yvonne asked.

"Yvonne, I don't know Kim Novak."

Yvonne's face fell in disappointment. "You don't? You don't know Kim Novak?" she asked incredulously. "But ya'll both live out there in Hollywood. Don't you see her at parties?"

"So far we haven't run into one another." She wished people would stop asking her about people she'd never met.

"Well, don't that beat all," Yvonne mused. "I thought for sure you'd know Kim Novak."

"I met Christopher Isherwood a few times," Topsy offered, wondering how much this monstrosity had cost.

"I don't care much for the Brat Pack," Yvonne confided.

Topsy sighed. *Give 'em what they want.* "I met Yvonne de Carlo once."

"Why-vonne de Carlo!" Yvonne screamed. "What did she say when you told her I was named after her?"

She looked up at Yvonne, standing in a sea of clashing violets and magentas. "She said they should have named you 'Kim' after Kim Novak," Topsy said gently.

"To go with my house!" Yvonne nodded excitedly. "Aw, well, I guess I don't care what my name is just as long as they spell it right!"

Topsy nodded and smiled and smiled and nodded. She wondered if Bobby still wore jeans and boots. Had he been to Neiman-Marcus, bought ascots and tuxedos? Did he wear silk underwear and Georgio Armani suits?

"Now look up yonder!" Yvonne directed. "There's twenty bedrooms and ten are suites. Each one has a bathroom and a dressing room and the suites have kitchenettes. I already invited the Peanut Butter people to stay here! That is five bed-sleeping places per floor, not countin' the top floor, a-course. Now, come on, 'cause I want to show you the top floor!"

Topsy's head was swimming. *No telling what he wears now,* she thought. *My mind is probably not creative enough to imagine it!*

She followed Yvonne into the nearest elevator. Yvonne pushed the button, and as Topsy and Yvonne were carried upward inside the plastic bubble, Topsy was simply too flabbergasted to speak. As the elevator doors opened, Yvonne said, "This here is the master suite."

Bobby's bedroom. Hideous curiosity mixed with a raging desire to see no more overwhelmed her.

They stepped inside.

The master suite contained an Olympic-sized swimming pool and a tennis court, in the middle of which sat a gigantic canopied bed. At the foot of the bed was a jacuzzi. Umbrellaed tables and chairs surrounded the pool. The umbrellas were closed.

"I know you're not supposed to open up a umbrella in the house, so look!" Yvonne pushed a button and the entire ceiling slid back, folding into itself, revealing the sky. As the ceiling disappeared, all the umbrellas unfolded and snapped into place.

"It's a water bed," Yvonne said.

"What?" She was trying not to laugh. She was trying not to cry.

"The mattress. On the bed. It's one of them water beds to help me relax. I have a terrible time tryin' to sleep. Don't you just love a canopy bed? I do."

"Unbelievable," Topsy whispered, trying not to imagine what unmentionable acts had gone on in here and unable to help herself. She looked from the swimming pool to the jacuzzi to the tennis court to the umbrellaed tables and chairs. *The backseat of an old Ford just wasn't big enough for him...* She wondered if he and Yvonne used gadgets and things. She wondered what Yvonne had done to get on top.

"*You got to prove it," he had said. "You got to prove it...* "

"Well, it's convenient to have all this stuff right here. I could have put it out in the yard, but ever-body does that. I don't know what to do about the yard," Yvonne said, wandering around the room. "What was that suggestion of yours? Something about a boat?"

"A moat."

"*I will*," she had vowed. "*I will . . .* "

"*Will you do anything I tell you to*?"

"*Anything . . .* "

Yvonne smiled brightly. "Oh, yes! The drawbridge idea! Now see, I just hop out of bed, throw back the roof, jump into the pool, play a little tennis, take me a jacuzzi, then I sit down under one of the umbrellas and eat me my breakfast, lunch and dinner right up here. They send it through the wall."

"The dumb waiter." Did they do it on the dumb waiter? It was big enough for an orgy.

"José? Naw, he's not dumb, he just cain't speak English too good. When he learns how to, then he'll leave and I'll have to teach another one how to work the car and drive and English and ever-thing. It's a mess. The whole thing's a mess . . ." Yvonne's voice trailed off for a moment. "But the food comes up through this hole in the wall here. See it?" Yvonne opened the device with glee. "Another hotel idea!"

Why a hotel? Topsy wondered anxiously. *I live in a hotel . . . WHAT DOES THAT MEAN*?

Suddenly Yvonne turned to Topsy and whispered conspiratorally, "There's a kitchen down yonder on the bottom floor somewhere, but I have never seen it, never been in it, and I don't ever intend to go! I told 'em, just build me the biggest and the best goddamn kitchen in the state of Texas and I am assumin' that all is A-okay or somebody would have said somethin', 'cause when I said I wasn't never settin' foot in a kitchen again as long as I live, I meant it! When I grew up I didn't even have runnin' water!" Yvonne grabbed a breath and continued. "And it had better be bigger than Catsy Ivanhoe's, too! I *hate* her! She's always been rich ever since the day she was born!" Yvonne had been talking louder and louder and faster and faster, and finally she looked at Topsy with infinite irritation and snapped, "Oh, what do *you* know about bein' poor?"

Topsy looked at Yvonne, surprised. This hotel wasn't about *her*. It was about being *poor*. Well, she'd never been rich, but she'd never been poor. She remembered how Yvonne had spent all her spare time cooking and cleaning for her demented relatives. She remembered how Yvonne had never ever owned a new dress. All the Flowers women had rotated clothing. And they wouldn't have had those things if Lottie and Irene and other women in the town hadn't taken their old things over to the Flowers shack. Yvonne Dee Flowers had worn

Mary Jane Shady's hand-me-downs for the first eighteen years of her life.

Yvonne vehemently hit another button and the levolored blinds disappeared into a neat band.

It was amazing. All the walls were glass.

"And you'll do anything I tell you to?"

"Anything."

"And no more."

"And no more . . ."

"And no less."

"And no less . . ."

"And you'll never tell what happened this night, now or ever after. Amen."

"That's my landin' strip," Yvonne said, pointing to what appeared to be a huge highway in her backyard. "I think the moat will look real nice around the house. I wish it was built already so the Peanut Butter people could see it when they come in today. Don't tell Catsy Ivanhoe about the Playmobile idea or she might build a drawbridge first—"

Amen . . .

Topsy was worried about Yvonne. Yvonne was not the same cheerful person she had been talking to this morning.

"I won't tell her. I promise." She wondered how much of this house was Bobby's idea. She wondered if Yvonne Henderson had ever fucked a dog and found out about it later. She wondered if Bobby was still a pervert. Was he out there molesting innocent little cheerleaders, lonely housewifes, old maid schoolteachers, rodeo queens? Her head started its rat run. *I don't know what he does! He lives in a hotel! He married Yvonne! He made me fuck a dog! SOMETHING IS WRONG WITH HIM*!

"Alice Catherine Shoemaker," Yvonne mocked. "Married this big dark Indian named Bo Ivanhoe. He has all that land between here and Notrees the government give his daddy 'cause he was a Indian and they struck oil and believe me, Mary Jane, all Mrs. Indian Ivanhoe wants out of her life is to have a bigger teepee that me. Can you imagine marryin' a *Indian*? People who've had money their whole lives long just think they can do anything and get away with it. Could you help me put these wings on?"

Topsy looked up, startled. Yvonne was holding a set of gold mesh wings toward her.

"You're going to wear these? With your outfit?" Topsy asked dubiously.

"Uh-huh. Help me get my arms through. See how it attaches in back?"

"Wait a minute," Topsy said, fumbling with the hooks. *This isn't happening,* she thought. *Tell me I'm not in this hotel-house helping Bobby's wife put on a set of butterfly wings*!

Yvonne walked away from Topsy and toward the intercom. "Louisa!" Yvonne screamed, pressing a button. "Louisa! Hasta la vista! Pronto!" She turned to Topsy and sighed. "Have you ever noticed how Mexskins just disappear into thin air? Where the hell is she?"

"I'll do it," Topsy said. "I don't mind."

"Oh, wait!" Yvonne said. "I forgot the rest of my top!" She walked into a closet the size of Topsy's hotel suite at the Mayflower and came back holding a gold breastplate with two jeweled gold bugs dangling from each sculpted nipple.

Topsy gasped.

Yvonne looked up. "It's beautiful, inn't it?"

"What *is* it?" Topsy whispered.

"It's a Yellow Jacket outfit!" Yvonne grinned. "And looky at this! See the hat!" She held up the antennaed, bejeweled, beehive hat.

Topsy was stunned. She thought she had seen everything in the wardrobes of Western Costume, in the Metropolitan Museum's Costume exhibits, in Busby Berkeley movies. But she had never seen anything like this. Every detail was spectacular. Each jewel was real. But it didn't belong at a Pep Rally. In an Erté, maybe. In *La Cage Aux Folles,* certainly. In Paris in the early part of the century at one of those balls. Of course, Yvonne would need a hive of real bees to go with it . . . But Uncertain? No. In Uncertain it had no place to go.

"My, God, Yvonne," Topsy said. "You could have bought Dallas for what you paid for this."

"I could have," Yvonne grinned, wiggling into the breastplate. "I should have." She placed the beehive headpiece on top of her head and turned to look in the mirror. "Oh, wait!" She returned to the closet and in a moment stepped out wearing a collection of maroon and gold turkey feathers around her neck. "Okay!" she said. "I'm ready to go! What do you think?" Yvonne eyes sparkled in anticipation.

Topsy thought carefully. *Should I tell her*? She looked at Yvonne, eagerly waiting for her approval. The headpiece had slid slightly to one side and was pulling Yvonne's red wig with it. *I can't say it,* Topsy thought. *I don't even know the words . . .*

"*YOU CAN'T TALK! . . . IF IT DOESN'T COME IN A SCRIPT, YOU DON'T KNOW WHAT TO SAY!*" . . . That's what he'd said . . . Ralph Painter, The Perfect Agent . . .

"I want to know how I look!" Yvonne suddenly demanded. "Tell me how I look!"

"Stunning . . ." murmured Topsy Dingo Wild Dog.

"Really?" Yvonne asked, all grins again.

Topsy nodded. "Really," she mumbled. "I'm stunned . . . "

"Why, thanks!" Yvonne cooed. "If you got glamoured up, you could look like this too!"

Dazed, Topsy followed Yvonne out of the master suite and into an elevator. *He must like her to look like this,* she thought. *I never had a chance . . .*

As they were descending, Topsy looked down and saw a small lithe figure floating through the hall. The waist-length hair filled with ribbons and roses told her it was the strange, beautiful girl who had spoken to her earlier.

"Who's that?" she asked Yvonne as the splendid creature wandered down the hall.

Yvonne looked out of the plastic enclosure sharply.

"Bambino!" she cried. "Bambino!" She turned to Topsy and muttered, "White trash makes the worst servants! I'm tryin' to teach her Spanish, so she'll think more like a Mexskin!"

They reached the first level and the door opened. Like a hornet flying out of her nest, Yvonne took off down the hall. "Get back in that kitchen!" she called out to the splendid creature, who just kept moving. "You just vamoose into that la co-cina mooey pronto!"

Baby took one look at Yvonne's butterfly wings, jeweled beehive hat, gold breastplate and feathered accessories and burst into a peal of delighted laughter. Her hands fluttered excitedly in the air.

As Yvonne flew after her, Topsy watched them disappear down the hall. Baby Flowers' echoing laughter tumbled through interiors and bounced off the walls like the lone mocking howl in a funhouse.

Topsy looked around anxiously. Never in her craziest daydreams had she expected anything remotely resembling this house. Bobby was obviously indulging Yvonne in all her fantasies, now that he had so much money. She wondered how he had gotten it. She cursed herself for not reading those letters. She wished Yvonne would come back so they could leave.

She must have done everything he ever told her to, Topsy shuddered. *WONDER WHAT IT WAS*?

She looked around uneasily. For the first time she became aware of the stillness of the house. Now that they were almost out the door, she hoped desperately to escape confronting Bobby. Maybe he had forgotten all about her. Maybe he wasn't going to say anything after all. Maybe he'd gone out of town on business. Maybe he was down the hall, locked up in some monumental study studded with antlers and deer heads and dog tails. She didn't want to know. She just wanted to get out.

She moved through the large room, unnerved by the sound of her footsteps hitting the tile floors. The waterfall gushed monotonously.

As she passed it, something occurred to her. *I have never died in a waterfall . . .* she thought, recalling each horror film. *I have never been killed in water. . .*

Chills ran over her.

Her heart bolted.

She could feel something approaching her.

I want out . . . she thought desperately.

She couldn't move.

Before her was the planter. Behind it, the front door. She stared at the planter. Dozens of birds stared back.

"Okay." She heard Yvonne's voice behind her. "Okay. That's it."

She waited, paralyzed. Yvonne secretly hated her. She was going to kill her. She would die in Bobby's house, killed by Bobby's wife. Of course. This is why she had come back. She was about to die . . .

Yvonne walked slowly up beside her. She seemed subdued.

"Too much . . ." Yvonne mumbled. "Too much . . . " She reached up and pulled her beehive headdress off. It fell to the floor. She released the catch on the breastplate and dropped it in a chair. "Too, too, too, too much . . . " She slipped off the wings, stepping on them as she stepped over them. She unsnapped the feathered necklace and let it fall. She looked up at Topsy tiredly. "Mary Jane. I have to tell you. It's too much . . . "

Topsy looked at Yvonne apprehensively. Yvonne wasn't about to kill her. Yvonne wasn't even looking at her. And Yvonne looked like she was about to cry. "Yvonne?" Topsy said. "What's the matter?

Yvonne? Are you about to cry?" *Cry in the car,* she thought. *Please. Cry in the car. . .*

Yvonne let out a long pent up wail. "They're goin' to make fun of me!" she wept. "They're goin' to make fun of me!"

Oh, God. Topsy grabbed Yvonne Henderson and held her fast.

"You don't know what it's like when people make *fun* of you!" Yvonne bawled.

"Oh, yes, I do," whispered Topsy Dingo Wild Dog.

Yvonne Henderson looked up at Mary Jane Shady and started to cry again. "How could you know?" she sobbed. "Nobody ever made fun of *you*!"

"Oh, yes they did," said Topsy Dingo Wild Dog.

"Who?" sniffed Yvonne Henderson. "Who?"

"Well . . ." Topsy hesitated, carefully considering. "My agent for one."

"That agent made *fun* of *you*?" Yvonne asked incredulously.

Topsy nodded.

"Well, fire his ass!" Yvonne said. "Do it this afternoon!"

"Listen, Yvonne," Topsy said gently. "I didn't want to tell you this because I know you're counting on me —"

"I sure am!" Yvonne nodded. "You're comin' back is goin' to clear my slate! People think I've done somethin' important gettin' you back here!"

"Yvonne, I'm sorry to tell you this," said Topsy. "But I expect to get fired this afternoon—"

Yvonne Henderson's eyes grew wide. "You're kiddin'," she said. "Tell me you're kiddin'."

Topsy shook her head.

Yvonne started to bawl.

"I'm sorry," Topsy said helplessly. *I shouldn't have told her. I should have waited. Left town. Left the country. Left the planet . . .*

"They cain't fire you!" Yvonne shrieked wildly. "I'll kill 'em! I'll kill ever one of 'em!"

Topsy stared at Yvonne, who was going into a frenzy. "I was just kidding," she said quickly. "But you felt so bad and everything—"

"You said that just to make *me* feel *better*?" Yvonne asked. "Well, it made me feel *worse,* but I appreciate the effort. Nobody ever tried to make me feel *better* before." She picked up the wings and tossed them on the chair. "I'm goin' to save these for our ride in the loser's car! I don't want to show off all my surprises in one appearance!"

Topsy watched as Yvonne walked over to a closet, opened the door, and pulled out a canary-yellow, full-length, turkey-feather coat trimmed in yellow ostrich feathers and lined in antique Chinese silk.

Startled, Topsy realized that it was *exactly* the same as her very own *purple* turkey-feather coat with the ostrich-feathered collar. Faintly, she sat down in the closest chair.

"Okay, I'm ready!" Yvonne cried happily. In her bright red wig and her bright yellow turkey-feather coat, she looked just like a new-born bird. "I think this looks just right for the Pep Rally, don't you?"

Topsy stood up slowly and followed Yvonne Henderson out the door. *Birds of a feather,* she thought weakly. *Birds of a feather*. . .

CHAPTER FORTY-FIVE

IRENE SHADY was just about to call Scoot Widders on the phone and see how she was doing with creating a float when her sister-in-law walked through the front door with a cardboard box in her arms.

"Here," said Lottie as she put her purse down on the desk and walked toward Irene with the box. "This was waitin' at the post office this mornin'. I went ahead and got it."

Irene stared at Lottie. "Is that all you got to say to me?" she asked indignantly, grabbing the box. "You have been gone for twenty-four hours and all you got to show for it is this cardboard box!"

"Don't throw it at me," said Lottie calmly. "Ole Mrs. Coconot from Goldsmith's in it, and I picked it up just in the nick of time, too, 'cause Bonnie Gene and Ozell is right behind me. I guess he wants to make sure we got his mama out of the mail."

Before either of them could say another word, the bells on the front door jingled and Mr. Bonnie Gene Coconot and his sister, Ozell, from Goldsmith came through the door, dressed in Sunday suits they had bought at a garage sale five years ago.

"Hidy, Bonnie Gene," said Irene and Lottie Shady. "Hidy Ozell."

"Hidy, girls," whispered Bonnie Gene Coconot, taking off his cow-boy hat.

"This is the worst thing that ever happened to me," cried Ozell Coconot, as she grabbed a Kleenex out of the box she was carrying.

She dabbed her eyes with the tissue. "The worst thing that ever happened in my entire family—"

No, you're the worst thing that ever happened to your entire family, Irene Shady thought maliciously. *That ole woman died just to get away from these two. Imagine! A brother and a sister off livin' together just like they was married and nobody ever thinkin' a thing about it neither! But that ole woman knew what was goin' on. Took a trip to California and died to keep from havin' to come back and face another minute of these two, is exactly what happened! Could have just gone to a rest home, if these stingy kids would have paid for it*!

Out loud she said sympathetically, "We just picked her up this mornin'."

"*I* picked her up," said Lottie, ripping open the cardboard box. "*I'm* the one who picked her up."

"Oh, Lord, why did she do it?" Bonnie Gene asked the ceiling of the Uncertain Chapel of Memories. "I just don't understand why anyone would have to go and die out in *California* . . ." His bulky frame started to shake and tears ran down his big round cheeks, falling on his leather string tie and bouncing off the little boot dangling from the middle of it.

"Irene's daughter lives out there in California part-time," Lottie offered.

For once in her life, Irene Shady did not want to talk about Mary Jane Shady. She wanted to get the Coconots taken care of and on their way, so she could concentrate on Mary Jane Shady *Day*.

"Inn't it full of Mexskins?" asked Ozell Coconot. "Inn't California full of Mexskins?"

"It's full of ever-thing you can think of!" Lottie cried, as she pulled crushed newspaper out of the cardboard box. "Sex! . . . Drugs! . . . Rock 'n Roll! . . ."

"And Mexskins," added Bonnie Gene.

"I hate Mexskins worse than trees," stated Ozell Coconot. "Both of 'em just scatter things all over ever-where. If Jesus loved me, I know he'd take a bolt of lightnin' and just clear out my whole yard."

Irene Shady looked at Ozell sharply. "I never knew one Mexskin to have anything but the most decent funeral you could imagine, complete with church chimes and chants."

"Funeral are the biggest events in a Mexskin's life," Lottie Shady nodded. "They sure know how to go all the way with a funeral."

"I certainly hope that you don't think we intend to give our mama anything but the best!" Ozell replied, determined not to be outdone by her inferiors.

"Anything but the best you *can* do, under the circumstances," Irene muttered, wondering when Lottie was going to have all the newspaper emptied out of the cardboard box.

Bonnie Gene shuffled from one boot to the other. "Well," he said. "We don't even know if Mama had any say so in this matter or not, Mrs. Shady and Miss Shady. It just ain't too clear what happened at all. See, our brother Haskell lives out there in California where your daughter had to live—"

"And what was he doin', but what ever-body out there does," Ozell interjected, "gettin' married *again* for the *third* time! I don't know what his problem is!"

At least he married outside the family, thought Irene.

"'Course Mama had to go out there to that weddin'," Bonnie Gene nodded. "There was nothin' doin' but for her to go out there to California—"

"Three Judies," Ozell interrupted. "Ever one of 'em named *Judy*!"

"And no sooner had Haskell and Judy—"

"*Judy! Judy! Judy!*" mocked Ozell.

"Walked down the aisle," said Bonnie Gene, "than Mama dropped dead of a heart attack—"

"Was she in poor health previously?" asked Irene Shady.

"Hell, no!" cried Ozell. "You'd drop dead, too, if your child got married three times!"

"She'd drop dead if *hers* got married *once*," said Lottie.

"*She* don't have any children," Irene sniffed, referring to Lottie.

Lottie Shady looked up and smiled. "I don't have no problems, neither!"

Irene grabbed the cardboard box out of Lottie's hands. "I don't either!" she cried.

"Ha!" said Lottie. "Ha! Ha! Ha!"

"Well, we do!" Ozell stated impatiently. "Ever-body in our whole family is about to split a gut over this. I'm embarrassed, humiliated, ashamed and chagrined!"

"I can see that," Lottie nodded.

Irene stared at the Coconots, frowning. *This is what it took to embarrass them*? she thought. *They don't know the meaning of the word*!

She yanked a plastic bag filled with ashes out of the cardboard box and held it up over her head like a prize. "Here she is!" Irene announced.

"Looks like some sorry grocery boy sacked her up," Lottie remarked. "Looky how they stuffed her in . . ."

"She's the only one in our entire family who ever got *cremated,*" Bonnie Gene grieved.

"She's the only one in our entire family who ever died outside the Central Time Zone!" Ozell moaned.

Lottie Shady took the plastic bag out of Irene's hand and walked to the foyer, where she held it up to the light. "This is the pitifulest thing I have ever saw in my life as a undertaker and I seen a lot, too, believe you me! I didn't even know her, but I wouldn't recognize her if I did." She walked over to Ozell and handed her the plastic bag. "I am just sick for ya'll."

"I don't want that!" Ozell cried, jumping back. "That's not my mama!"

"Wonder what made her go get herself burned up on purpose?" Lottie wondered. "We got such a nice selection of caskets—"

"There's a little fiberglass urn to go with it," Bonnie Gene sniffed, grabbing a Kleenex from his sister. "We bought and paid for a little fiberglass urn."

Lottie and Irene draped themselves like two vultures around the cardboard box.

"It's not here," said Irene Shady, shifting through newspapers.

"Not in this box," said Lottie Shady, shaking the empty box.

"But we *paid* for it!" said Ozell. "It was included in the price!"

"We *paid* for a little fiberglass urn and they's supposed to have put it in that cardboard box!" Bonnie Gene continued, taking a piece of paper out of his pocket. "Here's the bill."

"Let's see," said Irene, putting on her glasses. " 'One cremation: three hundred and twenty-five dollars—' "

"Cheap," stated Lottie. "We'd go under at them prices. Flat-out starve."

Irene read on. " 'Includes removal of body from place of death, filling out medical cause of death and signing of death certificate by the doctor, filing death certificate with the county health department, and any other necessary paperwork, transporting the deceased to the crematorium, a *single individual one-body-at-a-time* cremation service, placing the cremated remains in a standard urn, in-or-out of state mailing, burial at sea if desired—' "

"Burial at sea!" shouted Lottie Shady. "Whoever thought up *that*?"

" 'And one fiberglass urn with interlocking seal—' "

"A bargain!" cried her sister-in-law, slinging the plastic bag into Bonnie Gene's arms. "A flat-out bargain! That's a overall savin's of at least a thousand dollars! 'Course, here at the Uncertain Chapel of Memories, we drain and formaldehyde the body, do the hair, fix the nails, paint the cheeks, mascara the lashes, not to mention horrible accident repairs, serve ice tea and homemade cake and give you a fine selection of caskets, as well." Inspired, Lottie added. "Maybe we could interest ya'll in a casket?"

Bonnie Gene Coconot's head calculated quickly. He was beginning to think his mother had done them a favor.

Ozell threw her brother a look that confirmed his instincts.

"Are you sure that little urn isn't in there, Mrs. Shady?" Bonnie Gene asked far more calmly than when he had come in the door.

"Nope," Irene said. "Over and out. See for yourself." She handed him the empty box. "And I can bet you my top-of-the-line metallic-blue, velvet-lined, seepage, varmint and jewelry-proof coffin over there in the display area, that this cardboard box and that plastic bag is not your mother's idea of how to go—"

"Please," said Lottie Shady in her best undertaker voice. "Let us step into the slumber room and show you two of our best items—"

But Bonnie Gene Coconot had made up his mind. He wasn't about to spend a thousand dollars if he didn't have to.

"They're way too big," Ozell sighed. She was already envisioning a vacation for the two of them in Corpus Christi or Padre Island on the money they were about to save.

A big yellow light bulb went off in Lottie Shady's head. "Okay, you two," she said. "Come with me." She didn't want to have to deal with her sister-in-law before her niece arrived and she certainly wasn't about to let old Mrs. Coconot's death be a total morning's loss. "Your mama may have got done out of a first-class funeral, but we're goin' to see that she gets the very best that we can come up with today."

"And just what *is* the very best that we can come up with today?" asked Ozell dubiously, as Irene wondered the same thing.

"Just pick her on up and bring her with us," Lottie smiled, taking the plastic bag out of Bonnie Gene's hand and tossing it in the cardboard box. "Ya'll can drive me in your car and we'll get this fixed."

"How much is it goin' to cost?" asked Bonnie Gene and Ozell simultaneously.

"Two hunnerd dollars. For the idea," said Lottie.

"What idea?" asked Ozell.

"What idea?" asked Bonnie Gene.

"What idea?" asked Irene Shady.

A slow steady cat-like smile wrapped itself around Lottie Shady's face. "Bonnie Gene . . ." purred Lottie Shady. "Ozell . . . ."

The two Coconots waited in silent anticipation.

Lottie's eyes were lit with an ominous glow. "Ya'll are just goin' to have to trust me . . ."

Irene thought her sister-in-law had never looked more like a mortician.

Ozell and Bonnie Gene looked at each other and shrugged. Tickets to the Texas-OU football game in Dallas danced in his head. A evening at Billy Bob's at the Fort Worth Stockyards danced through hers.

"Well," said Ozell to Bonnie Gene Coconot. "I guess we just don't have a choice . . . ."

Out on Highway 158, past the Flowers' shack, past the gates to Catsy Ivanhoe's ranch, and just on the outskirts of Notrees, the old ex-Hopi Indian Catsy Ivanhoe had hired to hand-paint her dress, watched, amused, as Catsy stepped into her Rolls Royce and turned on the ignition. In the back seat was her dress which the old Indian had just finished finger-painting that morning. On her ears, tongues dangling from each pierced loop, were two live baby rattlesnakes.

"Don't touch them snakes, now," the old Indian warned, chewing on his toothless gums. "Don't be pettin' 'em nor nuthin'."

Catsy nodded impatiently as she checked the rearview mirror and waited for the shiny new red eighteen-wheeler roaring down the highway to pass her. She was anxious to be on her way.

"You come back here now and let me take 'em off when you're finished with that party," the old Indian nodded. "They's fine, just a-danglin' like I got 'em, but don't go messin' with 'em or nuthin'. They's poison, don't forget—they *kill* when they bite. No joke."

Catsy gave a sharp nod, saw that the highway was cleared, and gunned her accelerator.

"Don't tell me what to do with a snake," she muttered to the Indian's vanishing image in her mirror. "I *know* how to handle a rattlesnake . . ."

* * *

Scoot Widders closed the doors of her garage, cackling with excitement. She had moved her car out on the street in the middle of the night to make room to build what had become, by the crack of dawn, The Mary Jane Shady Float.

"Okay, girls," she told the twins, "ya'll better go on home now and get ready. You've did a remarkable job in such little time! Just *remarkable*!"

"What am *I* gettin' out of this is what I want to know," grumbled Verona Widders as she stomped towards her grandmother's car, recklessly hauling Morona along by their mutually shared crown.

"Slow down!" Morona cried, shuffling desperately for balance. "Quit draggin' me!"

"You'll see," Scoot promised. "It wasn't for nothin', I can promise you that!"

"I don't care what it is," Verona complained, rubbing her hands which were sore and stiff and not slowing down for a minute. "If I never see another cemetery again, it will be too soon!"

"Hush your mouth, Verona!" Morona shushed. She stopped abruptly in her tracks, jerking Verona backwards and bringing them both to a jolting halt. "If anybody finds out we took all these flowers out of the cemetery, I won't get to be Homecomin' Queen!"

"Gladys Turner's ole sister sure got a bunch of ugly ole pink carnations laid out all over her," Verona muttered, tugging them both back into motion. "When I die, I want to be laid under some kind of a big ole green plant." She opened the door of Scoot's orange Ford and started climbing in, as Morona stumbled in behind her.

"But I don't like green plants," Morona Widders cried, falling into the car and on top of Verona. "I don't want to be covered up with a big ole green plant!"

"Ya'll stop worryin' about that now, girls," Scoot told her granddaughters. She glanced in the back seat. "Got yourselves straightened out?" Morona disentangled her right leg from under her twin's left arm. "Good," Scoot said when she could clearly see both heads in her rearview mirror. "It's time to go on home and get ready. I promised Daddy I'd have ya'll back by noontime today, so ya'll will have plenty of time to get dressed and ready for the Pep Rally. I don't know what I would have done if they hadn't given the nominees the day off from school today." She started the ignition and waited a moment for the car to warm up. "Now. I don't have to tell ya'll how important it is *not to tell a soul* that we took every last flower off of every grave between here and Wink to cover up that Mary Jane Shady Float, now, do I?"

"Naw," said Morona.

"Naw," said Verona.

"Okay," said Scoot, backing the car out the driveway. "We got a deal then."

"What deal?" grumbled Verona. "I spent my day off flower robbin'. I never get to have any fun."

"You'll see," answered Scoot.

"You wouldn't have had a day off at all if it wasn't for me," Morona chided.

"I wouldn't have to go to that ole crownin' if it wasn't for you, neither!" Verona hissed. "I hate it! I don't want to go!"

"Yes, you do," said Scoot. "Ya'll both are goin' and ya'll both want to go."

"Grandma?" asked Morona. "Are you sure that Mr. Turner isn't goin' to mind it that we took his little boat?"

"Believe me," Scoot nodded emphatically, "the way we got it covered, Orville Turner is never goin' to recognize that boat!"

Lottie Shady climbed out of the car and waved good-bye to Ozell and Bonnie Gene Coconot. She counted the two hundred dollars they had paid her for her burial concept, then held it up in the air, waving.

Across the street, parked next to the Hoop and Holler Motel for a Dollar, sat Leo Diggs in his brand new red eighteen-wheeler truck, waving back. Lottie blew him a kiss and started inside. Leo toasted her with a styrofoam cup filled with hot coffee. He knew he didn't have much longer to wait.

"Awright, Lottie Shady!" hollered Irene Shady as Lottie walked in the door. "I don't know where you've been or what you've been doin', but we're puttin' the 'Closed' sign up on that door this minute!"

"Closed?" blinked Lottie. "I just made us two hunnerd dollars in thirty minutes!"

"How?" asked Irene, tiredly. "What in the world did you do with those poor ole woman's ashes?"

"Why, I took 'em over to the drugstore and had 'em giftwrap 'em," Lottie replied.

Irene's eyes grew wide. "You did *not,*" she said incredulously. "You did *not* take that plastic bag over there and tell the drugstore to gift-wrap it up."

Lottie grinned. "Gift-wrapped for glory! I gift-wrapped that woman for glory!"

"You did *not* let the Coconot's go and put their pore ole mother in the grave in a gift-wrap, Lottie," Irene whispered, appalled. "Please tell me that you did *not* let them put her in the ground that-a-way. . ."

"Well, not exactly," replied Lottie Shady. "I had 'em tie a little pink ribbon around her and Ozell had a little picture of her in her purse, so we cut off all but her head and glued it right on top."

"And you charged them two hunnerd dollars?" Irene asked, amazed. "They *paid* you two hunnerd dollars?"

"Half of it's yours," Lottie assured her, waving the money. "You know how cheap the Coconots are. They was lucky to get off so light."

Irene Shady thought about her share of the profit and decided an optimistic approach was in order. *The woman's cellophaned,* Irene thought. *What can I do*?

"Gift-wrapped for glory," sighed Irene Shady, reaching for the money.

Lottie Shady put her hand over Irene Shady's hand. "Wait a minute, Sister," she smiled sweetly. "Before I give you this hunnerd dollars, tell me: what the *hell* did you do with Lucie Garden's *body* and Wendell Butler's *corpse*?!"

CHAPTER FORTY-SIX

TOPSY, followed by Yvonne, hurried up the steps of the Uncertain Chapel of Memories. For the first time since she had arrived, she was glad to be back home. Compared to Yvonne Henderson's house, the Uncertain Chapel of Memories was beginning to look normal and safe. Ignoring the "Closed" sign on the front door, she rushed inside and was just passing the five blown-up cardboard figures of herself when she heard angry voices engaged in battle thundering their opposition from the slumber room.

Topsy and Yvonne both stood still as they realized that they had almost walked into the middle of an intense argument.

"We're never goin' to make it if you turn all the customers over to Deal Grimes!" Topsy heard her Aunt Lottie yell.

"Then *you* stick around and do your share and don't be goin' off and leavin' me in the lurch on what turned out to be the most important day of my life!" Irene shouted back. "The very idea of not workin' on a body because you didn't make your grades is bad enough, and here no one ever knew a thing about it either! Who'd ever have expected it! I have to *know* what to *expect* if I'm goin' to be able to *plan,* Lottie. How could you keep a thing like failin' the second grade a secret anyway? This puts *serious* doubts about you in my mind, and a person needs to trust a business partner, not to mention their very own sister-in-law! You still haven't mentioned a word about your whereabouts over the last twenty-four hours either! I'll bet you've got a whole slew of a secret life tucked away somewheres, and that is not a good way to live, either! These things have a way of poppin' up right at the wrong time, and if yesterday is any indication, I'm the one who ends up payin', as well as you! You inconveniencin' me at a time like this was just as expensive to me as the loss of them bodies to bury was to you! WE ARE PARTNERS, *SISTER!* Can you see my point!?"

"I can see you're implyin' I've maybe held back a thing or two," Lottie hollered, "and you know I've told you ever last thing that's ever happened to me, which is *NOT MUCH*! You wouldn't have buried someone who failed you in the second grade either, would you?" she demanded.

There was a little pause.

Topsy and Yvonne exchanged glances.

From where they were standing, just inside the doorway, they heard the Shady sisters each take a big deep breath.

"Well, okay," sighed Lottie Shady.

"Well, okay," sighed Irene.

Topsy waited for another moment, and hearing nothing, motioned for Yvonne to follow.

Beyond the red velvet curtain, pulled back by the heavy gold-braided cord, Irene Shady and Lottie Shady stood staring at one another in mutual exasperation. They were separated by silence and a navy coffin lined in baby blue. A yellow and cream-colored coffin formed the background. Topsy thought her mother and aunt looked like they were in the middle of a community theater production where one of them had forgotten her lines.

Yvonne and Topsy entered the slumber room unnoticed until Topsy spoke.

"Well, hello," said Topsy, making her way toward the middle of the navy blue casket where she intended to center herself between her mother and her aunt. She knew that one step in the wrong direction could set something off a week later.

"Honey, I failed the second grade and I want you to know it right this minute!" Lottie cried, hopping towards Topsy. She threw her hands on her niece's shoulders and stood on her tiptoes in an effort to try to look Topsy eye to eye. Her eyes were almost squinted shut. She couldn't see much this close up.

"I did, too," Yvonne offered. "I also failed two more, but I have so much on my mind I cain't remember which ones they was—"

"Fifth grade *twice*," Irene said without thinking and instantly regretted it. Yvonne's life was too full of failures to go reminding her of such long forgotten ones. "Well, the fifth grade *is* hard," she assured Yvonne, whose jack-o'-lantern grin had turned upside down. " 'Specially since you had Gladys. Ever-body'll pass more when she retires."

"Or dies," Lottie added hopefully. Lottie looked at Yvonne who was standing a good four feet away and blinked. "Why-vonne, you're lookin' like *somethin',*" she said, wondering how many birds it had taken to make such a coat.

"Well, thanks," Yvonne grinned, cheering up.

"Yep," nodded Lottie. "That's some canary." Yvonne burst into an aria of giggles as Lottie Shady fluffed the feathers on her coat. "*Tweet! Tweet! Tweet!*" She made a full circle around Yvonne. "I hope none of 'em knew how to *sing*!"

"Oh, these are ostriches and turkeys," Yvonne assured her. "They wasn't singers or talkers. They was just squawkers."

Irene Shady rolled her eyes and braced herself against the closest casket.

Lottie ambled over to Topsy, took five steps backwards into the parlor and looked her niece up and down from head to toe. "That's not much of a glamour hair-do, honey," she said. "And where'd you get that ole green rag from? You look just like *us.*"

"I think she looks fifteen," Irene said.

"No, you don't," Lottie assured Topsy. "You look pale, tired, ragged and real, real, real un-Hollywood-like."

Topsy thought she would cry.

"You should have seen her when she arrived," Irene said.

"I'd have *liked* to," Lottie retorted, "and if *somebody* had asked me to drive to the airport with them, I *would* have." She reached up and poked at her niece's stiff bouffant hair. "Another Annie Lovejoy catastrophe! Why don't you let me take a hose to it!"

"I'll run get you one of my wigs," Yvonne offered eagerly. "I got 'em by the hunnerds. You can have your pick. I keep a variety because I like choice, but I also have ones like my favorite stars. There's a Rita Hayworth one, naturally I have Kim Novak and Why-vonne de Carlo, also Morgan Fairchild, Dyan Cannon, Farrah Fawcett, Madonna, Dove Lightlady—"

"She's not wearin' a Dove Lightlady!" Irene stated.

"Thanks, Yvonne," Topsy mumbled. "I guess I'll just wear my own hair—"

"You can have this one I'm wearin' right now," Yvonne went on. She turned to Lottie. "It's supposed to be *her.* The red is not exactly the right red, but she's so little on the TV I guess maybe my hairdresser couldn't see her too good. I *told* him to make me *look* just like *her*!"

It'll take more'n a wig, thought Irene Shady.

It'll take more'n a wig, thought Lottie Shady.

I wish I had a wig to take off, thought Topsy Dingo Wild Dog. She could feel herself starting to sweat.

"Let's go upstairs and fix you up!" cried Lottie Shady. "I don't know what possessed you to want to play down your beauty, honey, but we're goin' to throw you in order right quick! I'm back and just in time, too, 'cause I intend to see that you get dressed and ready and have a head of hair worth wearin' to a Pep Rally and a face full of make-up to go with it!"

Topsy took a deep breath. *I look like who I am,* she thought. *My outsides match my insides . . .*

"Ever-body's got to use what natural gifts they got!" Lottie Shady threw a bony arm around her niece's waist and guided her toward the stairs. "Lookin' like Olive Oyl turned out to be the best thing that ever happened to *me,* honey," she said. "But it don't work for ever-body."

Topsy Dingo Wild Dog stared at her aunt, bewildered. All her life Aunt Lottie had claimed she was a visual failure. And now here she was, twenty years later, proclaiming that the very thing she had despised most in her life was the very best thing that had ever happened to her.

"We just never know when the very things we spend our whole lives wishin' to change are goin' to turn out to be the very things that *distinguish* us!" Lottie announced as they reached the top of the stairs.

Topsy stopped moving. She wanted to ask her aunt how she had made such a turnaround. She wanted to know how she had done it. She wanted to know what had happened. Something drastic must have happened. How long had it taken? Could it happen overnight?

"Why, Why-vonne, here, would give anything to look like you, wouldn't you, Why-vonne?"

"Uh-huh," said Yvonne obligingly. "I awready did the best I could—"

"Who did this to you?" Lottie asked, darting Irene a quick look of disapproval. "Was it Annie Lovejoy?"

Who did this to me? thundered Topsy's head. *WHO DID THIS TO ME*?! She could not take another step.

"What's the matter, honey?" Lottie asked her niece, who had stopped climbing the stairs and was staring into the *Poor White Trash, Part II* poster.

"I find white trash just depressing, don't you?" Yvonne shuddered. She took one look at the poster and darted up the rest of the stairs as fast as she could, leaving a trail of yellow feathers behind her.

Topsy tried to clear her head. She wondered if there was any possible way to turn an act of bestiality into a positive experience. *I should have taken EST,* she thought. *I should have read Terry Cole Whitaker. There I am out in California half the time, practically on the same side of town as Louise Hay and have I ever tried to heal my own life*? She wondered if there was time for her to be rebirthed, saved and reborn in the next fifteen minutes. *I need a guru*! she thought desperately. *I need a trip to India*! She tried to take a breath. *Why didn't I ask Christopher Isherwood!? All we talked about was ME!*

Her knees buckled.

. . . ALL YOU THINK ABOUT IS YOURSELF. EVERY QUESTION YOU ASK BEGS FOR AN ANSWER THAT DIRECTLY RELATES TO YOU. YOURSELF . . .

She swayed on the landing. "Aunt Lottie . . ." She wanted to ask what had happened to her aunt. She wanted to know what had happened to her. She wanted to understand something, anything. She needed to ask. *I WANT SOME ANSWERS*!

"What, honey?" asked Lottie, concerned.

Don't ask, her head said. *You made yourself a promise that you would not ask . . . not anyone . . . not about anything . . . YOU CANNOT ASK . . . DO NOT ASK*!

"What is it?" Irene asked, pushing Lottie aside. "Maybe you need somethin' to eat—"

"Or somethin' to drink," said Lottie.

"Or a nice hot bath," Yvonne offered.

"Are you nervous?" Lottie asked.

Topsy nodded.

"You're not nervous," Irene told her. She turned to Lottie and Yvonne. "She's used to crowds and attention. She cain't be nervous."

"I am *nervous*!" Topsy snapped. "I'm not used to anything! I never know what to expect!"

I snapped! I'm snapping! I'm coming apart! Here I come!

"I never know what to expect either," Yvonne chimed in. "But life's little mysteries is what makes life interestin'! Just play things by ear! That's what I do!"

Irene and Lottie exchanged a look which Topsy didn't miss.

They are worried, she worried. *They are worried about me . . . What do I do? What do I do? What am I going to do? WHAT AM I GOING TO DO*?

She saw three spectators standing there in her bedroom: three people with *expectations*.

Topsy Dingo Wild Dog grabbed onto Lottie Shady desperately. "Aunt Lottie!" she cried out. "If you were me right this minute, *what would you do*?"

Lottie Shady looked at her niece and smiled. She reached in her purse and pulled out a container. "First I'd take some of this nervous-wreck medicine," she said, handing Topsy the bottle, "for when you are a nervous wreck."

"Nervous-wreck medicine?" Yvonne Henderson asked. "What kind is it?"

"They're kind of round and kind of white and kind of hard," Lottie patiently explained. "And then I'd do what Yvonne suggested. I'd take a nice hot bath—"

"Is that Valium?" Yvonne asked, reaching for the bottle. "Can I have one?"

VALIUM. VALIUM. VALIUM. Topsy could almost feel it.

"Oh, let's all have one!" said Irene Shady, grabbing the bottle.

She could feel her muscles relaxing, the tension declining. *VALIUM. MAGIC. VALIUM . . .*

Irene frowned at her daughter. "You already took a shower. Why do you need a bath?"

"She wants to relax for the Pep Rally," replied Lottie Shady. "Don't get in the tub with her! Let her relax!"

Topsy watched the bottle of pills. Her eyes were on the bottle. "Give Yvonne a pill," she heard herself say to her mother. She took the bottle from Irene's hand. *Don't shake. Open it. Give Yvonne one. And take the rest. Take it. You deserve it. Take them all . . .*

"You better pass," said Irene Shady pointedly.

"Why?" asked Yvonne. "I'm not drivin'."

"I mean *you*, Mary Jane Shady," said Irene Shady, taking the pills and opening the top. "You don't need no pills. Ever-time anybody in our whole family takes a pill, they do somethin' crazy."

"Like the time you hit that preacher," Lottie nodded.

Ignoring her sister-in-law, Irene poured several pills into the palm of her hand. "Here, Yvonne. How many do you need?"

Yvonne grinned back. "I'm nervous for *her,*" she explained, indicating Topsy. "I'm a nervous wreck for *you*, Mary Jane!"

Why is she nervous for me? Topsy wondered, agitated. *Why the hell is she nervous for me? Why should SHE be nervous? What could make HER nervous? She married my boyfriend, she got the house, the swimming pool, the tennis court and the servants, she's sitting in the back seat of a chauffeured limousine, all dressed up in a bunch of fine, expensive clothes, and now she's taking my fucking pill and ABOUT TO HAVE MY NERVOUS BREAKDOWN*!

Yvonne daintly picked out a pill and put it in her mouth. "What *are* these things anyway? I never seen any like these before."

"I told you," said Lottie Shady. "It's nervous-wreck medicine. For when you are a nervous wreck." She scooped up a couple and popped them in her mouth. "I think I'll have a few, too!"

Irene handed the pills in her palm to Yvonne, keeping one for herself and then she passed her daughter the whole bottle. "Well! If ya'll think this nervous-wreck medicine is goin' to change our lives, then let's *all* live it up!" She threw her head back and dropped the pill in her mouth.

Topsy watched, stunned. *We're all falling apart! Everybody is snapping*!

"Oh, goody!" sang Yvonne. "I just love nerve pills and I always love to try somethin' *new*! When I had my little breakdown that time, the doctor gave me a whole bunch of stuff that made ever-thing seem just like a daydream, but then I ran out and nobody would give me another prescription." She put another pill in her mouth. "I hope these make you see bright colors!"

Topsy glanced at Yvonne, who had wandered over to a bookcase and was now admiring a complete set of Madame Alexander Little Women dolls, still dressed in their original outfits.

What 'little breakdown'? she wondered. *Did she have to be committed? How bad was it*? She looked at Yvonne and wondered if she had really ever recovered.

"What did they end up sayin' was wrong with you anyway?" Lottie Shady asked Yvonne cautiously. "Were they able to account for what happened?"

It's HIM, thought Topsy. *It's* HIM *and* HE *caused* IT . . .

"Oh, gosh . . ." sighed Yvonne Henderson, who looked as if she might be thinking, "They *told* me . . . but you know . . . it's like the fifth grade . . . I guess I just *forgot* . . . ." Grinning, Yvonne shrugged her shoulders and turned back to the dolls.

Topsy looked at Irene and Lottie who were just standing there, staring silently at Yvonne. *They are stoned,* she thought incredulously. *They have taken those pills and now they're getting stoned*! She clutched the pill bottle in her hand. *Well, I'm taking the rest of these! I'm not sticking around for this! I'm killing myself!* She walked out of her bedroom and started down the hall toward the bathroom. *At least I won't have to wonder what happened,* she told herself. *At least I can stop* THINKING . . .

Yvonne's voice broke through her thoughts. "Mary Jane, while you're bathing, do you think I could hold one of these dolls?"

Topsy stopped moving and turned around to see Yvonne standing out in the hall in her yellow turkey-feather coat and spangled dress, gazing at Topsy with eyes large and fascinated and reverent, as if she were viewing something awesome and precious. Yvonne Henderson was staring at her in the same way Topsy had stared when first gazing at Monet's *Water Lilies.* There was no mistaking that look. Yvonne *admired* her. She felt sick with deceit. She looked at Yvonne, standing there, in yellow bird feathers and maroon and gold sequins, ridiculous and devoted. She wanted to apologize. She wanted to tell Yvonne she was sorry Yvonne had had to wear her old hand-me-downs, and sorry if Bobby had made Yvonne try to look like *her,* or *be* like her. She wanted to tell her she was sorry she wasn't worth trying to emulate in the first place and sorry if Yvonne had suffered a nervous breakdown trying to. She still didn't know what had happened to Yvonne's life with Bobby, or how life had treated Yvonne at all over the past twenty years, not really. All she knew *for sure* was that Yvonne was counting on her *now. Today.* She felt horrible. She wanted to die. The only thing that made her feel one bit better was the bottle which she held in her hand.

"Yvonne," whispered Topsy Dingo Wild Dog. "I would love for you to hold those dolls . . . "

"I wish I had somethin' for you to hold!" cried Yvonne Henderson. "You want to hold my coat?"

Topsy smiled wanly. *Don't tell her you've got one just like it . . .*

"Oh, my goodness!" said Yvonne. "The way you're standin' there in the hall now, half-sad and half-smilin', you look just like you did when you was playin' that mermaid, *Ondine* . . . I will never forget that as long as I live," Yvonne continued. "Oh, you fell in love with a human bein' and then you tried to be a human bein', and just nothin' worked out, 'cause you just weren't meant to be human! Then *he* died and you went back just to like you was and things was fine once you got back in your own waters . . . "

Topsy stared at Yvonne speechlessly.

"Now, don't let me keep you!" Yvonne grinned. "I'm goin' to go play with those dolls while you go on and take your bath! Just relax and close your eyes . . ." Yvonne's bright jack-o'-lantern grin faded into her painted face. She stood quietly for a moment, and when she spoke, her voice almost trembled. "I cain't thank you enough for comin', Mary Jane," Yvonne said softly. "This is the most important day of my life . . . "

Topsy Dingo Wild Dog gazed at Yvonne wistfully. "You're welcome, Yvonne. But try not to get too excited. It might not turn out like . . . you planned . . . "

"Oh, yes it will!" cried Yvonne Henderson, her upside-down mouth once again all grins. "I have real good luck at things turnin' out like I plan!"

CHAPTER FORTY-SEVEN

TOPSY COULD HEAR the continued mingling of their voices as she opened the door to the large, spacious bathroom. It was as clean as the best hospital. An operation could be conducted right on the floor. Nothing had changed since earlier in the morning. Nothing had changed in the past twenty years. There was that same floral pattern on the same towels and washrags. There was the same soap dish painted with bluebonnets she had given to her mother on Mother's Day in 1957. The same flowerless bud vase sat on the back of the commode, a gift to Irene one Christmas from Gladys Turner. The clotheshamper was empty. Irene Shady never had dirty laundry.

Numbly, she emptied the contents of the pill bottle into her mouth. She took the plastic glass from its plastic dispenser next to the mirror on the medicine cabinet, filled it with water and swallowed. She took another sip and swallowed again. She placed the plastic glass back in its container.

And then she prepared to die.

First, she filled the old claw-footed tub with lilac-scented Avon bubble bath, then she dropped the skirt and sweater set on the floor, then she stepped out of her underwear and into the tub. She half-heartedly scrubbed the red line on her chest and finally just gave up.

Maybe whoever works on the line under my left eye when they're embalming me can take care of this thing at the same time. Remove all red lines! Topsy giggled. *Why am I laughing? This isn't funny. It's horrible.* She couldn't stop laughing. Tears rolled down her cheeks and splashed into the tub. Would her mother do the undertaking or would Aunt Lottie drag her out of the tub and down the stairs and throw her on the table in the pantry before she was even cold? She giggled hysterically. *I'm practically ready to go! They don't even have to press my dress!* She envisioned Arabella du Noir and Ralph Painter standing out front with Dr. Smith and Judge Upchurch and all her family's friends. Would the Widders family be there, Scoot, the twins, Sammy and Kay? Would Scoot bring the float? Would they place her body on it, upright and stuffed, like one of Yvonne Henderson's birds? Would they drive her through the middle of town on the float, hitched to the loser's car? Would her mother finally, finally, finally have her parade? Would Gladys Turner read a speech? Would Yvonne cry? Would Kay cheer? Would Catsy care? Would Bobby come? Who would tell Herman? Who would call Herman? Who would even *think* about Herman? She hadn't. She had forgotten all about Herman.

The giggles became convulsions. The convulsions turned to sobs. Suddenly she was crying, overtaken by anguish and remorse. Who would look into her still, empty face and weep with heartbreak and pain and loss and despair? Who would wail and stomp and scream in protest and appalling rage? Who would grieve the way she had? The way she had when her daddy had died?

. . . daddy . . .

She swooned. Without warning, a gale of grief, monstrous, huge, dark and powerful, tore through her from some remote and distant, dark and foreign, hidden, buried crevice.

What's happening to me? she sobbed. *STOP LAUGHING. STOP CRYING. OH, MY GOD, I'M THINKING! DON'T START THINKING . . . There you go, about to THINK again. Don't do it. Don't think. Stop thinking. Stop laughing. Stop crying. Better stop. Stop. Stop. Stop. Stop. Have you stopped? Better stop . . . stop . . . stop . . . stop . . . stop . . . stop . . . stop . . . FEELING. STOP.*

But it wasn't so easy to stop.

"Om-m-m," she chanted. "Oh, Om-m-m-m." She started to giggle again. "Ho-hum-m-m-m!" She pulled herself down in the tub. "I'll die in a minute! All I have to do is just lie here and die!"

Submerged in a sea of warm lilac bubbles, she tried to make herself relax. She tried to tell herself it would soon all be over.

She tried to drive her mind away from that horrible stunning *passion* she'd just felt. She told herself she was better off to think about Herman, Arabella du Noir, her Mama and Ralph Painter. Better to concentrate on Yvonne Henderson and Peanut Butter contracts, wrinkles, floats and old dogged memories. Easier to think of Bobby Henderson . . .

And for a moment she forgot fear. *Nothing can get me,* she reassured herself. *I'm practically dead. Nothing can get me now . . .*

But in a moment, peacefulness was interrupted by just her awareness of it. And in that moment, she tried to remember when the last time was that she had felt safe and secure and relaxed.

"*WHENEVER A HUMAN BEIN' FUCKS A DOG, THAT DOG BECOMES PART HUMAN AND THE HUMAN GETS TO BE PART DOG . . .*" That's what he'd said. Bobby . . .

The pills didn't seem to be working. She couldn't relax. Startled, she wondered, *What if those pills aren't any good? What if I don't die?*

What if I don't ever get to relax! She had no idea when she started to laugh again. *I'm in Uncertain, Texas, with Bobby Henderson's chicken-feathered wife! My Aunt Lottie just told me she's happy to look like Olive Oyl! My mother is running the Hocker-Smockter Agency! Ralph Painter and Arabella du Noir are on their way to a Pep Rally! Siamese twins are about to be crowned Homecoming Queen! Uncertain, Texas, is about to find out I'm part dog and I might not even get to die*!

Topsy Dingo Wild Dog started to weep softly. Tears ran down her cheeks and dripped onto her half-hearted heart.

"*YOU JUST WEREN'T MEANT TO BE HUMAN* . . . " That's what she'd said. That's what Mrs. Bobby Henderson had said . . .

What if I live through this! she thought, harassed. *What if I live and have to go on*!

She looked at her hands, overwhelmed with monstrous possibilities. *At three P.M. you turn to claws* . . . She touched her mouth. *At three P.M. you become a muzzle* . . . She felt a thigh. *At three P.M. you HEEL. You SIT.*

She sat up sharply. Clarity was on the rise!

"Oh, my God," she whispered, hysterically. "This is *it*. This is it! This is it! This is how I get *through* it!" Her head clattered and raced and banged, spinning with delirium. "Why didn't I think of it before? I'll treat myself like a—a—pet!" She nodded, frenetically absorbed. "*Sit*, I'll say to myself! SIT! And I'll sit. *Stay*! I'll say! And I'll STAY. HEEL, HEEL, HEEL." Filled with frenzied hope and desperate designs, she got up and dizzily paced back and forth in the tub, splashing water and bubbles over the side. "SIT! SIT!" She sat. "STAY!" She patted herself on the head. "That's it, pal. Relax. Good *dog*!" She pounded herself on the head again. "*Good dog. RELAX! RELAX!*"

She fell into the water, panting. Exhausted. She was ready to roll over and relax when something caught her eye.

There on the shelf was the double-edged razor she had first shaved her legs with the night her daddy died.

Her daddy . . .

She could hardly remember her daddy. She had almost remembered him. Was it only a few minutes ago? Something had happened. She'd been thinking. What had she been thinking? But she hadn't tried to remember him. He had just come out of nowhere . . .

Probably MYSELF, she told herself. *I WAS PROBABLY THINKING ABOUT MY SELF* . . .

She tried to remember the sound of his voice, something he had said to her, what he looked like . . .

She couldn't remember a thing.

Puzzled, she strained to remember. Something. Anything . . .

Nothing. She remembered nothing.

Her efforts became urgent, obsessive, desperate.

In her head she saw a bright white light. In her mind she heard a buzz.

The words to the song tumbled into her head.

Drivin' down a dirt road . . .

She shook her head, wearily. "No, no, that's not it . . . "

After a six-pack picture show . . .

She pushed the song out of her head, and started over, but still she couldn't remember. She couldn't remember Robert Shady. Everytime she tried to think of him, to remember him, all that came back was that song and the white light and the buzz.

It had just been oiled the day before

I asked him please drive slow . . .

She shook her head. "No, no . . . "

She shut her eyes. Bobby. She could see Bobby. She could see his face, his eyes. She could hear his voice.

But she couldn't remember her daddy . . .

Something pierced the palms of her hands. *My hands . . .* She stared at her hands. Her fingernails were digging into her flesh. She observed this, completely detached. She watched the nails of her left hand abandon the imprinted, reddened palm. She watched the fingers uncurl as if they belonged to someone else. She watched them mark their destination, then, without hesitation, cunningly crawl through the air toward the silver, gleaming sharp-edged device, like a spider toward a fly.

But it wasn't until both hands hugged the razor's old familiar handle, that finally, finally, Topsy Dingo Wild Dog relaxed.

I'll just carve the other side of that heart out . . . she thought, calmly closing her eyes and cradling the razor. *And then I can relax . . .*

The bathroom door swung open softly.

"Hey. 'Member me?"

She made her eyes stay closed.

"I saw you on TV."

Bobby. It wasn't her daddy. It was Bobby.

Her eyes didn't open. She refused to open her eyes.

"You're the best," he said.

"Yeah, sure," she said. "The best what? The best cocksucker, the finest rubber-thrower, the fastest tape-remover from your class ring? The best allergy victim?"

Where was he? Where was her daddy? Why didn't he just come in the door and beat the shit out of Bobby Henderson?

"Hey," he said. "What are you so pissed off for? C'mere."

He was on top of her, she felt his mouth, she felt his hardness. He wrapped himself around her. She thought she would choke.

"TELL HIM TO STOP IF YOU DON'T WANT HIM DOING THAT." It was her father's voice.

"What?" she said, panicked. "What?"

"SAY 'NO.' YOU KNOW HOW TO SAY 'NO' DON'T YOU? DID YOU FORGET HOW TO SAY 'NO'?"

"Oh, my God . . ." she whispered. "I forgot . . ."

She could feel Bobby. He pinned her legs apart. He held her arms back. She thought she would suffocate. "Don't go!" she cried out.

"That's what I thought," Bobby said. "You want it. You want it . . ."

"Don't," she said to Bobby. "I mean *don't.*"

Splashing water flew over the tub and onto the floor.

He grabbed her and turned her over on top of him. He held her up on top.

"Here you are," he grinned. "Up on top."

She pulled away from him wildly, her head faint, her heart aching. She felt nauseated. Sick. Helpless. Bobby was holding her up in the air like Fay Wray in *King Kong*.

"Don't," she pleaded. "Don't, don't, don't . . ."

"C'mon, now. What's the matter with you? You're up on top like you wanted to be."

"I changed my mind!" she cried. "Let me go! I don't want to be on top! Stop!"

"DON'T EXPLAIN TO AN ANIMAL, MARY JANE. JUST SAY 'NO.' " Her father. He was there. He was somewhere.

"Relax. C'mere. What do you want? Don't you want it to be like the first time? C'mon, M.J. Lemme make you feel just like the first time . . ."

When he painted me with his tongue
Like I was a piece of art . . .

The first time? The very first time? Isn't that what she wanted? Not the last time. The first time . . . And what had Bobby said after the first time?—"*Bye, bye, little Bob* . . . "

"BYE, BYE, LITTLE MARY JANE . . . " Again, she heard her father.

She turned to find him, her arms reached for his voice, her hands, fistfuls of air.

That is when my friend . . .

Her neck cracked. Her arms whipped behind her, knuckles turned inside out, legs pulled apart, tongue jerked out. Her hair ripped from her scalp. Bobby was all over her. Pieces of her were all over Bobby. Only a tiny bloody muscle was left. She was a tiny bloody muscle pumping wildly, frantically to stay alive.

Something screamed. "*It hurts! I hurt*!"

He grabbed her neck and tossed what was left of her face aside. He snatched the tiny flagellating muscle and held it under the water.

She couldn't breathe. She couldn't see. She was choking on her heart.

"YOU BEGGED FOR IT! YOU WANTED IT!"

"*No*!" the bloody muscle sobbed. "*PLEASE, PLEASE, PLEASE, PLEASE NO! NO! NO!*"

"YOU SHOULD HAVE SAID 'NO' THE FIRST TIME," she heard her daddy say. "THIS ISN'T HOW YOU GET TO THE TOP."

"*No! No! No!*" She remembered how to say no. Why hadn't she remembered before it killed everybody?

"YES!" Bobby spat maniacally. "That's right. Beg me to stop. BEG. BEG ME TO STOP!" He picked up the heart and stuffed it in his mouth.

"*I AM BEGGING YOU TO STOP*!" she moaned inside his teeth. "*YOU'RE GOING TO KILL ME! YOU'RE GOING TO EAT ME UP! YOU'RE EATING ME UP ALIVE*!"

Bobby Henderson broke into maniacal laughter. "I don't have to, Topsy Dingo Wild Dog! Don't you know about half-dog women? They eat *theirselves* up alive!"

He swallowed the palpitating mass. And down she went. Down, down, down his abysmal caverns, through his esophagus, past slimy kidneys, inflamed liver, grinding though endless coils and trenches of sinewy guts and bottomless bowels. She slid into his rectum, dark, murky and putrid. A grunt exploded her through him in a combustion of odious fumes. She plummeted out of Bobby Henderson, a dump of trembling excrement, hovering in her own ruptured mire of sticky, slimy refuse.

"Daddy!" she screamed. "Daddy!"

"I'M SORRY, MARY JANE," Robert Shady told her patiently. "I'M DEAD NOW. I CAN'T HELP YOU." He sounded sad. "I'M SORRY YOU'RE LETTING YOURSELF BEING EATEN UP ALIVE."

"*Did I kill you*?" she asked frantically. "*Did I?*"

"No" he said, "YOU DID NOT KILL ME. OF COURSE NOT. WHAT A SELF-CENTERED IDEA. I DON'T KNOW WHAT HAPPENED TO MY HEART. ALL THE SAME I AM DEAD NOW. I AM NOT AVAILABLE. I AM NOT ALIVE. BUT YOU ARE."

Appalled, she gasped, "You mean I'm still *alive*?"

"THAT'S RIGHT," he said. "YOU ARE STILL ALIVE. YOU HAVE TO TAKE CARE OF BOBBY HENDERSON YOURSELF. YOU HAVE TO TAKE CARE OF YOURSELF, YOURSELF. YOU ARE ALIVE. YOU ARE ALIVE . . . YOU ARE ALIVE . . . YOU ARE ALIVE . . . YOU ARE ALIVE . . ."

Her eyes flew open, the water from the shower hitting her so hard in the face that she didn't even see the shower curtain as it whipped open.

"Mary Jane, are you alive?" Irene Shady asked, reaching down to turn off the water. "Gracious, mercy, what a disaster," she lamented, looking at the water on the floor. "Mary Jane, it would take you ten minutes to destroy Rome."

"I didn't do it!" Topsy cried, as she stood, then slipped, then stepped from the tub that looked like somebody's old forgotten pond. The razor fell from her hands, clanking out a metallic protest as it bounced off the porcelain and plunged to the bottom of the tub, silent and abandoned.

"You didn't?" Irene said, reaching for a mop. "Who did then?"

Topsy stood shivering on the wet mat. She knew who did it. "I did," she said quietly. "I did it."

"Well," Irene sighed. "I guess it could have been worse." She looked up at her daughter and smiled. Slowly the smile slid off her face. "Mary Jane," she said. "What's that red thing between your breasts?"

"Oh, *that,*" said Topsy Dingo Wild Dog, as her hands flew over her heart.

Irene Shady pushed Topsy's hands away. "It looks kinda like a half-tattooed heart," she said incredulously.

"It is," Topsy said simply.

"Forevermore," said Irene Shady anxiously. "Can they *remove* it?"

"I don't think so."

"Oh, my God," Irene whispered. "You better keep that *covered* up."

"Don't worry about it," said Topsy quietly. "I'm going to get it fixed."

CHAPTER FORTY-EIGHT

TOPSY DINGO WILD DOG looked into her mother's eyes and thought she had never seen such sadness.

Irene looked away. Then she looked down. She didn't know exactly where to look. Awkwardly, she turned and made a little half circle, vaguely pointing to the freshly pressed Peanut Butter Cup dress.

"I brought your dress in," she mumbled. "So you can go on and get dressed—" She started out the door.

"Mama . . . "

Irene turned back abruptly, facing her daughter directly. "What's *wrong*?" she asked quietly. "What's the *matter*?" Finally, she looked right into her daughter's half-hearted heart. What's *happened* to you?"

What happened? . . . Topsy's head echoed. *What happened*? . . .

"What's *wrong*?" Irene repeated. "You have not acted like yourself for one minute since you stepped off that plane—"

Act like yourself . . .

"But I'm *going* to," Topsy assured Irene Shady. "I'm okay." She smiled anxiously, desperate to please, to put her mother at ease, determined to act like *herself,* some *recognizable self,* some old familiar, contented and satisfying *self* that everyone, including her, would *recognize.* "I haven't changed. Really. It's the same old me, I'm just the same. The same old dress. The same old name . . ."

Smile. Topsy Dingo Wild Dog. Smile . . .

But she couldn't. She couldn't remember how. She couldn't remember her father's face. She couldn't remember her name.

Irene just stared at her daughter. "You can tell me," she said.

But Topsy knew she couldn't.

Irene looked again at the red line between her daughter's breasts. "What does that *mean*?"

Topsy knew Irene Shady did not want to know. It didn't matter. She had no idea what to tell her.

"Is it *Jewish*?" Irene asked.

"Mother!" Indignant.

"Well, I don't know," Irene snapped. "What do I know?"

Topsy reached for her bra. "Please," she said. "It isn't Herman . . ."

Silence. She put on the blouse. There. Finally covered.

Silence. She stepped into her panties, into her skirt. She attached the dickey to the blouse.

Silence. Topsy Dingo Wild Dog smiled her Mary Jane Shady smile. She thought her face would crack.

"There! Look. See. It's *me* . . . "

She was in her dress, dressed in gingham and ruffles, ribbons and bows. Pressed, starched, clean, unlined and white.

Perfect.

Silence.

Irene tore off some toilet paper and blew her nose, wadded up the tissue and tossed it in the wastepaper basket. It hit the rim but fell right in.

Irene looked up at her daughter and smiled tiredly. "It looks like you," she said bravely.

Topsy put her arms around her mother and kissed Irene's damp hair and her finely lined face.

"I'll be all right," she promised.

Goddamnit. Get all right. You're alive. Act like it. NOW.

"Well," Irene sighed, "I hope so." She reached up and untied the little bow attached to the dickey. She retied the bow to suit herself and dropped her arms to her sides. Topsy Dingo Wild Dog watched her mother evoke a very shaky Irene Shady smile. "Well," Irene said, reaching into her pocket. "I guess maybe you need one of these pills more than I thought."

Topsy stared at her mother incredulously. *I was all ready to die,* she thought in confusion. *I had myself ready! I was ready to go! Then here she comes . . .* She stopped abruptly. *Wait a minute,* she told herself. *Why AM I alive? I should have DIED from those pills but they didn't even phase me! I was about to carve my heart out*! She reached for the pills. "What are these things anyway?" she asked.

"Some kind of nerve pill, I guess," Irene said. "I don't know nothin', so I don't know . . . "

Topsy looked into her mother's palm. She picked up a white pill. "This isn't Valium," she said slowly. She hadn't even looked when she'd swallowed the pills. "It isn't Tylenol and Codeine. It's not a Quaalude. It isn't Ecstasy." *And I don't feel a thing . . .*

Irene peered at her daughter, concerned "What's 'Ecstasy'? " she asked nervously. "What's a 'Cool-Dude'? "

"What *is* this?" Topsy murmured. She turned the pill over in her hand, examining its shape and color and size. It looked familiar. Very familiar.

"What if it's somethin' real, real lethal?" Irene asked anxiously. "I knew I shouldn't have just popped it in! What a silly, stupid thing! Wonder if we're all goin' to get sick? What if one of us *urps* durin' the Pep Rally? How strong is it, do you think? I took *one,* Lottie took *two,* I don't know how many Why-vonne must have took—I think she ate a whole *handful*!" Irene groaned extravagantly and clutched her throat. "How many did *you* take, Mary Jane? How do you feel? Do you feel *sick* yet?" She fanned herself with her hand. "Oh, no, oh, no, I think I may feel *dizzy*!" She bowed her head and started to pray frantically. "Oh, Lord, please don't let it kill us! We need to go to that Pep Rally! We don't have time to die yet! We don't need to get sick yet, either!"

Topsy held the pill up to the light, staring at it closely. Her eyes grew wide. A series of soundless staccato jolts rumbled thorough her convulsively. And then she started to giggle.

"It's not *funny*!" Irene snapped. "What's so funny?"

"It's a *vitamin*!" Topsy gasped. "It's a High Potency, Advanced Formula, Complex-Complex, A to Zinc, essential to human nutrition, Multimineral, Multivitamin *vitamin*!"

Irene Shady screamed, "A *vitamin*?" She fell against the sink, cackling. "No wonder I didn't feel nothin'!"

Topsy Dingo Wild Dog cackled with her. She collapsed against her mother. She could hardly stand up. She couldn't sit down.

"I don't understand Lottie Shady and I never have!" Irene crowed, wiping the tears from her eyes. "I guess I never will, either!" She doubled over, her shoulders shaking. "What do you think *she* thinks these pills *do,* anyway?!"

Topsy could not answer. All she could do was laugh. *I tried to kill myself*! She hysterically succumbed to yet another onslaught of giggles. *I tried to kill myself on VITAMINS*!

"Wonder if she thinks she's on some kind of a *high*!" Irene whooped. "She's got Yvonne down on the floor in yonder and they're *both* playin' *dolls!*"

Topsy and Irene screamed together.

Laughing, they fell into each other's arms.

Slowly, they wiped away each others tears.

They looked into each other's eyes.

Silently, they grasped one another's hands.

They held on tightly.

And then they smiled.

And then they laughed.

Together.

Together, they laughed all the way down the hall.

When they reached the doorway to Topsy's room, there were Lottie and Yvonne, down on the floor, sitting in the middle of box after box of old school clippings, class albums, prom dinner menus, pressed corsages, party favors, scrapbooks, notebooks, every piece of jewelry Mary Jane Shady had ever owned from birth until she left home, and an entire set of *The Book of Knowledge*.

"See?" Irene whispered to her daughter. "See what I mean?"

"This is your life!" Lottie Shady announced, as she opened a box filled with old costumes from various high school productions.

"Looky," Yvonne said, gently touching the dolls. She had Meg, the oldest in the story, standing up beside Marmee, the mother. Jo was sitting, Beth's head resting on her lap. She'd positioned Amy a little distance away. Amy was the first of the collection Mary Jane had received. She had the most elaborate hair-do, her white blonde tresses plaited and elaborately coiffed.

"Here's your *Ondine* dress!" Lottie stated, holding up a tattered and faded, pale green, medieval-looking outfit and an old pair of dyed-to-match fishnet hose.

"I just love these dolls!" Yvonne said admiringly. "I read the book from the libery 'bout twenty times, I guess!"

"Didn't you have *Little Women*?" Irene asked and immediately wished she hadn't.

"I never had a doll in my life," Yvonne Henderson said simply.

Topsy wished she knew what to say. Of course Yvonne wouldn't have had a *doll*. She had hardly even had clothes. Topsy tried to imagine what it would have been like to grow up without a *Little Women* set. Without clothes. Without Aunt Lottie. Without a mother. Without a daddy. Without Bobby. . .

"This one's you," Yvonne continued, walking the Amy doll around. "See how she's the prettiest and a little apart from the rest because of it?"

"Which one's you?" Topsy asked Yvonne softly.

"None of 'em," Yvonne said flatly. "I'm just not in this story."

Topsy picked up another box of her dolls and pulled out a bride. "Here you are," she said, holding the doll out to Yvonne.

But Yvonne was looking at another doll. When she saw it, her eyes became so bright and wide, Topsy thought the electricity in them could have caused a blackout in New York City. "What's this?" Yvonne asked, picking up a doll Topsy vaguely remembered, but had long forgotten.

"Why, that's my ole doll," Lottie said, "by the name of Big Bertha. She's a trapeze artist and if you wind her up she'll turn somersaults over that little wire there."

It was a mechanical toy with a porcelain face cracked down the middle and crazed green eyes. It wore a short pink tattered skirt and had a red horsehair wig piled in a pompadour on top of its head. Her little smile revealed one chipped tooth and she was missing one leg.

"She's lost a limb, but she'll still go," Yvonne said, watching in delight and fascination as the toy flopped slowly over the wire.

Lottie had taken the bride and was walking it down an aisle she had created from folding up a white satin cape. "Why didn't you get a groom to go with this?" Lottie asked Irene.

"I did," Irene replied shortly.

"I'm lettin' that one go for now," Lottie Shady Diggs replied. "Remember I said it."

"I just cannot believe my eyes!" Irene remarked. "A grown-up ole woman down on the floor playin' dolls! *Please* get up before somebody comes in here and thinks we *all* lost our minds."

Lottie Shady jumped up and threw the white satin cape over her head and around her shoulders. "Here comes the bri-i-i-d-e!" she sang, dancing around the room, out the door and down the hall. "She's goin' for a ri-i-i-d-e!"

Topsy sat down at her dresser, took her cosmetics bag out of her purse and looked in the mirror. She pulled her hair back. It was softer. When it dried it would be all right. The hairdresser would take care of it anyway. She reached into the cosmetics bag. A touch of foundation.

A little rouge. A wisp of mascara. The make-up man would do the rest.

Yvonne sat on the floor, cradling the trapeze doll. "I bet Kim Novak'd like to look like you," Yvonne whispered, gazing at Topsy.

"I bet Kim Novak'd be on time for her own Pep Rally," Irene Shady said, checking her watch.

"I bet Kim Novak wouldn't even *go*," sang Lottie Shady, waltzing into the room. She danced back out again. "I didn't go to mine . . ."

They could hear her singing all the way down the stairs.

"Here comes the bride . . ." she chanted. "Here . . . comes . . . the . . . bri-i-i-d-e!"

"She's crazy," Irene told Yvonne and Topsy. "There is not another thing wrong with her except she is *stark, raving insane*!"

CHAPTER FORTY-NINE

"ROLL OFF THE TOP, James!" cried Yvonne Henderson, as Topsy, Irene and Lottie Shady walked toward her limousine. "Let's show Uncertain, Texas, we got Mary Jane Shady back in town!"

Irene watched intently as the limousine's roof slid back, silently and smoothly. She was wearing last year's Easter dress. Everything about it was blue.

Lottie Shady looked across the street toward the parked eighteen-wheeler and blew Leo Diggs a kiss when she was sure no one was looking. She had wanted to wear her pale pink shirtwaist with the tiny white stars and moons, but she hadn't been able to find it, so she'd put on her second best dress, a drip-dry that featured every flower she had ever heard of on the fabric, and then some.

"Irene," said Lottie as she climbed into the car. "I couldn't find my stars and moons dress anywhere. Do you know what happened to it?"

Irene was busy feeling the cowskin upholstery. "No," she lied, thinking how much better the dress had looked on Baby Flowers. "I haven't seen it. Look at this *cowhide* . . . "

It was almost two-thirty and the air was perfect.

No smog, no smoke, no crowds, no dog shit, no homeless people, no freeways, thought Topsy. *Simple* . . .

She and Yvonne sat on the jump seats facing Lottie and Irene.

"You ought to ride back here, Mary Jane," said Irene Shady.

"Yes, you should!" Lottie agreed.

"Then move over so she can sit here in the middle!" Irene told her sister-in-law.

"We ought to move to the jump seats and let Yvonne and Mary Jane both sit back here," Lottie said.

"I'll sit where you're sittin', Lottie, and Mary Jane can sit where you're sittin', Irene!" Yvonne Henderson suggested.

They pulled out of the driveway, drove past the Hoop and Holler Motel for a Dollar, made a left turn at the red light, which for once was not red, drove past the pony man's ponies, the fortune teller's tent and past the Widders' trailer-made-house without Yvonne, Topsy, Lottie or Irene even noticing. They were all too busy rearranging themselves in the backseat to even notice that not one of them had remembered to turn off the neon sign.

The limousine turned left off Highway 158 onto a dirt road.

Topsy saw the Flowers' dilapidated shack and shoddy yard full of tin cans, stickers, weeds, broken tools, flat tires, discarded Cracker-jack boxes and wildcats emerge in front of them.

Even the Flowers family, poor as they are, have a home, she mused. *And everyone knows every single one of them by name . . .*

"Hey!" Yvonne shot up out of her seat, plunged between Lottie and Irene and rapped the driver on the back of the head. Yellow feathers flew everywhere. "I told you and I told you, don't come this way! I didn't tell you to take any shortcut! Why didn't you drive through town where ever-body could see us, you half-brain!?"

The driver looked at her in confusion.

"Why am I always the only one who speaks English!" Yvonne cried in frustration. "He don't understand nothin' but 'open the door!' "

Hearing this, the driver screeched to a stop, jumped out and threw open Yvonne's door.

"No! No! No!" screamed Yvonne Flowers Henderson, as her seven rocking relatives all started to wave. "Goddamnit! Goddamnit! Shut the door!"

"Hidy, Why-vonne!" yelled Petunia.

"Hidy, Why-vonne!" shrieked Iris.

"Hidy, Why-vonne!" shouted Rose.

"Hidy, Why-vonne!" hollered Daisy.

"Hidy, Why-vonne!" squealed Daffodil.

"Hidy, Why-vonne!" screamed Poppy.

"Hidy, Why-vonne!" gurgled Mum.

Seven Crackerjack boxes waved in the air.

"Pronto! Pronto!" Yvonne cried, hysterically gesticulating in the back seat.

Seven grinning Flowers gesticulated wildly back.

Lottie and Irene Shady shook with silent laughter. Tears were pouring down Irene's face. Lottie was hiccoughing.

"Pee-e-e-ugh!" shuddered Yvonne, sliding down into the backseat as the car finally roared off. She pulled herself up slowly and never once looked back toward her disappearing relatives. "This whole town is full of fruitcakes!" she declared, as if she weren't related to every single one of them. "Everybody in Uncertain, Texas ought to be locked up!"

As Topsy looked behind her, seven little Crackerjack boxes were still waving in the air.

She turned around. They were crossing the intersection of Reading and Writing Avenues. Uncertain High School was right in front of them. It was a quarter of three. She was almost there.

"This is the most exciting thing that ever happened to me!" yelled Yvonne Henderson. She leapt to her feet and waved grandly as she saw the crowd of people standing in front of the school. "*Slow down,*" she told her chauffeur. "No pronto! Go *slow*!"

"Looky!" cried Lottie Shady, pointing to a huge banner draped across the entry of Uncertain High School which proclaimed:

WELCOME HOME, MARY JANE SHADY, OUR OWN UNCERTAIN STAR!

"Well, *finally,*" glowed Irene. She smiled at the crowd and waved and waved. "Wave, Mary Jane!" she said to Topsy. "They've all come to see you! Wave!"

Topsy Dingo Wild Dog waved.

"Smile!" Irene beamed. "Give 'em a big ole Mary Jane Shady smile!"

Topsy Dingo Wild Dog smiled her Mary Jane Shady smile.

The crowd waved.

A flurry of teenagers gathered around the car. "We want your name! Sign your name!" They held out autograph books, school annuals, pieces of paper, and newspapers, pens and pencils, crayolas and chalk.

Topsy Dingo Wild Dog took the books and papers one by one.

Carefully and slowly, over and over, she wrote the same thing: MARY JANE SHADY. MARY JANE SHADY. MARY JANE SHADY.

Tinsy Tabor grabbed Yvonne Henderson by the arm. "What's she like?" Tinsy wanted to know. "Has she *changed*?"

"Tinsy," grinned Yvonne Henderson, a yellow-feathered bundle of sequined information, "the only thing that hasn't changed about Mary Jane Shady is her name!"

Yvonne's chauffeur jumped out of the car and flung open the doors.

"I got her back!" Yvonne cried out to the crowd. "I got her home!"

Topsy Dingo Wild Dog stood up slowly. Topsy Dingo Wild Dog waved. Topsy Dingo Wild Dog smiled. And smiled. And smiled.

"Here she comes!" cried the crowd, as she stepped down from Yvonne's limousine. "Here comes Mary Jane Shady!"

HERE COMES TOPSY DINGO WILD DOG . . . smiled the waving, smiling Topsy. *HERE COMES TOPSY* . . .

PART
THREE

CHAPTER FIFTY

ANYONE DRIVING EAST OR WEST through Uncertain, Texas, on Highway 158 around three o'clock in the afternoon on Friday, September 13, 1985, would not have missed seeing Baby Flowers out walking.

Baby had waited until she had heard Yvonne's limousine drive off before wandering back down through the empty hall and into the deserted motel-like living room. She was hoping to find the cut-out lady, the one who looked exactly like the blow-ups over in the entryway of the Uncertain Chapel of Memories.

At first, when Baby found the house deserted, she thought the cut-out lady might have gone home, so she wandered from floor to floor and room to room, turning on and methodically switching the channels of thirty-seven television sets, hoping to find the cut-out lady in one of them. In her effort to see if Miss Peanut Butter Cup was back in her little kitchen, she flipped through flashes of *Hollywood Squares, Guiding Light, General Hospital,* and *Santa Barbara, Bewitched, Superman, I Love Lucy, Mr. Ed, Dobie Gillis, Lassie,* a *Tom and Jerry* cartoon. *Tic Tac Dough* and an old Judy Garland movie.

She had been gazing at *Meet Me in St. Louis* for almost thirty minutes before Judy Garland's bright happy smile reminded Baby of Miss Peanut Butter Cup. Then she remembered she had been trying to find her. She didn't remember why. She just wanted to *look* at her some more. After waving at those blown-up cardboard figures everyday of her life, Baby was fascinated with the real thing. She wanted to admire the cut-out lady's shining chestnut hair and china blue eyes and clear white skin. She wanted to listen to her smooth, silky voice.

" 'Creamy or Smooth . . .' " Baby whispered, practicing.

" 'Pure . . . rich . . . nutty . . . taste . . . Creamy Butter, Nutty, too . . .' " She stopped. " 'What?' " she mimicked, for that was the word the cut-out lady had said to her. " 'What?' . . ."

Baby wandered through the empty house several times, oblivious of the TV sets now blaring different programs out of every room, before she set off for the Uncertain Chapel of Memories.

She had reached the living room and was headed for the front door when something shiny caught her eye. Baby blinked. Near the planter, scattered across the cold marble tiles and over a chair, were several splendid ornaments.

The cut-out lady had left her presents!

Baby blinked again. Moving closer, she could see that these magnificent gifts looked like some of the splendid embellishments she had seen Yvonne wearing earlier.

Joyfully, Baby turned around three times. Baby's smile covered Baby's face. She moved steadily toward the decorations. She picked them up, one by one, and sat down on the floor to fondle them. She cradled the gold breastplate in her arms, marvelling at the coldness of its touch. She flipped the yellow-diamond and deep-red-ruby yellow jackets dangling from each spiky breastplate back and forth, her eyes following each sparkling, circular motion. Baby picked up the necklace of maroon and gold arched feathers, gently fingering the large red and yellow stones encrusted on the choker. She smoothed each feather with her hands. Then she tickled herself and tittered. She reached for the headdress. She placed the golden crown shaped like a small nest on top of her head, tucking some of her raven-hued, ribboned, flower-trimmed curls inside the diamond-studded gold netting. Five little pavé bejeweled yellow jackets dangled precariously over her forehead.

Standing up, Baby giggled in delight.

She circled around the goldfish pond three times.

Then slowly, she unbuttoned her new white dress, stepping out of it, and tossing it aside. It fell into the pond, startling Yvonne's freshly imported goldfish. She stepped out of her new slip and threw it in the air. It landed on a plant. She slipped out of her new panties and rolled them into a ball, hurling them toward the planter. They rested on the stuffed mockingbird's fully spread wings.

Baby Flowers stood giggling in the midst of the glittering treasures, almost naked. On her head was the headdress and on her feet were a pair of Yvonne Henderson's practically new tennis shoes. She wasn't used to wearing them, so she had forgotten to take off the shoes.

The next thing Baby picked up was the breastplate. She strapped it on backwards to fasten it. Then, she pulled it around and up over her own chest so she could see the spiky-molded gold-nippled breasts and the tiny sparkling bugs dangling from them whenever she looked down. Then, she picked up the exotic feathered necklace. She threw this over one shoulder like a boa and was parading around in a circle when, on a chair, she saw a set of fabulous wing-like things, dripping in gold pearls.

Baby Flowers knew how butterflies flew, and she knew just what to do with butterfly wings. She let the feathers fall to the floor as she picked up the wings. She put her arms through the gold-banded loops, effortlessly slipping the wings onto her back. Once more she picked up the collection of feathers. She didn't want to disturb her wings, so she attempted to wrap the plumes around her tiny waist. To her amazement, when she pressed the jeweled ends of the band together, they joined as if by magic! The weight of the jewels pulled the choker below her naval. Instead of a necklace, the arched maroon and gold-tipped quills formed a short-plumed skirt.

Baby Flowers walked out of the living room, out the door, and down the circular driveway, unnoticed by the other servants who were outback, busily sweeping off the runway in preparation for the out-of-town visitors. She walked down the road that led to the drive, across the cattle guard and through the double gates. She walked one mile down a dirt road. It was the same dirt road Yvonne's limousine, heading north, had ridden over a short time earlier. Baby was going south. She always walked south when she started to walk.

Soon she approached an old broken-down shack. She didn't look left and she didn't look right until her seven rocking relatives started waving and shouting.

"Hidy, Queenie!" yelled Petunia.

"Hidy, Queenie!" shrieked Iris.

"Hidy, Queenie!" shouted Rose.

"Hidy, Queenie!" hollered Daisy.

"Hidy, Queenie!" squealed Daffodil.

"Hidy, Queenie!" screamed Poppy.

"Hidy, Queenie!" gurgled Mum.

"Gotta Crackerjack?" smiled Baby Flowers, holding out her hands as she wandered closer. "Gimme some . . ."

As Baby approached, seven rocking chairs stopped rocking. Seven hands stopped waving. Seven mouths stopped talking. And seven silent Flowers rose in unison, dropped their Crackerjack boxes and wandered out toward the road. They gathered around their youngest member, gaping and staring in wonder and awe, as they tentatively touched the dazzling garments, oo-h-ing and ahh-ing.

"M-m-m-m . . ." hummed Petunia.

"O-o-w-w . . ." whispered Iris.

"A-h-h-h . . ." nodded Rose.

"Whe-e-e . . ." wisped Daisy.

"Wo-o-o-o . . ." cooed Daffodil.

"E-e-i-i . . ." chanted Poppy.

"Aw-w-w-w . . ." gurgled Mum.

"Whar yew *been,* Baby?" asked seven circling Flowers. "You been to the castle? You comin' on home? . . ."

Baby Flowers smiled and kept on walking.

"Whar yew goin'?" asked seven Flowers, trailing behind her. "Goin' back to the castle?"

"Parts Unknown . . ." said Baby gaily. "I'm goin' off to Parts Unknown . . . "

"Parts Unknown . . ." echoed seven voices, as seven Flowers shuffled along behind her. "We're all goin' off to Parts Unknown . . . "

"Parts Unknown . . ." smiled Baby Flowers. "I'm takin us to Parts Unknown . . . "

CHAPTER FIFTY-ONE

"DON'T WORRY about a thing!" Lottie Shady shouted to her sister-in-law and business partner, Irene Shady, as Irene prepared to step down from Yvonne Henderson's purple-colored Chrysler-Cadillac, coyote-horned and cowskinned-upholstered convertible limousine. "Me and José will be right by the landin' strip to bring the movie folks on over just as soon as they land!"

"Be sure to wait for *both* planes, Lottie!" Irene instructed her sister-in-law. "I don't want that agent from Hollywood runnin' around *loose* and talkin' the way he does! He's awready upset Mary Jane so bad I may kill him when I see him! I think he must have *forgot* that *he* works for *her*!"

"Okay, okay," nodded Lottie, who was anxious to be on her way. "Let me go now or they'll all be on the ground with nobody to meet 'em!"

"I sure hope Mr. Superintendent has a bus and a truck over at Yvonne's house like he promised," Irene worried. "He's inside the gym and goin' to give his speech and he may have forgot about the transportation!"

"It's all taken care of," Lottie assured her. "I got backups, too. Anyhow, Orville Turner ain't goin' to start on any speech 'til the cameras start to roll if I know Gladys."

Orville Turner had been the Superintendent of the Uncertain School System for thirty-five years and everyone knew he would continue as long as Gladys was alive. Every year for Homecoming, the biggest event of the year in Uncertain, Gladys Turner wrote out a speech which Orville read at the Pep Rally preceding the game. Every year, everyone was forced to give recognition to Gladys when her creative efforts reached all of Uncertain through Orville's annual speech.

Irene nodded, knowing full well that Gladys would let nothing, but nothing, stand between her and Homecoming and hearing Orville deliver the annual speech. "You're right about that speech of hers. If Gladys' sister had've died one day *later,* she wouldn't go into the ground until *tomorrow.*"

"Well, she's buried and *under,*" Lottie grumbled. "And Deal Grimes got the job—"

"Let's don't get started on that again!" Irene said. "You better hurry, now! Go on, go!"

She jumped out of the limousine, hurrying to catch up with her daughter, who was encircled by a small crowd of well-wishers and autograph seekers. Irene watched Yvonne Henderson standing in the middle of the circle next to Mary Jane Shady, answering questions and signing autographs, too.

What the hell does Why-vonne think she's doin'? Irene wondered, rushing toward them. She broke through the circle. stepping between her daughter and Yvonne. "I'm her mother!" she announced to the crowd. "Don't anybody want my autograph, too?!"

Lottie Shady and José were pulling away in Yvonne Henderson's limousine when Scoot Widders careened out of nowhere, jumped over the side and into a jumper seat.

The driver braked abruptly, sending Lottie into Scoot's lap.

Lottie blinked. She hadn't seen Scoot coming and she still didn't exactly know how Scoot had gotten into the car in the first place.

"Hidy, Lottie!" grinned Scoot, holding Lottie Shady in her arms like a baby. "Boy-hidee! I liked to have missed you!"

" 'Scuze me," said Lottie, unwrapping Scoot's arms and moving back into the backseat. "Where'd *you* come from?" she asked, wondering why on earth Scoot hadn't made an exception on such an important day, climbed out of her old faded Levis and denim jacket and put on something more appropriate for the grandmother of a possible future Homecoming Queen.

"Listen, here, I got that float ready! Me and the girls was up all night! It's a hell-of-a-thing, I kid you not! One of a kind, I assure you! Now, it's over in my garage all locked up! Lemme find the key!" Scoot stood up, tore off a boot, turned it upside down, picked up the key that fell from the toe, and handed it to Lottie. "I want to surprise Irene is why I didn't tell her about the float, see. That's why I'm tellin' *you,*" Scoot explained. "I'd like to see her get real, real *worried* and then real, real *disappointed* and then real, real *mad* and then real, real sort of *resigned* to it and then real, real *surprised* and then get real, real *happy* when she sees what she's got! Don't you?"

"I see her get like that ever-day," said Lottie Shady. "But if you want me to pick up that float for you, I will."

"Good!" said Scoot. "You'll recognize it right off! It's the only float in the garage!"

"Okay," Lottie nodded, hanging onto the key.

"Just hitch it onto this stretch-out car and pull it back over here with you! That way, when Mary Jane gets through in yonder, she'll have somethin' real, real *special* to drive off in!"

"Okay," nodded Lottie. "Will do."

"Thanks!" hollered Scoot, hopping back over the side. "Keep your fingers crossed for my twins, now!"

Lottie held up both hands with fingers double-crossed.

"That's the spirit!" raved Scoot Widders, running along by the side of the car.

"Hasta la vista!" Lottie Shady told Yvonne Henderson's driver. "Pronto, Tonto! Let's get out of here fast!"

Scoot Widders spun away from the car and dashed off toward the schoolhouse. She was dying to see her Siamese twin granddaughters crowned Homecoming Queen. But first, she wanted to torment Irene Shady. Or somebody.

The ceremony causing all the excitement was to take place inside the big two-story redbrick building which had been completed in 1929 for $225,000.00. In 1926, there had only been three children in the entire county within school age. By 1927, this number had increased to seven.

And then the boom hit. The school census of 1928 showed *one thousand two hundred and thirteen* students enrolled in the Uncertain School System.

Today the enrollment totalled four hundred and three.

Spread out over seventeen acres of land, every square foot had been paid for from the moment of its purchase and every red brick had been paid for before it was laid. The original building was fronted by a double staircase which led to two tall French doors on the second floor. A row of paned glass topped the doors, which were anchored on either side by rather grand marble pillars and topped by an arch of Romanesque design. The high school classes were upstairs. Junior high school classes were downstairs. The younger students entered the building through the double doors beneath the staircase at the front of the building. The grade school and kindergarten entered from the back.

Around 1936, several additions were made. First, a brand new football stadium was constructed around the already existing field. A field house was built with showers, lockers and an office for the coach. A separate structure was designed for the grade school, and next to that was the new Homemaking Cottage, complete with a kitchen for cooking and sewing machines for sewing. A wing containing a gymnasium was added to the right of the original building. To the left of the original building was added an auditorium, which housed a stage—the origin of Mary Jane Shady's disaster and triumph as an actress. It wasn't until the early '50s that Uncertain got a band hall. Connected to the backstage of the auditorium, the Uncertain High School band hall could have been designed for the New York Philharmonic. Acoustically perfect and specifically tiered, the band hall was the pride and joy and design of its band director of thirty-four years, Mr. Arkley Justice, who had come to West Texas from a military academy up North with a song in his heart, music on his mind and a marching drill straight from the Army.

Each spring, since 1951, Mr. Justice had gone to the Uncertain Grade School and examined the lips, mouths and tongues of each fifth grade student. Then he looked at their fingers for length, width and flexibility. There was no more choice about instrumental preference than there was about being in band at all. If a student was physically right for the brass, woodwind or percussion section, in Mr. Justice's opinion, he was forced to play the instrument of the band director's choice for the next seven years. Coach Jones could decide whether a boy would be a halfback, quarterback, fullback or not play football at all; Mr. Justice decided whether a person would play percussion, woodwind or brass. There was never much branching out either, for once Mr. Justice decided a person had lips and fingers fit for a clarinet or flute or trumpet, the farthest one could vary from that instrument would be due to a promotion for good work and this promoted the clarinet player to the oboe, the flute player to the piccolo, the trumpet player to the French horn. An aspiring drummer, starting out on the triangle, might one day find himself holding a coveted pair of drumsticks. A failing drummer would find himself holding onto a triangle. The players of these instruments at least were offered variation. A tuba player, no matter how good or bad, just played the tuba and that was it.

Mary Jane Shady had been a piccolo player until she took up with Bobby Henderson. After that, her piccolo practice faltering and her energies divided, she was demoted back to the flute. Bobby Henderson had been a tuba player. When he wasn't playing football.

After football season, both strings, first and second, came back into the band. Football was the only sport a player could devote his entire time to and not have to go to band class. The presence of basketball and baseball players in Mr. Justice's band hall was required during third period, but during football season, the players didn't have to go. The Uncertain Yellow Jacket Football Team was just as important in that town as the Dallas Cowboys were to the whole state of Texas.

Today was the biggest day of all. Today was Homecoming. It was the day of the crowning of the Uncertain Homecoming Queen. After the announcement at the gymnasium, where the coveted crown would be placed on her head, hers to wear through life (beginning with the parade), the Queen and her attendants would be cheered throughout the stadium and presented with armfuls of roses before the football game by the captains of the team. These young men then went out on that field with an outwardly sportsman like attitude and the inner intention to kill. They were bred to look heroic. And hopefully later, get laid.

Now, at three P.M. (the school let out an hour and twenty minutes early on Homecoming), the crowd of people who had gathered around Miss Peanut Butter Cup stopped chatting and asking for autographs as they watched the Uncertain High School band members winding, like a long lean water moccasin, single file across the school yard from the band hall on their way to several reserved bleachers in the southeast corner of the gymnasium. Some of the people began to move inside as the band members approached. Everyone knew that once the band was seated and tuned up, the Pep Rally would begin.

Although the Uncertain High School Band was known all over the school district and the entire State of Texas for being one of the best marching and concert bands in the Southwest, Mr. Arkley Justice could not boast of ever having turned out one musician who ever went professional. These players spent the sixth through twelfth grades following diagrams that took them eight steps to the left, four steps to the right, two steps backwards (or variations thereof) and lots of circles in between, all to the beat of "Grandioso" or some equally difficult piece, which then had to be *memorized,* for no member of the Uncertain High School band ever carried music onto the field or into the concert hall. Finally, all that effort memorizing fugues and marches and all that energy spent as a little winding speck of a letter that would hopefully spell out *UNCERTAIN* (or whatever) all over the football field just didn't seem that rewarding to anybody but Mr. Justice, who just kept collecting prize after prize at each new event where he took his band.

All metals and trophies, whether won by quartets, duos, solos or the entire Uncertain High School Band (and Junior High School Band), were placed in a gigantic case in the foyer by the auditorium. Groups up to four in number had their names listed beside the medals or trophies. More than that number, as well as prizes won by the entire band, simply had a small sign beneath the medal or trophy that read *Class of 1958, Class of 1965, Class of 1974*, and so on.

During marching and concert season, each student who had ever won a medal was allowed to wear it to all public events where the band appeared. Mr. Justice opened up the gigantic case and distributed the medals himself, and later collected and put them away again himself, first in the fall during marching season, and again in the spring during concert season. Between those times, if a musician wanted to see his medal or show it to someone who loved him (or said they did), family or friends or an interesting stranger, everyone could go to the big glass case and look at it.

During marching season, it mattered no more to Mr. Arkley Justice if it was one hundred and ten in the shade or twenty degrees below zero. His band members wore their maroon and gold trimmed uniforms whether it was raining or sleeting or hailing, whether there was a sandstorm, hurricane or tornado, or whether it was a dog day afternoon. If it rained, they got wet; if it snowed, they got cold; if it was hot, they just sweated, and if it was pleasant, they got lucky. Like today.

As Topsy Dingo Wild Dog watched the sixty-three band members advancing, she wondered if each member was still painstakingly and individually fitted for their uniforms, hats, gloves, belts and shoes. She wondered if they were still issued instruments according to the shapes of their lips and fingers. She saw the drum major at the front of the line. The only variation that distinguished her as leader of the band was her tall, dome-like white hat, the additional tassels on her shoulderpads and the extra gold braid across her chest. But in 1965, there had been a lot more to it than that.

The Uncertain High School Band had experienced only one real disaster during Mr. Justice's reign as its director. The year Johnie Sue Seven was drum major and got pregnant, but nobody knew it, and Johnie Sue had given birth to the baby in the Wink stadium's public bathroom right when the Uncertain High School Band was supposed to be on the field at half-time, was a disaster. Mary Jane Shady, who was a twirler, had grabbed Johnie Sue's hat off her head and yanked her whistle from around her neck, as Johnie Sue stumbled off the field and headed for the bleachers. Mary Jane Shady flew onto the field to save the show. But Mary Jane was so rattled by Johnie Sue's abrupt departure, that she marched off in one direction, while the band went in another, and Mary Jane never knew she wasn't leading a thing until she was clear down on the Wink ten-yard-line. With no one to blow the whistle, the band members didn't know whether to go ahead and make their formations or not. No one really needed the drum major's whistle to tell them when to circle and turn; they all knew their formations by heart. They just didn't know whether to go ahead and form or keep marching straight ahead, so some formed and some marched and some circled and all ran into each other all over the field and everyone agreed it was the biggest mess they'd ever seen.

Bobby Henderson had broken up with Mary Jane Shady for the umpteenth time that night, and Irene Shady said that she was just grateful it had happened on a foreign field. "If it had have happened in Uncertain and you marched off the wrong way like you did, I'd have whipped you!" Irene had told Mary Jane. "Surely you know which way the Uncertain goalpost is located!"

When Mr. Justice found out that Johnie Sue had given birth to a little boy at half-time, he didn't even say "congratulations." Johnie Sue Seven was banned from the band for not showing up when her presence was required and kicked out of high school for detracting from the game and disturbing the peace in a Wink, Texas public bathroom. She wasn't allowed to graduate from Uncertain High School either. Johnie never told who the father was and never bothered to get married. She named her son Major Seven and went to work at the Hoop and Holler Motel for a Dollar as a day maid, saying she had never enjoyed leading the band in the first place or going to school anyway. A job, a baby and independence suited her just fine.

That was in the fall of 1963. Mary Jane Shady had been a junior, and since grade school, had harbored aspirations to be drum major her senior year. But after the Johnie Sue Seven catastrophe, Mr. Justice had sent every aspiring candidate over to Dr. Smith for a physical examination before he would even let them try out for twirler or drum major. If Dr. Smith didn't send back a slip verifying the visibility of the presence of a hymen to his naked eye, the applicants were deemed unacceptable by Mr. Justice. Oh, a girl could try out, all right. But if she didn't get chosen, she left herself open to heated gossip and ugly speculation: Was she just not good enough? Or was she not a *VIRGIN*?

When Topsy's classmate, Alice Catherine Shoemaker, applied for drum major their senior year and was found unacceptable by Dr. Smith, Catsy's mother explained that Catsy had lost her cherry when she fell from the top of the monkey bars in the third grade and popped it open when she landed and straddled the bottom bar. Dr. Smith was the attending physician. Didn't he remember? Dr. Smith didn't remember and there were no records to prove it, since his second wife had burned down his former office in a fit of matrimonial rage preceding their divorce settlement. Not only did Catsy not get to twirl or lead, she got her drumsticks taken away—(Catsy was a drummer)—and was put on the triangle. Catsy's mother, Clyda Shoemaker angrily declared, "The triangle is a humiliating instrument if there ever was one!" She was so mad she went over to Odessa and bought Catsy the biggest bass drum she could find, and for one whole game, Catsy and Clyda Shoemaker stood outside the chain link fence that surrounded the Uncertain Stadium while Catsy banged her new drum and Clyda clanged a pair of cymbals together to demonstrate their protest. Clyda bought an extra pair of cymbals and invited her husband to join them, but he declined and sat in his regular place up in the stands, ignoring both of them.

Clyda Shoemaker took Catsy over to Midland and bought her a secondhand 1957 Thunderbird convertible. It was pink and white with a white tire case on the back. Clyda Shoemaker divorced her husband for not giving Dr. Smith and Mr. Justice a piece of his mind and for sitting like "a lump on a log up in the stands" and not taking part in their protest. She and Catsy moved to Wink where she enrolled Catsy in Wink High School. Catsy was elected Wink's Drum Major, Homecoming Queen and Senior Class Favorite, and the word in Wink was that Catsy even almost had a date with Roy Orbison right when he was getting famous and had come back home for a visit one weekend. Clyda Shoemaker never really got her revenge on her husband until she let Catsy marry Bo Ivanhoe. But Catsy's marriage to the Comanche Indian was almost a year later, and in the autumn of 1964, it was Catsy's trip to the doctor that made Mary Jane Shady think twice about trying out for drum major, or even twirler again.

She simply cancelled her appointment with Dr. Smith when she heard what had happened to Catsy, saying that she wanted to concentrate on her "acting career" her senior year. Leading the band was another dream she put away fast.

Mary Jane Shady's best friend, Milly Dee Waffles, became the Uncertain High School Drum Major. Kay Hobbs and Darnelle (Spider) Webb, the preacher's daughter, gave up twirling and became cheerleaders. Mary Jane Shady took up Bobby Henderson. Yvonne Henderson dropped out of school completely.

There were *no* twirlers in the Uncertain High School Band during the school year of 1964-65.

CHAPTER FIFTY-TWO

LOTTIE SHADY and Leo Diggs sat in the back of Yvonne's air-conditioned limousine parked next to the landing strip, holding hands as they peered out the windows, Lottie looking for a plane from the east, Leo on the lookout toward the west.

"Did you tell 'em yet?" Leo asked, as he gazed out the window.

"Naw. Didn't seem like the right time," Lottie replied. "I swear, if I'd have knowed Gladys Turner's sister was goin' to require servicin' day before yesterday and Mary Jane was comin' home for the first time in twenty years twenty-four hours ago and we were goin' to get us all this company from New York City and Hollywood, California today, I think I'd have picked us another time to elope."

Leo gave his new wife a long soft kiss, took a hit off the joint he had just rolled and gently blew smoke rings into Lottie's mouth.

"Well, we're hitched now forever, dear heart," Leo said. " 'Til death do us part."

"And that's why I'm goin' to do all the drivin' from now on, too," Lottie said, pushing her fingers through his wild wiry red hair. "You're too careless at intersections and corners. I could have had me a corpse as easy as a husband."

"Your drivin' is fine with me," Leo said dreamily. "But what are you goin' to do about the funeral home? You cain't drive an eighteen-wheeler all over the country and run your business, too."

"I don't intend to," Lottie smiled coquettishly. "I'm retirin' from the funeral home business and turnin' it over to Irene and goin' on the road for life with you!"

"We could get us a chauffeur like Why-vonne's here and let *him* drive," Leo joked, taking another hit. "You and me'd just sit in the back seat and *smooch.*"

He gently moved his hand up Lottie's leg.

"That's not a bad idea, Leo Diggs," Lottie whispered, quivering. She yearned for more of his touch and offered no resistance to his strong fingers as they slowly massaged her inner left leg. "If I didn't like to drive that new eighteen-wheeler so much myself I might consider it." Tingling, she wriggled closer, clamped her legs around his hand and pressed her face close to his. "Why don't you tell José to get lost for a minute. I want to look at somethin', honey."

Leo rapped on the glass dividing the driver and the passengers. "Hey, James ole buddy, turn up the air-conditioner, leave down the roof, tune in the radio to somethin' real, real country and get lost for a little bit, okay?" He took several joints out of his pocket, liberally tossed a few over the glass divider, and motioned with his thumb toward the house. "Vamoose, padner. Gracias."

The chauffeur's eyes grew wide when he saw the joints. He hurriedly scooped them up and jumped out of the car. "Gracias! Gracias!" exclaimed the driver, delighted with his good fortune.

Leo Diggs turned back to his new wife. He kissed her tenderly as his hands once more moved up her skirt. He pressed one against her lower stomach and held her buttocks with the other. Then, finding her waist, he leisurely pulled down her panty hose and tossed them to one side. As his bounteous lips enveloped her dainty posey-painted heart-shaped mouth, her bony arms dropped to her sides. She groaned as his mouth moved from hers to her tiny shell-like ears, and then to her long pencil-thin neck. As his plump pink tongue lazily found hers, she lifted her hands weakly, fumbled for his zipper and unzipped his pants. Out flew his equipment. She put both small hands around it, drew her head back, staring into his calm, gentle eyes for a moment before she looked down in wonder.

"That's the *biggest* one I've ever seen," Lottie whispered admiringly.

"It's the *only* one you've ever seen," Leo slowly smiled, stroking her face with pride. "And the only one you're ever goin' to see, too." He gazed at her eyelashes. He thought they were the blackest, curliest ones he had ever seen. "I swear, Lotta Baby, for a seventy-five-year-old virgin, a man would think you'd a been doin' it forever . . . "

"Well, it was worth waitin' for is all I can say," Lottie breathed, appreciatively stroking the miracle. "Open your shirt up, sugar, where I can see that kitty cat, too . . . "

Leo Diggs obligingly unbuttoned his shirt, revealing a chestful of red hair, skin whiter than Irene Shady's best pressed sheets, and his tattoo of Garfield the Cat. He held his shirt open proudly, for he knew she liked to look at him like this. Then he leaned closer and nibbled on her ear. "Your pussy or mine?" he whispered wickedly.

Lottie Shady burst into a medley of giggles. "You're just the wittiest thing I ever knew!" she raved, adoringly kissing the cat on his chest. "And I'm just in love with this Pecker!" She stroked Leo's member, crooning to it as if it were a pet. "G-o-o-d Pecker . . . He's standin' up for Mama . . . G-o-o-d Pecker . . . He's goin' to get a nice surprise!"

Leo moaned, blood pumping through him. He just loved it when she talked to him that way. "Lean back, Lotta Precious," he begged. "One of these pet's about to turn into a wild wild animal! Feels like it might be Pecker . . ."

Lottie reclined on the backseat of Yvonne's upholstery, coyly posing like every blonde in every World War II movie she'd ever seen.

"Where's my heart medicine?" she asked Leo flirtatiously. "I think maybe ole Pecker's givin' me another poundin' heart!"

"Here go, hon," Leo said, popping a vitamin into her mouth. "Let's stick with this nervous-wreck medicine! 'Cause if you ain't scared, you ought to be!"

"Are we in danger?" Lottie whooped, happily chewing up the pill. "I just love danger! How dangerous is it? Is it bigger'n both of us?"

"Oh, Gawd," he groaned. "It's *gettin'* bigger'n both of us! But I think the two of us together can tame that terrible beast!"

"I want to tame it . . ." Lottie whispered urgently. "Tell me what to do to tame that terrible Pecker . . ."

"Put your legs up, honey," moaned Leo Diggs. "This beast is too much for either one of us! I'm goin' to have to turn the wild thang loose!"

"Help! Help!" giggled Lottie Shady, as he lifted her legs into the air. "I'm just a prisoner of love!" she swooned as her feet arched and her toes pointed toward the skies.

"Help's on the way . . ." promised Leo Diggs, descending. "I'm sendin' up the troops, baby . . . Help's on the way . . ."

José had tuned in to WHIP in Odessa, where Johnny Horton was singing:

> "*It takes a pretty little girl and a jug of wine*
> *That's what it takes to make a honky-tonk mind,*
> *With the juke-box a-moanin' a honky-tonk sound,*
> *That's when I want to lay my money down . . .*"

Lottie just laughed and laughed as Leo approached her.

He lowered his voice to a growl. "You're my prisoner, baby. Get that smile off your face! Get that shirt off, too!"

"Oh!" blinked Lottie, delighted at this new turn in their adventure.

"Do it!" he ordered. "Do it *now*!"

"I'm just your prisoner!" she cooed happily as she fumbled with her buttons. "I'm just your prisoner of love . . ."

"My prisoner of love!" Leo echoed, wild-eyed. He pushed her hand away and unbuttoned the rest of her blouse, "Tok-e-yo Rose!" he cried, seeing her bare breasts. "Where's your brassiere?"

"I'm liberated!" Lottie hollered, throwing off her blouse. "You cain't keep clothes on Tok-e-yo Rose!" She sprang up, her legs coming around his waist. "Lay back, prisoner! I got you now, soldier! You're my prisoner, now, lover! What's your name, honey-bunny? Get this skirt off me, too!"

"Just call me Patton, Toke," quivered Leo, falling to his knees and unzipping her skirt.

"Patton!" repeated Lottie. "Well, good, I'm glad it's *you!* I been wantin' to give you some orders! Are you ready for my requests now? You can start with my toes!"

"I'll do just about anythang you say to, lady!" Leo swore, kissing her feet. " 'Cause Tok-e-yo Rose scares the shit out of me!"

"You better be scared, Pat!" She ripped off her skirt, tossing it over the trunk of the limousine. "Stand up at attention! And I mean *all* of you!"

He stood straight, tall and obedient, stiff and hard, as he yanked off his shirt, jerked down his pants, and threw his underwear aside, leaving him as unclothed as she was. "Your next order is to turn up that radio, fast!"

Thrilled to obey, Leo Diggs leaned over the divider and raised the volume. As he did so, Lottie Shady crawled up on top of the trunk of the car. "Ever-thang's *up*, my little spy," Leo called out. "Now what's your pleasure?"

He turned to see his new wife standing on the trunk of the car, where she had posed herself with her right arm extended toward the sky and her left arm cradled under her breast.

Leo Diggs stared at her, enchanted. He was looking at his other favorite heroine: The Statue of Liberty.

"Where's my *torch*!" cried Lottie Shady Diggs. "My kingdom for a *torch*!"

For a moment he couldn't move. He was too overwhelmed by what he was feeling. He simply thought that Lottie Shady was the most intriguing, beguiling, beautiful, funny thing he had ever met. Leo Diggs had never loved anyone in his life and his feelings almost paralyzed him. But only for a moment.

"Here it comes, mistress!" Leo leapt on the trunk with her, and with arms strong as tree trunks, lifted Lottie into the air and held her there. "I love you, Tok-e-yo . . ." he whispered. "I love you, Olive Oyl . . . I love you, Lottie . . . I love you, Liberty . . . "

"I love you, too," Lottie mumbled in an amorous haze of unbridled anticipation. "Now what are you goin' to do with all of us?"

"I'm thinkin' . . ." he murmured, gently swaying, as he cushioned her in the air. His hands cradled her buttocks, his fingers fondled her delicately from the back. "I'm thinkin' I'm goin' to take ever bit of you for a little joy ride . . . " He stood still for one moment and then thrust forward. She gave a little gasp as she felt him firmly entrench himself inside her. With her legs wrapped around his waist, Leo swung her in and out from him, in and out, in and out, as Johnny Horton sang out over the radio:

I'm a honky-tonk man
And I cain't seem to stop
I love to give the girls a whirl
To the rhythm of an ole jukebox
But when my money's all gone
I'm on the tel-e-phone, a-hollerin',
Hey, hey, mama, can your daddy come home!"

As Leo and Lottie exploded in mutual pleasure on top of the limousine, they joyfully burst into song with Lottie swinging in the air, singing, "Hey, hey, daddy, your mama's come home!" and Leo swinging Lottie back and forth, singing, "Hey, hey, mama, your daddy's come home!" at the top of their voices.

And that is the first thing Arabella du Noir, Senior Vice-President of the Hocker-Smockter Advertising Agency, the largest advertising agency in the world, saw as she descended from her Lear Jet, which had landed totally unnoticed by anyone in the Welcoming Car.

CHAPTER FIFTY-THREE

IT HAD BEEN twenty years since Mary Jane Shady had had mouth to mouth and finger to finger contact with a piccolo or flute. As Topsy Dingo Wild Dog watched the last of the band members disappear into the right wing of the school on their way to the gymnasium, she saw a familiar figure, tall and gangling, trailing leisurely behind them. His hair had thinned slightly. His face had creased and wrinkled. But basically, he had not changed at all. It was Mr. Justice, her old high school band director.

She immediately felt a stab of guilt. She hoped he wouldn't say anything about the time she led the band off in the wrong direction. She hoped he wouldn't mention how she had been demoted back to the flute after being a potentially outstanding piccolo player. She was glad that he never knew how often her maroon and gold uniform, hat, gloves, tassels, gold braid and all, had been dumped in a sea of sand, a garden of mesquite bushes, out by that oil well after countless football games. When she went there with Bobby. To celebrate with Bobby. To console Bobby. Until she'd climbed on top of Bobby. . .

"Whoa!" Irene Shady called, as if stopping a horse. "Lookie here, Arkley!"

Mr. Arkley Justice turned to wave, but he never finished that gesture. He nodded at Irene hurriedly. He didn't seem to notice Topsy at all. Arkley Justice was staring at Yvonne Henderson. He was unable to take his eyes off Yvonne.

"Don't you recognize Mary Jane?" Irene cried, wishing that Yvonne had not worn that yellow fowl-feathered coat.

"—here from New York City and Hollywood, California, and they're comin' too!" Yvonne squealed. "Maybe ya'll can spell her name out durin' the half-time show!" Yvonne's hand flew over her mouth. "Oh, gosh! I hope I didn't spoil some kind of a surprise!"

Mr. Justice squinted his eyes and peered hawkishly at Yvonne. "I know *you,*" he said accusingly.

"Of course you know her!" Irene cried. Exasperated, she grabbed onto her daughter's arm and pulled her closer to the band director, who was still staring at Yvonne.

"*Me*?" Yvonne laughed. "I wasn't in the *band*!"

"*She* wasn't in the band," Irene echoed. "But *she* was!" She thrust her daughter forward.

"You didn't even finish high school, did you?" Arkley Justice asked Yvonne Henderson curtly.

"Naw," sighed Yvonne, her smile fading.

"And when you *were* in school, you didn't participate in school activities, did you?" the band director interrogated.

"Naw . . . " Yvonne looked away, hurt.

"Mary Jane was in the band," Irene offered quickly, determined to obtain the director's attention. "Remember when she led the band off toward the Wink goalpost that time and made such a fool of herself?"

Topsy and Yvonne looked at one another in mutual dismay.

Arkley Justice turned to Topsy at last. "Oh, yeah," he said flatly. "You're that flute player."

"She played piccolo one year!" Irene reminded him. "One year she was a piccolo player!"

"Uh-huh," he nodded with a smirk. He looked back and forth from Topsy to Yvonne, staring at the two of them as if they were a couple of bugs. Finally he turned to Irene. "God knows best," he grimaced. Shaking his head hopelessly, he walked off and disappeared through the tall open doors.

What was that? wondered Topsy Dingo Wild Dog. *Does he know? Does he know? Does he know? WHAT DOES HE KNOW*?

Irene Shady was miffed. Not only had Mr. Justice made no effort to defer in any way to her daughter's present status and claim to fame, Arkley Justice had devoted all his attention to Yvonne Henderson.

"Arkley is gettin' old," Irene declared. "Needs to be re-placed before he dies on us and all the half-time show formations go with him in his head!"

He could hardly even look at me! Topsy Dingo Wild Dog thought nervously. *He knows SOMETHING! I know he knows SOMETHING!*

"He's always been stuck up!" complained Yvonne Henderson. "I'm glad I didn't waste a minute in his stupid ole band!"

Yvonne and Irene were still discussing how much the Uncertain High School Band had gone down lately as they entered the foyer. Topsy followed in a daze. She didn't even see the oval glass case that stood in the middle of the floor.

Inside, was the gift from the graduating class of 1965. It was a gigantic yellow jacket, the symbol of Uncertain High. Made from a base of coat hangers and covered with papier-mâché, the yellow jacket stood three feet tall and five feet wide in the case. It looked like a big angry fly that had just gotten stuck on fly paper and was wildly trying to escape. The senior art class had been responsible for this creation. Each student had taken turns painting the fly gold to become a yellow jacket. Then they painted maroon stripes down the yellow jacket's body. Somebody thought it should have wings, and Darnelle Webb, daughter of the minister of the Uncertain First Methodist Church, went to her daddy and got wings someone had worn as an angel in a Christmas pageant once. They had been silver at the time; the art teacher instructed her students to take turns spraying them gold, and those were the wings that adorned the yellow jacket now.

"Wonder what this year's class will give?" Yvonne wondered. It occurred to her that after she finished wearing them, she might donate her breastplate, feathers, headdress and wings.

"It will be hard to beat that," Irene declared. "For pure-dee ugly, that glued together bug is hard to beat. It's not the right color, neither," she continued critically. "A yellow jacket is all black on the body with yellow stripes around the middle. Who ever heard of a maroon and gold yellow jacket in real life?"

Relax, relax, relax. Arkley Justice is not going to take the piccolo away from you again! That already happened! It's too late to be a drum major! It's too late to twirl a baton! It's too late to be a virgin! It's too late to not be a dog fucker! It's too late to give a shit! STOP CARING! STOP THINKING! She made her eyes focus on the glass case and the papier-mâché bug. She stared at the huge tormented yellow jacket, caged and angry and desperate to get out.

"Why didn't ya'll change the colors to match the insect?" Irene demanded. "Make our colors black and yellow so it'd make sense."

"Black and yellow are Andrews' colors," Yvonne said. "Did you know Andrews is in a different district now, Mary Jane? We're back down to Wink's size again. We don't play Andrews no more. Inn't it sad?"

"What's their symbol?" Irene asked. "They're black and orange. What's black and orange?"

"It's somethin' Halloween," Yvonne mused. "I cain't recall for sure. Do you know what Wink's symbol is, Mary Jane?"

Topsy just stood there, staring through the glass case. She hadn't thought of colors or symbols or mascots for twenty years.

"She don't know," Irene said to Yvonne. "She's off on her cloud."

"It's a wildcat," Topsy stated matter-of-factly.

"That's right!" Yvonne squealed, as if Topsy had just answered the Sixty-Four Thousand Dollar Question. " 'Skin the Wildcats! Skin the Wildcats! Skin the Wildcats!' I knew it was in the feline family!"

"We're not playin' Wink!" Scoot Widders called out, flying up from behind. "They're not in the game tonight! We're playin' *Pyote* and their symbol is a *coyote,* so ya'll better be yellin' 'Kill the Coyotes! Kill the Coyotes! Kill the Coyotes!' "

She pronounced coyote "kie-oat" and Pyote, "pie-oat." So did everyone else.

Like a boxer in training, Scoot danced around, prancing from Irene to Yvonne to Topsy, giving each a short, light punch on the arm. "Oh, my stars and feathers!" Scoot whooped. "Who cares about a dadburned ballgame anyway! I'm about to have me a *Homecomin' Queen* in my family, I just know it!"

"We're a-rootin' for you, Scoot," Irene said. Attempting to pull Scoot over to the side, she lowered her voice, "What about the float? Is it ready to go?"

Scoot's face fell. "Aw, hell!" she yelled. "I *knew* I forgot somethin'! Goddamnit, Irene, I am *so* sorry!" Scoot's face looked like a big sad baboon's. "Now don't hold it against my girls, okay? You said you'd innerduce them to all the right people and all! I hope you'll still keep your word even if I am a no-good forgetful son-of-a-bitch!"

Irene Shady looked severely disappointed. "You sure are!" she agreed. "How could you let me down that-a-way?"

"Honey, if you had Siamese twins a runnin', you'd be mixed up, too!" Scoot said.

"Scoot Widders, could you please watch your language?" admonished Gladys Turner who had walked up behind them. "This is a temple for higher minds, you know!"

Ignoring Gladys and turning to the others, Scoot announced proudly. "Aw, it's a shoo-in! There ain't much competition to speak of. Maria Rodriquez is the only one that caused me to lose a wink of sleep." She leaned close to Topsy and confided, "She's the little *Mexskin* girl, you know." Then she turned to Gladys mischievously. "Oh, yes! We have a great big *Mexskin* population in here now, don't we, Gladys?"

"Ask Why-vonne," Gladys retorted, running her eyes over Yvonne's coat in obvious disapproval. "She ought to know! She's got most of 'em over at her place, a-wipin' and a-sweepin'!"

"Somebody's got to do somethin' with 'em," Yvonne shrugged. "I'm just tryin' to give them somethin' to *do*."

"Oh, sure!" Gladys hissed. "You're the one sneaking them in the country! They don't just hop by the hundreds like a mess of mosquitoes right over the border and land in Uncertain, Texas, all by themselves! They are everywhere you look!"

"Yeah," nodded Yvonne. " 'Cause ya'll won't let 'em in school—"

"That's right!" Scoot cackled. "I been noticin' they ain't too many *third* world types in this here high-minded temple!"

Gladys turned to Scoot and explained in a tone of formal superior authority, "There is a state *law* against going to school in the State of Texas if you are an illegal wetback or the child of one—"

"Oh, horseshit!" Scoot Widders cried. "Horseshit! Bullshit! And monkeyshit! That is Gladys Turner bullshit *shit*! That rule's been changed and you know it!"

"The rule's been *changed*?" asked Yvonne bewildered. "And you're still keepin' out the wetbacks? Like you did the niggers?"

"Oh, that's just some crazy woman in Dallas, Texas, by the name of Claudia Guiterrez who's trying to get away with that!" Gladys protested. "She's a *demented white* woman from Dallas, Texas, who *mar-*

ried this *Mexican* music man named Manuel Guiterrez! That demented white woman joined up with some uppity-up communist political man and all those over-breeding Catholics and worked like the She Devil she is to change the law so all those little wetbacks could go to school just like any ordinary person!"

"I thought that's what school was for," stated Irene Shady irritably.

"Well, they may be doing that in *Dallas,* but we're not having it in *Uncertain*!" Gladys declared. "See what happens when interracials marry? Before you know it, *anybody* can get an education!"

"I saw that Mrs. Guiterrez on *Good Mornin' America,*" Scoot Widders cried. "She's *right*! You're wrong! She's right!"

"Why on earth do you care, Scoot?" Gladys Turner harped. "I counted up and there are only twenty-seven of 'em in the whole school *at this time,* which was enough to get Maria nominated, but hardly enough for a *win*, so you don't even have a problem today! *I,* on the other hand, am in *constant jeopardy*! I have to *teach* them," Gladys pouted. "Or *try* to!"

"What the hell are they goin' to learn from *you*?" Yvonne Henderson grinned.

"Nothing! Because those little wetbacks don't want an education!" Gladys announced. "They just want to take our jobs away from us!"

"Well, we could use a turnover!" Irene declared.

"Are you saying I'm not doing a good job?" Gladys demanded.

"Oh, shut up, Gladys!" Irene snapped. "No Mexskin is goin' to take the fifth grade away from you! Nobody but *you* wants the fifth grade!"

"Ha!" said Gladys Turner. "I am the only one who does not underestimate these Mexskins! Niggers are different. Niggers are *lazy*. They're all doped out. Mexskins are *ambitious*! They're going to overpopulate us, take away our jobs and we're all going to have dark-skinned neighbors and one day one of your grandchildren will bring one home and *marry* them and then you can all stick it up your *enchiladas*! But they are going to start with our *jobs*!"

"If one takes away your fifth grade class, why maybe Why-vonne here will give you a job drivin' *her* around in that stretch-out car!" Scoot joked.

"I wouldn't give her the time of day!" Yvonne muttered.

"And I wouldn't accept anything you had to give away, either!" Gladys retorted. "You are white trash, white trash, white trash! You belong with the Mexskins! I bet that's where you got that coat!"

"Nasty, nasty, nasty," grinned Yvonne Henderson. "Listen! There's not no word for what you are, Gladys Turner!"

"Well, there *is* one for you!" Gladys glowered.

Yvonne Henderson's grin slid off her face. She looked at Gladys Turner quietly. "I know what word you're thinkin'," Yvonne said in a deadly calm voice. "And I'd think *real, real* careful about it before I *said* it if I was you."

Gladys gave a little shudder before she began to stammer nervously. "Well, I think it's *horrible* the way they're invading us here! And I am going to do everything I can to stop it, and Mr. Superintendent is, too! This is a *white* people's town and a *white* people's school and we're going to have us a real *white* Homecoming Queen, too!"

"Good!" said Scoot. "Pardon me if I'm prejudiced!"

"I don't mean *them*!" Gladys replied, eyes like steel. "We're not having any *freaks* wearing that crown!" She turned to Topsy. "And the best thing you could ever say about *your* class, Mary Jane, was that *yours* had the pleasure of being the last class to graduate from Uncertain High School without one *nigger* in it! I cannot tell you how proud I am of the fact that we kept full integration *out of here* until 1965! Believe me, it has been downhill ever since! Siamese twins, Mexskins, niggers!" She glowered at Yvonne.

"Oh, go on and say it, Gladys," Yvonne Henderson taunted, grinning again. "Say it and I'll *kill* you!"

Irene, standing beside the papier-mâché yellow jacket in the glass case, began to sing loudly:

> *"Jesus loves the little children*
> *All the children of the world*
> *Red and yellow, black and white,*
>
> *They are precious in His sight*
> *Jesus loves the little children*
> *Of the wor-r-r-r-ld!"*

"Have you gone crazy, singing Sunday School songs at the Pep Rally, Irene Shady?" Gladys Turner screamed.

"Probably," Irene said. "But not as crazy as you! Anyway, we aren't at the Pep Rally yet. It's in yonder and we're out here, and before you know it, you're goin' to miss Orville give your speech, Gladys."

"No, I won't," Gladys said. "He's going to wait until *everybody* gets here."

"Oh," Irene said, feigning surprise. "You mean the *Peanut Butter People.*" Irene shot Topsy and Yvonne a look that read: *What did I tell you*? "Well. You better hurry on in yonder with the *white* folks."

"You know who I mean, since you arranged everything," Gladys snapped. "And arranged it before I had my coffee, too," she added accusingly. Her eyes thinned into two narrow mean slits. "We'll just see who has to worry about the Mexskin invasion today, Scoot Widders," she snorted. She turned to Topsy. "We may have Siamese twins and a Mexskin running, but we don't have a *nigger* and we don't have a *Jew*!" She turned to Yvonne Henderson. "And we don't have *you*!" She turned on her heels and stomped back inside the gym.

Topsy felt her head begin to scream, clang and jangle. Shrill, piercing vibrations penetrated her skull like a dentist's drill. Banging thuds resonated within her like an attack from a madman's hammer... "*We don't have a nigger and we don't have a Jew!... We don't have a nigger and we don't have a Jew!...*"

A slow horrifying hiss, like the onslaught from a rampage of locusts, rioted through her ears. *Dog fucker! Dog fucker! We've got you!*

From inside the gymnasium, a chorus of voices began their own low, rhythmic chant:

"We are the Yellow Jackets...

Nobody prouder...
If you can't hear us
We'll yell a little louder..."

The band was warming up. The Pep Squad had started their cheers. The Pep rally was beginning.

Topsy Dingo Wild Dog stood paralyzed and terrified. Waiting.

Variations of Gladys Turner's death danced in front of Irene Shady's eyes. She saw Leo Diggs running over Gladys with his truck, smashing her to bits like he had her wooden sign. She visualized the fifth grade class hitting Gladys over the head with a window stick, flinging her out the window and throwing spit wads at her. She saw Gladys tarred and feathered by the black population. She saw millions of Mexicans stuffing hot tamales and enchiladas down Gladys' throat until she choked on them. "Say Gracias," the Mexicans chanted to Gladys in Irene's head. "Gracias," Irene heard Gladys choke.

The band broke into "Grandioso."

I forgot how to play it! Topsy thought, desperately searching through her head for flute fingerings, piccolo scales. *How could I forget something so familiar? How could I forget something I spent years perfecting*? Drums pounded. Clarinet reeds shrieked. Piccolos screamed. *PERFECT. PERFECT. YOU'RE NOT PERFECT. PERFECT. PERFECT . . . . You forgot how to play the flute, you got kicked off the piccolo, YOU ARE THE ONE WHO LED THE BAND OFF IN THE WRONG, WRONG, WRONG DIRECTION! YOU'RE RESPONSIBLE FOR BRINGING ARABELLA DU NOIR TO UNCERTAIN, TEXAS! YOU FUCK UP! YOU LOSER! YOU DOG FUCKING DOG FUCKER!*

Topsy Dingo Wild Dog was shaking.

Yvonne Henderson was crying.

Topsy put her arms around Yvonne. She thought of Herman. She thought of Arabella du Noir. She thought of Bobby. *Gladys Turner is going to love hating a dog fucker. . .* she thought numbly. *I'm going to unify this whole town: I'll be the ONE THING they ALL get to hate . . . .*

Scoot saw Irene Shady standing trance-like, whispering "Gracias, gracias." She gave Irene a poke.

The chanting inside the gymnasium grew louder and clearer.

"We are the Yellow Jackets . . .

Nobody prouder. . .
If you can't hear us
We'll yell a little louder!"

Topsy's head screamed, a twisting whirlpool of malicious voices.

We don't have a nigger!
We don't have a Jew!
Dog fucker! Dog fucker!

We've got YOU!

It started at the peak of the clatter.

Cold.

Glacial.

Detached.

Calm.

I GOT YOU OUT OF HERE ONCE, she heard a voice say. *I'LL GET YOU OUT AGAIN . . . .*

"I wish I knew more Spanish," Yvonne sniffed. "I wish I'd a-wore my butterfly wings!"

Irene snapped out of her trance. "Ever-body ought to make a effort to learn their language, too." She reached in her handbag and handed Yvonne a Kleenex.

"Unos! Duos! Trace! Quantos! Cinquos! Seace!" Scoot Widders sang. "I can count to five in it!"

MARY JANE SHADY? Topsy's head pounded. *MARY JANE! IS THAT YOU*?!

"Ouch!" cried Yvonne to Topsy. "You're about to squeeze me to pieces!"

"I'll tell you what, Scoot," Irene told Scoot. "I'm beginnin' to realize that I hate Gladys *so bad* that I'm goin' to have to root for those twins, even if you have let me down with that float!"

Cries and whispers, echoes of her own inner voices collided, spiraling through her head, juxtaposing with the chants from the crowd.

"We are the Yellow Jackets . . .

Nobody prouder . . ."
Mary Jane Shady . . .
Yell a little louder . . .

"I think she hates Siamese twins more than niggers and Mexskins," Yvonne Henderson agreed.

"Aw, hell, I was kiddin'!" Scoot admitted. "I got the float! Lottie's bringin' it back with her and the Peanut Butter people! I was pullin' your leg! It was kind of a joke!"

Irene Shady frowned. "Well, it wasn't very funny!"

I GOT YOU OUT OF HERE ONCE. I'LL GET YOU OUT AGAIN.

Topsy Dingo Wild Dog shivered violently, pillaged with mercurial hope. The maniacal laugh which followed was like windchimes hurled through a glass house in a hurricane.

"I don't know what you're laughin' about," Irene Shady told her daughter. "This whole thing has been *livin' hell* to organize!"

"Let's just *stick together* and turn *all* our jokes on Gladys Turner, ya'll, where we can do some kind of worthwhile damage!" Yvonne Henderson suggested, blowing her nose.

"I'm with you!" shouted Scoot. She turned to Topsy. "Who are *you* stickin' with?"

"Mary Jane Shady. . . " Topsy breathed, praying desperately that she was really there and that she wouldn't go away. "Mary Jane Shady . . . Mary Jane Shady. . . "

"Always thinkin' of *yourself,*" frowned her mother. "Always, always, *always* just a-thinkin' of *yourself*!"

CHAPTER FIFTY-FOUR

JOHNNY HORTON was going full blast on the radio. A Mexican in a rented tuxedo sat slumped over the steering wheel of a huge red eighteen-wheeler truck, which was parked next to a large strange structure that gave the appearance of a big redbrick schoolhouse with modern hotel overtones.

Directly in front of her was a bizarre-looking purple convertible limousine, which was covered with a weird collection of skulls and horns and upholstered in the skins of an animal whose origin she couldn't recall at that moment. On the trunk stood a totally naked fifty-odd-year-old man with a tattoo of Garfield the Cat on his chest and hair red and wiry as a burning bush all over his head and body, penetrating the living daylights out of a woman who, not only was the spitting image of Olive Oyl, but was seventy-five years old if she was a day. Not only were these two maniacs both singing at the top of their voices, they were laughing like a couple of wild hyenas.

Arabella du Noir almost cried. She had prayed the better part of her corporate career to be approached in exactly the fashion she was currently witnessing.

I miss the South, Arabella thought irritably. *Goddamnit, I hate to admit it but some things are just hotter South of the Mason-Dixon and wilder East of the Pecos . . .*

Arabella du Noir always worked from the left side of her brain, however, and that was the part that took over now. It occurred to her that the limousine looked faintly familiar. At any rate, she was ready to work.

"Gary, get out the hand-held camera. Quick!" she snapped. "Wong! Sound! FAST! I want this local color for a start."

Gary, a curly-haired cameraman who was always loaded down with the latest Panavision had to offer, stood ready and waiting along with Wong Tai, a transplant from Hong Kong and Arabella's favorite sound man. These gentlemen had traveled all over the world with Arabella du Noir. They were equipped to shoot anything on the word "action." And they knew Arabella: it would come without warning. Anytime. Anywhere.

"*Excusez-moi, Madame,*" Arabella's four-foot two-inch dark-haired French secretary, Pierre, said to his boss. "*On a besoin d'une décharge*! Should we ask for a *release*?"

"*Taisez-vous,* Pierre!" Arabella snapped. "How many times have I told you NOT to interrupt me when I'm *working*!"

Pierre glanced nervously at the couple on top of the trunk.

Johnny Horton was singing:

> *"I'm livin' fast and dangerously*
> *But I've got plenty of company...*
> *When the moon comes up and the sun goes down,*
> *That's when I want to see the lights of town... "*

He had started again on the chorus by the time Leo and Lottie noticed they had company.

"Oh, Lord! Look, Leo!" Lottie whispered, aghast, as she saw the camera and fifteen people gathering around them in a circle. "They're here! They're here! Put me down, hon! It's the Peanut Butter people!" She grabbed her new husband's neck, leaned in close, speaking fervidly into his ear, "Honey, this has the potential of bein' the most embarrassin' moment of my life, and yours, too, I 'spect, if we let it! But I know a thing or two about human nature! If we don't act embarrassed, then neither will they! So let's just pretend this is a *ordinary* thing to have happened and *act like it was just exactly the thing to be a-doin' under the circumstances*! Okay? Good!"

Leo Diggs looked around, disengaged himself from his wife and lifted Lottie down from the trunk to the ground with the care one would take in handling a porcelain doll.

"Howdy," Leo said, jumping off the trunk, grabbing his pants and extending a sunburned arm. "I'm Leo Diggs and this here's my wife, Lottie Shady Diggs."

"Howdy," Lottie said, shading her eyes from the sun with one hand and offering a handshake with the other. "I'm Lottie Shady Diggs, Mary Jane Shady's aunt on her daddy's side, and we're your Welcomin' Committee to Uncertain, Texas." She turned around to look for her clothes. " 'Scuze our appearance. We was entertainin' ourselves while we was waitin' on ya'll." She picked up her skirt and put it on. "We don't usually carry on like this normally, but everbody's at the Pep Rally and we just got married yesterday but nobody knows it yet, so we're just havin' a little celebration and doin' whatever we have never done before but wished we had and we sure hope we didn't offend nobody." She stepped into her skirt, zipping it up as quickly as possible.

One South Bronx cameraman, one Chinese sound man, one Russian defector boom man, a best boy from North Africa, the script secretary from Queens, a gofer who had just graduated from the American Film Institute, the gaffer who was from Berkeley, both East coast pilots and their assistants who hailed originally from Tuscon, Arizona, Macon, Georgia, Tallahassee, Florida, and St. Paul, Minnesota, as well as a hairdresser who'd been born and raised in East Los Angeles, a makeup man from Germany and three other crew members from midtown Manhattan, as well as Arabella du Noir, her French secretary and his Belgian assistant, who all thought they'd seen *everything,* realized in a single collective moment that they had not.

"I know, I know," Lottie said, straightening her clothes. "I been to one World's Fair, two goat ropin's and even seen a gobbler fight over in Jal, New Mexico once, and I ain't *never* saw anything like what you just seen *neither,* but like I said, we're the Welcomin' Committee so *welcome* anyway!"

CHAPTER FIFTY-FIVE

INSIDE THE GYMNASIUM, Mr. Arkley Justice was warming up his band. Clarinet players were licking their reeds or replacing split ones with new ones, the trombones were moving their "arms" back and forth like men sawing down trees, trumpet players flung spit out of their mouthpieces, the flutes lined up the three silver sections of their instruments, pursing their lips in anticipation like children preparing to blow bubbles. Lydell Olson was the first-chair piccolo player, and she just pretended she was blowing smoke rings, little bity ones, and never gave another thought to any of it. The drummers hit their sticks against their drums lackadaisically. Every now and then one of them would make a roll. The only one in the percussion section seriously warming up was Sally Sims. Sally was a sophomore and had been assigned the triangle again this year. She was desperately afraid if she didn't do her best, she might get kicked out completely and end up in the Pep Squad. Sally had never managed to hold onto a pair of anything throughout an entire piece, and now she clung for dear life to her triangle and its stick, hoping and praying that neither would fly out of her hands, forever sealing the demise of what was left of her musical future.

Next to the band sat the Pep Squad. Dressed in maroon skirts and gold V-necked sweaters with a big maroon "U" stitched over the front, the Pep Squad was made up of every girl in Uncertain High who had *not* been selected to be in the band, or who had been kicked out of it. Like orphans brought out for a special excursion, the Pep Squad sat apart and in their own section, fulfilling the duty expected of them—chanting cheers.

It was the duty of Miss Palmer Jordan Pullet, the girls' physical education teacher and sports coach, to oversee the group during football and basketball seasons. Miss Pullet tolerated the Pep Squad with the spirit of one forced to board the Titanic, all the while knowing its fate right from the start. She simply hated every single person in the Pep Squad. And if the girls didn't have the talent or coordination to make the band, they certainly weren't going to have a chance of getting on her volleyball team. She had been stuck overseeing the "losers" of Uncertain High, and to Miss Palmer Jordan Pullet, this was a sickening situation.

Miss Pullet was also in charge of the cheerleaders, however, and that was the part which made the whole thing tolerable, even putting Miss Pullet in an enviable and prestigious position. It was just as important to be an Uncertain High School cheerleader as it was to be the drum major or one of the twirlers. And just as the football players were allowed to forego participation in band during football season, so were the girls chosen as cheerleaders. Certainly no cheerleader was chosen from the Pep Squad.

There were four main cheerleaders and each had an assistant. In addition, there were four sub-assistants. This meant that there were twelve girls down on the gymnasium floor or out on the field leading the cheers. Unlike the drum major or the twirlers who had to be beautiful or at least halfway attractive to lead the band, Uncertain sometimes had cheerleaders whose faces could stop a clock. There was never any question as to whom Miss Palmer Jordan Pullet would choose as cheerleaders: The main cheerleaders were selected from her A string volleyball team, their assistants from the B team, and the other four were selected from the second strings of each.

Miss Pullet considered a good set of lungs and outstanding athletic ability the only assets worth considering in a cheerleader. She herself had reminded more than one person in Uncertain of one of those pictures hanging up in the post office. Irene Shady once told her husband Robert that if she didn't know better, she'd swear that Palmer was an ex-convict. What everyone did know, however, was that prior to becoming the girls' P.E. teacher at Uncertain High, Palmer Jordan Pullet had spent two years in the Shrine Circus as an acrobat, touring all over the Gulf Coast from Nuevo Laredo clear down to Biloxi, Mississippi, and that's where she'd learned all the tumbling tricks she had implemented into her cheerleaders' formations over the years.

Miss Palmer Jordan Pullet was just as famous in her field as Mr. Arkley Justice was in his, and the combination of the show the two of them, always competing to out do one another, came up with, was better than Ringling Brothers, Barnum and Bailey, anytime. Lots of people who didn't even live in Uncertain and didn't even like football came from neighboring towns all over West Texas just to see what new thing Palmer and Arkley had created.

And now, as Irene Shady led her daughter, Yvonne Henderson and Scoot Widders into the gymnasium, they all stopped and stared at the cheerleaders, who were stacked up in the air on top of one another like Chinese checkers, the top one somersaulting to the floor in double rolls, followed by the rest of the set, only to begin a new formation, as the crowd chanted along with the Pep Squad:

"Two bits!
Four bits!
Six bits!
A dollar!
All for Uncertain!

Stand up and Holler!"

Miss Palmer Jordan Pullet threw an impatient glance toward the Pep Squad, as the group reluctantly stood, lackadaisically waving their maroon and gold pom-poms. "YELL, YOU PANSIES!" Palmer boomed in her big bass voice. She carried a megaphone, but never used it. She'd never needed it.

The coach directed her attention back toward "her girls" on the floor. Half were doing cartwheels. The other half caught the cartwheelers by their ankles and lifted them into the air, the girls on top balancing their feet on the shoulders of the girls below, and all giving the effect of a double-line of cutouts unfolded and suspended in space. The crowd "oh-ed" and "ah-ed" and "ow-ed" and applauded, and of course, stood and yelled as loud as they could on "All for Uncertain, Stand Up and Holler!"

Topsy Dingo Wild Dog lost herself and Mary Jane Shady as she gazed at the cheerleaders. She had forgotten how *complicated* Uncertain school activities were. And for a moment, her personal complexities paled as she watched the Uncertain High School cheerleaders fly through the air and land on each other's shoulders. She admired the way they made it look so effortless. She admired their skill, their grace, their dedication and dare-devil style. And then she wondered what on earth they would do with all that after Uncertain High School. Go to college? Go to work? What happened to the ones who *stayed*? She wondered what happened to old small-town cheerleaders who never left town. And old Homecoming Queens and old Prom Queens and old Class Favorites who chose to *stay.* What did it mean to get married, have children and stay home? *Were they happy*? Did they go to work in banks, insurance companies, grocery stores, teach school, get into macrame, numbered paintings, bingo and bar-be-que, ladies' clubs and *like* it? Did they sew and cook and clean *and* run businesses, too? Did they know where things were and WHAT THEY WERE SUPPOSED TO DO? WERE THEY ORGANIZED? WHAT DID THEY THINK ABOUT?

THEY HAVE SCHEDULES AND COMMITMENTS AND OBLIGATIONS. They aren't still pursuing silly childhood dreams . . . LIKE YOU ARE . . . Making themselves crazy trying to be WHAT? Trying to achieve WHAT? Trying to get WHERE? . . .

She suspected that most people didn't think too much about what *was*, that they left what *was* to photograph albums, and faded pressed flowers glued into scrapbooks, packing away their memories along with carefully boxed evening gowns, worn once in a lifetime, then closeted in attics forever. She suspected that if it weren't for Homecomings and Pep Rallys and perpetual reunions that most people would just forget about this part of the past and get on with it.

MOST PEOPLE GROW UP... THEY DON'T TRY TO MAKE A CAREER OUT OF THEIR CHILDLIKE IMAGINATIONS... THEY ARE BUSY DOING GROWN-UP THINGS, ADULT THINGS...

Then she looked at Yvonne. She remembered Yvonne down on the floor with all those dolls and second-hand memories. And she didn't know what to think.

" 'Scuze us, 'scuze us!" Deep voices, ringing with importance, cut through the cheers, as several men carrying heavy-duty cables and a twenty-foot step ladder marched past Topsy, Irene, Yvonne and Scoot.

"Oh! Is it *them*?" Yvonne cried. "Are the Peanut Butter people here?"

Don't think... Topsy told herself sharply. *This isn't a good time to think...*

That's right, don't THINK, said someone who sounded exactly like Mary Jane Shady. *You better shut up and let me* THINK...

"Come on!" cried Irene Shady, reaching out to move her along. "Come on! Come on!"

Topsy gasped as she stared into the stands. A sea of faces, waving arms and shouting voices ricocheted back.

This is IT, *Topsy told herself anxiously. What am I going to do? What am I going to do? What am I going to do?*

You're going to smile and nod and nod and smile, Mary Jane told her. *That's easy enough. And that's all I want you to do.*

What are YOU *going to do? What are* YOU *going to do? What are* YOU *going to do?* asked Topsy frantically.

I'm going to smile and nod and nod and smile with you, smiled Mary Jane Shady. *Just nod and smile and smile and nod. That's* ALL *you have to do.*

Oh, my God, oh, my God, oh, my God, groaned Topsy, smiling. *This is hard. This is really hard to do...*

Shut up and smile and stop babbling, Mary Jane told her. *I cannot give this my best smile if you insist on regurgitating your mental garbage into my head. I can't think!*

You have to THINK *to* SMILE? Topsy asked, bewildered. *I have to do that! I have to do that, too!*

Yes, sighed the smiling Mary Jane Shady. *I have to when I'm with* YOU . . . .

Her mother's voice cut into her head. "Those are *our* men," Irene said. "I recognized Otis Medcalf and he's the janitor here, and ole Jimmie Meeks was holdin' up one side of the ladder, or tryin' to, and he's the Junior High School bus driver. Orville's gettin' the electricity ready to go like I instructed him to," she stated with expertise. "Now ya'll go on up and sit in the stands and I'm a goin' down on the floor here and make sure ever-thing gets hooked up right." Deserting the group of women, she walked right out on the middle of the gymnasium floor, weaving her way through twelve flying cheerleaders as she proceeded to tell Otis Medcalf and his assistants how to plug in and turn on the electricity.

Deserted! grumbled Topsy, looking after her mother. *She dragged us here and now look! Abandoned!*

Will you come on, please? pleaded Mary Jane Shady. *I'm really getting tired of you.*

Likewise, Topsy muttered, following Scoot and Yvonne, as they moved toward the section of the bleachers that had been reserved for the former students of Uncertain High School and the families of the students.

She moved into the stands. *Just follow Yvonne. Smile and nod. Nod and smile. That's all they expect you to do . . .*

Next to the section filled with ex-students sat the Pep Squad. Gathered on the opposite side of the gymnasium was the entire student body of Uncertain High School, as well as some of the Junior High School Students.

Scoot Widders led the way into the bleachers as if she herself were running for Homecoming Queen and was still trying to get votes. There wasn't a soul in sight that Scoot did not shake hands with, accepting congratulations from all, even though the winner had yet to be announced and the event had yet to take place.

Yvonne clung to her yellow-feathered coat, as people reached out to touch the plumes.

"Watch my head for me, M.J.," Yvonne told Topsy. "One of these little assholes from church will grab my wig if they can!"

Topsy smiled and nodded and nodded and smiled, staring zealously at Yvonne's wig.

I'm hot! she told Mary Jane Shady fervently. *I'm hot! I'm hot! I'm burning up hot!*

No, you're not, Mary Jane replied. *You're not hot.*

You're not hot! babbled Topsy Dingo Wild Dog. *You're not hot! You're not a star! You're not a star! And you're not hot! YOU'RE NOT HOT!*

"Mary Jane Shady!"

Topsy and Mary Jane jumped as they saw former drama teacher, Judy Jones, who was decked out in an outfit that rivaled Yvonne Henderson's. Nearing fifty and bearing an amazing resemblance to Gloria Swanson in *Sunset Boulevard,* Mrs. Jones had costumed herself from bits and pieces of her favorite shows.

"Mrs. Jones!" smiled Mary Jane Shady.

Appalled, but smiling with her, Topsy waved hello, too.

"This silver lamé dress was a costume from *Present Laughter,* my senior class production of 1959!" Judy Jones screamed. "This black feather boa I have flung around my neck was an accessory from *The Madwoman of Chaillot,* the second-place winner in Regional Competition held in Lubbock in 1963! And these three-inch-long rhinestone earrings hanging precariously from these precious ears were costume jewelry worn by the actress playing the Eliza Doolittle part at the ball in my only attempt at a musical, *My Fair Lady,* 1972!"

"And her make-up looks like she's been cornered in a conspiracy between Why-vonne here and Deal Grimes over at the One Call Does All Permanent Rest Center!" Scoot Widders whispered into Topsy's ear.

"*Our Star*!" Mrs. Jones gushed dramatically. "*Our Star*! I'm the one who discovered her!" she cried, grabbing Topsy by the arm. "I'm the one who's responsible for what's happening here today!"

She is responsible! Topsy Dingo Wild Dog's head said. *Look at her! What a maniac! I listened to a raving lunatic!*

"No, you're not," said Yvonne Henderson. "*I'm* the one who's responsible for what's happenin' here today!"

"My twins are responsible," Scoot said, backing away from Judy Jones. "*They're* responsible for what's about to happen here today!"

"But I discovered her!" Judy Jones screamed. "If it weren't for me, there would be no Miss Peanut Butter Cup!"

She said I was talented and I believed her! She told me "YOU ARE AN ACTRESS!" and I believed HER! SHE SAID I WOULD MAKE IT AND I BOUGHT IT! Where is my mother? Where the hell is my crazy, crazy mother? She and Judy Jones are responsible for this! They did this to me! THEY DID ME IN!!!

OH, SHUT UP, said Mary Jane Shady. *Stop blaming everyone else. You did yourself in.*

Me? Topsy thought anxiously. *ME? ME? I? I? I did myself in? I did myself in?*

"No! No! No!" Judy waved her arms in the air as if attempting to flag down a cab in a snowstorm in Chicago. "I'm referring to the *Star of Uncertain!* Remember *Anastasia?!*" Judy cried.

I remember! Topsy's head jangled. *I remember! I remember! I remember! AND I DON'T WANT TO REMEMBER!*

Your hysteria is driving me crazy! Mary Jane Shady snapped. *You're going to fuck this up.*

Me? Topsy repeated, an echo. *Drive who crazy? Drive me crazy? Me? Me? I? Do us in? Do us in? Do us in? You? Me? You? I?*

SHUT UP. SHUT UP. SHUT UP. SHUT UP.

"Remember our victory!" shouted Judy Jones.

No! No! No! rattled Topsy. *No! No! No! No!*

"Hey." A slow low voice drawled behind her. " 'Member the Alamo?"

It's him! Topsy screamed. *It's him!*

LET ME . . . said Mary Jane Shady. *Please. LET ME* . . . .

Bobby . . . whispered Topsy Dingo Wild Dog. *Bobby. . . Bobby. . .*

YOU ARE GOING TO DO US IN! roared Mary Jane Shady. *Goddamn you! Help me! Help me . . . .Help me . . . .*

Topsy turned.

Helpless.

Mary Jane's heart stopped. Her eyes closed. She stood paralyzed.

Topsy whirled.

"Bobby!"

CHAPTER FIFTY-SIX

"PIERRE! Champagne!" Arabella du Noir motioned gracefully to her secretary. "*Vite, s'il vois plaît*!" In her white Chanel suit trimmed in black, the tall, splendid looking woman reminded Lottie Shady of Diana Ross. She reminded Leo Diggs of an elegant black swan.

Arabella gave her group a collective impatient glance. "Well, move!" she told them, as the group broke into working clusters. "*Tout de suite*!"

"Claude! Champagne! *Vite, s'il vous plaît*!" Pierre cried out to his assistant.

"Champagne! Champagne!" echoed Claude as he hustled inside the Lear Jet.

"Where's Miz Dune-war?" Lottie Shady asked Arabella du Noir while buttoning up Leo Diggs' shirt. "Couldn't she make it?" Lottie wondered, looking around.

"I'm Arabella du Noir," Arabella du Noir said patiently.

Lottie missed two buttons on Leo's shirt. "Why, you're *colored*!" she observed, peering up at Arabella.

"Why, so I am," Arabella agreed amiably.

"And purty, too, inn't she, Leo?"

"She sure is," Leo nodded cheerfully. "I knew right off she was the boss."

"That's 'cause he's a nation-wide traveler," Lottie explained. "Leo's more up on things than me. But I sure am glad to see such a fine-lookin' dark woman in such a high uppity-up position, although I surely did not expect it."

"I'm usually a surprise," Arabella acknowledged.

"Me, too," Lottie nodded. "Almost nobody 'spects to buy a casket from a person who's the spittin' image of Olive Oyl. But how I look can sometimes even make a person feel better. If they're real upset about somebody dyin', at least they can be glad they don't look like *me*!"

"I know what you mean," smiled Arabella wryly. "It's a rare day when my clients tell me they wish they were *black*."

Lottie Shady looked at Arabella du Noir curiously. "What's it like to be *colored*?" she wondered, peering at Arabella's creamy skin. " 'Cause I wouldn't call that color *black*."

"Well," replied Arabella, finding Lottie's directness disarming. "First of all, people always expect you to be able to *sing*."

"And can you?" Lottie Shady wanted to know. "Is it a natural thing?"

"No," sighed Arabella. "I just can't sing a thing."

"*Voilá*!" Claude said to Pierre, as Claude emerged from the plane with a silver ice bucket carrying a magnum of Bollinger Vavielles Vignes Françaises.

"*Voilá*!" Pierre said to Arabella, as he presented the champagne.

"Glasses!" Arabella commanded.

"Glasses!" Lottie cried.

"I love women who give orders," grinned Leo.

"*Des verres, s'il vous plaît*!" Arabella repeated.

"Day very, silver plate!" echoed Lottie Shady.

"*Des verres, s'il vous plaît*!" Pierre demanded.

"*Des verres, s'il vous plaît*!" Claude disappeared.

Lottie Shady clapped her hands with joy. "Oh, those boys just do whatever you tell 'em to, don't they, honey?"

"They sure do, honey." Arabella grinned.

"Well, I guess I'm just lucky," smiled Lottie, gesturing towards Leo, " 'cause mine treats me like that, too!"

"Good . . ." murmured Arabella, as she watched Leo Diggs straightening his wife's skirt. "Let's drink to that . . . "

"It's not cookin' sherry, is it?" Lottie wanted to know. "Last time I drank that stuff I didn't remember a *thing*. 'Member, Leo? I didn't hardly 'member you and you're hard to forget."

I'll bet he is, thought Arabella. She turned away to Gary, the cameraman, to make sure he was "getting everything."

Wong Tai, the sound engineer, had his eye on Boris Rudinsky, the boom man.

"What's that?" Lottie asked the man holding the long steel pole.

"This is a boom," Rudinsky explained. "It has a microphone on the end of it. It's so we can pick up your voices. For sound."

"Looks like a fishing pole," Lottie remarked. "Don't get it in my hair. I wouldn't want to get messed up for the picture."

"Part of my job is to keep it *out* of the picture," Rudinsky explained, staring dubiously at Lottie Shady's coiffeur, which looked like a mangled bird's nest.

Sylvie Notions, the script secretary, had brought her fold-out chair off the plane and was arranging colored pencils, loading a Polaroid and setting a stopwatch all at the same time.

"I admire a person who can do more than one thing at a time," Lottie said to Sylvie. "When I formaldehyde people at the funeral home, I'm always havin' to juggle this and that. I'm a undertaker," she explained to Sylvie, who had dropped the watch and all twelve pencils and was putting the film in upside down.

"*Voilà*!" cried Claude, hurrying forward with a silver ice bucket containing the champagne.

His boss, Pierre relieved him, removing the paraphernalia from Claude's arms. "*Voilà*!" Pierre cried, offering the wine to Arabella du Noir.

"*Voilà*," Arabella smiled.

"Walla! Walla!" Lottie Shady echoed.

Leo Diggs took the bottle of champagne and examined it appreciatively. "Now this is *spirits,* Lottie," he told his wife. "It's made out of real old grapes without a bit of vinegar, and you're goin' to like this fine," he assured her. Turning to Arabella du Noir, he added graciously, "Me and Mrs. Diggs thank you kindly." He paused. "Oh. Our first names is Leo and Lottie. Call us by those, if you can 'member to."

Arabella du Noir smiled and said, "Thanks. And please. Call me Belle."

"We sure will," Lottie promised. "I know I can remember that 'cause my favorite ice cream's Blue Belle's chocolate chip fudge."

Pierre's assistant, Claude, almost fell down the steps of the plane with an antique silver tray holding fifteen seventy-five-year-old Waterford glasses when he saw Leo Diggs take the three hundred and fifty dollar bottle of champagne, remove the wire with his teeth, spit it to the ground, and proceed to wrap his lips around the cork.

Arabella du Noir thought her heart would fly through her chest as she watched Leo Diggs remove the cork slowly with his mouth, sucking it smoothly out of the bottle. *Oh, my God, somebody do that to me*... The cork slid gently into his orifice and he displayed it, without a nick or sound, at the tip of the longest tongue Arabella thought she had ever seen. *Does this man have a brother*? she wondered as she visualized Leo Diggs' tongue caressing her instead of the wine cork.

"He just has *more* tongue tricks!" Lottie Shady giggled.

There is no equality, Arabella du Noir thought forlornly to herself. She raised her glass, smiled at Leo and his wife, and offered a toast. "Cheers!"

As Pierre poured the champagne, Claude fetched another bottle.

"Are you sure you're getting this?" Arabella asked Gary irritably.

"Yeah, sure, Ms. du Noir," Gary assured her. He nodded toward his assistant, who was maneuvering another hand-held camera from a different direction.

"What about the car fucking? Did you get *that*?" Arabella asked.

"Everything. Tarzan and Jane. Geriatric Acrobats Performing the World's Oldest Tricks in Extraordinary West Texas Fashion, Johnny Horton captivated by the one and only Boris Rudinsky on sound—"

"*Captured,*" Arabella corrected. "Not *captivate. Capture.*"

"We got it, okay?" Gary sighed. "Who's the spic in the truck?"

"Don't be racist, Gary," Arabella sighed, sipping her champagne. "I'm sensitive."

"Okay, Miss Belle," Gary grinned. "Move your honky ass over and I'll get a close-up of Senor Mex-i-can taking a 'nap.' "

Turning to the newlyweds, Arabella remarked, "Your chauffeur is having a siesta."

"Yeah," Leo said, swallowing his champagne in one gulp. "Weed."

"M.J.," Arabella smiled knowingly.

"Naw, she's at the Pep Rally," Lottie explained. "José's passed out on dope. But don't worry. Me and Leo are goin' to drive."

"Is this a *typical* country automobile?" Sylvie Notions, fascinated, asked in her thick New York accent.

Arabella turned to look at the car. A vague feeling of familiarity needled her. She felt as if she'd seen the car before somewhere. "Is this your car, Lottie?"

"Lord, no! It's Why-vonne Henderson's car," Lottie explained, "and there ain't *nothin'* typical about her!"

Just as Lottie was about to tell Arabella about Yvonne Henderson and her limousine, Sylvie looked up and her mouth dropped open in shock.

"What is it, Sylvie?" Arabella asked. "Do you see the other plane?"

"Sky!" Sylvie replied, staring above, wide-eyed. Her voice was filled with awe. "*Sky.* I see *sky*. . . "

"Surely they got sky in New York City, don't they?" Lottie asked. "Skies are all over the world. I ain't never been all over the world, but I know they're there. I see 'em in the background on TV."

"We can't see it very well because of the tall buildings," Arabella explained. "We miss the full expanse."

"How tall can a buildin' be?" Lottie frowned thoughtfully. She looked at Sylvie. "You ever see a star?"

"In the movies and at the Hayden Planetarium," Sylvie said sadly. "I see Dustin Hoffman a lot," she added. "And Madonna."

"I mean a *real* star!" Lottie Shady cried.

"You mean up in the *sky*?" Sylvie Notions questioned.

"You ain't never seen a *real* star?" Lottie was flabbergasted. "This means you ain't seen a *shootin'* star or the Big Dipper or the Little Dipper or *nothin'*!"

"I've just missed everything!" Sylvie Notions agreed woefully.

"Well, if you never seen a sky before or a star before, you missed *somethin'*!" Lottie agreed. "But we'll fix that tonight," she promised, looking up into the clear cloudless celestial blue heavens. "Oh! Looky! Here comes the other one!"

From the west, a tiny dot grew larger and larger as it came closer and closer.

"Pierre! Claude! *Débarrassez la table, s'il vous plaît*! Clear everything!" Arabella ordered. She turned to Leo and Lottie. "Is that truck our transportation?"

"It's *our* new truck," Lottie told her, motioning toward the shiny new eighteen-wheeler. Painted on the side in bold black letters inside a huge yellow heart were the words:

THIS RIG'S LEO AND LOTTIE DIGGS

"That's my weddin' present," Lottie grinned.

"Fabulous!" Arabella exclaimed in genuine admiration. "If you will drive it over here, we'll have the men start loading."

"Mr. Superintendent sent a bus and a trailer and they're in front of the house, if we need them," Lottie added.

"We'll need the bus," Arabella nodded. "We won't need the trailer."

"Good," Lottie sighed, " 'cause I promised to stop by Scoot Widders' house and pick up a float."

"For the parade?" Arabella asked.

"Uh-huh," Lottie said. "That equipment will fit into our truck and the crew can ride in the bus."

"Excuse me, Ms. du Noir," the East coast pilot interrupted. "What about my plane?"

"Oh, just park it anywhere," Leo told him. "We'll leave José here to look after things."

The pilot gazed gravely at Leo. "You mean with that man in the tuxedo passed out in that truck?"

"Don't worry," Leo told the pilot. "He'll be okay in about ten seconds."

Leo excused himself, poured a glass of champagne for José in the Waterford glass he had placed on the trunk of the car, took several Black Beauties out of his pocket, opened José's mouth, stuffed them down the driver's throat and poured the champagne after the pills.

"Nap time's over, sonny," Leo said, giving the chauffeur several gentle taps on both cheeks. "Hello, José. Come in, James." Leo turned to the pilot. "He'll be right with you," Leo said. "Promise."

The other Lear Jet had landed, pulled up beside its twin, opened its doors and flushed forth its steps.

Arabella prepared herself for Ralph Painter.

"Here comes the human *slug,*" muttered Arabella du Noir. Of all the people she did not like, she liked Ralph Painter the least. Of all the agents that she loathed, she loathed Ralph Painter the most.

But as Arabella du Noir stood out on the runway unshielded by chalets, villas, Seventh Avenue or Madison Avenue, as she looked into the enormous blue billowing clouds moving lazily through the vast expanse of sky over an endless panorama of white desert dust, her thoughts turned to Mary Jane Shady and how *far* she had come from this flat, unpopulated prairie. And she thought of *herself* and how far she had come.

We drop our accents, get the right addresses, buy the right designers, learn a few languages, acquire a few charities, find a prestigious job and forget where we come from . . . FORGET WHO WE ARE . . . For the first time, she felt every effort of her own journey.

Mary Jane Shady must be exhausted, Arabella mused, as she watched Ralph Painter get off the plane. *I know I am. And I only have to deal with people like this son-of-a-bitch once or twice a year. . .*

CHAPTER FIFTY-SEVEN

THE LIGHTS in the gymnasium dimmed. Newly-famous Roy Orbison from Wink, Texas stepped onto the floor, accompanied by his band, *The Wink Westerners,* recently renamed *The Teen Kings.* Sunday suited young men with carnations stuck in their buttonholes, clumsily extended their hands to young ladies attired in billowing gowns that entire families had sacrificed for.

Her clear china blue eyes looked into Bobby's. Filled with hope that he would let her make him happy and the wild anticipation of getting to try, she stood before him, proffering herself. Her innocent sweet self. Draped in a strapless fountain of cascading silk organza, she stood ready and waiting to be his forever. So easy... so *easy*...

For what did she ask of him in return? What did she want from him? It was nothing. Really *nothing.* Only that he make her happy, too...

His blue, mysterious, half-laughing, half-brooding eyes gazed back at her. Challenging.

But she knew him now. He just liked to give her a hard time. Play the game *his* way. So he'd feel he was in control or something. Boys. Always causing trouble. Always having to have things their way. But at least she knew *that* now. She had *that* figured out. He'd taken away the jacket so he could give it back. He'd taken away the ring so he could give it back. He'd gone away so he could come back. But he'd come back. He would always come back. He always did... She stared up at him, wondering what was going on up in his head, wondering what he had planned for tonight. *I'll always take him back, no matter what,* she promised herself. *That's what love is... it's NO MATTER WHAT...*

Roy's band had started to play. Bobby extended his hand. She took it and followed him onto the gymnasium floor. She put her hands around his neck, swaying to the music. *Oh, Bobby... I'll never leave you....*

Roy started to sing:

"Tell me one more time...
Put your hand in mine...
That you love me like you used to do...
Tell me one more time that you want me...
One more time break my heart in two...
Tell me one more time...
With your hand in mine...
That you need a love so sweet and true...
Tell me one more lie...
I'll cry you one more cry...
Tell me that you love me one more time..."

Don't listen, Mary Jane Shady told Topsy Dingo Wild Dog. *He's not here. Roy's not here. This isn't a prom. You're not there...*

Topsy Dingo Wild Dog swayed as Roy sang on:

> *"One more time . . .*
> *Tell me that you care . . .*
> *One more time, honey, I'll be there . . .*
> *Tell me just once more . . .*
> *Like you did before . . .*
> *That you need a love so sweet and true . . .*
> *Tell me one more lie . . .*
> *I'll cry you one more cry . . .*
> *Tell me that you love me one more time . . ."*

Get out! Mary Jane Shady urged. *You're in the past! GET OUT!*

"Tell me one more time . . . ." Topsy's head sang.

Oh, Jesus! groaned Mary Jane Shady, disgusted. *I'm leaving!*

"No!" Topsy pleaded urgently.

THEN LET ME HANDLE THIS! Mary Jane Shady insisted.

The prom attendants dispersed, fragmenting into oblivion. The lights grew brighter, hotter. Roy Orbison disappeared along with his song. But Bobby's voice was still behind her. His voice was still clear and strong.

"Welcome home, girl."

Twenty years of anguish, dread and remorse turned into a blazing smile. Twenty years of performing before a live audience automatically transformed fear into challenge. She was no longer alone in the dark rooms of Topsy Dingo Wild Dog's head with tumultuous memories and malignant rampaging fears: she was surrounded by hundreds of people. She was at the Pep Rally in Uncertain, Texas.

Topsy Dingo Wild Dog cringed.

Mary Jane Shady was *on*.

She turned casually, gracefully, and said warmly, "Hi . . ."

A close-up might have caught it. But the people standing next to her noticed nothing. She didn't flinch when she saw Sammy Widders. There was a moment's recognition, a slight adjustment containing only the least element of surprise.

Bobby Henderson was nowhere to be seen.

"Hi, Sammy," Mary Jane Shady smiled.

Sammy! Topsy Dingo Wild Dog raved. *It's Sammy! Sammy Widders!*

Sammy stood, right behind her, his eyes dancing and warm. He was handsome, tan and trim in his Levis, Larry Mahan boots, white starched shirt with a row of dancing cowgirls embroidered across the front yoke, and the same silver belt buckle shaped like the State of Texas that he had always worn. He looked at Mary Jane Shady's outfit and grinned, amused. "Wow," he drawled, gazing at her, impressed. "Holy shit, you're a Peanut Butter *star.*"

Sammy picked her up, twirled her around and gave her a hug before putting her down.

A sudden rush of genuine affection for these strange and familiar people and surroundings flooded through her.

Simultaneously, they both burst into laughter.

"Welcome home, Butter Cup," he grinned. "We been missin' you."

How *unexpected* came this compelling swell of fondness. "Me, too, Sammy." She was surprised. She meant it.

Home. Home. Home. She was home.

"Sammy!" Kay Widders snapped. "Sit down!"

Yes, she was home.

"Fuck off, Kay," Sammy smiled to his wife.

Yes, indeed. *Home.*

Mary Jane Shady looked at Kay and Sammy Widders and remembered them down on the gymnasium floor twenty years before, dancing so close that Orville Turner had taken Sammy aside and told him to make some space. She remembered Kay's dress. It had been cactus green, Sammy's favorite color.

"Sammy, I mean it," Kay Widders said. "I forbid you to talk to her. She's goin' with a *Jew.*"

She looked at Kay and wondered when Kay had started caring who went with who. Was it after the twins? Was it before?

"What's 'at?" Sammy asked.

"A *Jew,*" Kay hissed.

"I heard you the first time, Kay. Now what the fuck's your problem? If it hadn't been for the Jews we wouldn't have had Lenny Bruce, inn't that right, M.J.?"

I could be sitting right here in these bleachers in a marriage just like this one . . . Mary Jane thought bleakly. *This is what happens to old cheerleaders who never leave . . .*

"Is that right?" asked Yvonne Henderson.

"Lenny *who*?" Scoot Widders questioned. "Did he graduate with ya'll?"

"I *guarantee* it," Sammy grinned. "And we sure wouldn't have had Jesus Christ, and I *know* you think a lot of *him,* Kay."

"Sammy. . . " Kay Widders was grinding her teeth so hard that they squeaked.

"Anyway, Jesus was a fairy, hon, didn't nobody ever tell you that?" Sammy asked his wife. When she started to speak, Sammy pointed a finger at her and smiled, "If you don't be nice I'm gonna come all over your face." He turned to his mother. "Hey, Mama." Sammy gave Scoot a swift pat on her butt. "Sit down and relax. The votes are *in.* Ya'll want a beer?"

"No, thanks," said Mary Jane, numbly. *Why do they put up with each other*? she wondered. *Why don't they leave one other? Why do they tolerate this?*

Sammy looked at her disbelieving. "*You* don't want a beer?"

"No *drinkin',*" Kay stated.

You would have put up with it, too. You would have gladly put up with it if Bobby had asked you to . . .

"Kay," Sammy smiled. "Do you want to *live*? Be nice." He reached down under his place on the bleachers right in the second row, opened up a Coors from his ice-chest and handed it to Mary Jane. "Have a cool one, M.J. Here you go—"

But maybe he's changed . . . maybe Bobby is different now . . .

"Well," mumbled Topsy. "Maybe—"

NO, said Mary Jane Shady. *NO!*

She wondered what had happened to Sammy and Kay. She wondered what had happened to Bobby and Yvonne. She wondered what had happened to her and Bobby. What had happened to all of them? Where was the turn? When had it all changed?

Topsy looked away, nervously. *Why am I acting like a baby about this?* she wondered irritably. *I'm almost thirty-six years old. I can have a drink if I want one . . .*

Kay Widders was scowling at her. "*No drinkin'*!" she hissed. "*No drinkin'*!"

Topsy Dingo Wild Dog turned her Mary Jane Shady smile on. "Kay," Topsy Dingo Wild Dog said sweetly. "Do you mind—"

I mind! snapped Mary Jane Shady. *I mind.*

"Well, I don't mind," Sammy grinned. "And what I say is what goes. Whatever you want, Star. I got this all stocked up for you!"

"*. . . And what I say is what goes . . . and what I say is what goes . . . and what I say is what goes . . .* " echoed Sammy's voice.

Don't do it, warned Mary Jane to Topsy. *Don't do this to me . . .*

Who wouldn't want to drink if they were about to run into Bobby Henderson? Topsy asked Mary Jane Shady, annoyed. She turned to Sammy. "Well, then," continued the smiling Topsy Dingo Wild Dog, "I don't mind if you don't mind . . ."

"*EVERYTIME ANYBODY IN THIS FAMILY TAKES A DRINK, THEY DO SOMETHING CRAZY. . .* " Irene Shady's voice cut through her Mary Jane Shady smile and her Topsy Dingo Wild Dog head.

Her hand fluttered to her temple, dropped to the neckline of her Peanut Butter Cup dress, where her fingers fidgeted in agitation with the very top button.

" 'Member that time when I won that trophy for pushin' you and Harla Elaine out all over the stage?" Sammy laughed. "Boy! We got drunk that night, didn't we, M.J.?"

"I think I'd like . . . some . . . air . . ." said Mary Jane Shady.

Why is he bringing that up? Topsy thought anxiously.

You don't remember that night very well, do you? . . . mused Mary Jane Shady.

"Oh, what a scene!" cried Judy Jones. "It's one of the best pieces I've ever done!"

"Don't remind her of the one and only time she ever lost!" cried Yvonne Henderson. "She's the star! She should have won! She should have won!"

"She was building up to her senior year!" Judy Jones exclaimed. "She won everything that year!"

Three gold statuettes flew into her head, three trophies from her triumphant senior year, the year she won District and Regional and State. *I took the Best Actress Award*! she remembered flabbergasted. *My God, I forgot I won*! Her head started to reel. *I won every everything there was to win and I got just as drunk every time I won,* she thought, confused. *Why'd I get so drunk if I won? . . .*

YOU KNOW WHY, said Mary Jane Shady simply.

I hate you, said Topsy to Mary Jane Shady. *Everytime you come around I stop having any fun*!

CHAPTER FIFTY-EIGHT

A DASH OF PINK appeared in the portal of the plane.

Wearing a pink sweatshirt and matching pink shorts, pink socks and a pair of custom-ordered pink Reeboks, Ralph Painter adjusted the gold chains around his neck, making sure that his most recent Gucci acquisition was resting outside of his new sweatshirt. Meticulously manicured and perfectly tanned, he moved firmly down the steps of the plane. In one hand was a pink ostrich attaché case and clipped to his waist was a pink portable telephone.

"Who's that big pink thing?" Lottie Shady asked Arabella du Noir. Coming toward them was the most color-coordinated man she had ever seen. "He looks like a big pink popsickle!"

"Only much, much messier," Arabella warned.

"Bella!" Ralph called out, measuredly ambling down the steps to meet the woman whose decisions made possible his condo in Beverly Hills, his sailboat at the Marina, his annual trips to Spain to watch the bullfights and cruise the bullfighters. "Bella, *darling*!"

Arabella stared at his pink shirt, which had AA, CA, NA, GA, PA and OEA written all over it. "New logo?" Arabella asked, as Ralph Painter approached.

"Oh, one of my *client's* gave this to me. *Kippy Witt,*" Ralph confided, mouthing the actress' name. "She got it at the *You-Know-Where* Clinic. Oh, my dear, she was in for *everything*. See?" He pointed to the shirt. "Alcoholics Anonymous, Cocaine Anonymous, Neurotics Anonymous, Gamblers Anonymous, Pills Anonymous, Overeaters Anonymous . . ." He flashed Arabella a flattering smile, revealing a mouthful of perfectly capped teeth. "A's are *in,* Arabella, A's are *in*!"

"Ralph." Arabella did not bother to keep smiling. "Please save the private details of your client's trauma for the article which I'm certain you surely must have sold to *People* Magazine before your plane left the ground—"

"I *did*!" Ralph nodded, delightedly running his manicured fingers through his silver-blond toupee. "Isn't it *wonderful! Addiction is in*! Her price went up $500,000 dollars just like that! I could have gotten more, except she never tried to commit suicide."

"I always ask more for suicides," Lottie Shady nodded. "I usually get it, too."

"Oh, *ugly*!" Ralph Painter whispered to Arabella, staring at Lottie. "Ugly! Ugly! Ugly!"

"It sure is," Lottie agreed. "Now, the first one was back in 1949—"

Ralph brushed Lottie aside. "Someone will be with you in a moment, dear. See that lady with the Polaroid." He pointed toward Sylvie Notions. "Just give her your name. She'll call you." Shuddering, he moved away from Lottie Shady. "It's beyond *quaint,* isn't it? What would you call it? Walking, talking folk art? Cartoon life? I can't use it."

"Huh?" said Lottie.

"You're not right for this job, dear," Ralph Painter told her. "You're too tall, too short, too thin, too fat, too light, too dark, and frankly you seem a bit neurotic. And, darling, with *your* looks you can't afford to be neurotic. Wait for Robert Altman. I'm sure he'll have something for you in one of his comebacks—"

"*Ralph*!" hissed Arabella.

"And *you're* too soft," Ralph told Arabella. He turned back to Lottie. "Olive, dear. Please. Miss Oyl. Get lost. Goodbye. Thank you."

"Hold on, Pink Boy," interjected Leo Diggs.

"Are you part of this shoot?" Ralph asked, irritably giving Leo a hasty glance. "Could you excuse us? Please?" He turned back to Arabella. "*Actors. Really.*"

"Speaking of suicide," Arabella said carefully. "I'd like a word with you."

"Oh, for Christ's sakes!" Ralph groaned, chewing on a manicured nail. "She didn't kill herself, did she? I told her to get on a plane and go to Palm Springs, get in a cab and drive over to Park. I *told* her I didn't care *where* she went, just get her fucking face fixed. But she's a stubborn little cunt. I told her *that,* too—"

"Ralph!" Arabella wanted to scream.

"Mary Jane Shady is going to be the death of me, Arabella. Absolutely the death. Now you know I don't usually go *dumping* on a client. But you're a sensitive person. Look at you. You've *got* to be with your background—"

"You mean race," stated Lottie. "I think he means *race,*" she told Arabella.

"I think he does, too," Arabella nodded.

Ralph Painter turned to Lottie. "Get lost. I mean it. Someone will give you your call. We're trying to do business here. *Go away*!" He turned back to Arabella. "Well, she's just too *old* for the job. Mary Jane has had it. I knew it when I saw those last headshots. This isn't a surprise. It's clear why I'm here. Don't worry, I have the best client list I've had in years. Ten girls from towns with less than one thousand people. See, I know what you like." He opened up his attaché case and pulled out a stack of photographs. "Look at these. Randi Turner, Comfort, North Carolina, population *300,* okay? Cute, huh?" He shoved the picture to the bottom of the stack. "Larger town? Bigger tits? Maeve Hiller, East Rochester, New Hampshire, population 1,100." He shoved that picture to the bottom of the stack. "Want something kinkier? You know, a Carol Kane from Bazaar, Kansas, population 64? Tizzy Lamar. A doll. Not much upstairs, but cute to look at. Don't worry. She talks. You know Kansas, a nice Midwestern accent—"

"Suicide!" exclaimed Lottie Shady. "Mary Jane didn't try to commit *suicide*!"

"That's because she doesn't know what's good for her!" Ralph Painter snapped. "Who *are* these people?" He asked Arabella. "Where's the A.D.?"

Turning to Leo and Lottie, Arabella said, "Leo and Lottie, this is Ralph Painter of the Painter Perfect Agency in Hollywood. Ralph is Mary Jane's *agent*. And I don't think any further explanation is necessary."

Lottie Shady and Leo Diggs each gave the agent a short nod.

Ralph Painter nodded back curtly.

"I don't believe you've had the pleasure of meeting Mary Jane's aunt and uncle, Mr. and Mrs. Diggs. Have you? Ralph?"

The agent paled. Arabella's eyes had become two dark pools, shooting pains all through Ralph Painter's left side from his temple to his fingertips and especially on the left side of his chest, which he now massaged with nervous intensity.

Hoping to divert her own annoyance, Arabella added thoughtfully, "Mr. and Mrs. Diggs were just married yesterday."

"How charming!" Ralph blubbered, anxiously taking the cue. "How *exciting*! And *I* missed the wedding! If only I'd *known*!"

"We eloped," Lottie explained. "Nobody knows yet and we'd be real appreciative if ever-body here could keep it a secret—"

"*Why*?" Ralph asked, feigning interest.

"Ralph," Arabella said. "This is the last time today you're going to be told something *twice*. Their wedding is a secret and *that is that.*" She turned back to Leo and Lottie. "Please excuse me."

"I'm so sorry about the confusion!" Ralph told Lottie Shady hurriedly. "Your distinct looks, that aquiline nose—*anyone* would have mistaken you for an actress!" He turned to Arabella. "I'm right about Altman." He swiveled back to Lottie Shady. "I'll call him in ten minutes." He wheeled to Leo Diggs. "Mister. You are married to a *star*!"

"Come here, Ralph," said Arabella.

"Oh, yes, yes, of course, *yes,*" smiled the sweating, fawning palpitating agent. "Yes, yes, yes, yes, *yes*!"

Leo Diggs and Lottie Shady stared at the pink-suited man as he trailed, puppy-like, behind the tall beautiful black woman.

"If I didn't know better, I'd say thangs are just about to get real *weird,*" said Leo Diggs.

"I have always been suspicious of a man who paints his fingernails and wishes somebody would commit suicide," agreed Lottie Shady. "Unless, of course, he's in the undertakin' business. And that man ain't."

"I don't know," mused Leo Diggs. "I think he might be one of them California flesh-burners you was just tellin' me about . . ."

The warm Texas sun combined with his innate fear of Arabella du Noir was sending beads of perspiration through Ralph Painter's pancake make-up. "Oh, now you're going to tell me I've offended the rednecks!" Ralph Painter complained.

"Let's don't set limits on your offensiveness, Ralph," Arabella retorted. "You are simply offensive. Period. End of subject."

"What if they offend *me*?" Ralph whined. "Everybody thinks it's fine to offend me!"

"I'll put them on my payroll. And stop whining."

"Bella!" Ralph protested.

"I loathe familiarity," Arabella warned. "*Don't* call me Bella."

"All right, Arabella," Ralph whimpered.

"And *don't* call me Arabella."

"Then what *am* I going to call you?" Ralph pouted. He knew what he wanted to call her, but looking at her, Ralph thought the flames from her blazing smile could burn a hole right through him.

"You lied to me about Mary Jane Shady," Arabella du Noir said softly. "You knew how old she was from the beginning."

"So what?" Ralph asked incredulously. "What do you want from me? I'm an *agent. You* got what you wanted from her. *I* got what I wanted from her. She got what she wanted from *both of us*. We all got what we wanted. If her looks had held up for a couple of more years, if she'd taken care of herself for the past few years, you'd be renewing her contract instead of dropping her. What difference does it make? I'll get you another girl. A twelve-year-old. I'll even find you a fucking virgin! What's the matter with you? It's show biz. I haven't committed a crime. Nothing *unusual* is happening. So she's getting dumped today. She's lucky. She had a few good years and that's all any woman's got. *She's lucky she got paid for any of it.* Sooner or later it's always over. If she wanted a steady job, she should have been an anthropologist. The public doesn't want wrinkles. The public doesn't buy wrinkles. It's not my fault. I am a wrinkleless supplier of carefree faces, bouyant smiles and hope-filled eyes. If I were in the wrinkle business I'd be running a dry cleaners. If I could promote 'sad' I'd have represented Faye Dunaway and Tennessee Williams. Listen, I'm a happy shallow guy. I wear a pink suit and hang a telephone around my waist so clients won't forget me. I'm repulsive on purpose. But it works. Doesn't it?" He grinned amiably at Arabella du Noir. "Want to see these headshots?"

She stared at the agent, disgusted. But more than that, she was disturbed. Something else was bothering her badly, something she couldn't really specify. Every word Ralph Painter had said was true. It was a business of youth and perfection and always had been. So why was she feeling so rotten about firing Mary Jane Shady? She had fired hundreds of people without blinking an eye.

"Hey! Hey! Hey! What-do-you-say!" José cried, hopping out of the side of the truck in his very wrinkled tuxedo. "Look who's here! Hollywood! New York! East Coast! West Coast! Big Apple!" He began running in circles around the limousine. "Tinseltown! Man! What a trip! I'm José Garcia, but you can call me James and you can call me Jimmy, but just call me your driver-chauffeur-tour guide who's been employed by Mrs. Why-vonne Henderson to see that you all get all around Uncertain, Texas in this finely designed purple-painted Chrysler-Cadillac-Chevy-engined cow-seated special-stretch from Midland's number one most outstanding dune-buggy-helicopter creator." Turning, he circled the car from the opposite direction. "We get about one-half miles to the gallon and can go two hundred and seventy-five miles an hour if the wind blows right—"

"Is the camera *on*?" Arabella shouted at Gary. "Turn the goddamned fucking camera *on*!"

"Have some faith, Belle," Gary said. "It's never been off."

"Uh-oh," Leo said, observing José, as he dropped to the ground and began a series of rigorous push-ups. "He's goin' to really mess up that monkey suit."

"Lock up the planes," the East coast pilots said to the West coast pilots.

"He don't need a *plane,*" Lottie remarked. "Wherever he's goin', he'll get there by *hisself.*"

"—so everybody climb in and *let's go-o-o-o*!" José hollered, jumping to his feet and breaking into a wild Spanish dance.

"He's *cute,*" Ralph whispered to Arabella du Noir. "LET'S GO!" he shouted to José.

"Come on, Ralph," said Arabella du Noir. "*Now.*"

"*Why*?" asked Ralph Painter. "We're stuck here. I want to have some fun!"

"Have I told you in the last five seconds that you make me want to puke?" Arabella asked wearily.

"Not in the last five *seconds,*" Ralph grinned.

"Ralph—" Arabella warned.

"Oh, lighten up!" Ralph Painter said, giggling uncontrollably at his own joke. "No pun intended! No pun intended!"

Thoroughly disgusted, Arabella du Noir turned on her heels to walk away.

Nigger cunt! Ralph Painter thought to himself. *Black poison pussy nigger*!

Arabella du Noir turned around. "I can read minds, Ralph."

The agent paled with paranoia. "H-h-h-how" he stammered.

"Voodoo," she told him. "I inherited it instead of sickle-cell anemia. I hate to be frivolous with my talents, Ralph," she said. "But you have just unloaded one account! *Me*!"

Ralph Painter was afraid he was going to pee right through his new pink shorts. "*Why*?" he asked, momentarily shaken.

"Because I feel *mean,*" Arabella replied. "And because I hate men in pink suits. And because I hate people who ask *why* when they know *why*!"

"I didn't mean that 'why'," Ralph apologized quickly. " '*Why*' is a part of my business language. It's an occupational hazard. I can't help it. I may not be able to overcome it in one day! Give me a break!"

"You better hope I don't," she retorted as she walked away.

Regaining his unrelenting work-induced instincts, he hurried after her. "Oh, you don't mean it!" Ralph Painter insisted. "You *need* me,

Madame du Noir! I have the best client list on either coast and you know it! I'm a necessary evil, Countess, dear! Flesh Peddler Extraordinaire is written all over your card, too, you know!"

Arabella du Noir stared at the agent coldly. "I need *nothing* from you," she told Ralph Painter. "Mary Jane Shady is the only client you have ever had on *any* list worth hiring for *anything*. You were lucky to have her. And she deserved far better than *you*!" Irately, Arabella threw herself into the back of Yvonne Henderson's limousine.

The agent yanked his pink telephone off of his waist. "What's the number in that limousine?" Ralph Painter called out to Leo Diggs.

"Drive!" Arabella told Leo. "Please, just drive!"

"I'll catch you!" Ralph hollered after them, as Leo drove Arabella away. "I've got what you need! And you'll take me to lunch, too!"

What the hell do I care anyway? Arabella thought irritably. The huge clear sky loomed overhead, a pricking reminder, again, of one very young, very awkward, very tall skinny girl years ago, back in North Carolina, leaving home. Going off alone. Armed with one bus ticket, fifty dollars, a lot of faith, total naïveté and grandiose intentions. But knowing with all her heart there was more to the world than that sky. Arabella du Noir felt tears come into her eyes. *Oh, no . . .* she thought anxiously. *Really! How stupidly sentimental*! She reached in her handbag for a handkerchief.

"Excuse me," Arabella said to Leo Diggs. "Could you put the top up on this thing?"

She could not bear to look at the sky.

Lottie led the procession in her and Leo's new eighteen-wheeler, carrying all the equipment, as well as Sylvie Notions, who'd never ridden in the front of a big truck before.

The pilots, crew members and Ralph Painter rode in the school bus, driven by one of the East coast pilots. They left the West coast co-pilot with José, who was running up and down the landing strip as if he were in preparation for Olympic competition. Category: Human Flight.

Leo Diggs brought the top up on Yvonne's convertible and slid down the window divider so he could talk to Arabella du Noir as he drove her to the school.

"Now," said Arabella, attempting to clear her mind as she settled into the backseat. "Tell me. How did you and Lottie meet?"

"Oh," grinned Leo Diggs. "That was a good one . . . ."

CHAPTER FIFTY-NINE

FUN! snapped Mary Jane harshly. *I make YOU stop having FUN? You have wrecked my life for twenty years and now you're going to tell yourself I don't let you have FUN? You are demented, you know it! DEMENTED!*

I'm a nervous wreck, a nervous wreck, a wreck, a wreck, a nervous wreck! babbled Topsy Dingo Wild Dog. *I can't smile another minute! I can't smile another minute!*

And I can't take another minute of a day with YOU in it, Mary Jane Shady retorted. *You LIKE being in a state of delirium, that's your problem! You are a genuine mental case, pure and simple! You ought to be locked up! And I would certainly love to locate the key! You LIKE being crazy, you LIKE all this insanity. If you didn't LIKE it, you wouldn't do it. You'd shut up, disappear, go away. . .*

You sound just like me, Topsy said. *You sound just exactly like me!*

I AM you, idiot! I am YOU too! Only I don't LIKE it! I HATE it! But YOU love it! Otherwise you would stop. Quit. Lay off. Leave me alone. Go away. Please . . . please . . . please . . .

I can't stop, I can't stop, I can't stop. I'm scared. Aren't you scared? Don't you feel tall? Don't you feel old? Don't you feel cold? Don't you feel tall? Don't you feel old?

. . . oh, yes-s-s . . . feel sorry for yourself . . .

You are so cold! YOU ARE COLD, COLD, COLD!

. . . you LOVE that . . . that feels so-o-o good . . .

FUCK YOU, MARY JANE. FUCK YOU.

. . . uh-huh. Right. Fuck ME. Fuck YOU. Fuck IT. Isn't that next? ''Oh, fuck it? To hell with everything? FUCK IT That's good. That'll work . . . Go on . . . I KNOW WHAT YOU WANT!

They're going to fire you! They're going to fire you! You're getting fired! You're getting fired! They're going to fire you! They going to fire you!

. . . I'll get another job . . .

Where?

. . . I've always worked. I'll get a better job . . .

How?

. . . I'll . . .

Where? Where? How? How? Who's going to hire YOU? Who's going to want YOU? Where are you going to find one? How are you going to get one? You'll never work again. You'll never work again. You'll never work. You won't work. It won't work.

I'LL GET ONE! screamed Mary Jane. *I'LL GET ONE! I'LL GET ONE! TRUST ME!*

TRUST YOU?! shrieked Topsy Dingo Wild Dog. *That's a good one! TRUST YOU? Why should I trust YOU? I mean, listen, think about it! You got tattooed, too!*

That is YOUR tattoo, stated Mary Jane Shady. *That tattoo is YOUR tattoo. YOU'RE responsible for that tattoo.*

You said we were the same! You said you-are-me-and-I-am-you! That makes it YOUR tattoo, too! Anyway, I don't remember! I DON'T REMEMBER GETTING THAT TATTOO!

That is exactly my point, if you'll SHUT UP and listen! shouted Mary Jane Shady. *If you start DRINKING you could end up with legfuls and armfuls and buttfuls and breastfuls and facefuls of blood-red-jagged-shattered-heartbroken tattoos!*

I don't think I'd do THAT . . . protested Topsy.

YOU FUCKED A DOG ONCE! wailed Mary Jane Shady. *IT COULD HAVE BEEN A GORILLA! IF YOU START DRINKING, YOU MIGHT FUCK A WHOLE ZOO!*

CHAPTER SIXTY

ALICE CATHERINE and Bo Ivanhoe were pulling up in Catsy's black, Silver Cloud Rolls Royce convertible just as Leo Diggs' truck and the Uncertain School Bus double-parked as close to the back doors of the gymnasium as they could get.

"That must be Hollywood," Catsy said to Bo, who had refused to drive. "Well, shit. We're too early to make a good appearance. Let's drive over to Wink and look at that sink hole or somethin'. I don't want to *mingle* in the crowd!"

Catsy was dressed in a short, tight, white suede sheath which stopped five inches above her knees. Rivers of fringe fell from the heavily padded shoulders to her wrists. The old ex-Hopi Indian, who had moved to Notrees from Arizona, had finger-painted every design of every Hopi Indian doll he could remember all over the dress and sewn black turkey feathers all around the V neckline when he wasn't changing tires. Some of the smudges remained on the dress, but Catsy thought they were part of the design.

Catsy Ivanhoe's belt was her most prized possession. It had been in Bo's family for years, and was exquisitely designed silver, inlaid with turquoise the size of silver dollars. Indeed, the links were silver dollars, and the most rare in existence; circa 1804. Bearing the bust of Miss Liberty on one side and the Heraldic spread Eagle on the other, there were perhaps only a dozen of these coins in the world. Worth two hundred thousand dollars each, Catsy was wearing seven of them. Four Liberties and three Eagles was the way she had elected to wear the links today. When Bo's grandfather had worn the belt, he had turned all the Eagles on the outside and all the Liberties on the inside.

Maud Frizon, who made all of Catsy's custom-ordered boots, had created the cobra-skinned, jade green pair she wore today. Beginning at the ankle and running all the way up the leg was the Ivanhoe's brand symbol, a simple "I." The stem of the "I" was implanted with turquoise to match the belt, while the top and bottom of the "I" were sprinkled intermittently with lapis and turquoise.

From Catsy's earlobes hung the two live baby rattlesnakes, their tongues pierced that morning to fit through rings for Catsy's ears. The rings themselves were loops of turquoise, opals and lapis. Around Catsy's neck was a simple choker, a gold coiled cobra.

She wore her waist-length jet black hair plaited in three long pigtails down her back. Bouquets of orchids, magnolias and camellias, which she grew and cut from her hothouse at the ranch, were intertwined with three waist-length ribbons made of threads of eighteen-carat gold.

She had overdressed and she knew it.

"Bo," thirty-seven-year-old Catsy Ivanhoe had smiled ambitiously. "I been thinkin' . . . "

Bo knew right away there was about to be trouble. *Expensive* trouble.

"If Mary Jane Shady can be a movie star, then why cain't *I*?"

He stared at her evenly. "You're already the highest paid actress in the world, Catsy. I been financin' your act for years, honey."

"All I need is to be discovered!" Catsy whined. "I already got me a Rolls Royce car and all the right clothes and my very own hairdresser! I can act as good as Mary Jane Shady can!"

"You sure can," Bo nodded, adding to himself, *'Cause you sure fooled the hell out of me . . .*

"Of course," she added sweetly. "I'll need a part . . . ."

Bo Ivanhoe hit the roof. "And I guess you'll expect me to end up financin' some blood-suckin' Hollywood movie!"

"Half of your money's mine, Bo!" Catsy reminded him. "Half of everything you own is mine, mine, mine!"

"Well, you're not goin' into movie-makin'. Not with your money. And not with mine," Bo told her. "You got almost as much talent as Pia Zadora. Let's don't advertise it." He had refused to talk about her silly scheme and had refused to go to any local Pep Rally. "If you're so bored, then try cleanin' house! Try cookin' a meal! Try somethin' other than shoppin', shoppin', shoppin' and travelin', travelin', travelin'! You been around the world three different times in the past three months. If you didn't interduce yourself, I wouldn't even know you!"

"Oh, you don't like me anyway," Catsy had complained. "You're glad when I'm gone and you know it."

This he couldn't deny.

Bo Ivanhoe was sick and tired of Catsy. He'd been sick and tired of her for years. He hated the way she dressed, no matter what she had on. He hated the way her mind worked, always scheming and undercutting. He loathed her nasal twang. The only thing he liked about her was that he didn't have to sleep with her. He had only slept with her once—the night of their honeymoon. She hadn't said a word. She hadn't closed her eyes. She had just laid there, her skin as cold as a snake's. As cold as her eyes. When he'd finished, she'd said, "Is that it?" She hadn't even taken off her clothes.

He had given her the belt as an engagement gift. He had added her name to half of everything that was his as a wedding present. And she hadn't even taken her clothes off. She had never even shut her eyes. "Is that *it*?" she had said. Cold as a snake. Bo Ivanhoe had never mentioned that night, ever. Not even once. Not to Catsy, not to anyone. His disappointment in being so self-deluded, in being so *duped*, had been staggering.

He had never been shopping with her. He had never gone around the world with her. He didn't even go into Uncertain with her. The only place Bo Ivanhoe went with Catsy was to the bank, to the attorneys and to the business manager's over in Midland. He certainly did not intend to go to a Pep Rally with her. And he wasn't about to finance a film career.

But that morning when Catsy had gone to the Ex-Hopi Indian's to pick up her dress, Bo had come home and found seventeen-year-old

Maria Rodriquez, the upstairs maid's daughter, in tears. Ordinarily, she would have been in school, but she was running for Homecoming Queen and all the nominees had been given the day off. Maria was crying because her mother couldn't afford to buy her a thing to wear to the Pep Rally. Bo had taken the young woman up to Catsy's wing of the house, where Maria was trying on Catsy's clothes when Catsy walked through the door. Catsy didn't bat an eye. She walked right past Maria and Bo and hung up her new dress as if nothing had ever happened. Then she turned to Bo, ignoring Maria. "Get this Mexskin out of my closet this minute, Bo Ivanhoe! I'll have to get it fumigated! And give her ever garment you laid her skin next to!"

"Hold on, Miz Ivanhoe," protested Maria. "You're makin' a mistake—"

"Get that spic cunt out of my wing and off my ranch!" Catsy hissed. "Go back south of the border, *puta*!" Catsy spat.

"Hey, fuck you, too, lady," shrugged Maria Rodriquez. "I came up here by invitation, you know."

When Bo Ivanhoe took Maria home, he sent with her a three hundred thousand dollar wardrobe, the promise of a trip to Mexico City, and four years of college tuition guaranteed to be paid to the institution of her choice. It was the only way he knew how to begin to apologize.

"Thanks for the stuff, Mr. Ivanhoe!" Maria had told Bo. "I don't care if I win or not! I'm goin' to college with all my new clothes!"

If Maria Rodriquez had not been running for Homecoming Queen, nothing new would have happened. But Catsy used this to her advantage. "If you don't get dressed up and come with me and show up for Hollywood and finance my movie *this minute,* I will tell ever person in that Pep Rally crowd that you screwed that Mexskin nominee *this mornin'* right on my closet floor! Nobody likes a child molester, Bo Ivanhoe! She's underage and they'll hang you up by your toenails!"

"You don't need me at any Pep Rally," Bo said. "Go by yourself."

"*No,*" Catsy insisted stubbornly. "*You are goin'! I want you to go*!"

He knew no one would believe he was a child molester. But Maria Rodriquez was the first Mexican to ever be nominated for Homecoming Queen in the history of Uncertain, Texas. He didn't want her triumph or participation in the ceremony to be marred by Catsy's vindictiveness. And he knew his wife. She had no limits.

So there he sat in her black Rolls Royce, dressed in a plain white silk shirt, white silk pants, and white ostrich boots. On top of his head was his great-great-grandfather's headdress, which he'd never had on in his life. An assemblage of white ostrich feathers paraded all the way down to his boots. Catsy had added two hundred and fifty perfectly cut and matching pear-shaped one-carat diamonds across the top of the band. She'd stuck his arms through a white vest made of the finest chinchilla, and around his neck tied a bow tie solidly dotted with diamonds. White suede chaps over silk pants were snapped together with diamonds matching the headdress and bow tie.

He knew why Catsy had wanted him to go with her: It was the ultimate humiliation. He had never felt sillier in his life.

Catsy's eyes glistened, hard and cold. "I don't care who you fuck, *Chief.* Just don't do it in my *closet* next to my *clothes*."

Bo Ivanhoe looked at the heirloom hanging around his wife's waist. He wanted to choke her with it. *I'll choke her with the Eagle side first,* he thought. *Then I'll finish her up with the Liberties* . . . .

"Don't move too fast, Bo," Catsy hissed. "I don't want anybody to miss seein' you in your new clothes!"

CHAPTER SIXTY-ONE

"HEY!" Someone was snapping fingers in front of her face.

She froze when she saw the badge. Paralyzed, she gazed at the holster. It had seemed like an eternity. It had happened so quickly. She had expected this for two days. She had expected it forever. And now here it was.

"C'mere," demanded the officer.

All six feet of a big boned woman, her hands folded across her mighty bosoms, stood towering in front of her. The heels of her Larry Mahan boots bit the concrete floor impatiently. The woman was wearing khaki pants and a shirt and a big badge. One impressive revolver was strapped around her waist.

"Are you asleep or what?" asked the officer. "You heard me. C'mere."

"Okay," she murmured, grateful to be taken away. Grateful that at last she was being arrested. Grateful that it was happening now. Before the ceremony. Over.

She rose in one advancing movement, her spine straight and proud.

"I knew you was trouble from the time you took the role of Mary away from me in the Christmas pageant at church—"

"What?" she asked puzzled, looking at the officer for the first time. "Excuse me?"

"You're not gettin' anything else of mine, neither!" the woman warned. "I mean it!"

She peered at the face before her. Tall. Familiar. Aggressive. "Christmas Pageant?" she mumbled. "Church? . . ."

"Cute," frowned the woman. "You was always real, real, real, real *cute.* Like that time you painted my angel wings. I guess you thought *that* was cute."

"Wings?" repeated Mary Jane Shady.

Wings? echoed Topsy Dingo Wild Dog.

"First you took the part of Mary in the Christmas Pageant of 1956. We was ten years old. You remember *that.*"

I don't remember. . . thought bewildered Topsy Dingo Wild Dog.

"I don't remember. . ." confessed baffled Mary Jane Shady.

"How quick and fast we forget, Sweet Miss Innocent. If I remember, you remember. You remember Mary the Virgin in the Christmas Pageant of 1956. You knew how bad I wanted it, too. You remember my angel wings. And you cain't possibly have forgotten that cat."

"Sit down, Darnelle," said Scoot Widders. "I cain't see through you, honey."

DARNELLE!

Recognition swept over her. *Darnelle*! It was former cheerleader and State Champion volleyball player, Darnelle "Spider" Webb, daughter of the minister of the Uncertain Methodist Church and the tallest girl in the senior class. They'd been twirlers together before the "virginal examination" had been imposed on the student body.

"Spider!" gasped Mary Jane Shady. Of course it was Spider. Who else would show up dressed like that? "God, am I glad to see you!" Spider had always loved a good joke.

"We'll see about that," stated Darnelle "Spider" Webb.

She looked at Spider's badge and entered into the drama with frenzied spirit. "You're arresting me for playing a virgin, right?" Topsy heard Mary Jane tease. "Okay, Spider. Can we do this quietly?"

"I don't give a shit how we do it," Darnelle "Spider" Webb retorted. "But you're not takin' away any goddamned cat."

"She's takin' it back to Hollywood, California with her!" Yvonne Henderson informed Scoot, Judy Jones and Sammy.

"Like hell and over my dead body!" The woman stopped tapping her foot and spread her legs apart, rocking back and forth ominously.

Topsy's head did a slow turn. *I think Spider's serious . . .*

She can't be serious, thought Mary Jane Shady. *Spider was never serious . . . .*

Then this must be a new Spider, Topsy Dingo Wild Dog said, *because she's serious about that cat . . . .*

"Spider!" cried Yvonne Henderson. "Are you talking about the Gladys Turner cat?"

"Move it to the right, Spider," Sammy Widders told the woman. "Unless you want to sit down and have a beer."

"You know the cat I'm referrin' to," Spider smirked. "You know the very exact cat."

"She married Orville, Jr.," Yvonne told Mary Jane. "That's why she's upset about that cat—"

"I should have been playin' Mary," Spider growled, ignoring Yvonne, as well as Sammy's offer and request.

"Is she really mad about this?" Mary Jane Shady asked, stunned.

"You can talk to me," said Spider Webb Turner. "I'm here. I can hear you. And I'm mad as hell, I can assure you!"

Has she been mad at me for twenty years? Topsy wondered. *How can you stay mad at someone for twenty stupid years*?

"You're too tall to play a virgin," Judy Jones stated.

"Bullshit!" the patrolwoman hollered. "Virgins can be any size!"

"I'll drink to that," Sammy said, crushing his beer can flat with one hand.

I cannot believe she is still thinking about THAT, *thought Mary Jane Shady. My whole life is falling apart and she's wrapped up in virgins and wings, Christmas pageants and cats*!

Sammy continued. "Anyway, you were a damned good Joseph and I ought to be pissed 'cause you beat me out of that. I could have had a career, too, Spider. Ask Judy. I got *talent*. Right, M.J.? Sit down. Spider. Have a few beers. You don't need no cat."

When am I getting arrested? thought Topsy Dingo Wild Dog. *Somebody put me away.* PLEASE! *If I see it again, I'll strangle that fucking cat*!

I did *not* play Joseph. I was a fuckin' wiseman and you know it. I carried myrrh, you carried frankincense and—"

"I carried gold," Sammy said, reaching for another Coors. "Lester Evans carried the frankincense and ole Delmer Dean carried the myrrh. You played Joseph."

"You are so full of shit you cain't remember the fuckin' Christmas Pageant of 1956, Sammy Widders!" Spider retorted.

The Christmas Pageant? THE CHRISTMAS PAGEANT? Now they're back to the fucking Christmas Pageant of nineteen-fucking-fifty-six? What about NOW? What about TODAY? What about THIS MINUTE? WHAT ABOUT ME? What happened to Friday the Thirteenth, nineteen hundred eight-five? wondered Topsy Dingo Wild Dog irritably.

"You played Joseph. I remember that. Who could forget it?" Sammy took a swig. "Have a beer, Spider. You were great."

Count your blessings, warned Mary Jane Shady. *They're not talking about dogs. They're into wisemen and cats . . .*

"I hope you burn up in hell right this very minute for playin' Mary," Spider told Mary Jane.

Competition, competition, competition, thought Mary Jane, exhausted.

"You were a terrible, horrible virgin," Spider went on.

I was a terrible, horrible virgin, agreed Topsy Dingo Wild Dog.

"That's because she didn't have any practice!" Sammy Widders laughed. He turned to Spider. "But you were a good Joseph," Sammy said.

I didn't like being a virgin . . . Mary Jane thought forlornly.

"You said I was a *great* Joseph," Spider countered.

"Did I say that?" Sammy asked. "I thought I said you would have been a great *virgin.*"

"I would have been if I'd a-had the opportunity," Spider went on.

"I never even wanted to play Mary," protested Mary Jane Shady.

"That's what they all say!" Sammy gauffawed.

"—and the only reason I was not a angel at the time was because Bubba Brown was supposed to be Joseph and as a reward his daddy let him drive to church and when Bubba's veil slid over his eyes, that was when he sent parts of Penny-lope Higginbothum all over the Uncertain Assembly of God—"

Angels, virgins, wings, cats, angels, virgins, wings, cats . . .

"Hair went north, eyeballs south, arms east and legs west," Scoot commented.

Hair yanked . . . eyeballs jerked . . . legs pulled . . . arms twisted . . .

"She died on Easter and it was three years later," Yvonne said. "Bubba had the chicken pox is why he wasn't there."

"You remember the durndest things, Why-vonne," Scoot frowned.

"I know," Yvonne sighed.

Nobody cares how many Peanut Butter eaters you've charmed . . .

STOP THINKING, Mary Jane warned.

They sure don't care how many Broadway stars are in love with you either!

"Better stop thinking . . ." Mary Jane whispered.

"Them wings was mine!" Spider was tapping her boot again. Her fingers shot out at Topsy.

Wings, wings, wings . . . we're back on the wings . . .

"I'm sorry, I'm sorry, I'm sorry," Mary Jane Shady apologized.

"Wait! Wait! Wait!" Judy Jones cut in. "Look at this with *optimism,* Darnelle! You must be the *only* person in your entire church who didn't have to wear the wings at one time or another," Judy Jones beamed encouragingly. "You got to be *different.* You never had to play an angel and sing 'hallelujah, hallelujah' over and over, plus you would have had to try to look *small,* which would have placed you right in the failure category. Everyone would have said, 'Isn't Darnelle a *big* angel?' Or 'Isn't Darnelle a *huge* angel?' Or 'Isn't Darnelle an *enormous* angel!' " Two black chicken feathers from Judy's boa attached themselves to her lower lip. Matter-of-factly, she disengaged them, leaving two streaks in her Revlon lipstick. She slapped the loose feathers back on the boa as if she expected them to stay there. "They might have even said, 'Darnelle makes a *terrible* angel,' " Judy continued. "And you would have, too, because you are simply too overstated in height to be a believable angel!"

Spider glared at Judy Jones. "You're not making me feel any better."

You're making me crazy! screamed Topsy Dingo Wild Dog.

You're making me insane! bellowed Mary Jane Shady.

"Judy?" Scoot asked. "Did you *graduate*?"

"We are on my professional ground here," Judy Jones informed Scoot. "I know what I'm doing."

No, you don't! You don't know what you're doing!

"Well, *she* doesn't," Spider stated, pointing at Mary Jane.

"Darnelle, honey, fold yourself up somewhere," Scoot said. "You're blockin' out six cheerleaders standin' where you are."

"You're not takin' that cat out of Uncertain, Texas," Spider told Mary Jane without budging an inch. "Got that? Got *that*?"

Tell her. . . urged Topsy.

"Listen, Spider—" began Mary Jane Shady.

"Why?" asked Yvonne. "Why would you deprive that cat of a chance to ride in a plane all the way to Hollywood and live with the stars?"

Speak up! begged Topsy.

"It's not—" started Mary Jane.

"That cat don't need to ride in a plane to Hollywood or anyplace else and everybody knows movie stars are reckless," Spider shot back. "That cat knows more good people right here in Uncertain, Texas than it will ever meet in Hollywood, California. It don't know a soul out there and it's not goin' to go!"

Tell her, urged Topsy Dingo Wild Dog. *Tell her, tell her, tell her she's right . . . she gets the cat . . . it's not going to go . . .*

"I don't want—" tried Mary Jane.

"You're just holdin' this against Mary Jane because she played Mary and you didn't," Yvonne said. "You shouldn't deprive the cat because your daddy made you play Joseph, Darnelle."

"Ever-body told you you was a real good Joseph, too," Scoot Widders offered. "Now move, hon. I come here to see my Siamese twin grandbabies get crowned and your six-shooters are just about where their heads should be if they was to appear. And you *are* too tall for a angel."

Too tall, thought Topsy.

Too short, thought Mary Jane.

Too thin . . .

Too fat . . .

Too TWO . . .

"I bought that cat as therapy for my mother-in-law and you cain't tell me she don't need some!" Spider persisted.

"What kind of therapy?" Scoot, Yvonne, Mary Jane Shady and Topsy Dingo Wild Dog all asked at the very same time.

"To take her mind off them little dishes she's got collected all over the place. That and herself and runnin' the fifth grade and this town is all she ever thinks about," Spider stated.

"*All you think about is yourself* . . . "

"Well, she loves them little dishes," Scoot told Spider. "She's half scared to death that kitty is goin' to break one of 'em and if it does we'll never hear the end of it. We'll all need therapy. What kind of therapy is *that*?"

"*All you ever care about is yourself. . .* "

"She's got to train it, see," Spider told Scoot. "That's what's goin' to take her mind off them dishes and the fifth grade and this town."

"*Every question you ask begs for an answer that directly relates to YOU. YOUR SELF. . .* "

"It ain't goin' to work, Darnelle," Scoot sighed. "Once one dish is broke, she's goin' to take it right out on the rest of us. You don't have no kids in the fifth grade, but them twins could get married after they get the Homecomin' crown, and then *they'd* have kids who'd end up in Gladys' fifth grade and a few years from now all this therapy is goin' to just destroy my whole family. Send the cat to Hollywood. It cain't hurt nothin' out there."

"That cat is stayin' here in Uncertain, Texas! It can break dishes it is awready used to and not somethin' that belongs to some stranger it's never seen before a day in its life!" Spider Webb screamed.

You're not trying hard enough! Topsy warned. *You're not trying! You're not trying!*

"Spider—" She made one last effort.

"Oh, shut up!"

"*You're fucking rude! That's your problem*!"

"You're screaming," whispered Mary Jane Shady. "Can you *please* listen to me quietly?" she pleaded.

"You are selfish, selfish, selfish!" accused the officer.

I am selfish, selfish, selfish!. . . despaired Topsy Dingo Wild Dog.

"And I don't give a shit what you're tryin' to say! You're not takin' my cat away!"

I am dying, dying, dying . . . moaned Mary Jane Shady. *This is it. NO EXIT. . . I am being exhausted to death by a set of old wings, the part of a virgin and a tiny, silly, little cat . . .*

"If you'll shut up, Spider," said Yvonne Henderson, "I got some new wings I can let you have."

Spider looked at Yvonne with interest.

Mary Jane Shady looked at her with hope.

"And anyway," continued Yvonne. "If I can forget about *her and Bobby,* you can forget about that goddamned cat!"

You are so stupid! Topsy Dingo Wild Dog screamed to Mary Jane Shady. *Naïve, infantile retard! Slug-stupid no-brain! Did you really think this was about Christmas pageants and sprayed gold wings and*

Gladys Turner's cat? It's about YOU *and* BOBBY HENDERSON *and that* DOG, IDIOT!

I knew it . . . whispered Mary Jane Shady, beaten. *I knew it wasn't about that cat . . .*

CHAPTER SIXTY-TWO

ARABELLA DU NOIR had totally drifted into a daze in the back seat of the limousine, as she listened to Leo reminisce about his first encounter with his new wife. She hadn't noticed when they'd stopped by Scoot Widders' house. She didn't even remember Leo getting out of the car and hitching a float to the back of the limousine. She was imagining herself in Lottie's place—cushioned in a navy blue coffin at midnight . . . swinging through the air on top of a limousine in broad daylight . . . .*Seduced.* She was imagining being seduced. It beat the hell out of thinking about Mary Jane Shady. It beat the hell out of thinking.

"I hadn't never actually did it in a casket before," Leo said, as he got back into the car. "And it was Lottie's first time and all, too, and what with her sister-in-law maybe appearin' any minute, she could have just got cold feet, but that sister went somewhere and when she did, Lottie Shady lost ever inhibition she'd ever had in her whole entire life, and I never knew I had any at all, but I guess I did, 'cause to tell you the truth, I *did* think twice before I hopped in that coffin—I mean I didn't want her to hurt herself—but that's where we fell in love!"

"You just fell into it . . ." Arabella encouraged.

"Well, no, now, we had a few drinks, you know, to get us started and all. A few drinks never hurts. And then I usually keep a few little uppers and a few little downers handy and maybe a popper or two."

"What?" asked Arabella, shocked. "You *medicated* her?"

"Just some nervous-wreck medicine," Leo explained easily. "A little poundin'-heart medicine." He shrugged. "I thought she might be scared. She's older than she looks, you know."

"What are you saying?" Arabella sat up abruptly. "Are you saying you doped and drugged her?"

"I'm sayin' I took care of her," Leo clarified. "See, what women like is to be taken care of," he explained. "And a seventy-five-year-old virgin is a most particular thing. Even with a regular type gal, most men just leap in, take what they want, and leave the woman to adjust as best she can, see." He looked back at Arabella. "Tell me if this inn't your experience."

"No, it wasn't." Arabella replied. "My husband was very considerate. Very."

"I bet he was a foreigner, then," Leo offered.

Arabella nodded. "French."

"I knew it!" Leo grinned. "I got myself half my technique from watchin' them little Marshmellow Master-ninny movies. Now he's I-talian, but them Frenchies is the same. Take Wives Montand, for instance—the King of France." He shrugged. "See what I mean? Everbody appreciates a thoughtful guy. Well, I travel in a different circle, but I apply what I learn at them fine arts foreign movie houses up in Dallas to ever purty woman I meet. Wives and Master-ninny take out the champagne, get out the fish eggs—but I'm in my truck—I don't always have a fresh supply. I got to be ready another kind of a way, see. So say a little gal's got a headache or a case of gnawin' nerves—and at first they always do. Why wouldn't they? They been workin' all day, most of 'em, and some of 'em all night too. Been puttin' up with onnery men, sick kids, loathsome customers. So what I do is make sure I got somethin' handy to give 'em. I found out long ago, just give 'em *one* to get 'em started—"

"One *what*?" asked Arabella, who had been accustomed to roses, champagne, diamond bracelets. Houses.

"One upper. One downer. One popper. Dependin' on their personality and what kind of life they're engaged in at the moment and what kind of a temper that life has put them into. Then what I do is talk to 'em a little. And then I shut up and listen a *lot*. That gets 'em to *relax*. Most people, nobody has *listened* to since the day they was born. Nobody knows what colors they like, or how they feel around sundown or what their favorite tune or TV show is, even. I make it my job to find out. Then I make sure they're in a *setting* that's real seductive in a *unusual* kind of a way. That casket is a prime example. That was good," Leo grinned. "That was *real* good. I sort of lucked out on that casket. For some reason, people just get a kick out of foolin' around where they *work*. Now they're a little high, they've talked a bit, they're gettin' relaxed, you know. And *then* I switch to vitamins. I substitute. Understand? And then guess what? It's shake, rock, rattle and roll!"

Arabella shook her head to clear her thoughts. "You mean Lottie thinks she's getting high on pills and she's just taking *vitamins*?" Arabella asked, astounded.

"Lady," Leo Diggs laughed. "Lottie Shady ain't had nothin' but me and vitamins since the night we met! And she's havin' the time of her life, too! Mrs. Leo Diggs don't know it, but what with all them vitamins, and all my lovin' she's the healthiest woman alive!"

"Placebo!" gasped Arabella du Noir.

"Got some in the glove compartment," grinned Leo Diggs.

Arabella du Noir lay back in the limousine and laughed until she could not stop. "That is the most loving, charming story I have ever heard in my life!"

"I love a wild and happy woman," Leo nodded. "And Lottie Shady is the *wildest,* happiest woman I ever did meet! I knew I had to marry her right fast! I been on cafe counters, bingo tables, and bowlin' alleys, in grocery store aisles, a fur storage locker and of course, all over the rodeo! But I ain't *never* been in a casket! I figger a woman who *starts* with me in a casket, just has no limits of places to go!"

Arabella du Noir had not thought about love in a long, long time. But coming face to face with the sheer affection Leo had for Lottie, and she for him, it was impossible for her not to think of her own late husband, Roland du Noir. His world had been as different from Leo Diggs' as was imaginable. But aside from their differences in style, the two men had one thing in common: *They loved women.*

In that moment, Arabella du Noir missed Roland du Noir more than she ever had before. Arabella suddenly felt very, very sad. And lonely. The quietness of the empty streets and the brightness of the vast sky were unsettling, overwhelming.

What am I doing in the middle of the West Texas desert? she wondered. *Alone*?

Arabella du Noir stared at the banner draped above the doors as they approached the schoolhouse.

WELCOME HOME, MARY JANE SHADY, OUR OWN UNCERTAIN STAR.

Arabella stared at the sign, troubled. *Oh, my God, I've got to fire her...* Guilt flooded through her. *Will you stop it? Quit, please. Enough. It's your job. You're doing your job. You just came to do a job. Pull yourself together. You've been all over the world,* she told herself. *You've seen everything. You've done everything. You've had everything. And this is nothing new . . . I'm the lucky, lucky, lucky Countess du Noir. Here to intimidate, fire and humiliate . . . Conscienceless. Unfeeling. Insensitive. Effective. Masterful, Arabella . . . Powerful. Countess . . . Lucky Mary Jane Shady! She gets to be fired by me!*

She stared at the sign. *Our Own Uncertain Star . . .* She missed her husband. She hated the advertising agency. She missed her mother. She ached for Mary Jane Shady. *What in the hell is the matter with me*? She just could not pull herself together. *I shouldn't have come here,* Arabella thought, depressed, but no longer surprised. *I just shouldn't have come . . .*

Leo was opening the back door.

Arabella, got out. Elegantly.

Leo admired her cool refined grace.

From across the street, Catsy Ivanhoe said to Bo, "Look. A *nigger* gettin' out of Why-vonne Henderson's car. When poor people like Why-vonne get rich they think they can do just anything in this world and get away with it!"

"So far, she has," replied Bo.

"Well, I'm sick to death of Why-vonne Henderson!" Catsy stated. "She's pulled one stunt after another just to get attention and it's time *somebody* put a stop to it!"

"Why, Catsy," muttered Bo Ivanhoe. "If I didn't know you better, I'd say you had plans for Why-vonne up your fringe."

"On my *ears,* Pow-Wow. On my *ears*. I'm white-trash patienced out." Catsy glanced across the street. "That's got to be the maid, that's all there is to it. But why was she ridin' in the *backseat*? See how Why-vonne lets this town look bad? She lets the help ride in the backseat! Oh, look! Yvonne's given that nigger maid one of her old dresses! A Chanel if I'm seein' right! Well, I cain't believe it! All the help is endin' up with *our clothes*!"

"Maybe the *white folks* want to get out of here and go with you to the Dairy Queen and grab a bite," Bo said sarcastically. "I know your dyin' to meet Hollywood. Go on. Go." He glanced toward Yvonne's car. His head stopped moving. His eyes stopped moving. His heart started pounding and his mind stopped thinking. Bo Ivanhoe had just seen Arabella du Noir.

"They're *show business* people, Bo," Catsy said reprovingly. "It's one thing to let them make our picture, but we certainly don't want to sit down and have a *meal* with them."

"We don't?" Bo uttered, completely distracted. Arabella du Noir was the most graceful, elegant lady he had ever laid eyes on.

"Even at the Dairy Queen," Catsy replied. "I'm the royalty of Uncertain, Texas, Bo Ivanhoe, and don't you forget it."

"Oh, I wouldn't forget *that,*" Bo said under his breath. "You're royalty! You're royalty! I paid! I paid! I know! I know!"

"Hidy!" Lottie waved, coming up behind them. "Leo, I hope you didn't drive Miz Dune-war crazy with your drivin'!"

"He was perfect," Arabella replied. Turning to Lottie, she kissed her and gave her a hug. "It's been a long time since I've seen two people so much in love."

"We're in the repulsive stage awright!" Lottie Shady grinned. "It's the up side of love, honey! And I'm glad you approve!" She planted a big kiss back on Arabella's mouth.

Catsy Ivanhoe stopped in her tracks when she saw Arabella du Noir touch her lips to Lottie Shady's.

"That's Irene Shady's ole sister from the Uncertain Chapel of Memories gettin' kissed by that nigger maid!" Catsy gagged. "Did you see that that nigger kiss that ole woman?"

"I sure did," Bo whispered. It was taking every bit of composure he could muster not to go galloping across the street and throw himself at Arabella's feet.

"Oh, puke!" Catsy shuddered as she watched Lottie Shady kiss Arabella. "Puke! Puke! Puke! Puke! That ole bag of bones is kissin' back that *nigger*!" Liberties jangled, fringe shook, and two baby rattlesnakes swayed. "I'm pukin', Bo, I'm pukin'!"

"Catsy, precious," said Bo Ivanhoe. "Your raw heart would gag a maggot."

Ralph Painter, the entire crew, the pilots, Pierre, Claude and Sylvie Notions had all emerged from the bus and truck and were staring in utter amazement.

They had *never* seen Arabella du Noir show affection in any way, shape or form to anyone before. They had never seen her kiss or hug *anyone*.

They had never seen a float that was made of hundreds and hundreds of dead, wilted, crumbling brown flowers, stuck into chicken wire that was formed, shaped and designed to look like a giant jar of Peanut Butter, either.

And they certainly had not expected to see a black Rolls Royce emerge, drive up, and deposit two people who looked like a couple of extravagantly costumed rock stars.

Arabella turned to thank Leo, and in turning spotted Catsy and Bo Ivanhoe. She swayed. Regaining her balance, she raised her hand against the sun, squinting in an attempt to reassure herself that she wasn't seeing things.

"Oh, good," smiled Ralph Painter. "The extras. Good. Classy. I like it."

CHAPTER SIXTY-THREE

THEIR double-coiled brains collided.

Traitor! shrieked Topsy Dingo Wild Dog. *I let you come back and you deceived me! You deceived me! You deceived me!*

You fucked that dog, Mary Jane whispered.

You fucked it, too, Topsy snapped. *I DID IT. YOU DID IT. WE DID IT. WE FUCKED IT. WE FUCKED THE DOG. THE DOG IS FUCKED. I'M FUCKED. YOU'RE FUCKED. WE'RE FUCKED. OUR JOB IS FUCKED. YVONNE IS FUCKED. ARABELLA IS FUCKED. YOU'RE FUCKED. I'M FUCKED. WE ARE FUCKED. I AM FUCKED. YOU ARE FUCKED . . .*

You should have said NO! Mary Jane reprimanded. You have never, never known how to say NO!

Ha! laughed Topsy. *That's a good one coming from YOU! It's your fault that we're here at all, wearing this shitty Peanut Butter Cup garb, smiling our frozen, fake smile, trying to act like we're only twenty-eight, never fucked a dog and don't have a tattoo!*

Did it never occur to you NOT to try to keep him? Mary Jane demanded. *You were willing to do ANYTHING, ANYTHING HE WANTED YOU TO!*

YOU FUCKED IT, TOO, Topsy repeated. YOU FUCKED IT, TOO. I DID IT. YOU DID IT. WE DID IT. WE FUCKED IT. WE FUCKED THE DOG. THE DOG IS FUCKED. I'M FUCKED. YOU'RE FUCKED. OUR JOB IS FUCKED . . .

. . . *No, no, no*! begged Mary Jane Shady. *Not again! Shut up, shut up, shut up, shut up, no, no, no, no, no, no, no . . .*

. . . *You think you can drag yourself in here, hopscotch around your worse transgressions, things, that in your next life, are going to bring you back as a SLUG at best, and find some kind of absolution just because you FINALLY showed up? You have a tricky mind, Mary Jane Shady, but I didn't stick with you for nothing! I've spent years preparing for you, you devious little dog-snatching pervert deviate!*

Die! begged Mary Jane Shady. *Die . . . die . . . die . . .*

No. No. No. I'm not committing suicide. I WILL NEVER KILL MYSELF UNTIL YOU ADMIT THE TRUTH! AND I KNOW YOU! YOU WON'T DO IT! YOU WON'T DO IT! YOU WON'T DO IT! YOU WON'T DO IT! YOU WON'T DO IT!

STOP STOP STOP STOP STOP STOP STOP STOP STOP STOP STOP! rattled Mary Jane Shady as Topsy Dingo Wild Dog loomed larger and larger and larger.

Gigantic. Elephantine. Huge. Awkward. Stupid.

Mary Jane Shady was fading and dizzy. Topsy Dingo Wild Dog was clear and huge.

"Isn't Mary Jane pretty?" Judy Jones' voice clanged and jangled from somewhere close by. "Doesn't she just look . . ." Judy paused to find the word she wanted.

Topsy Dingo Wild Dog shut Mary Jane Shady's eyes.

" . . . *Let me assure you, your future is not looking too bright. Those new headshots that Marty took last week came back and what do you think came out in every single shot? A line, just under your left eye. A line, Mary Jane, as in WRINKLE, CROW'S FOOT, AGE. GET THE PICTURE?*"

"*Give her an 'O'!*" hissed Kay.

"*Give her an 'L'!*" screeched Spider.

"*Give her a 'D'!*" screamed Yvonne.

"*What have you got?*" laughed Ralph Painter.

"*NOT SO HOT*," sighed Arabella du Noir. "*She's just too OLD!*"

" . . . *Young*!" Judy cried.

Kay Widders stared into Topsy Dingo Wild Dog's face. Her eyes burned as brightly as a wild fire. Her head turned on its neck like a wooden-jointed toy whose parts fitted too closely together to move with ease. She slowly unclenched her teeth just enough to say, "When did you get your face worked on, Mary Jane?"

But Mary Jane Shady appeared not to hear.

" . . . *Ladies and Gentlemen of Uncertain, Texas, here to crown this year's Homecoming Queen is Miss Mary Jane Shady. She has distin-*

guished herself in many ways, but never more so than now. Friends, Miss Mary Jane Shady is an aging dog fucker. You will recognize her by the line under her left eye, the tattoo over her heart and the tail growing beneath her Peanut Butter Cup skirt . . . "

She felt the tail. It was under skirt. She looked at her hands. They were claws.

Drink! Drink! Drink! Drink! pleaded Mary Jane Shady to Topsy Dingo Wild Dog. *DRINK! DRINK! DRINK!*

"She's two years younger than you are, Kay," Yvonne Henderson retorted. " 'Member? You did like ever-body and passed one grade at a time and you're thirty-seven. I'm the same age as Mary Jane only I failed a buncha grades and that's what aged *me* prematurely. Mary Jane skipped two because she's *smarter—younger.* She is thirty-five and looks twenty-five because she takes *real, real, real* good care of herself—and she cain't help it if she's a natural beauty and inn't *two hunnerd pounds overweight like you are*!"

Before anyone knew what happened, Kay Widders had reached up and yanked Yvonne Henderson's red wig right off her head.

"ARE YOU CRAZY!?" Sammy hollered. "She'll *kill* you!!!"

"I would!" Scoot screamed. "Kay! Kay! Give her back her hair!"

Claws! Topsy whispered violently. *Claws! Claws! Muzzles! Paws!*

Yvonne stood in her full-length, canary-yellow, turkey-feathered coat. A headful of wispy white hair punctuated by one lone blatant bald spot accentuated her clownish faceful of make-up. She drew herself up with quiet dignity. "You may keep that hair, Kay Widders," she said in a hushed still voice. "And furthermore, there is *nothing* in this world you could do to humiliate *me.* So if that is what you were aimin' for, *you failed.*" Yvonne opened up her purse. It looked as if she might be pulling out a gun.

But Yvonne took out another red identical wig and proceeded to pull it over her white-tufted head. "I *expect* the worst, and am therefore as prepared for it every minute in my life as I can be." Yvonne turned to Mary Jane. "Is this on right?"

Speechless, motionless, Topsy did not move.

SIT. SIT. STAY. STAY.

"I told you some asshole from church would pull it off, didn't I?" Yvonne asked, looking straight at Kay. She leaned right into Kay's face. "Kay. You're just not *original.*"

"I had Siamese twins!" Kay hissed defensively.

"And *Sammy's* responsible for that!" Scoot Widders hollered.

"Come on, ya'll, sit down and ever-body *relax,* hear?" Sammy pleaded. He turned to Mary Jane and explained apologetically. "Same ole sixes and sevens. Never a minute's peace. Let's get drunk. Who wants a beer?"

"We're *sittin',*" Yvonne said. sitting down right between Sammy and Kay. Scoot Widders made herself comfortable as Judy Jones wormed in next to Scoot. None of them said another word to Kay Widders, who never said another word at all, but just sat there, holding Yvonne's extra wig in her hands, like a woman fondling a tarantula.

Bobby Henderson turned Yvonne's hair SNOW WHITE, thought Topsy Dingo Wild Dog, aghast. *What in the world has he done to her to turn every hair on her head* SNOW WHITE*?!*

She looked around, desperately.

What difference does it make anyway? Mary Jane Shady responded grimly. *Once they know what a dog* YOU *are, nothing else is going to matter. . .*

Silently, she reached for the beer.

CHAPTER SIXTY-FOUR

BO IVANHOE wanted to reach up, remove the headdress he was wearing and toss it in the backseat of Catsy's Rolls Royce. He wished he could take off the chinchilla vest, get rid of the chaps. Get rid of Catsy. Once he had seen her, Bo Ivanhoe's eyes never left Arabella du Noir. He crossed the street in four large strides with Catsy struggling to keep up.

As she hurried after him, the heel of one of her cobra-skinned boots caught in a niche in the pavement, loosening the heel. "Bo! Bo! Wait! Wait!" called Catsy, as her foot slipped precariously on the pavement.

Arabella gazed at the man coming toward her. *He'd be so attractive out of those feathers*! Arabella thought, distractedly. She turned to Pierre. "*S'il vous plaît, aidez cette dame avec sa botte*! Help that lady with her shoe!"

Pierre snapped his fingers and called to Claude, "*Aidez cette dame avec sa botte, s'il vous plait*!"

Just as Bo reached Arabella, Catsy grabbed him by the arm. "Did you hear me? I told you to wait up! I almost broke my neck on that ole boot!"

"*Excusez moi, s'il vous plaît,*" Pierre said grandly, pushing his assistant, Claude, aside and attempting to assist Catsy with her boot. "*Je suis Pierre Dumont, secretaire privé de Madame Arabella du Noir, Vice-President de la Hocker-Smockter Corporation Affaire Mondiales . . .*"

"Huh?" Catsy asked. "Speak English! Come again?"

"Secretary," Pierre replied in flawless English. "To Madame Arabella du Noir."

"What is he talkin' about?" Catsy asked irritably. "Where are the Hollywood people?" she wondered, looking around. She quickly unzipped her boot and handed it to Arabella du Noir. "See if you can tighten my heel, okay? And hurry! I am here to get in the movies and I am unbalanced without two shoes!"

"Catsy," Bo said quietly. "The gentleman is making an introduction—or *trying* to—"

"I can act as good as Mary Jane Shady can," Catsy declared to no one in particular and the collective crowd in general. "Anybody can do what *she* does—" Catsy's red harsh mouth twisted into an ugly smirk. Her eyes flashed as brightly as an ambulance's lights. Her voice, jolting and shrill, was as abruptly upsetting as a siren, as she suddenly threw herself into a sidewalk demonstration of her talents. "Creamy Crunchy Peanut Butter! For sale! Right here and now! We got it smooth! We got it nutty! But we got it!" Attempting to balance herself and achieve a look of seduction all at the same time, Catsy lowered her voice to what she hoped would be a sexy growl. "And *you're* goin' to git it!" she snarled.

That is the scariest thing I have ever seen in my life, thought Arabella du Noir.

"Where's the Hollywood representative?" Catsy's eyes darted from person to person, looking for someone in charge. "I've got the money. I can make my own picture, starrin' *me* if somebody will just talk to me in English!" Exasperated, she turned to Arabella impatiently. "Did you fix it yet?" she asked Arabella, who was simply standing, holding Catsy Ivanhoe's boot. "If you're sick of workin' for Why-vonne Henderson, we got a openin' out at the ranch," Catsy said, peaking in feverish superiority. "Do you fry with lotsa grease? I'm on a new low-cal diet they put me on at the Greendoor, so I cain't have any grease—"

Without batting an eye, Arabella replied evenly, "I'm happy where I am."

"I just offered you a job workin' for *me*!" Catsy snapped. "If it's money you're concerned about, I can beat Why-vonne's price! You be there Monday mornin' at seven o'clock sharp, ready to steam!"

"I'm steaming now," purred Arabella.

"How dare you sass me!" shrieked Catsy Ivanhoe. "Get over yourself, you cheeky nigger! And I'm not waitin' 'til Monday! You can start *now*!"

The entire company gasped, then broke into pandemonium.

"Madame!" cried Pierre, hurrying toward Arabella.

"Madame!" cried Claude.

"Oh, shit!" groaned Sylvie Notions.

Lottie shot between Arabella and the Ivanhoes like a bolt of lightning. "Gary!" Lottie called to the cameraman. "Ya'll *on*?"

"We are indeed, Mrs. Diggs," Gary called back.

"Oh!" smiled Catsy Ivanhoe, delighted to see a camera. "Are ya'll takin' a picture of *me*?" She pushed Arabella out of the way. "Could you *move*?"

Arabella stepped aside, unsmiling.

Unsmiling, Bo Ivanhoe stood beside her.

"Wait!" cried Catsy. "Gimme my shoe!"

"Oh, get *him* in the picture," Ralph Painter squealed. "Get that cute Indian in there, too!"

"I'll handle this, Ralph," Arabella said tightly. In one swift movement, she broke the heel off the boot. Turning to Catsy, she said in an exaggerated "Mammy" voice, "*Aw, lawsy, mercy, missy, now looks what I's did*!"

"You broke my boot, you stupid Aunt Jemimah!" screamed Catsy, as Gary moved his camera into a close-up.

"That's beautiful," the cameraman encouraged. "Just great . . ."

"Really?" asked Catsy, momentarily forgetting Arabella. "Why, *thanks*!"

Ralph Painter doubled over, laughing.

"Catsy!" growled Bo Ivanhoe, throwing off the headdress. "I'm through with you!"

"Mr. and Mrs. Bo Ivanhoe, I'd like ya'll to meet Madame Airybell-uh Dune-war, head of the largest advertising agency in the entire whole world, and she's in charge of *Hollywood,* too!" Lottie said hurriedly. "And Miz Belle, this here is Bo Ivanhoe, a real rich Comanche

Indian, and his wife, Alice Catherine, but everybody calls her Catsy. Guess why?"

"Charmed," said Arabella, smiling sardonically.

"What is this? Some kind of a joke?" Catsy gasped.

"*Continuez a tourner*!" ordered Arabella du Noir . "We'll watch *this* on the eleven o'clock news!"

"*Continuez a tourner*!" cried Pierre.

"*Continuez a tourner*!" shouted Claude.

"Keep the fucking camera rolling!" the assistant director told Gary Cohen. "We're gonna be on the eleven o'clock news!"

"Listen!" Catsy cried frantically, realizing her severe faux pax. "I never would have said that except I ate a bad raw sea creature three days ago in Galveston! I've got a wild, wild fever! I've been pukin' for seventy-two hours! I could have died! Couldn't I have, Bo!"

"No," said Bo. "I don't think so."

"How unfortunate," Arabella said coolly. "Claude! Pierre! *Madame Ivanhoe est gravement malade*!" she called to her assistants. "*Donnez-lui le* poison, *vite, s'il vous plaît! Faites tout ce qu'il faut, qu'elle ne souffre plus, cette chienne*! See if Leo has something. *J'espere que ça la tuera.*"

Claude handed Pierre a glass of Perrier and Leo handed Catsy a pill. He didn't understand a word of French, but he understood Arabella du Noir.

"*Voilà*!" Pierre said. "*Pour la dame malade.*"

"Oh, I want one, too!" said Ralph Painter. He winked at Bo Ivanhoe. "I'm getting my period!"

But Bo Ivanhoe was paying no attention. He was taking off his chaps.

"Oh, my, look at *you*!" Ralph whistled, watching Bo. "Look at *him,*" he said to Arabella. "He's *cute*!"

"Give Ralph a pill," Arabella told Leo Diggs evenly.

Leo reached into his pocket. "These is for the *real, real* sick," Leo assured Arabella.

"Oh, thanks," Catsy breathed, taking the pill and drinking the water. "Now," she smiled, her invidious lips curving into their amphibian demeanor. "I am *so* sorry!" As Catsy brushed the sweat from her brow in a spiraling fierce swish, Arabella thought she could almost hear Catsy rattle. "And I apologize, too, for callin' you a *nigger,*" she whispered, slithering up closely to Arabella, "when anybody can see you're some kind of a Moroccan or a Egyptian or maybe from Peru?"

Arabella du Noir, satisfied that all was being captured in glorious technicolor and perfect sound, smiled her practiced, patient smile. "No," she said. "You were right the first time. I'm an ordinary all-American native nigger."

"Oh, but you're not ordinary!" Catsy gushed. "You've got a foreign name!"

"She's a countess!" Ralph Painter shouted out.

"From *where*!" Catsy gasped, wide-eyed and impressed.

"France!" Ralph retorted.

"*A Paris-France Countess*!" Catsy shrieked, stunned. "We got somethin' in common!" she cried. "We are *both* royalty! Did you get yours out of the Neiman-Marcus catalogue?"

Arabella stared at Catsy silently.

"It's in their 'For People Who Have Everything' section this year!" Catsy babbled. "Those poor ole rich families all over Europe are auctionin' off their Dukes and Duchesses! Neiman's has got it on page two hunnerd and seventy-three, so I got a Rumanian Baroness one for myself and a Transylvanian Countess for my mother! Come Christmas, I'll have it all! Where'd you get yours from?"

"*From* the Count!" giggled Ralph. "*From* the French Count!"

Catsy leaned in closely to Arabella and said in a voice that implied they were both life-long princesses, "And is the Count joinin' us today?"

"The Count is *deceased,*" Ralph tittered.

"*Dead*?" Catsy asked, as the pill filled her head. Dizzily, she began to giggle, too. Tottering unsteadily, she looked at Arabella and said, "Is that why you're always in black?"

A deadly smile crossed Arabella du Noir's face.

Ralph Painter saw it and laughed even harder.

Bo saw it and muttered acerbically, "It's that ole raw sea creature from Galveston—"

Sylvie Notions saw it and said to Arabella, "It's taken me five minutes to hate this woman worse than Puerto Ricans." She gave Arabella pleading look. "Can we go inside and get this over with? I don't even care anymore if I see a big or little dipper or a shooting star or not. I just want to do my job and go *home.*" She added in the lowest whisper she could manage, "For God's sake, don't tell anyone here I'm *Jewish.* I'll never get out alive!"

Arabella du Noir looked from person to person, emotionless. *I knew when I got here, I'd get screwed,* she thought. Her eyes rested on Catsy Ivanhoe's reptilian face. *But it's not going to be by YOU . . .*

CHAPTER SIXTY-FIVE

DRINK IT . . . whispered Mary Jane Shady. *Drink. Shut up. Drink . . .*

We'll stop after this, promised Topsy Dingo Wild Dog.

Just one. To relax. To make you stop thinking . . . agreed Mary Jane Shady.

Just one . . . swore Topsy.

Just one . . . Mary Jane nodded.

They lifted the drink upward.

Together.

Together they promised they would only drink one.

The door of the gymnasium opened.

Mary Jane let go. Topsy dropped everything.

Together they rose.

Together they fled.

CHAPTER SIXTY-SIX

"HOLY SHIT!" Sammy Widders dropped his can of Coors right on the toe of Spider Webb Turner's left boot when he saw Arabella du Noir enter the back door of the Uncertain gymnasium. Bo and Catsy Ivanhoe were right behind her. Ralph Painter was right behind Bo.

"Catsy's brought her maid!" Judy Jones screamed.

"What's that?" Yvonne Henderson cried.

"That's Hollywood!" Scoot yelled.

"That's a nigger!" Kay Widders hissed.

"That's pussy!" Sammy Widders smiled.

Lottie hopped in front of Arabella, Catsy, Bo and Ralph to search for her sister-in-law. If she'd looked up, she would have seen her, for

Irene was standing on the top of a fifteen-foot stepladder, viewing all below through Otis Medcalf's binoculars.

When she saw Ralph Painter, Irene changed the focus fast. If everything hadn't turned into a blur, she would have yelled, "Who's that?" from the top of the ladder. Instead, she only got out the "W-h-o-o-o" which came out more like "o-o-o-o" as she fell fifteen feet from the top of the ladder and landed right into the ready arms of all four main cheerleaders who were perpetually prepared for such things.

"Miz Dune-war, I want ya'll to meet my sister-in-law, Irene Shady," Lottie said. "This is Mary Jane's mother." Lottie moved in between the cheerleaders. " 'Scuze me, girls." She gave Irene a shake. "Irene, Miz Dune-war and Hollywood is here."

Irene opened one eye slowly. "I think I dropped Otis's sightseers," she said to Lottie.

"Naw, they're still hung around your neck," Lottie told her.

"Are they broke?" Irene asked.

"Naw," Lottie said.

"Ever-thing just went dark up there," Irene said.

"Ever-thing is still real *dark,*" Lottie whispered.

"What?" Irene cleared her throat to whisper back. "I seen that Silverado blonde in them pink shorts—a very inappropriate dress code for this affair, in my opinion. Couldn't Miz Dune-War have gotten a bit more dressed up? I wish she wouldn't bleach her hair—"

"That ain't her," Lottie said, glancing toward Ralph Painter. "That's that agent."

"*No*!" Irene whispered, shocked. "Why is he dressed up like a *woman*? How *embarrassing*! Where's Miz Dune-war?" she asked Lottie, searching the crowd.

"Well," Lottie Shady nodded toward Arabella. "That's her."

"Oh, look at those pretty clothes!" Irene whispered appreciatively. "Miz Dune-war's got taste and style and—" She looked closer. "I swear, if I didn't think somethin' was wrong with my eyes, I'd swear that Miz Dune-war is not a Caucasian girl."

"Ain't nothin' wrong with your eyes," Lottie assured her.

A big grin spread over Irene Shady's face. "I don't believe it!" she told her sister-in-law. "This just ain't goin' to be Gladys Turner's day!" A worried look came over her face. "It might not be Miz Dune-war's day neither," Irene mused. "No tellin' what's goin' to happen *now*!"

"Don't worry about Miz Dune-war," Lottie confided. "She's sweet as honey, sharp as a knife and tough as nails all at the same time. She's awready had a run on Catsy Ivanhoe!"

"Well, set me up straight!" Irene commanded the cheerleaders. "Let's go say hello to the world's leader of the biggest advertisin' agency in the whole wide world!"

The cheerleaders sat Irene down on the floor.

"This here is Miz Dune-war," Lottie told Irene.

"I'm just not at my best when my feet aren't on the ground," Irene explained to Arabella, as she extended her hand in greeting. "But at least you can see our cheerleaders know what they are doin', Miz Dune-war!"

"That was a very impressive fall," Arabella remarked amiably. "Flexibility must run in your family."

"I keep in shape," Irene said. "It's from liftin' dead people." She looked at Lottie pointedly. "By *myself.*"

Arabella did not even lift an eyebrow.

"I told her we was undertakers," Lottie smiled. "She knows all about that."

"Not ever-body in the whole family's a movie star," Irene grinned.

Ralph Painter started to laugh.

"What is *that*?" Irene Shady asked. "Did it have one of them operations or *what*?"

Lottie turned to Arabella. "Don't tell Irene about me gettin' married yet," she whispered. "This ain't a good time."

Ralph Painter smiled condescendingly at Irene. "I'm Mary Jane's agent," he announced importantly.

"Whatever," smiled Irene. "You are just in time to go over yonder to that woman who looks like a convict, get that megaphone and take it to that couple over yonder who look like they think they're about to do somethin' important—"

"Excuse me?" Ralph Painter smirked.

"The couple comin' out on the floor—see 'em yonder—they're dressed by the same person who dressed you—"

"Look, lady, I'm not your servant!" the agent huffed indignantly.

"You're Mary Jane's agent, ain't you?" Irene Shady asked.

"That is precisely who I am," Ralph Painter replied haughtily.

"That makes you the servant," Irene told him. "You are the hired help. Go get the megaphone."

"What?" Ralph Painter asked, peering at her. "I am the *what*?"

"You're the nigger, Mr. Perfect," Arabella purred. "Step over and fetch it, boy."

Ralph's face broke into a leering smile. "You can't humiliate *me* that easily," he told Irene Shady. "I'm from L.A., honey. I live in *Hollywood.*"

All activity on the gymnasium floor abruptly came to a halt.

A short, chubby man with thinning hair pulled across one side of his head came out onto the floor accompanied by his twin, a short dumpy woman with thinning hair pulled across her head. Orville Turner and Gladys Turner were wearing matching pink and white seersucker suits. Gladys was wearing a skirt and Orville was wearing slacks. Otherwise, they were one and the same.

"Who is that?" Arabella asked Irene Shady, as the Turners placed themselves in the middle of the floor. Gladys held a handful of pages in one hand, as Orville wiped his glasses with a tissue.

"That's Mr. and Mrs. Superintendent of Schools." Irene explained. "Don't let her skirt throw you. She's definitely the one wearin' the pants. Looks like a couple of Kewpie dolls, don't they?"

"No, they don't," disagreed Lottie. "They ain't that cute."

"He's about to read her speech," Irene informed Arabella. "It's written fifth-grade style."

"Hey, Gary!" Lottie called. "Turn yourself this-a-way! Hey, Wong!" she yelled. "Lower that boom!"

Irene turned to Arabella with a grin. "Did we welcome you to Uncertain?"

"You certainly did," Arabella smiled. "You certainly did."

"Who's *that*?" Spider Webb Turner asked, as she watched Ralph Painter approach Palmer Jordan Pullet.

"Who's *that*?" Sammy asked, as he watched Arabella du Noir laughing with the Shady sisters.

"Who's *that*?" Irene Shady called to Lottie over her shoulder. She'd just caught sight of a red-headed man who looked for all the world the spitting image of that truck driver who'd devastated her sign two days before. "I seen a red-headed man!"

"I'll check with Gary and the boys to make sure they're set," Lottie said hurriedly, pretending she had no idea who Irene was referring to. "We sure don't want to miss Gladys's speech!"

"I seen *that* red-headed man!" Irene cried. "What's he doin' still in town?"

"One of them pilots has red hair," Lottie stammered feebly. "Carrot-colored. Like *I Love Lucy!*" She was biting both thumbnails to the quick.

"I believe that *is* one of the pilots, Irene," Arabella remarked, covering up for Lottie. "I believe he must be one of the West coast pilots."

Lottie stopped chewing on one thumb.

"Well, don't get up in the air with him!" Irene Shady shouted. "If he's who I think he is, he's flat-out dangerous!"

"He cain't hurt nothin' in the air, Irene!" Lottie Shady said. "It don't have no intersections!"

"They got rules up there!" Irene yelled. "Somebody has to fly *over* and somebody has to fly *under*!"

Lottie blinked. "What the hell are we arguin' about, Sister!" she cried. "Let's just hope they're flyin' over *our* corner and a little ways backwards or a little ways forwards!"

"The greatest prestige our class had was graduatin' without one nigger in it," Kay Widders was telling Spider Webb Turner, as she watched Sammy looking at Arabella du Noir.

Spider's attention had shifted to the opposite side of the gym, however. Her eyes narrowed as she saw Ralph Painter move toward Palmer Jordan Pullet.

"I ain't handin' my megaphone over to a stranger," Palmer was saying to Ralph Painter.

Over Palmer's shoulder, Ralph saw a tall khaki-attired figure jump over the stands and start across the floor towards them. "Is that your husband?" he asked innocently.

Palmer took the megaphone and smashed it over Ralph's head. Just as Spider reached them, Ralph fell to the floor in a pink heap.

"What's goin' on here?" Spider asked Palmer.

"I don't know if she insulted me or if she insulted you!" Palmer replied. "But I'm sick of these beauty-parlor club-ladies comin' in and tellin' me what to do!" She handed her friend the megaphone. "Take this over yonder to your daddy-in-law so he can say what we're all waitin' to have over with. I'll keep my eye on her." She couldn't resist giving Ralph Painter a kick.

"I'll be right back," Spider told Palmer. "There's about to be trouble."

"What kind of trouble?" Palmer asked.

Spider Webb Turner ran her hand up to her throat and loosened her collar. "Mary Jane Shady is tryin' to steal my cat."

"Did you get—" Arabella began.

"We got Ralph getting smashed," Gary said. "He's still down. What's next?" Through his lens he saw the tall woman with the badge take the megaphone from the short woman in a cheerleader outfit, walk across the floor and hand it to the identical looking couple. The man took the megaphone, cleared his throat and in a monotone, began to read from his notes:

"Welcome to Uncertain
Welcome here today
Homecoming opportunity
Is yours to build like clay.
From the halls of Yellow Jackets
Little Dirt Daubers grow
To fly Uncertain's colors
With wings of maroon and gold.
We welcome every color
Except a very few
And with those exceptions
We welcome you."

Orville looked at Gladys uncertainly. She poked him and he continued:

"It's the spirit and the friendship
We've gathered to observe,
The fellowship of people
We've all heard.

To welcome all the old Yellow Jackets
Who've come from far away
No matter how far they stray
They cannot stay away.

We see them here today.''

Orville adjusted his glasses and turned a page.

''We welcome present Yellow Jackets,
They were once like you.
They'll give the world a better chance
In case you might have failed to.
If you did, then shame on you.

Each Yellow Jacket's had their chance

From the fifth grade on
To make the world a better place
In thought and deed and song.

So let us sing now praises high
For such a sacred thing.
And there is no better singer
Than the Yellow Jacket's sting.''

"Peugh!" Irene said. "Gladys has outdid herself." Gladys handed Orville another sheet of paper.

''So here's to the cheerleaders

And here's to the band
Here's to the A Team
The grandest in the land.

Here's to winning,
Or even if we fail
Here's to our failure
In it we'll prevail.

Here's to our colors,
Here's to our song
Here's to our school
Uncertain and strong!''

"On Uncertain, on Uncertain, lift those colors high," the entire student body stood and sang, "We're not hurtin', 'cause we're from Uncertain and carry our banners h-i-g-h-h-h-h! Over highways, over bye-ways, life will always b-e-e-e-e-e-e a happy memory o-o-o-o-o-f that school we know and l-o-o-o-o-v-e! Our colors! Our song! Uncertain and strong!"

"WIN! WIN! WIN! WIN! WIN! WIN! WIN! WIN! WIN! WIN!"

Ralph Painter opened one eye and saw nothing but a sea of pompoms. Two hit him in the face at once.

Oh, that turns me on! he thought feverishly. *I'm turning on! I'm turning on*!

"WIN! WIN! WIN! WIN! WIN! WIN! WIN! WIN! WIN! WIN!"

The student body continued to scream, as the cheerleaders jumped up and down. The band played on until Orville Turner signaled them to stop.

"I know that's my favorite song and I am sure it is yours, too," Orville cleared his voice and smiled out at the crowd. "Now at this time, it is customary to bring out the Homecoming Queen nominees, those fine young women who are going to distinguish themselves in our representation at tonight's game, and then to announce the winner, as is traditional. But at *this* time, I'm going to divert from what is the customary agenda, since we have a special guest with us. Those of you who know me, know it is my custom to refer to my papers so I can say exactly what is on my mind at the time, but since I have not written out this next part, I am going to take the liberty of turning this part over to my imagination, so please bear with me." Pleased with himself, Orville smiled again. "Now we have out-of-towners," he told the crowd. "They flew in a few minutes ago and thanks to the accommodation of Mrs. Why-vonne Henderson's landin' strip out in her backyard southeast of town, these folks were able to join us from Hollywood, California, and New York City, homes of the stars, to be here at the hometown home of one of *their* stars, Miss Mary Jane Shady, as she returns to her family and friends and share with us all her glamour and glory and success and splendor as America's favorite Queen of Creamy, Crunchy Peanut Butter, Smooth and Nutty—"

"Get a close-up of M.J.," Arabella told Gary.

"Impossible," he said.

"Why?" she snapped.

"Because she's not there," Gary replied.

CHAPTER SIXTY-SEVEN

WELL, YOU ALMOST did it that time! Mary Jane Shady told Topsy. *I can't listen to you for a minute! You had that beer in your hands, you were about to DRINK—*

Did you see my hands? Topsy asked hysterically. *I was growing a TAIL! I was about to HOWL!*

Mary Jane leaned heavily on one of twelve polished and shining washbasins in the Uncertain High School Girls' Room.

"Oh, my God," she moaned, her head in her hands. "I cannot handle this. I cannot handle you." One hand fluttered nervously, and like a frail sick bird that could no longer cling to its nest, fell, and landed in a small clutched pile of fingernails and flesh atop the cold white enamel sink. The index finger limply inched forward. Then recessed. And moved forward again, testing itself for life.

Mary Jane looked at the sink in front of her. The knotted hand miraculously made a stunning recovery, and with direct and graceful force swept its index finger across the tile.

Clean . . . so clean . . . how do they keep everything so CLEAN? . . . It's practically antiseptic . . . She couldn't find a speck of dirt, lint, anything on her finger. The spotless high school bathroom could have been her mother's.

She tried to fill the basin with water, but someone had revolutionized the Uncertain plumbing system while she'd been away. There were no longer any rubber stoppers for the sink. The water just poured down the drain, just poured down.

Topsy watched it rush from the faucet and disappear, aghast. *How are you supposed to drown in here*? she wondered. *I can't even get enough water in one place long enough to drown myself . . .*

"Hey," said a voice, a different voice, a familiar voice.

Don't turn, Topsy . . . Mary Jane Shady warned.

"Huh?" she spun around.

"I brought you a present," the new, old voice said.

"Goddamnit, Bobby, get out of here. You can't come in the Ladies' Room."

"*Girls*' Room. It's '*girls*,' hon. You go in the '*Ladies' Room*' when you're all grown up, know enough not to be stupid—"

"*YOU HAVE TO TAKE CARE OF BOBBY HENDERSON YOURSELF . . . YOU HAVE TO TAKE CARE OF YOURSELF, YOURSELF . . .* "

"I'm *not* stupid!"

"Yeah, you're pretty stupid," he said with a grin in his voice. "If you's smart you'd have turned this water off," he continued, watching the basin overflow all over the floor.

"That's twice today you've made me do that!" Topsy cried irritably.

Who made you do it? hissed Mary Jane Shady. *WHO is 'who'*?

"Well, that was dumb, hon, but nothin' that cain't be fixed. So clean it up," he told her.

WHO is YOU . . . Mary Jane warned. *YOU* are *WHO*!

"Okay," she murmured submissively.

Okay . . . mocked Mary Jane Shady. *Do you hear yourself . . . do you hear yourself saying "okay" "okay" "okay" "okay"*?

Her eyes grew wide. It seemed just like yesterday when she had said this to him before . . . Not today . . . But before . . . Another bathroom? School? In the 1954 Ford convertible by the oil well . . .

He'll turn you into that dog again! He's going to turn you into a dog!

"Here's your graduation present," Bobby said.

"Oh, thanks. Sorry I don't have yours on me," she apologized.

"You will," he laughed. "Open it up."

SAY NO. YOU REMEMBER HOW TO SAY "NO." SAY IT: NO. NO. NO.

It was a big white box, tied with a big white bow with two white school bells attached. She tore it open.

Mary Jane stared at the contents. *Give it back. Give it back. Give it back.*

"Wow," Topsy said. "Twelve bars of Lux soap. Wow."

Bobby grinned. "Go on."

Oh . . . Mary Jane moaned. *Don't go on* . . .

"Oh," Topsy blinked. "Four clean old rags . . . "

"Sterilized," he affirmed.

No way, muttered Mary Jane Shady. *No fucking way* . . .

"Gee. Arm and Hammer Baking Soda. That's great." She looked back down. "Vinegar!"

Mary Jane gave a short laugh. *Don't drink it.*

I won't! Topsy replied.

"Think that'll do the job?" he asked.

"Well, you could have got me a broom," she smiled.

"What for?" he snapped. "What do you need a fuckin' broom for if you got me?"

"What are you talkin' about, Bobby?" Topsy asked, bewildered. "I just meant if these are my graduation presents so I can be gettin' ready to set up our house when we get married after we graduate, I might need a broom—"

FOOL! FOOL! screamed Mary Jane Shady. *You don't want a house! I hate grass! You don't want a husband! You can't handle a commitment! You can't even commit to ME!*

"What house keepin'?!" Bobby yelled. "I'm goin' to college! How many times do I have to tell you that? These aren't household supplies, you stupid, silly West Texas cunt! This is to clean yourself up with!"

I'm going to kill him . . . Mary Jane thought calmly. *I am going to kill this son-of-a-bitch . . .*

Bobby's voice circled around Topsy's head. "Lux soap to wash with, 'cause you know I'm allergic to Lux and that makes me allergic to you!"

Topsy was dizzy. Topsy was sick. "Oh, right," she said.

Right, right, right, mimicked Mary Jane Shady. *You'll never get it right*!

"That's right," he said. "Now. Nice white dishtowels to wash yourself off with, that come directly out of my own mother's washer, so I *know* they're clean," he pointed out.

"YOU HAVE TO TAKE CARE OF YOURSELF, YOURSELF. . ."

"My mother had to use lye soap on 'em four different times after you touched me. That's why they got holes in 'em. But they're clean."

STOP IT! screamed Mary Jane Shady. *DON'T LISTEN TO THIS! DON'T!*

"Scrub your mouth with the bakin' soda. Right before you kiss me is a good time to use it—"

DON'T LISTEN! begged Mary Jane. *DON'T! DON'T! DON'T!*

"Uh-oh. I almost forgot. Carbon tetrachloride. Be sure to drink that. Cleans out your insides. Drink the whole thing."

HE'S GOING TO KILL YOU! Mary Jane cried. *HE'S KILLING ME! HE'S KILLING YOU!*

"YOU HAVE GOT TO TAKE CARE OF YOURSELF, YOURSELF. . . YOU HAVE GOT TO TAKE CARE OF BOBBY HENDERSON YOURSELF. . . "

"I don't think you've got much of a future with me," Bobby Henderson told Mary Jane Shady. "Have you ever considered suicide?"

"No . . ." whispered Topsy.

Say it again! demanded Mary Jane Shady. *Say it loud! Let me hear it! Say NO, NO, NO, NO, NO, NO, NO!*

"NO!" screamed Topsy. "NO! NO! NO! NO! NO! NO! NO!"

YOU ARE CRAZY, BOBBY HENDERSON, said Mary Jane Shady. *CRAZY. CRAZY. CRAZY. ALL YOU THINK ABOUT IS YOURSELF. ALL YOU EVER TALK ABOUT IS YOURSELF. EVERY QUESTION YOU ASK BEGS FOR AN ANSWER THAT RELATES DIRECTLY TO YOU, YOUR SELF. BUT DO YOU WANT A STRAIGHT ANSWER? NO. YOU THINK YOU CAN DRAG US IN HERE, HOPSCOTCH AROUND YOUR WORST TRANSGRESSIONS, THINGS THAT IN YOUR NEXT LIFE, ARE GOING TO BRING YOU BACK AS A SLUG AT BEST, AND FIND SOME KIND OF ABSOLUTION JUST BECAUSE YOU SHOWED UP? YOU HAVE A TRICKY MIND, BOBBY, BUT WE DIDN'T STICK WITH THIS FOR NOTHING. WE HAVE SPENT YEARS PREPARING FOR YOU, YOU DEVIOUS HORRIBLE MANIAC PERVERT. OH, BOY, HAVE WE CONSIDERED SUICIDE! THE ANSWER TO THAT IS YES. BUT I'M NOT GOING TO KILL MYSELF. AND SHE'S NOT GOING TO KILL HERSELF. WHY SHOULD WE KILL OURSELVES WHEN ALL WE HAVE TO KILL IS YOU?*

"You're as sick as your secrets, sister," grinned Bobby Henderson. "And you're going to stay that way. You'll never kill me. Not until you face yourself. And that's one thing you will never, *never* do. I'll tell you another thing, too. I'm *not* the *problem* here, Topsy Dingo Shady—Mary Jane Wild Dog. But you just keep tellin' yourself I am, if that's what you've got to do—"

Water from the basin welled over the side and onto the floor. Topsy Dingo Wild Dog looked at it in horror. Mary Jane Shady looked at it and laughed. Tears ran down their faces. Mary Jane ran in each stall and pulled all the toilet paper off their rolls, weaving white streamers from stall to stall, as Topsy, right on top of her, frantically tried to clean up the mess.

"*You'll never kill me! Not until you face yourself and that's one thing you'll never do!...* "

Mary Jane turned on more faucets. Topsy turned them off.

YOU'RE AS SICK AS YOUR SECRETS, AS SICK AS YOUR SECRETS, SICK SICK SECRETS... YOU ARE SICK, SICK, SICK....

Mary Jane took a red lipstick from her purse, grinding it into the mirror.

OH! howled Topsy Dingo Wild Dog. *OW-W-W-W-W-W-W-W-W*!

Mary Jane scrawled the thick letters across the mirror.

MARY JANE SHADY IS A DOG FUCKING DOG FUCKER!

Then she began adding crooked, cracked hearts.

The door to the Uncertain High School Girls Room opened.

The lipstick fell from her hands.

"Mary Jane?" said Arabella du Noir. "We're ready for you."

CHAPTER SIXTY-EIGHT

MARY JANE SHADY left Topsy Dingo Wild Dog and her cracked hearts smeared across the bathroom wall.

She moved through the past, through fear, away from Bobby Henderson, and right into her Peanut Butter Cup persona the minute she heard the voice of Arabella du Noir. She reached the door before Arabella had even finished speaking. She stepped out into the hall before Arabella stepped in, closing the door behind her.

"Ms. Du Noir." She spoke softly. Her china blue eyes gazed at Arabella with a quietness that she hoped gave her a modium of composure. "I hope I haven't kept you waiting."

Don't explain anything... Mary Jane told herself. *Don't ask her if she notices your lines... Don't ask her when you're getting fired... And don't ask her if anyone has been rude to her yet... SHE'LL TELL YOU. LET HER TELL YOU. YOU'RE HERE TO DO A JOB. DO WHAT YOU ARE PAID TO DO.*

In her freshly pressed pale blue shirt-waisted dress with the full white apron trimmed in eyelet, her thick chestnut-colored hair pulled back from her face, Mary Jane Shady stood before Arabella, doing her best to look like what she was paid to look like, making every effort to appear to be what she was paid to be.

Arabella held her gaze, studying the face before her. *She's no longer right for this job*... Arabella thought to herself. *It isn't the skin... it's still flawless... It isn't the bone structure... still fine*... It wasn't a sagging neckline. In fact, Arabella could barely detect the sign of a line. Arabella stared into the china blue eyes. *It's a depth*... Arabella thought, intrigued. *Now this is interesting... She's just not SIMPLE enough anymore*...

"How was your trip?" Arabella asked. Her smooth smoky voice caressed her words. Her eyes twinkled with a mixture of curiosity and a tinge of humor.

"Fascinating," Mary Jane replied softly. *When I grow up,* she thought, *I want to be just like you*...

"I'll bet," Arabella smiled.

As she took Mary Jane by the arm and walked with her toward the gymnasium, she wondered what would become of Mary Jane Shady. What happened to other former Miss Peanut Butter Cups? Did they go on to TV series, become spokespersons for other commercials? Or were they destined to forever be identified with Creamy Crunchy labels and little gingham dresses? Ingenues, grown too old for their parts? Did they return to regional theater, get married, retire on their considerable earnings, never making the bridge into real stardom. Not because of talent, and not because of looks, but because they were just not special enough. And then there were those, like Mary Jane, who had everything except timing. Arabella thought, perhaps, like her, Mary Jane could become an executive. Not because of talent, and not because of looks and not because she wasn't *special,* but because she had simply been too tall, too short, too white, too *black* too soon.

Too late . . .

Airy Belle Williams from Durham, North Carolina, looked at Mary Jane Shady from Uncertain, Texas, and wished she could promise her some hope for her future.

She watched Mary Jane move onto the floor like a gallant race-horse. Hair shimmering, eyes shining, her ebullient demeanor brought the exhilarated crowd to their feet, screaming.

Arabella's cool hazel eyes had missed nothing. Not the hearts on the wall. Not the slogan. She didn't have a clue what any of it meant and she really didn't care. She was far more interested in how Mary Jane Shady handled herself.

And as she watched Mary Jane Shady walk into that Pep Rally, she thought of one word: grace.

You can develop style, Arabella thought to herself. *But you have to be born with grace . . .*

"Oh, good! Here she comes!" Orville Turner cried out over the megaphone. "Some functions don't change, no matter how famous you get," he observed with a smile as Mary Jane joined him and Gladys.

"Ladies and Gentlemen, men and women, children and youngsters of Uncertain," Orville read solemnly from another sheet of Gladys' paper. "It is the dream of ever Yellow Jacket who ever left the comforts of home for foreign territories North, East or further South or further West, to strive for somethin' greater, or otherwise, why go? To break the umbili-cord of home and friends you have known all your life and go out there where you have no idea if they are goin' to empty your trash on the right day of the week or even at all, stop at the red light or keep goin' and run right over you like you was an armadillo, where people live right on top of each other in buildings three times as high as our water tower and in basements with bars like a jail, where you have to pay somebody to drive you around in yellow cars that don't belong to you, don't belong to them, and don't have a good set of shock absorbers, neither, is a brave thing to do. I have been to New York City and *that* is what goes on *there.* I know of what I speak. I and other members of the Texas Superintendents' Association attended the 1971 Association of School Services Convention in nineteen hunnerd and seventy-one. We stayed at the Taft Hotel, right in the middle of town, and it is a city under a roof in itself that reminded me of Bo and Catsy Ivanhoe's house out south of town—"

"Ranch!" Catsy hollered out.

"I'm the one with the hotel look!" Yvonne Henderson yelled from the stands.

Orville looked up from his pages. "Well, okay. Anyway, one day after we had finished our breakfast there in the Taft Hotel Coffee Shop, we took ourselves a walk down the street. And just like we do here at home, we said good mornin' to ever-body we saw. 'Good mornin',' we said. 'Good mornin'.' 'Good mornin'.' 'Good mornin'.' 'Good mornin'.' Do you know how many people there was on that one street? *Millions.* 'Good mornin'.' 'Good mornin'.' 'Good mornin'.' 'Good mornin'.' We said 'Good mornin' ' to ever single person we saw. And do you know what? *Not a single one of them said 'good mornin' ' back*!"

Orville took a deep breath as he gave his audience an opportunity to absorb this.

"Now my point is this: The North is not a very friendly place. You have to be tough and strong to stick it out there. It can be tough, rough and even deadly. I've even heard of people stickin' knives in people over a stick of Juicy Fruit." Orville let this sink in. "And so to go live in a place like that and in Hollywood, California, and I've never been *there,* but I'm sure it is the same thing but with trees, a person had better have a firm grounding in *what is right and what is wrong* or they'll get mixed up and never know what hit them and if you ever watch the news you'll know it could be anything. Well, our own Mary Jane Shady has been out there in that world and has arrived back here in one piece, so we know what works. She's brought some of her friends with her, so we know it is possible for people who don't come from Uncertain, Texas, to go to Hollywood, California, or New York City and get out in one piece, too. We don't know how they did it unless they started out there and grew up used to it. Maybe she taught them how *she* did it. And we know how *she* did it. *She* did it by being the *best* Uncertain Yellow Jacket that she knew how to be. Now, you may ask, how do *I* conduct my life in an Uncertain way? Here is how:

"Number one: By being strong.

"Number two: By being resolute.

"Number three: By making an outline. (Every Uncertain Yellow Jacket learns how to do this in the *fifth* grade.)

"Number four: When in doubt, go the *Book of Knowledge*. If you don't find what you need, call the telephone operator. That's what we teach here from our football players right on down the line, and the same principles that work in Uncertain, Texas, will work anywhere and with anything and anybody can do 'em, too."

Orville's tone was full of reverence. "We are proud of Mary Jane Shady. We are proud of her mother, Irene Shady, and we are proud of her aunt, Lottie Shady, too—"

"She just got married!" Ralph Painter called from where he was lying in a heap on the floor. Palmer stuck the tip of her cheerleader boot on the tip of his tongue and its white tassel flew in his left eye, so the word "married" was lost on almost everyone. But it was not lost on Gladys.

"That man lying on the floor—did he say she got *married*?" Gladys asked Irene anxiously.

"S-h-h-h!" Irene replied. "Orville's not through!"

"Is she or not?" Gladys insisted.

"We're missin' your speech, Gladys," Irene snapped.

"Are you, Mary Jane?" Gladys whispered frantically. "You didn't go get married to that *Jew* and not tell anybody, surely! Please don't tell us you eloped with a heathen when Mr. Superintendent is about to introduce you as a *success*!"

"—So let's give a big welcome to a star that did it the Uncertain Way. Here she is, Miss Mary Jane Shady, a real Yellow Jacket who hasn't forgotten how to say 'good mornin'!"

Topsy heard the crowd applaud politely. Mary Jane Shady heard the crowd roar. She felt confused and speechless. She couldn't even remember if she was really wearing her Peanut Butter Cup dress. She looked down. Shoes. She saw shoes. And the hem of a blue and white dress. Had she remembered the apron? The dickey? Where was Arabella du Noir?

"Good morning! Good morning! Good morning!" Topsy gushed, smiling and waving to the crowd.

Too much, warned Mary Jane Shady. *Calm down . . .*

Mary Jane Shady just smiled and smiled and smiled until she was sure that Topsy would not speak. "It is wonderful to be . . ."

Topsy's voice was coming out of her mouth. "Ladies and gentlemen of Uncertain, Texas," Topsy was saying out loud. "I'm not who you think I am! I'm—"

Topsy felt Irene Shady's elbow in her ribs. "Just say you're happy to be a star!" Irene Shady told her daughter. "And don't apologize for who you are!"

Topsy swallowed hard and Mary Jane continued. "I'm sure I'm not who you think I am, but whatever you think is fine with me—"

Whew! breathed Topsy.

Shut up, said Mary Jane. *Don't bother me. This isn't that easy . . .*

Irene Shady grabbed the megaphone. "She's as good a star as she knows how to be is what she's sayin'," Irene announced. Her chin lifted a bit. Her eyes narrowed. "And she's real, real, happy, too!"

Orville looked back down, adjusted his glasses and lifted the megaphone to his lips. "It isn't every day that the Peanut Butter Queen of America is here to introduce the nominees for Homecoming Queen of Uncertain High School and we are happy to honor back Mary Jane Shady, our own Uncertain star!" He was beaming at her as if her presence was the most important thing in his life. "But first," Orville Turner said, "why don't you introduce us to your friends who have joined you here today."

Topsy Dingo Wild Dog froze.

Mary Jane just stood there.

She looked at the group gathered around on the gymnasium floor. She saw Gary, the cameraman. She saw Wong, holding the boom. There was Sylvie Notions in her fold-up chair. Standing next to Bo Ivanhoe was Arabella du Noir.

Tall, elegant, beautiful Arabella.

Oh, my God, thought Mary Jane Shady. *THIS IS IT.* She stared as hard as she could at Arabella. *Think tall*, she told herself. *Think elegant. Be beautiful . . . Be like her . . .*

From the other side of the gymnasium, Arabella stared back at Mary Jane Shady in admiration. *She's splendid . . .* Arabella thought. *She's just splendid . . . We're* BOTH *splendid . . .* She glanced around coolly. *We both got the hell out of here . . .*

"Ladies and Gentlemen of Uncertain, Texas, it is my privilege to introduce to you a person who has taken the world of advertising and limned it into an art," Mary Jane Shady said softly. "She put color in the air, America in Levis, me in Peanut Butter, and I feel confident that she will somehow change your lives, too. It is my pleasure to introduce to you the Senior Vice-President of Hocker-Smockter, and one of the greatest creative minds in the world. I'm sure you'll give a big Uncertain welcome to Ms. Arabella du Noir!"

The crowd went mad with cheers. The bank played. The Pep Squad swayed and cheerleaders flew through the air.

Arabella du Noir stepped forward.

The crowd fell silent. The band stopped. The Pep Squad sat down in unison. And two cheerleaders fell right on top of Ralph Painter.

Irene Shady grabbed the megaphone. "That don't sound like a very friendly Uncertain welcome to me!" she said to the silent crowd, who was staring in wonder at Arabella.

Arabella du Noir was a study in composure.

Look at her, Mary Jane told Topsy, as they observed Arabella admiringly. *LOOK AT HER . . .*

She knows what to do, thought Topsy. *She knows when NOTHING IS EXACTLY WHAT TO DO*!

Irene Shady cleared her voice. "This lady I am attempting to innerduce is the most important person you all are goin' to meet in your lives today!" she announced.

The crowd listened intensely.

"Airy-bell-uh Dune-war is the great American dream," Irene Shady told them. "She grew up in a little town just outside of Durham, North Carolina, a town no bigger than Uncertain, Texas. When she was fifteen years old, with a bus ticket in her hand and fifty dollars donated by her mother's employer, a Mrs. Estelline Wiggins, who I am goin' to add, whether I appear to be braggin' or not, she tells me reminds her of *me,* she set off to find out what else was in the world other than the sky!"

"How did you know all this?" Gladys Turner asked Irene Shady.

" 'Cause I asked her," Irene snapped. She turned back to the crowd. "When Miz Dune-war left Durham she didn't know she was one day goin' to be lunchin' with Princess Margaret and meet her a count for a husband—"

"A *count*!" gasped the crowd.

"*Princess Margaret*!" shrieked Catsy Ivanhoe, who was, by this time, feeling deathly ill.

"She didn't know her future would be in designin' racks and racks of one-of-a-kind clothes. She didn't know she'd have houses in France and Italy and Spain and London, England and New York City—"

"Spain!"

"France!"

"Italy!"

"London!"

"New York City!"

"—and she sure didn't know she would be at a Pep Rally in Uncertain, Texas. Now Miz Dune-war has been around the world a time or two! And she thought there was nothin' she hadn't seen, until she seen some of *you*!"

The crowd listened attentively.

"Airy-bell-uh Dune-war discovered Mary Jane Shady," Irene continued. "She made her what she is today—America's Peanut Butter Queen! It's not no fantasy! There she is, standin' right there! Your own Uncertain star!" Irene paused dramatically before she asked, "Will *you* be the lucky new star Arabella du Noir discovers and takes back to Hollywood with her?!"

"What?" asked Topsy.

"What?" asked Mary Jane.

"What?!" asked Arabella du Noir.

The crowd swooned.

"Because that is what is about to happen!" Irene cried. "*Somebody* is goin' to get to go back to Hollywood and BE A STAR, and don't forget it either as you say 'howdy' in a BIG, WARM FRIENDLY UNCERTAIN WELCOMIN' WAY to Miz Airy-bell-uh Dune-war!"

The crowd went mad with cheers.

The band played.

The Pep Squad swayed and the cheerleaders flew through the air.

Ralph Painter moaned.

Arabella du Noir laughed.

Catsy Ivanhoe screamed. She was so carried away, she forgot her earrings were rattlesnakes and pulled one off in her hand. Leo Diggs' demerol was so effective that she never even noticed when it bit her.

Scoot Widders was hopping up and down in her seat. She could hardly wait for the nominees to be announced.

"Don't work yourself up too much," Kay Widders told her mother-in-law. "The woman's a nigger and niggers side with Mexskins."

"Who do you think she's goin' to take back?" Palmer Jordan Pullet asked Spider Webb Turner.

"I don't know," Spider spat. "But I can tell you one thang. It ain't goin' to be my cat!"

"Do you think she will choose from the nominees?" Gladys Turner asked Irene Shady anxiously, as Orville handed Mary Jane Shady the list.

"I'm not sayin'!" Irene grinned. She turned to her daughter. "Okay, honey, go ahead and read 'em out!"

This is just UNREAL! thought Mary Jane Shady.

What does this mean? wondered Topsy Dingo Wild Dog.

It means we lost our fucking job! said Mary Jane. *It means we are about to be Butter Cupped Up!*

You said you'd find us another job! Topsy said. *You said you would take care of us!*

I can't. . . said Mary Jane Shady.

Why?!

Oh, God, thought Mary Jane. *I'm going to cry*. . .

Oh, cry! Topsy Dingo Wild Dog retorted impatiently. *Go ahead and feel sorry for yourself! I'll find another job! I'm sick of this*!

Mary Jane Shady held back her tears.

Come on! snapped Topsy, exasperated. *Give me that list*!

CHAPTER SIXTY-NINE

" 'OUR FIRST NOMINEE is Anastasia Smith,' " Mary Jane Shady read from the page Orville Turner had handed her. " 'Better known as Annie for short, Annie is the daughter of Dr. and Mrs. John P. Smith of 210 Melogo Drive.' "

That's Dr. Smith's daughter, Mary Jane told Topsy. *If her mother is that ex-showgirl from Las Vegas, she won't stand a chance . . . Wonder how she got nominated? . . . Old Dr. Smith must be old enough to be her grandfather. Wonder what an ex-showgirl looks like*? She glanced up into the stands, but the closest thing she could see that looked like an ex-showgirl was Yvonne. Puzzling over why no one had pointed out this infamous character who had torn down the Doctor's house with a bulldozer and started over again from scratch, she continued.

" 'Annie is a member of the Future Homemakers of America, the Daughters of the American Revolution, and of course, the Uncertain High School Band. She is a piccolo player.' "

H-m-m-m . . . A hard worker, thought Mary Jane. *She's got to be a hard worker if she's a piccolo player.*

" 'She was Freshman Class Favorite, Sophomore Class Favorite, Junior Class Favorite and will probably be Senior Class Favorite. She's just real popular here in Uncertain which is one good reason why she's in this contest today.' "

This copy is shit, thought Topsy distractedly.

That showgirl mother isn't hurting her a bit, Mary Jane mused.

" 'But what Annie's most proud of is her parents. Her daddy John is one of Uncertain's greatest doctors. An outstanding humanitarian not just in his office, but right in his own home, Dr. Smith married Anastasia's mother, the former Harla Elaine Lewis, a previous polio victim—' "

NO! Topsy screamed inside Mary Jane Shady's head. *NO! NO! NO! NO!*

" 'Yes,' " Mary Jane Shady read slowly, " 'No one will ever forget Harla Elaine's gallant acting as she swept top honors falling to the depths of high drama to receive *The Outstanding Actress Award in Freshman Class District Permian Basin Dramatic Competition* in 1962.' " Gladys had underlined the last twelve words in red ink.

No, said Topsy Dingo Wild Dog. *We will never forget THAT.*

"Here comes the Smith family!" Irene Shady cried.

And sure enough, walking out on the floor as surefooted as an Eagle Scout, came an older, blonder, but steadily moving Harla Elaine Lewis. There was no sign of a wheelchair, iron lung, or even a set of braces. Just a pretty woman accompanied by a tall, distinguished-looking man some years older, but extremely handsome. He certainly did not look like anyone's grandfather.

That bitch married a doctor, thought Topsy. She had remembered him as being very old. And there he was, a handsome life-saver with his recovered wife.

The first thing I'm doing with you is getting you the other half of that heart, Mary Jane Shady said. *Get over yourself,* PLEASE. *That woman was crippled*!

" 'And now, everybody, here is Anastasia Smith,' " Mary Jane continued. " 'Named for the play where her mother knocked everybody off their feet!' "

Cheers and applause greeted Anastasia Smith, as she glided out on the floor in a frothy gown, her blonde hair cascading from a waterfall of curls that bounced in counter-rhythm with her ivory-hued breasts. Breasts just bleating to burst from chiffon and tulle of red, white and blue. Breasts that stood like a patriotic welcoming committee, prominent, heavy and ready to go as far as they could.

"Now, Annie," Orville Turner smiled. "It says here your favorite tune is *Anastasia,* your favorite color is red, white and blue, your favorite flower is the Lily of the Valley and your favorite food is French fries."

Topsy groaned. *I hate her already. She's so young she can still eat French fries*!

Anastasia nodded her head and all her curls bounced happily around her face.

Sick, sick, sick, Topsy thought.

Vomit, puke, I hope she dies! Mary Jane Shady added.

"What are you the proudest of?" Orville asked.

I never end a sentence in a preposition, Topsy and Mary Jane said silently.

"Well, I'm a real good piccolo player," Annie Smith replied. "And my daddy's real proud of *that.* And this year we're revivin' *Anastasia* for District Competition, and I'll get to play me, and Mrs. Jones' daughter Janet is playin' the part my mother won for, and 'course Mother's real proud of *that.* But what I'm the most proud of—" Anastasia's voice almost dropped to a whisper. It was choked with emotion. "What I'm most proud of is my parents. My daddy took my mother to Ewell Crownover, the famous healer, when he had done everything else he knew how to do. Not only did Brother Crownover heal my mother so she could get up and walk, the very next night my mother danced on the stage of the Desert Inn Hotel in Las Vegas, Nevada with Corinda Cassy and the Cowgirls for Christ who was makin' a special appearance there. I'm glad to tell you who I'm proud of!" Harla Elaine Lewis Smith's daughter cried. "I'm proud of God!"

The crowd went wild.

"You said Dr. Smith's wife was an ex-showgirl from Las Vegas!" Mary Jane Shady accused Irene Shady.

"No, I didn't," Irene denied. "Gladys said that."

"Well, she was," Gladys retorted. "For one night."

Topsy moaned. Anastasia was approaching her.

"Miss Shady," Annie Smith said in a low throaty voice. "My Daddy and Mother and me want you to have this."

And with that, she placed the Outstanding Actress Award of 1962 in the hands of Topsy and Mary Jane, who stood absolutely still and speechless, staring at the girl in front of her.

She was awesome in her beauty. Blond. White. Perfect teeth. Five-feet six-inches tall. One hundred and four pounds. Seventeen years old.

The West Texas accent can be gotten rid of in six months, a year at the most, with good coaching . . . The modulation, the pitch are perfect . . .

Topsy and Mary Jane looked at Arabella du Noir and knew exactly what Arabella was thinking. Anastasia Smith was a perfect Peanut Butter Queen.

PERFECT, said Topsy and Mary Jane. *SHE IS PERFECT, PERFECT, PERFECT. . .*

"Well, thank you," Mary Jane managed to say.

"You're welcome," Anastasia Smith smiled. Mary Jane and Topsy stared at her shining, flawless teeth, dazzling between her youthful soft full lips.

Orville Turner smiled benevolently. "This is a moving example of a real Uncertain experience," he said.

Everybody cheered as Anastasia moved to stand next to her parents, who were standing on the other side of Gladys Turner, who handed Mary Jane Shady a new sheet of paper.

Irene took the trophy from her daughter and started to shine it with the hem of her dress as Mary Jane once more started to read.

" 'Our next nominee is Maria Rodriquez, daughter of Lupe Rodriquez, who is employed as an upstairs maid by Mrs. Catsy Ivanhoe—' "

"Not no more!" shouted Lupe from the stands. "She fired me this mornin'! And she called Maria somethin' terrible, too!"

A rumbling of voices from the back far side of the gym could be heard.

Gladys looked nervously in that direction. "Hurry up, Orville, and bring the girl out before those Mexskins start anything nasty!" Gladys whispered. "Oh, I hate those Mexskins! And I hate that white woman in Dallas who is letting them in our schools!"

"Peugh!" said Irene Shady, sniffing around. "I smell somethin' funny—"

Gladys shot Irene a concerned look. "Is it *me*?" she asked anxiously. "Oh, *no*! I bet all this excitement is causing me to sweat!"

"Oh-h-h!" Irene whispered, moving away from Gladys. "Your pores are just cryin'!" Irene looked appalled. "You better go with Dr. Smith to Las Vegas, Nevada and see if he cain't get you up on a stage a-dancin' with the Cowgirls for Christ and let Brother Crownover fix you up with God so he can make you stop stinkin'!"

"I don't believe in faith healers!" Gladys cried. "You know this is a sore subject with me! You know that faith healer killed my sister! Is it really me you're smelling?"

"I know I smell somethin' that smells *real real bad*, Gladys!" Irene Shady confided. "If somebody asked me, I'd have to tell 'em that you stink in seven different languages!"

"Oh, *no*!" Gladys's scowled. "Orville!" she hissed. "I'm going to the bathroom for a minute while you ask Maria what her favorite things are. I know what they are, so I can miss this part!"

Gladys turned and waddled past Lupe Rodriquez, giving absolutely no indication of noticing either her or her daughter, who was standing beside her.

"You get that bitch Catsy Ivanhoe out here and make her tell what she did to Maria!" Lupe Rodriquez was saying. "Where is she? I saw her! I know she's here!"

The crowd looked around, searching for Catsy Ivanhoe, who was nowhere to be seen.

"It doesn't matter, Mother!" Maria cried. "I'm goin' to *college*! Let sleeping dogs lie!"

"If it wasn't for Bo Ivanhoe, Maria wouldn't even be goin' to college!" Lupe announced. "And she wouldn't have a trip to Mexico! And she wouldn't have any new clothes! And I'll tell you another thing, too: Catsy Ivanhoe has dirty underwear!"

The crowd buzzed, excitedly exchanging comments.

"Well, we're all real sorry Maria's mother is out of work, but we're sure somethin' will come up, so let's not let it spoil our day," Orville said hurriedly. "We should be real proud of Maria, the first Mexskin to be nominated for the Homecoming Queen in the history of Uncertain

High School, which goes to prove there is a first time for every Uncertain thing."

Chanting was heard from the Mexican section.

"CATSY! CATSY!
WE DON'T CARE!
AND WE DON'T WANT YOUR UNDERWEAR!"

Arabella du Noir turned to Bo Ivanhoe. "Dirty laundry, huh? . . . So you got yourself a little sweetie?"

Bo Ivanhoe stared straight ahead. "Please," he said quietly. "Don't insult Maria."

"HOORAY FOR MARIA!
NO INDIAN GIVER!
WE KNOW MARIA!
SHE DIDN'T DELIVER!"

"I guess Mrs. Ivanhoe must have left," Orville interrupted. "Come on out here, *quick,* Maria," Orville called. "And let's get on with the show!"

Maria Rodriquez stepped out wearing a new red James Galanos suit, a pair of red Maud Frizon high-heeled shoes and a red leather Claude Montana jacket. In her dark wavy hair, she had pinned a red rose. Her tall, lithe body moved like a shot of white lightning with every indication of Mount St. Helena on the verge of eruption. She filled the floor like a master matador, waving to the stands as she shouted, "Olay!"

"Maria is a three-time State Champion Volleyball player," Orville read.

Twelve cheerleaders, the Mexican section, Palmer Jordan Pullet and Maria's mother cheered.

"She is a member of the Spanish Club," Orville recited.

"Not any more!" Maria smiled, parading around in her new clothes. "I quit!"

"Why'd you do that for?" Orville Turner asked.

"Because I know Spanish better than the teacher!" Maria laughed.

"Oh." Orville examined his page. "Well, I hope the rest of this is right." He looked at the print Gladys had typed. "Maria's favorite hobbies are sleeping. Her favorite song is *South of the Border,* her favorite food is refried beans—"

"No, it isn't!" said Maria indignantly. "My favorite hobby is horseback riding and my favorite song is *Bolero*! Who wrote this anyway? Mrs. Turner?"

"Now, now," Orville said in a rush. "Just tell us, then, what you'd like to eat—"

"*Your wife*!" Maria laughed gleefully. "And for dessert, I'll have Catsy Ivanhoe!"

The entire gymnasium went into an uproar.

"We're goin' to skip the question about what Maria wants to be when she grows up," Orville confided to Mary Jane.

"No, we're not," said Mary Jane Shady and Topsy Dingo Wild Dog. "We are not going to skip a thing." She turned to Maria Rodriquez.

She's beautiful . . . thought Topsy.

And smart . . . thought Mary Jane.

And funny . . . added Topsy.

Ethnic is in. Arabella might go for this. She could replace me on the spot . . .

"Maria, what is your ambition in life?"

Maria looked at Mary Jane Shady admiringly. "To be like you," she said simply. "I want to be like you."

Oh, shit! Topsy told Mary Jane Shady.

A PERFECT ANSWER, agreed Mary Jane. *JUST PERFECT . . .*

She's got it, Topsy sighed.

"And that's our second contender," Orville told the crowd. He looked around, hoping Gladys would return.

"Go on, Orville," Irene urged. "Let's get on with it."

"I'm waitin' for Gladys. She's got the next pages," Orville said.

"You don't need pages for this part," Irene told him.

"Yes, I do!" Orville insisted. "I need to read what I'm sayin'!"

Irene looked at him impatiently. "Well, we cain't wait forever and that's how long it's goin' to take for Gladys to get cleaned up!"

"Why?" he asked. "What's wrong?"

"She's gone to the bathroom because of 'you-know-what'." Irene motioned under her arms.

"Oh-h-h . . ." Orville bit his lip. "I wish she had left me those papers."

"Never mind, I'll do it," Irene reassured him, moving him aside.

Up in the stands, Scoot Widders was pounding on Sammy on her right and Judy Jones on her left.

"Kay, why don't you come and sit where I am?" Judy Jones invited, trying to dodge Scoot's excited arms. "I know you want to be with your family at such a big moment."

"Haven't you been watchin', Judy?" Scoot hollered. "The family goes out on the floor with the kids! You're the pageant expert! How could you forget *that*!"

"I don't do *pageants,*" Judy explained. "I'm in charge of *plays.* Gladys does the *pageants.* Anyway, this isn't a *pageant.*"

"Well, whatever it is, let's get ready to go down!" Scoot said to Sammy and Kay.

Kay looked at Sammy for the first time in half an hour. "She's not goin' down there with us, Sammy," Kay said.

"Don't talk about my mama like she ain't here, Kay," Sammy told her.

"She ain't goin'!" Kay cried. "We are none of us goin' to go! I will not have Mary Jane Shady puttin' a crown on my girls! We are not participatin' in this event! And you had better stop them *right now*!"

"Kay," said Sammy. "If you don't shut your mouth, I'm goin' to stick my dick in it!" He turned to his mother. "You want to go, Mama?" he asked Scoot, who was already standing up.

"Oh, honey!" Scoot Widders said to Sammy. "I have lived ever day of my life for this minute!"

"NO! NO! NO! NO! NO!" Kay Widders screamed wildly. "I won't have it! I WILL NOT HAVE IT!"

"That's exactly what you said the day they was born," Sammy grinned. "C'mon, Mama," he told Scoot. "Got your boots on?" He finished his beer, slung his arm around Scoot, then lifted her in his arms, over his shoulders, and hoisted her up on his back, piggyback style.

"Whoop-eee!!!" cried Scoot. "Go, Sammy, go!!!"

"Our next nominee is Morona Widders," Irene informed the crowd, who applauded wildly. "She is the granddaughter of Mrs. Scoot Widders and the daughter of her parents, Mr. and Mrs. Sam Widders, Jr., who were both classmates of *my* famous daughter Miss Mary Jane Shady here—" Irene stopped speaking when she saw Scoot riding Sammy's back. "Where's Kay?" she asked Sammy.

"She cain't make it," Scoot said. "Forget Kay!"

"Kay ain't comin'!" Sammy grinned. "Hang on, Mama!"

Irene hoped Scoot Widders wasn't going to slide right off Sammy's back. "Sammy is a partner in the Uncertain Blow-Out and Nipple-Up Service here in town with Bobby Henderson—"

Bobby. . . Mary Jane's heart turned over.

So what. Topsy stared straight ahead.

"—or he *was* his partner until the—uh—*accident.*" Irene cleared her throat.

"What *accident*!" Mary Jane Shady cried.

"What *accident*!" echoed Topsy Dingo Wild Dog.

Irene looked at her daughter calmly. "What do you mean *'what accident?'* I wrote you all about it—"

"What? What? What?" whispered Topsy and Mary Jane.

"Irene," Orville nudged. "The people are waiting."

"Mama, *tell* me!"

"I *did,*" Irene said patiently. "Maybe from now on, you'll read my letters." She turned back to the crowd. "Why-vonne, hon, stand up and wave so ever-body can see you're okay!" Irene shouted up to Yvonne Henderson.

"Hi, Hollywood!" grinned waving shining Yvonne Henderson. "Hi, little ole New York, New York, New York!"

Arabella du Noir saw a full-length, canary-yellow, feathered coat. Then she saw a bright red wig. At first she was reminded of Woody the Woodpecker's sister. Then Arabella closed her eyes and the details of the customized limousine flashed through her head. Where had she seen that Holstein upholstery before? And the yellow feather coat? Where had she seen that woman?

"Sylvie, where have I seen Yvonne Henderson's car before?" Arabella du Noir asked Sylvie Notions.

"*People* magazine," Sylvie replied. "I was just about to comment on that car the minute we arrived and then I saw that couple up on top of it and got distracted and then I looked up and saw that sky and forgot all over again! George Jones has one. It was in *People* magazine, 'Inside Country', page one-thirty-nine, May twenty-first issue, Volume twenty-one, Number twenty—"

"No, no," Arabella murmured, distracted. "That's not it . . . "

"George's car has horns that moo when he honks the horn, real horns on top of the hood," Sylvie noted. "Yvonne's hood ornament is a coyote head. I haven't heard the horn get honked. I don't know if it screams like a coyote or not—"

"It wasn't *People,*" Arabella said, thinking aloud. "It was—"

"Welcome to Uncertain, Texas!" Yvonne screamed out, as she waved from the stands. "I'm just real glad I got here *alive*!"

Arabella du Noir gasped. She weaved. She shook her head to keep from fainting. Suddenly she knew *exactly* where she had seen Yvonne Henderson's car before. And she remembered *exactly* where she had seen Yvonne Henderson.

"Oh, this is too fabulous!" Arabella moaned. "Too, too, too, too *fabulous*!"

"You're not going to choose *her* as the new Miss Peanut Butter Cup, are you?" Sylvie worried. "Don't you think she's too old?"

"Yes! Of course!" Arabella was almost hugging Sylvie. "Where's Gary?"

"Here," the cameraman said. He was right behind her. "I'll take the hot little brunette. Wong wants the blonde who owes it all to God—"

"Are you getting that woman up in the stands in the yellow fur coat and the red wig?" Arabella asked.

"You mean Big Bird?" Gary asked. "Sure. Want some more footage? More local color?"

"You mean Why-vonne Henderson?" Lottie asked, coming up behind Arabella, Sylvie and Gary. "That's Mary Jane's best friend here. Mary Jane used to go with Why-vonne's husband. 'Course that was way before Why-vonne and him got married. Why, Why-vonne and me were just playin' dolls together this very afternoon—"

"Excuse me, Lottie," said Arabella du Noir. "Where is Mr. Henderson now?"

"Well, he ain't *here,*" Lottie replied. " 'Cause he's dead as a doornail."

"Dead!" Sylvie Notions gasped.

"Yep," Lottie nodded. "Why-vonne killed him about six months ago."

"You mean that woman standing up there in a full-length bird-feathered coat is a *murderer*?" Gary was zooming in for a close-up.

"Not exactly," Lottie told them. "She claims it was self-defense."

"But she *killed* him," Arabella said.

"Yep. She sure did," Lottie acknowledged.

"And what's going to happen to her?" Sylvie questioned.

"Oh, nothin'," Lottie shrugged.

"Nothing! She killed her husband!" Gary protested.

"Well, now, there's a reason for that," Lottie told them, and Arabella, Sylvie, and Gary could hardly wait to hear it. "Oh, shoot! Now that you asked me, it went right out of my head!" Lottie said. "Leo, honey boy, c'mere!" Lottie called to her new husband.

"What's up, sugar?" Leo smiled.

"When Why-vonne killed Bobby and all, what did I tell you they said caused her to do it?"

Leo smiled at his wife fondly. "You said they said, 'She's a *maniac depressive.*' "

"And I guess she was pretty depressed, too," Lottie added. " 'Cause she hacked that ole boy to death sixty-one times with her best kitchen knife."

"That's what it said in the *National Enquirer,*" Arabella nodded. "That's exactly what it said . . . "

CHAPTER SEVENTY

"AH-H-H-H-H!!!" Sylvie Notions let out a piercing scream.

"Calm down, Sylvie, you didn't even know him." Arabella du Noir had never seen Sylvie so shocked.

"OH, MY GOD," Gary Cohen choked.

"You're from New York," Arabella snapped. "*A MURDER A DAY IS AN APPLE AWAY.* What is it!"

"That's what I want to know!" Gary cried. "You get paid one million dollars a year to have an answer for everything. So just turn around and tell me: WHAT IS IT?!"

Arabella turned around. And for the first time in her life, she was utterly, totally, completely and absolutely speechless.

"That's the next nominee," Lottie told them. "The one on the left, I mean. The one on the right is her Siamese twin sister. She's not runnin' for queen or anything. She just come along for the ride."

Morona Widders moved eagerly forward, dragging a very reluctant Verona with her. The twins wore matching lime green taffeta dresses covered in stiff net around the shoulders that made two trains like ponies tails down their backs. Kay had ordered the dresses from the Bridesmaids' Section of the Sears and Roebuck Catalogue, and all her ulcers had erupted because not only had the dresses failed to arrive until two days before the ceremony, she then discovered the mail order department had sent one size-twelve and one size-fourteen.

This meant dragging both girls down to the cleaners to have one of the dresses taken in. Morona insisted that Verona have the alteration done on her dress since she wasn't a nominee. But Verona refused. She said she wouldn't have to be wearing an old green fishnet if it weren't for Morona and she wasn't going to stand still for anybody to stick pins in *her.* Kay had sided with Morona, and Verona got altered.

"Morona Widders is a member of the Uncertain High School Band, where for the past three years, she has won First Place at State in the Oboe Duet Competition," Irene announced.

"I won, too!" Verona hollered.

"Be quiet, Verona," Morona nudged her sister. "You're not runnin'!"

"I don't care!" Verona retorted. "There wouldn't have been no 'duet' without *me*!"

"She is also a member of the Debate Club, the Future Homemakers of Tomorrow and the President of JOINED TOGETHER: An Association of Teenage Siamese Twins in the Permian Basin Area of West Texas."

"And also the Vice-President, the Secretary, the Treasurer and the Members," Verona added. "We *are* JOINED TOGETHER. This is it."

"Will you *please shut up,* Verona!" Morona pleaded. "Nobody cares what you're sayin'! You're not the nominee!"

"I don't need a crown to be a queen," Verona replied loftily.

"Morona's favorite hobby is Solitare," Irene said.

"Ha, ha, ha," said Verona.

"Her favorite color is—"

"Black," said Verona. "Like that lady—" She pointed toward Arabella du Noir.

"Lime green," said Morona. "Like my dress."

"Her favorite song is—"

" 'I Want To Be By Myself.' "

" 'You'll Never Walk Alone.' "

"Her favorite food is—"

"Turnip greens," said Verona.

"Peach ice cream," said Morona.

"And her favorite flower's—"

"Baby," the twins answered together.

"What?" Orville asked.

"Baby Flowers. The girl with the Crackerjacks. She's our favorite Flowers," Verona said.

"Oh," Orville mused. "Is that your choice of flowers, Morona?"

"Uh-huh," Morona nodded.

"Okay, then," Orville said. He motioned for Irene to continue.

"Now, Morona Widders, what in the world are you going to do when you grow up?" Irene asked as carefully as she knew how.

"Get married and have babies," Morona smiled.

"Over my dead body!" Verona hollered. "I've come out of the womb with you, gone to school with you, caught every disease you've ever had—measles, mumps, chicken pox twice, been dragged through debate, dragged through band, dragged through homemaking and learned five whole parts in *The Miss Firecracker Contest* so you could play *Firecracker* and almost kill both of us tryin' to twirl a baton, but I have *no intention* of standin' around and watchin' while you get married and have *babies*!"

"Well, that's what I'm goin' to do," Morona smiled sweetly.

"No, you're not!" Verona said. "We are goin' to Hollywood with that nigger lady over yonder and be a movie star! They got all the blondes and Mexskins they need out there, but I'll bet you both our heads, there ain't nobody like us West of the Pecos River!"

Oh, God no! It was all Topsy could do to keep Mary Jane Shady from fainting. *She's right! Who could beat a gimmick like Siamese twins to sell Peanut Butter or anything else*!

"I am not goin' to Hollywood!" Morona screamed.

"Well, I *am*!" Verona cried.

"I'll be your agent!"

Ralph Painter had leapt to his feet and was making his way through the Smiths and the Rodriquezes and was passing Irene, Mary Jane and Orville Turner.

"Hi, there," he smiled to Sammy and Scoot. "I'm Ralph Painter of the Painter Perfect Agency in Los Angeles, California. That's area 213-737-3328 and that spells PERFECT and that's my business. PERFECTION. I represent the most beautiful, successful women in the world, women who turn heads, and believe me, that's what we have here! A couple of head turners!"

"Yeah," sighed Sammy, gazing coolly at Ralph. "Seems like I heard that before somewheres—"

"I'm not a bit surprised, I'm not a bit surprised," Ralph gushed. "Now what are their names again?"

"Verona and Morona!" Scoot screamed, scrambling off Sammy's back. "Oh! I knew it! I knew it! I knew it!" She grabbed Irene around the neck. "Oh, what a pal! What a lady! You did just what you said you would! How can I thank you enough, Irene Shady!"

"When Verona and Morona walk into Hollywood, and I'm talking BIG TIME here Mr.—uh—?"

"Widders. Sam Widders."

"When they walk in, Sammy, nobody is going to forget them. *Ever,*" Ralph promised.

"Usually don't," Sammy nodded, staring down at his boots.

Verona smiled, edging up closer and closer to Ralph, dragging Morona with her. "Whenever I see anybody I ever met, even just once, if I say 'Hi, remember me?', they *always* do!"

"Cute!" giggled Ralph. "Isn't she cute?"

That old joke! Topsy said to Mary Jane.

What an asshole, Mary Jane muttered, staring at Ralph. *So smarmy. . .*

"Oh, you two are just unforgettable, that's what you are!" Ralph sang.

That old song! scoffed Topsy.

Do you believe this guy? asked Mary Jane.

Get rid of him first thing, Topsy said. *No matter what. This guy goes. What a putz*!

"Oh, you girls are going to take Hollywood by storm," Ralph promised. "They've never seen anything like *you*! Original, unique, different, distinct—"

"But I don't want to leave Uncertain," Morona whimpered.

"And be rich, famous and successful?" Ralph asked. He turned to Sammy and winked. "Mr. Widders—*Sam*—can you talk some *sense* into one of these heads?" Ralph smiled.

"Probably," said Sammy. "But I'm not goin' to."

"Sammy!" Mary Jane Shady asked. "*Where is Bobby*?"

"What the hell is Ralph doing out there?" Arabella asked. "Conducting business?"

"You want me to tell him to stop it?" Sylvie asked.

Arabella gazed across the floor. Ralph, totally disheveled, was standing between a set of Siamese twins, a cowboy, and a feisty dungaree-clad woman, who, in her excitement, hit Ralph Painter right in the heart everytime he spoke.

"No," Arabella said. "I will."

When Scoot saw Arabella coming she yelled, "They're chosen! I knew it from the day they was born! They're chosen!"

"Sammy!" Mary Jane Shady cried. "What happened to Bobby!"

"I'm not goin' outside the City Limits!" Morona Widders screamed and kicked Ralph Painter as hard as she could.

"Yes, you are!" Verona kicked her twin and with her right hand, reached up and pulled Morona's hair. Morona socked Ralph in his left eye, and Verona, wildly attempting to sock Morona in the face, socked Ralph in his left eye. He fell on top of both of them, dragging them to the floor.

"They're beating each other up!" Sylvie Notions gasped, running up to Arabella. "They're beating *themselves* up!"

"All Siamese twins do that," Arabella replied. "Every set I've ever met."

"It's *Anastasia* all over again," Sammy sighed. "It must be in their blood."

Ralph was strangling on streamers of green net.

"They're going to kill Ralph if you don't stop them!" Sylvie said.

"I know," Arabella responded, turning back and walking toward Lottie and Leo.

"He was a scum. He deserved it," Sammy told Mary Jane.

"A no-good shit," she agreed. "What a liar. What a manipulator. I still can't believe how I let him set me up—"

"Is that what he did to you?" Sammy asked.

"That's exactly what he did to me," Mary Jane nodded. "And worse." She stepped to the other side of Sammy, as Verona, Morona and Ralph tumbled by in a big ball of green net.

"Girls!" called Scoot Widders to her granddaughters. "Act like *ladies,* goddamnit! Act like *ladies*!"

"But I loved him," Mary Jane admitted. "Who knows why—I can't even stop thinking about it—"

"*How*?" Sammy asked, bewildered. "I thought you had better sense than that. How could you *love* a shit like *that*?"

She shrugged, trying to sort out her thoughts. "I kept thinking he would change . . . And you know, he was so different in the beginning . . ." She looked at Sammy thoughtfully. "Maybe I made the good part up. Maybe I've just remembered the beginning like I wanted to . . . Maybe I thought I could make him change . . ." She looked away. "If you knew what happened, you'd understand why it's just about driven me crazy—"

Sammy shook his head, stepping out of the way of the rolling green ball. "I'd dump him, M.J., no shit," he advised. "I mean, look at you—you're good lookin', you're on TV, you got plenty of cash—and you're with *that* creep?" he scowled, pointing toward Ralph. "He's a scumbag. It makes you look bad. How can you let him touch you? Just thinkin' about it gives me worms!"

Mary Jane looked at Ralph. *"Him?!"* she asked incredulously. "I'm not talking about *him,* Sammy! I'm talking about *Bobby*!"

"Bobby?" Sammy asked blankly. "You're not still with *Bobby—*"

"Well, yes, in a way I am. That's what I've been trying to tell you—"

Sammy Widders looked at Mary Jane Shady as if she were crazy. "Mary Jane, Bobby's dead," he said. "Why-vonne killed him six months ago."

She couldn't speak. She couldn't move. She only faintly heard Sammy Widders' voice.

"I thought you knew that, M.J. I mean, *shit,*" Sammy said, "I thought *ever-body* knew that. I mean, *hell,* it was in the papers! It was on the *news*!"

CHAPTER SEVENTY-ONE

We were drivin' down the dirt road
After a six-pack picture show . . .

Balls of tape flashed through Mary Jane's mind. She was unwinding balls and balls of tape from around a huge senior class ring. The ring was taller than she was.

It had just been oiled the day before
I asked him please drive slow . . .

"C'mon, M.J., lemme just put it in for a minute *One* minute . . . ." Bobby's voice.

'Cause if I was gonna put my head down
Underneath that steerin' wheel . . .

Inside the ring there were twelve bars of Lux soap, four clean rags, Arm and Hammer baking soda, a bottle of vinegar and a container of carbon tetrachloride.

I didn't want a broken neck
To interrupt my meal . . .

"That's all he said," Bobby said. "Said I was, I repeat, allergic to you . . . ."

To the rhythm of the oil pump
My heart was beatin' wild . . .

"And for health reasons I cain't see you no more . . ."

I felt just like a bluebonnet
Tumbleweed prairie child . . .

"So gimme back my ring and my jacket . . ."

When he painted me with his tongue
Like I was a piece of art . . .

"And a little ole kiss for ole time's sake . . ."

That is when my friend . . .

Neck cracked. Arms whipped behind. Knuckles turned inside out. Legs pulled apart. Tongue jerked out. Hair ripped from scalp. Pieces of Bobby. Pieces of Bobby were all over. She grabbed his neck and tossed what was left of his face aside. Only a wizened dried-blood particle was left. Hardened and splintered, she snatched the muscle and squeezed it until it cracked . . .

* * *

"HHHHHHHHHH—EEEEEEEEE—AAAAAAAAA—RRRRRRRR—T!" howled Topsy Dingo Wild Dog from inside the ring filled with tears.

The ring broke.

Tinkling laughter, like fluid music gushed through the ring.

Far away, came the howl. Then the laughter. Then the howl.

What a joke! howled Topsy Dingo Wild Dog. *What a gigantic, hilarious incredible JOKE*!

I HAVE TORTURED MYSELF FOR TWENTY FUCKING YEARS OVER THIS! Mary Jane Shady laughed hysterically.

I'VE BEEN CRAZED FOR SEVENTY-TWO HOURS OVER SOMETHING THAT COULDN'T EVEN HAPPEN! Topsy Dingo Wild Dog shrieked.

I'M A JOKE! I'M A JOKE! I'M A STUPID, STUPID JOKE! Mary Jane Shady guffawed.

You got me dead drunk over this! Topsy Dingo Wild Dog barked. *You got me so upset that you turned me into a crazed maniacal DRUNK*!

YOU GOT DRUNK! screamed Mary Jane Shady. *I didn't drink! I don't drink! I haven't had a drink in twenty fucking years! I haven't had a thing to drink since the night you fucked that stupid dog!*

We got a tattoo, moaned Topsy Dingo Wild Dog. *Oh, God, we didn't have to get that tattoo . . . .*

You got the tattoo . . . laughed Mary Jane Shady. *I wasn't there! That was YOU*!

WHAT WILL WE DO? giggled Topsy Dingo Wild Dog. *WHAT WILL WE DO? WHAT ARE WE GOING TO DO?*

Oh, God, let me think . . . tittered Mary Jane Shady. *I must look like a FOOL lying here*!

If you were Helen Hayes, this wouldn't be happening, Topsy told her. *Helen Hayes would know what to do . . .*

Helen Hayes walked quietly out from somewhere in Topsy and Mary Jane's head.

My, Topsy and Mary Jane thought. *She's awfully small . . . .*

Miss Hayes approached Topsy and Mary Jane with a serene smile.

I can't do this! Mary Jane told Helen Hayes. *I don't know the part! I know the subtext but not the text! I don't know the lines!*

I don't know ANYTHING! Topsy Dingo Wild Dog added.

"You're afraid of appearing unprofessional, aren't you?" Miss Hayes smiled.

Yes!

Yes!

"Well, that's good," Miss Hayes smiled. Then she shook her head. "There are far too many unprofessionals in the business today."

I'm scared, Topsy said.

Do you still get scared? Mary Jane wondered.

Miss Hayes nodded and smiled.

What do YOU do? Topsy and Mary Jane asked.

"I pretend I'm HELEN HAYES," Helen Hayes said. "And that is what you should do, too."

Huh? Topsy and Mary Jane asked.

"Just pretend you're YOU. Then eventually you can be you. And that is when you become REAL."

What is REAL? Topsy and Mary Jane wanted to know.

"I need props for this," Helen Hayes said. "I need a Velveteen Rabbit—"

I'll be the Velveteen Rabbit, Mary Jane Shady volunteered.

"Good. You're the Velveteen Rabbit," Helen Hayes told her. "You have good instincts."

What am I? Topsy asked.

"You're the Skin Horse," Helen Hayes said.

I'd rather be the Velveteen Rabbit, Topsy said.

"I know, but you're not," Helen Hayes told her. "Now listen carefully as I tell you your parts:

"What is REAL!" asked the Rabbit one day when they were lying side by side near the nursery fender. "Does it mean having things that buzz inside you and a stick-out handle?"

"Real isn't how you are made," said the Skin Horse, "It's a long thing that happens to you. When a child loves you for a long, long time, not just to play with, but REALLY loves you, then you become Real."

"Does it hurt?" asked the Rabbit.

"Sometimes," said the Skin Horse, for he was always truthful. "When you are Real you don't mind being hurt."

"Does it happen all at once, like being wound up," he asked, "or bit by bit?"

"It doesn't happen all at once," said the Skin Horse. "You become. It takes a long time. That's why it doesn't often happen to people who break easily, or have sharp edges, or who have to be carefully kept. Generally, by the time you are Real, most of your hair has been loved off, and your eyes drop out and you get loose in the joints and very shabby. But these things don't matter at all, because once you are Real you can't be ugly, except to people who don't understand."

"I suppose *you* are Real!" said the Rabbit. And then he wished he had not said it, for he thought the Skin Horse might be sensitive. But the Skin Horse only smiled.

"Once you are Real you can't become unreal again. It lasts for always."

The Rabbit sighed. He thought it would be a long time before this magic called REAL happened to him. He longed to become Real, to know what it felt like; and yet the idea of growing shabby and losing his eyes and whiskers was rather sad. He wished that he could become it without these uncomfortable things happening to him."

Helen Hayes smiled. "Got it?" She kissed Topsy on one cheek and Mary Jane on the other. "Good luck!" Helen Hayes said. "I'm very proud of you!"

As she started to disappear, Topsy and Mary Jane cried out, *Wait! I don't know if I got it!*

"Well, you have to work at it!" Helen Hayes said. "I mean, after all, that *is* what we were talking about, isn't it?"

And she was gone.

Mary Jane Shady heard the howl from somewhere far, far away.

Down in the deep recesses of her throat, she felt vocal chords vibrating, twisting, pulling.

And then she heard his voice.

" '—it doesn't happen all at once,' said the Skin Horse. 'You become. It takes a long time. That's why it doesn't often happen to people who break easily, or have sharp edges, or who have to be carefully kept—' "

Reading. His voice was *reading*.

" '—Generally by the time you are Real, most of your hair has been loved off, and your eyes drop out and you get loose in the joints and very shabby. But these things don't matter at all, because once you are Real you can't be ugly, except to people who don't understand—' "

"*I suppose you are Real*?" Mary Jane Shady asked her daddy.

And Robert Shady smiled. "*Once you are Real you can't become unreal again. It lasts for always . . .* "

His face.

She saw her father's face. His sweet, gentle, laughing eyes, his loving caring face.

The face dropped.
Black. Void. Nothing.
She had lost his face. She couldn't find his face.
A horrible, slow grinding noise followed.
His voice. She had lost his voice.
Hard. Cold. Metallic.
A coffin. She was staring into a coffin.
And then nothing.
She saw nothing. She heard nothing.
She ran.

He'd died all by himself with a bit of help from her. But she didn't know that. Irene Shady had fainted and Mary Jane Shady had shaved her legs and headed right back to the oil pump with Bobby Henderson as fast as she could. Lit by the stars, she rode him, laughing at the moon . . .

drivin' drivin' dirt road six pack picture show . . .

No! No! That's not it! She tried to push the words away, but they tumbled ahead defiantly.

oiled oiled day before please please slow slow . . .

Lit by the stars. Laughing at the moon.

In her head she saw a bright white light. In her mind she heard a buzz.

" 'The Rabbit sighed . . .' "

'Cause if I put my head down under that steering wheel . . .

" 'He thought it would be a long, long, time before this magic called Real happened to him . . .' "

I didn't want a broken neck . . .

" 'He longed to become Real, to know what it felt like . . .' "

I DIDN'T WANT A BROKEN NECK . . .

" 'AND YET THE IDEA OF GROWING SHABBY AND LOSING HIS EYES AND WHISKERS WAS RATHER SAD . . .' "

to interrupt . . .

" 'HE WISHED THAT HE COULD BECOME IT WITHOUT THESE UNCOMFORTABLE THINGS HAPPENING TO HIM . . .' "

felt just like . . .

" 'HE WISHED THAT HE COULD BECOME IT WITHOUT THESE UNCOMFORTABLE' " . . . *bluebonnet tumbleweed child* . . . " 'THINGS HAPPENING TO HIM . . .' "

Robert Shady sighed. " '*The Rabbit sighed.* He thought it would be a long time before this magic called Real happened to him. He longed to become Real, to know what it felt like, and yet the idea of growing shabby and losing his eyes and whiskers was rather sad. He wished that he could become it without these uncomfortable things happening to him . . ."

Mary Jane Shady and Topsy Dingo Wild Dog sat in the middle of the gymnasium floor in Uncertain, Texas.
Together.
Together, they heard Robert Shady's voice.
Together, they saw Robert Shady's face.
For the first time, they grieved.
Together.
And for the first time, they felt joy.
They howled and they wept.
Together.
Together, they wept and they howled.

CHAPTER SEVENTY-TWO

THE TWINS HAD stopped rolling. Ralph Painter was sitting up. Arabella du Noir stared at Mary Jane Shady, mesmerized.

"Stunning!" Arabella whispered. "Look at the neck, the arch, the stance . . . Listen to that voice! That cry, that wail . . . Remarkable! The *depth* of expression . . . *Brilliant*!" She turned to Bo Ivanhoe, who was speechless. "Bo," said Arabella, "you have just watched a pro."

"Mary Jane, get up!" Irene Shady said. She bent down to help her daughter. "Lottie!" she screamed. "C'mere!"

"There's broken hearts all over the bathroom wall in bright red lipstick!" Gladys Turner cried, waddling over to Orville as fast as she could. "O-w-w-w-w!" squealed Gladys, seeing Mary Jane Shady. "She's down on the floor! She's down on the floor!" Gladys stood over Mary Jane, gawking. "Oh, Irene, I cannot let your crazy daughter take that cat back to Hollywood, California or New York City with her!" Gladys babbled. "And for heaven's sakes, get her up off the floor!"

"Move, Gladys!" said Irene Shady. "Nobody wants your ole cat. Let it break ever dish in your collection for all we care!"

She shoved Gladys away with all the force she had used on the minister of the Uncertain Assembly of God the day her husband had died. Irene Shady had no idea what was the matter with her daughter. She did not know what was causing her to laugh and making her cry. She did not know what had made Mary Jane Shady go and get a tattoo of half a heart imprinted on her chest. She didn't know what had brought her to her knees. But she remembered the only time in her life that she had been knocked to the ground. She would never, never, never forget the profound agony of that day when her husband died and her world fell apart and she thought she would never ever have the strength to recover, never have the desire to get up and go on. All Irene wanted was to tell Mary Jane that whatever it was, she would live through it. Whatever it was, she had to get up. She had to go on. She wrapped her big strong arms around her daughter. She held Mary Jane's face in her hands and kissed her daughter's tears. "Honey, it's okay," Irene Shady said. "Whatever it is. I don't care what. We'll get through it. I promise. Together. I'm here for you no matter what. . . "

Seeing Morona, Verona and Ralph, Gladys started babbling again. "What's going on here? What is it? What *is* it? Why is everybody down on the *floor*?!"

"Let her get some air," Leo Diggs said. "Ever-body back off. Let her get some air."

"You back off!" Gladys Turner yelled. "I don't even know who you are!"

"He's my new husband, Gladys," Lottie said. Patting Mary Jane's cheek with one hand, and holding Irene's hand with the other, she seized the moment to break the news. "Now don't get mad, Irene, but I eloped yesterday while you was off at the airport and I'm retirin' from the funeral home and leavin' it all to you to go on the road with Leo for life!"

"And you're tellin' me this *now*!" Irene screamed. "You chose this very minute to tell me this news!"

"Well, I wanted to tell you sooner—" Lottie began.

"You *lied* to me about the second grade, didn't you?" Irene shouted, getting up and stepping over Verona and Morona and Ralph. "You never failed a *thing*!"

"Well, now, no, I didn't," Lottie admitted. "But I'm real sorry about that." She decided not to remind Irene that she had never even attended school in Uncertain, Texas.

"And you are leavin' me while you high-tail it all over the country with this romancin' sign-bashin' truck driver!"

"That's why I'm goin' to do all the drivin' from now on," Lottie explained. "But I'm leavin' *you* the business."

"*I hate the death business*!" Irene screamed. Her hands knotted in agony. Tears flooded her eyes. She felt her daughter's grief. She knew her daughter's pain. And she knew how helpless she was to relieve it. "I have *always* hated the death business!" she mourned. "I may *retire*!"

"I'll take over!" Yvonne Henderson offered, putting her arms around Irene. "I'm used to death! It don't bother me a bit!"

The back double doors of the gymnasium opened. A tall, elegant figure dressed in a black cashmere coat, gray pants, a perfectly pressed pink turtle-neck shirt and a splendid pair of black patent leather slippers stepped in. Wrapped around his neck was a black and silver silk ascot.

"*What* is going on here?"

Arabella turned when she heard the familiar deep baritone voice. "Herman. . . " She extended her hand. "Did you come in from Manhattan?"

"Chicago," Herman said. "I tried to tell her I'd be here right after the show—" He peered into the gymnasium. "This looks absolutely *pagan.* Where's M.J.?"

"Over there. With the natives," Arabella replied, indicating the huddle surrounding Mary Jane Shady. "I'm sure she's going to be all right, but—"

He did not need to hear more. Without another word, he strode across the floor.

All of Uncertain, Texas, gasped in glee.

"It's *him*!" they whispered. "It's a Real Star!"

"M.J." Herman said softly. He sat right down on the floor beside her.

"Are you the Jew?" Gladys Turner asked. "Are you the one who's the *Jew*?"

"That is her *boyfriend,* I will have you to know!" Irene Shady told Gladys Turner. "And you can treat him and *us* with a little more respect, too!" Grabbing the megaphone from Orville Turner's hands, Irene stepped forward and spoke into it.

"Herman Top, the famous Broadway *Jew* has come all the way from New York City to see Mary Jane Shady!" Irene cried. "He is her boyfriend and she wasn't expectin' him and when she saw him she liked to have dropped dead from the shock! And *that* is what a *happy, happy love life* will do to you, too!"

Gladys Turner gasped, aghast.

Topsy Dingo Wild Dog opened one eye.

Mary Jane Shady opened the other.

Mary Jane Shady looked from Herman to her mother.

Topsy Dingo Wild Dog stared with her.

Then they both began to smile.

Oh, my! said Topsy and Mary Jane together. *My first Real smile*!

Irene Shady looked down at her daughter and winked mischievously.

"L'Chaim . . ." whispered Mary Jane Shady.

"What does that mean, Mr. Top?" Irene Shady asked Herman Top.

"*To Life* . . . " said Herman gently. "It means *to Life* . . ."

"Oh, don't say *that,* honey!" cried Lottie Shady Diggs, coming up behind him. "We'll go out of business a-rootin' for life!"

CHAPTER SEVENTY-THREE

CAREFULLY, Herman Top lifted Mary Jane Shady into his arms. Softly, he kissed her eyes, her nose, her mouth.

"Let's take her into the bathroom," Irene told Herman Top. "Get her some wet towels."

"Need some help?" asked Leo Diggs. "Be glad to help."

"I've got her," Herman said, "if you can just clear some of these people away. . ."

"Here, honey!" said Lottie Shady. "Let me give you some of this nerve medicine!"

Mary Jane smiled weakly. Irene rolled her eyes, shook her head and followed Herman Top.

No sooner were they inside the Ladies' Room, when Orville Turner dashed inside, hopping from one foot to the other.

"Irene!" he squeaked. "Lottie! Help! Help! Come here, *quick*!"

"What is it, Orville?" Irene yelled back. "What is it *now*? What's wrong? What's wrong?"

"Oh, Irene!" squealed Orville. "Oh, Lottie! Oh, dear! Oh, *dear*! I think we've got Baby Flowers out here!"

"*Baby*!" cried Irene and Lottie in unison.

"What's she *wearin'*?" Irene asked.

"I don't *know*!" Orville screeched. "I really don't *know*!"

"Whose baby?" Herman asked. "Who's Baby?"

"That's who got Bobby Henderson killed lookin' for parts unknown," Lottie yelled, flying out the door.

"What?" said Mary Jane Shady. *"What?"*

"I wrote you that!" Irene cried. "I wrote you pages and pages and pages of every single detail all about *that*!" Suddenly her eyes lit on the letters scrawled across the mirror.

MARY JANE SHADY IS A DOG FUCKING DOG FUCKER

"Jealous! Jealous! Jealous! People are jealous, jealous, jealous!" Irene cried, grabbing a paper towel and smearing the lipsticked letters together. "This just happens to her all the time!" she told Herman Top. "And it's about to upset her to death, too!" She turned to her daughter and said in a huff, "There's a lot worse things in life than what that sign said, Mary Jane Shady!" She hurled the paper towel in the wire basket container. "Think about it, honey! If they really wanted to insult you they should have wrote: MARY JANE SHADY WAS BORN WITHOUT *TALENT!*"

She turned and vanished out the door.

Herman Top stared at the red letters and the broken half-hearted hearts scrawled across the mirror.

" '*Mary Jane Shady is a dog fucking dog fucker?*' " He stared into the mirror. "That's a pretty mean thing to say . . . "

She said nothing for a moment. "Herman. . . "

He looked back at her.

Slowly she removed the dickey of her Peanut Butter Cup dress.

"You're taking off your clothes?" he asked. "Here? Now? Do you think that's a good idea?"

She pulled back the top of her dress.

He stared into her half-hearted heart.

"I did it . . ." said Mary Jane simply. "I wrote that up there . . . those are my cracked hearts. . . "

"*Why?*" he asked.

"I was trying to remember . . ."

"That football player? The one who looked like Humphrey Bogart? The one with the twelve-foot cock?"

"I was trying to remember . . . how I forgot . . . what I was trying to remember . . . "

"What?" he asked. "You're not making sense. I don't understand . . ."

"And there was this *dog* . . . "

He stared at her blankly. "You mean the cowboy?"

She shook her head. "Worse. Much worse. Think *horrible.* Think *really, really bad* . . . "

"I don't know how bad to think," he said. "How bad is *horrible*? How bad is *bad?*"

"I got *involved* with this dog . . . "

He said nothing.

"So if you don't want to hear this . . . I mean if you want to just leave . . . "

"Mary Jane, you can't shock me. I was married to Denise La Trelle, remember? So where is the cowboy?" Herman asked. "Is he around?"

"Dead," she whispered. "Dead, dead, dead."

"In your head?"

"Yes," she said. "But I mean, he is also *d-e-a-d.*"

Herman Top let out a long long sigh. "Boy," he whispered. "Oh, *boy.*" Looking down, he spoke softly. "About this dog thing. This isn't still going on, is it?" he asked. "You don't still have a *thing* for this dog . . . Do you?"

"I never even knew that dog—" she began. She was scrambling for words. "I mean—it's not like he *asked* . . . " She wanted to explain. She wanted to give some explanation. She wanted him to know what had happened. "Bobby Henderson set me up—" She wanted to blame him. "*He* did it . . . " But it felt so futile, so stupid, and so wrong. "It was my fault. If I hadn't been—if I had been—" she stammered. And finally, she just quit. "Herman," she said. "*I am responsible.*"

Gently, he put his arms around her.

Then she started to cry. "Oh, Herman," she whispered. "I thought I turned *into* a dog—"

"Oh," he nodded, anxious to comfort her. "Well. I see," he said. "Maybe you probably *thought* if you were a dog, things would be better. Maybe. I mean, maybe you thought if you were a dog probably somebody human would love you or something—"

She looked at him in wonder.

"I mean, that's what *I* would have thought. I think . . ."

He's going to love you no matter what you say, Mary Jane, said Topsy Dingo Wild Dog.

It's going to take more than a dog to drive him away, Mary Jane told Topsy.

Herman Top stood in the bathroom of Uncertain High School in Uncertain, Texas, gazing into a roomful of glaring white porcelain littered with unrolled toilet paper and lipsticked mirrors. Before him stood his reason for coming there. Slowly he lifted his hand and softly trailed his finger down the red line of her half-hearted heart.

"Mary Jane, I'm competitive. I can't help it," Herman admitted quietly. "But this can't be about *winning.* So I win," he shrugged. "If you don't want it, too, what have I won?" She said nothing. He cleared his voice. After a moment he spoke again. "But listen. Unless you tell me to *leave,* that you don't *care,* that you don't want *us,* I'm not going to give up."

She just sat there on the floor and stared.

He sighed. "Oh, what do I know? There are worse things than doing it with a dog, Mary Jane. I mean, for God's sakes, wait until I tell you about this orchestra that was *uniformly* out of *tune* in Chicago!"

The door to the bathroom flew open. Yvonne Henderson flew in.

"They're *all* out there!" Yvonne Henderson screamed. "All seven of them *idiots*! And Baby Flowers, that demented piece of white trash, is wearin' my brand new expensive custom-ordered, special-delivered butterfly wings!"

"Yvonne," said Mary Jane Shady. "What happened to Bobby?"

Herman Top's mouth fell open. "Look!" he said, seeing Yvonne's feathers. "She's wearing *your* coat!"

Yvonne looked at Herman Top and let out a piercing scream.

CHAPTER SEVENTY-FOUR

YVONNE HENDERSON flung her arms around Herman Top, sending a burst of yellow feathers all over his cashmere coat. "I have seen you on *The Tonight Show*!" Yvonne Henderson squealed. "And I am so excited that you are here in person that I am afraid I am just about to die!"

Herman was too startled to say a word.

"How did Bobby *die*?" asked Mary Jane Shady. "Yvonne. How did Bobby die?"

Yvonne paid no attention. "Can I get your autograph?" she asked Herman, her tone rising to a high feverish pitch. "And a great big picture to put on my wall?"

"Yvonne!" cried Mary Jane.

"Can you believe she is out there wearin' *my* new butterfly wings?" Yvonne asked Herman Top. Her voice, brimming with hysteria, was like an icepick jabbing at her words. "They're part of *this* costume! I was savin' 'em for the parade!"

"Yvonne!" Mary Jane grasped Yvonne by the arm and spun her around.

There were tears in Yvonne Henderson's eyes. But there was no sadness. And there was no excitement. What Mary Jane saw was undiluted rage. Yvonne's words purged from her mouth, a long continuous self-perpetuating flame, a sizzling hot uninterrupted blaze.

"Drugs. He was on drugs. He was always on drugs. It started in high school. He got 'em from his mother's medicine cabinet. You know she had that cancer and all that pain and he got hooked. And he didn't know he was hooked. But when he took that stuff he just went crazy. And then the remorse, 'cause he'd do terrible, terrible horrible things. And he'd be so sorry. And then he'd do stuff to hisself that made him feel worse."

Yvonne looked at Mary Jane, expressionless. "I know what happened to you. I know what he did to you. I didn't know it way back then. I didn't find out 'til much, much later. But the day after you left town, when he asked me to marry him, well I was so *flattered*." She gave a short self-deprecating snort. "I didn't understand it, but you know, of course, I *wanted* him. I married him." She looked down. "I wanted to be like you, Mary Jane. I wanted to *be* you . . .

"I didn't know I was some kind of punishment. For what he did to you." Her voice cracked with anguish.

"And smart. Oh, God, he was smart. And money. Bobby could make money. He made *lots* of money. Now I say I'm not crazy, but ever-body knows, I'm not very smart . . . "

She looked at Herman Top. "Listen. I been in ever kind of mental hospital you can imagine, but I am *not* crazy. The only crazy thing I ever did was wait so long to kill that son-of-a-bitch.

"It was when those drugs got so bad he started usin' up the money. I could see what was happenin'. So I went to this big famous attorney there in Houston. I said, 'Mister, you have got to help me. My husband is a dope-fiend. Now what can I do?' And he said, 'Lady, do you have access to his accounts?' And I said, 'No.' And he said, 'Does he handle all your business?' And I said, 'Yes.' And he took a big ole gun out from his desk and he said, 'Here. Shoot the son-of-a-bitch. We'll lose in a divorce trial, but I can get you off scot free for first degree murder in the State of Texas.'

"Well, I got out of there fast. But the next time he went on one of his rampages, he did somethin' so *horrible,* I could not even believe it. I walked in my kitchen, where I had swore I would *never, never* go—"

She looked at Herman again. "I grew up poor and the kitchen is the only place I ever have refused to go—" She turned back to Mary Jane. "And he had Baby—" Yvonne looked at Herman. "She's this little retarded thing that lives down the road—" Yvonne stopped. "Oh, shit." She was weeping. "And he had turned that ole dog loose on her." Her body shook with sobs. "The same ole mongrel he'd turned a hunnerd times on me . . . And then he told me what he'd done to you." She stopped crying. Her voice became a low slow seething hiss. "He said I was *his punishment.* And that he was punishin' Baby, too . . ."

Yvonne collapsed in Mary Jane's arms. "I killed him! I stabbed him over and over and over and over and over and over and over and over! And I'd do it again! I'd do it again! I'd do it again! Only I wouldn't wait so long! I wouldn't wait so long to kill that son-of-a-bitch!"

CHAPTER SEVENTY-FIVE

Baby Flowers wandered out onto the gymnasium floor, followed by seven crooked-teethed, stringy-headed, bald-spotted relatives. Still strapped on her back were the splendid butterfly wings, dripping in pearls.

Petunia, Iris and Rose had divided the feathered necklace between them. Daisy was wearing the gold-plated breastplate. Daffodil had on one of Yvonne's practically new tennis shoes and Poppy was wearing the other. Mum was wearing the headdress. But beneath their new accessories, all seven Flowers still wore their old tattered clothes.

The only thing Baby was wearing were Yvonne's wings and a few strings of pearls.

"*BABY!!!*" Irene and Lottie cried when they saw the practically naked girl wandering toward Arabella du Noir.

Arabella's seasoned eye watched Baby Flowers' supple, undulating promenade with heightening fascination, as Baby wafted gracefully toward her.

"Parts Unknown . . ." Baby whispered to Arabella. "Can you tell me where Parts Unknown is?"

Arabella looked at the magnificent face with rapt admiration. She reached up, took the girl's chin in both her hands. Then she stepped back.

Her eyes absorbed Baby's face. It had been years since she had seen such purity; such perfection; such perfect, youthful grace.

"*PERFECT*," she said. "*PERFECT* . . ."

"She's not dependable!" Harla Elaine Lewis Smith yelled.

"None of them are," Arabella replied.

"She's a scandal!" Lupe Rodriquez hollered.

"They all are," Arabella smiled.

"*SHE'S RETARDED*!" Scoot Widders yelled.

"*PERFECT*," Arabella said. "Just too perfect." She smiled at Baby and held out her hand. "I saw you on the news," she said quietly. "About six months ago."

Baby smiled that smile.

"You look like Ava," Arabella told her.

"In the cow car," Baby nodded. "They took me and Why-vonne to town in her cow car."

"I've been looking for you," Arabella told her.

"Why?" Baby asked. "You know where Parts Unknown is?"

Arabella nodded.

"Will you take me there?" Baby asked.

"You bet I will," Arabella du Noir promised.

"Does it have Crackerjacks?"

"Nothing but."

EPI-
LOGUE

A FULL CREW of newspaper people, television cameras, and reporters from all over the country stood outside the Uncertain Chapel of Memories. Lottie Shady and Leo Diggs stood talking to Scoot Widders. Sammy Widders chatted with Bo Ivanhoe, as Morona and Verona posed for various photographers. Wendell Butler's family had finally arrived from Georgia to pick up his body, and Deal Grimes of the One Call Does All Permanent Rest Center had brought them over to the Uncertain Chapel of Memories so they would have plenty to talk about as they drove back home.

"It's a good thing he ended up with me," Deal assured Wendell Butler's widow. "Otherwise, he'd just lay in the Chapel of Memories and *rot.*"

They turned their attention to the reporter who was doing a series of "taped" interviews, as he began speaking to Yvonne.

"What do you think of the story of your life being made into a movie, Mrs. Henderson?" the reporter asked Yvonne Henderson.

Wearing a full-length, purple beaver coat with a mustard-colored, mink-tailed hat and racing green, high-heeled shoes, Yvonne Henderson grinned back. "I want to make it in Hollywood any way I can!"

"Don't you want to be in the movie, too? A cameo, perhaps?" the reporter questioned.

"Oh, no!" Yvonne laughed. "I cain't act! I'm a undertaker! And I awready had my first customer, too. Catsy Ivanhoe, bless her sweet soul, died from rattlesnake bites complicated by self-imposed suicide with a Demerol pill right when they was tryin' to decide exactly *where* to put the Homecomin' Crown on Morona Widders' head! She had crawled out the backdoor of the gymnasium and nobody even knew where she'd disappeared to until the next mornin' when the janitor was cleanin' up! Inn't it *sad*? But it has a happy endin'. Her husband, the bereaved widow-man, Bo Ivanhoe, is carryin' out Catsy's wishes to make picture shows in her memory. He's financin' this one, along with me, a-course. And he's goin' to oversee it along with Arabella Dunewar. See, I'm not too good with figures. Anyway, I don't like to count. But I just *love* dead people! And that's why I bought this place lock, stock and barrel from Irene Shady. She's playin' herself in the picture. She's the one who embalmed my husband when he up and died, and they are usin' the real location—here—for the picture. I 'spect Irene won't be doin' any more bodies 'cause she's goin' on out to Hollywood after this to be the new Creamy Crunchy Peanut Butter Granny Queen!"

"Thank you, Mrs. Henderson," the reporter said. "And here comes Irene Shady. Mrs. Shady, the former undertaker, is undertaking a brand new career. Are you looking forward to moving to Hollywood, and what are your plans?"

"My first plan is to look up Johnny Carson," Irene Shady said, speaking directly into the camera. "I want to straighten him out on a thing or two."

"What could that be?" asked the reporter. "What's in store for John?"

"He needs to know how Dove Lightlady got her name, and I'm goin' to tell him quick!" Irene Shady told the lens. "See, the first part Mary Jane got from a little canary. Now it was a good enough name for a canary. . ."

"Oh, please excuse me, Mrs. Shady," interrupted the reporter. "But here comes Mary Jane Shady and the big screen's newest producer, Countess Arabella du Noir!" He smiled, graciously ending the interview and turning to Mary Jane Shady.

"America's *former* Peanut Butter Queen!" He navigated around Irene, moving closely up to her daughter, and putting a friendly arm around Arabella. "Miss Shady, how do you feel about your mother taking your place as the *new* Peanut Butter Queen of America?"

"Perfect," smiled Mary Jane Shady. "Just perfect."

"And how do you feel about Arabella du Noir's new discovery, Baby Flowers, playing you in the movie. Don't you want to play *yourself?*"

"The role of *Mary Jane* is a cameo," Arabella explained, nonchalantly moving out of the reporter's embrace. "Baby Flowers will be portraying her more or less as a fantasy figure from the past. The part of *Yvonne* is the lead," Arabella explained. "That's why Mary Jane's playing *Yvonne*. She's the star."

The reporter turned back to Mary Jane. "And if we may intrude on your private life. Are you and Herman Top engaged to be married? What are your plans?"

"I don't know," smiled Mary Jane Shady. "We're sort of taking things one day at a time . . ."

"And how did you choose Mary Jane Shady to star in your first feature, Ms. Du Noir?"

"Sheer luck," said Arabella.

"Yours?" the reporter asked Mary Jane Shady.

"Oh, no." Arabella du Noir looked at Mary Jane Shady and hugged her affectionately. "Mine. The luck was all mine . . ."

As Arabella moved Mary Jane away from the cameras, away from the reporters, they could hear Yvonne saying, "If he'd a-just not brought Baby in my new kitchen after he swore to me he'd never give me a reason to have to set foot in there, I wouldn't have minded so bad. And then he turned on the garbage disposal and tried to put *me* in it!"

"And that's when you got the kitchen knife?"

"I turned off the disposal first. That's when he got the knife!"

"And *then* what happened? After he got the knife?"

"Hell," Yvonne laughed into the television camera. "I'm not goin' to tell you the end of the picture!"

"Oh, here comes Baby Flowers, the new Arabella du Noir discovery! Baby!" the reporter cried. "What approach will you use to get into your part?"

Baby smiled that Baby smile. She didn't look left and she didn't look right. She turned around in a circle and blinked into the sun.

"Are you studying the classics? Joining the Actors Studio? Are you familiar with Mary Jane Shady's work? Do you work from the inside out, or the outside in? Where will you go to get what you need to play this part?"

"Parts Unknown . . ." smiled Baby Flowers, wandering off. "I'm goin' off to Parts Unknown . . . "

THE END